SPECIAL MESSAGE TO READERS

Cecelia Ahern was born and grew up in Dublin. She is now published in nearly 50 countries, and has sold over 25 million copies of her novels worldwide. Two of her books have been adapted as films, and she has created several TV series. She and her books have won numerous awards, including the Irish Book Award for Popular Fiction for *The Year I Met You*. She lives in Dublin with her family.

You can discover more about the author at www.cecelia-ahern.com

LYREBIRD

In the south-west of Ireland, rugged mountains meet bright blue lakes and thick forests. Deep in the woods, a young woman lives alone, forever secluded from the world, her life a well-kept secret. She possesses an extraordinary talent, the likes of which no-one has seen before: a gift that will earn her the nickname Lyrebird. When Solomon stumbles into Laura's solitary existence, her life is turned on its head. Pulled from her peaceful landscape to the cacophony of Dublin, she is confronted by a world desperate to understand her. But while Solomon knows the world will embrace Laura, will it free her to spread her wings — or will it trap her in a gilded cage? Like all wild birds, she needs to fly free . . .

Books by Cecelia Ahern
Published by Ulverscroft:

PS, I LOVE YOU
HOW TO FALL IN LIVE
THE YEAR I MET YOU

CECELIA AHERN

LYREBIRD

Complete and Unabridged

CHARNWOOD
Leicester

First published in Great Britain in 2016 by
HarperCollins*Publishers*
London

First Charnwood Edition
published 2018
by arrangement with
HarperCollins*Publishers*
London

A catalogue record for this book is available
from the British Library.

ISBN 978–1–4448–3766–7

Published by
F. A. Thorpe (Publishing)
Anstey, Leicestershire

Set by Words & Graphics Ltd.
Anstey, Leicestershire
Printed and bound in Great Britain by
T. J. International Ltd., Padstow, Cornwall

This book is printed on acid-free paper

For Paula Pea

It is not the strongest of the species that survives, nor the most intelligent. It is one that is most reponsive to change.

Attributed to Charles Darwin

Prologue

He moves away from the others, their constant chat blending into a tedious monotonous sound in his head. He's not sure if it's the jet lag or if he's simply not interested in what's going on. It could be both. He feels elsewhere, detached. And if he yawns one more time, she'll have no hesitation in calling him out on it.

They don't notice him break away from them, or if they do, they don't comment. He carries his sound equipment with him; he'd never leave it behind — not just because of its value, but because it's a part of him by now, like another limb. It's heavy but he's used to the weight, oddly is comforted by it. He feels a part of him is missing without it, and walks like he's carrying the audio bag even when he isn't, his right shoulder dropped to one side. It might mean he's found his calling as a sound recordist, but his subconscious connection to it does nothing good for his posture.

He walks away from the clearing, away from the bat house, the cause of the conversation, and moves towards the forest. The fresh cool air hits him as he reaches the edge.

It's a hot June day, the sun beats down on the top of his head and is baking the naked flesh at the back of his neck. The shade is inviting, a group of midges do high-speed set-dancing in paths of sunlight looking like mythical insects.

The woodland floor is cushioned and springy beneath his feet with layers of fallen leaves and bark. He can no longer see the group he left behind and he tunes them out, filling his lungs with the scent of refreshing pine.

He places the audio bag down beside him and leans the boom mic against a tree. He stretches, enjoys the cracks of his limbs and flexing of his muscles. He lifts off his sweater, his T-shirt rising up with it, revealing his stomach, then ties it around his waist. He pulls the hair bobbin from his long hair and ties it up tighter in a topknot, enjoying the air on his sticky neck. Four hundred feet above sea-level he looks out over Gougane Barra and sees tree-covered mountains extending as far as the eye can see, not a sign of a neighbour for miles. One hundred and forty-two hectares of national park. It's peaceful, serene. He has an ear for sound, has acquired it over time and has had to. He's learned to listen to what you don't immediately hear. He hears the birds chirping, the rustle and crack of creatures moving all around him, the low hum of a tractor in the distance, building work hidden in the trees. It's tranquil, but alive. He inhales the fresh air and as he does he hears a twig snap behind him. He whips around quickly.

A figure darts into hiding behind a tree.

'Hello?' he calls out, hearing the aggression in his voice at being caught off guard.

The figure doesn't move.

'Who's there?' he asks.

She peeks out briefly from behind the trunk, then disappears again, like she's playing a game of hide-and-seek. An odd thing happens. He now knows he's safe but his heart starts pounding; the reverse of what it should be doing.

He leaves his equipment behind and slowly walks towards her, the crunch and snap of the floor beneath him revealing his every move. He makes sure to keep space between them, making a wide circle around the tree she hides behind. Then she comes into full view. She tenses, as if readying herself for defence, but he holds his hands up in the air, palms flat, as though in surrender.

She would almost be invisible or camouflaged in the forest if it weren't for her white blonde hair and green eyes, the most piercing he's ever seen. He's completely captivated.

'Hi,' he says, softly. He doesn't want to scare her away. She seems fragile, on the edge of fleeing, perched on her toes, ready to take off at any moment if he takes a wrong step. So he stops moving, feet rooted to the ground, hands up flat, as if he's holding up the air, or maybe it's the air that's holding him up.

She smiles.

The spell is cast.

She's like a mythical creature, he can barely see where the tree begins and she ends. The leaves that act as their ceiling flutter in the breeze, causing rippling light effects on her face. They're seeing each other for the first time, two complete strangers, unable to take their eyes off each other. It is the moment his life splits; who he was before he met her and who he becomes after.

Part 1

One of the most beautiful and rare and probably the most intelligent of all the world's creatures is that incomparable artist, the Lyrebird . . . The bird is extremely shy and almost incredibly elusive . . . characterised by amazing intelligence.

To say that he is a being of the mountains only partially explains him. He is, certainly, a being of the mountains but no great proportion of the high ranges that mark and limit his domain can claim him for a citizen . . . His taste is so exacting and definite, and his disposition so discriminating, that he continues to be selective in these beautiful mountains, and it was a waste of time to seek him anywhere save in situations of extraordinary loveliness and grandeur.

Ambrose Pratt, *The Lore of the Lyrebird*

1

That Morning

'Are you sure you should be driving?'

'Yes,' Bo replies.

'Are you sure she should be driving?' Rachel repeats, asking Solomon this time.

'Yes,' Bo replies again.

'Is there any chance you could stop texting while you're driving? My wife is heavily pregnant, the plan is to meet my firstborn,' Rachel says.

'I'm not texting, I'm checking my emails.'

'Oh well then,' Rachel rolls her eyes, and looks out the window as the countryside races past. 'You're speeding. And you're listening to the news. And you're jet-lagged to fuck.'

'Put your seatbelt on if you're so worried.'

'Well, that's reassuring,' Rachel mumbles as she squeezes her body into the seat behind Bo and clicks her seatbelt into place. She'd rather sit behind the passenger seat where she can keep a better eye on Bo's driving, but Solomon has the seat pushed so far back that she can't fit.

'And I'm not jet-lagged,' Bo says, finally

putting her phone down, to Rachel's relief. She waits to see Bo's two hands return to the wheel but instead Bo turns her attention to the radio and flicks through the stations. 'Music, music, music, why does nobody talk any more?' she mutters.

'Because sometimes the world needs to shut up,' Rachel replies. 'Well, whatever about you, *he's* jet-lagged. He doesn't know where he is.'

Solomon opens his eyes tiredly to acknowledge them both. 'I'm awake,' he says lazily, 'I'm just, you know . . . ' he feels his eyelids being pulled closed again.

'Yeah, I know I know, you don't want to see Bo driving, I get it,' Rachel says.

Just off a six-hour flight from Boston, which landed at five thirty this morning, Solomon and Bo had grabbed breakfast at the airport, picked up their car, then Rachel, to drive three hundred kilometres to County Cork in the southwest of Ireland. Solomon had slept most of the way in the plane but it still wasn't enough, yet every time he'd opened his eyes he'd found Bo wide awake spending every second watching as many in-flight documentaries as she could.

Some people joke about living on pure air. Solomon is convinced that Bo can live on information alone. She ingests it at an astronomical rate, always hungry for it, reading, listening, asking, seeking it out so that it leaves little room for food. She barely eats, the information fuels her but never fills her, the hunger for knowledge and information is never satiated.

Dublin based, Solomon and Bo had travelled to Boston to accept an award for Bo's documentary, *The Toolin Twins*, which had won Outstanding Contribution to Film and Television at the Boston Irish Reporter Annual Awards. It was the twelfth award they'd picked up that year, after numerous others they'd been honoured with.

Three years ago they had spent a year following and filming a pair of twins, Joe and Tom Toolin, who were seventy-seven years old at the time. They were farmers who lived in an isolated part of the Cork countryside, west of Macroom. Bo had discovered their story whilst researching for a separate project, and they had quickly taken over her heart, her mind and consequently her life. The brothers lived and worked together all their lives, neither of them had ever had a romantic relationship with a woman, or with anyone for that matter. They had lived on the same farm since birth, had worked with their father and then taken it over when he passed away. They worked in harsh conditions, and lived in a very basic home of humble means, a stone-floored farmhouse, sleeping in twin beds with nothing but an old radio to keep them entertained. They rarely left the land, received their weekly shopping from a local woman who delivered their meagre items, and did general housekeeping. The Toolin brothers' relationship and outlook on life had torn at the heartstrings of the audience as it had the film crew, for beneath their simplicity was an honest and clear understanding of life.

9

Bo had produced and directed it under her production company, Mouth to Mouth productions, with Solomon on sound, Rachel on camera. They'd been a team for the past five years since their documentary, *Creatures of Habit*, which explored the falling number of nuns in Ireland. Bo and Solomon had been romantically involved for the past two years, since the unofficial wrap party of the documentary. *The Toolin Twins* had been their fifth piece of work but their first major success, and this year they had been travelling the world going from one film festival or awards ceremony to another, where Bo had been accepting awards and had polished her speech to perfection.

And now they're on the way back to the Toolin twins' farm which they are so familiar with. But it is not to celebrate their recent successes with the brothers, it is to attend the funeral of Tom Toolin, the youngest brother by two minutes.

'Can we stop for something to eat?' Rachel asks.

'No need.' Bo reaches down to the floor on the passenger side, dangerously, one hand still on the wheel as the car swerves slightly on the motorway.

'Jesus,' Rachel says, not able to watch.

She retrieves three power bars and throws one to her. 'Lunch,' she rips hers open with her teeth, and takes a bite. She chews aggressively, as if it's a pill she must swallow, food for fuel, not food for enjoyment.

'You're not human, you know that,' Rachel says, opening her power bar and studying it with disappointment. 'You're a monster.'

'But she's my little inhumane monster,' Solomon says groggily, reaching out to squeeze Bo's thigh.

She grins.

'I preferred it when you two weren't fucking,' Rachel says, looking away. 'You used to be on my side.'

'He's still on your side,' Bo says, in a joking tone but meaning it.

Solomon ignores the dig.

'If we're going to pay our respects to poor Joe, why did you make me pack all my gear?' Rachel asks, mouth full of nuts and raisins, knowing exactly why but in the mood to stir things up even further. Bo and Solomon were fun like that, never completely stable, always easy to tip.

Solomon's eyes open as he studies his girlfriend. Two years together romantically, five years professionally and he can read her like a book.

'You don't actually think that Bo is going to this funeral out of the goodness of her heart, do you?' he teases. 'Award-winning internationally renowned directors have to be receptacles for stories at *all* times.'

'That sounds more like it,' Rachel says.

'I don't have a heart of stone,' Bo defends herself. 'I re-watched the documentary on the flight. Do you remember who had the final words? Tom. 'Any day you can walk away from your bed is a good day.' My heart is broken for Joe.'

'Fractured, at least,' Rachel teases, gently.

11

'What's Joe going to do?' Bo continues, ignoring Rachel's jab. 'Who can he talk to? Will he remember to eat? Tom was the one who organised the food deliveries *and* he cooked.'

'Tins of soup, beans on toast and tea and toast isn't exactly cooking. I think Joe will easily be able to take up the gauntlet,' Rachel smiles, remembering the men sitting down together to shovel hard bread into watery soup in the winter afternoons when darkness had already fallen.

'For Bo, that's a three course meal,' Solomon teases.

'Imagine how lonely life will be for him now, up that mountain, especially in the dead of winter, not seeing anyone for a week or more at a time,' Bo says.

They allow a moment of silence to pass while they ponder Joe's fate. They knew him better than most. He and Tom had let them into their lives and had been open to every question.

While filming, Solomon often wondered how the brothers could ever function without each other. Apart from the market, and tending to their sheep, they rarely left the farm. A housekeeper would see to their domestic needs, which seemed an inconvenience to them rather than necessity. Meals were taken quickly and in silence, hurriedly shovelling food into their mouth before returning to their work. They were two peas in a pod, they would finish each other's sentences, move around each other with such familiarity it was like a dance, but not necessarily an elegant one. Rather, one that had been honed over time, unintentionally, unrealised. Despite its lack of grace, and maybe because of it, it was beautiful to see, intriguing to watch.

It was always Joe and Tom, never Tom and Joe. Joe was the eldest by two minutes. They were identical in looks, and they gelled despite the difference in personalities. They made peculiar sense in a landscape that didn't.

There was little conversation between them, they had no need of explanation or description. Instead their communication relied on sounds that to them had meaning, nods of the head, shrugs, a wave of the hand, a few words here and there. It took a while for the film crew to understand whatever message had passed between them. They were so in tune they could sense each other's moods, worries, fears. They knew what the other was thinking at any given time, and they gave the beauty of this particular connection no thought whatsoever. They were often bamboozled by Bo's depth of analysis of them. Life is what it is, things are as they are, no sense analysing it, no sense trying to change what can't be changed, or understand what can't be understood.

'They didn't want anybody else because they had each other, they were each enough for one another,' Bo says, repeating a line she has said a thousand times in promotion for her documentary but still meaning every word. 'So am I chasing a story?' Bo asks. 'Fuck yeah.'

Rachel throws her empty wrapper over Bo's shoulder.

Solomon chuckles and closes his eyes. 'Here we go again.'

13

2

'Wow,' Bo says as the car crawls towards the church in its stunning surroundings. 'We're early. Rachel, can you get your camera set up?'

Solomon sits up, wide awake now. 'Bo, we're not filming the funeral. We can't.'

'Why not?' she asks, brown eyes staring into his intently.

'You don't have permission.'

She looks around, 'From who? This isn't private property.'

'Okay, I'm out,' Rachel says, getting out of the car to avoid being caught up in another of their arguments. The tumultuous relationship is not just with Solomon, it's anyone who comes into contact with Bo. She's so stubborn, she brings the argument out in even the most placid of people, as though the only way she knows to communicate or to learn is by pushing things so far that they spark a debate. She doesn't do it for the enjoyment of the debate; she needs the discussion to learn how other people think. She's not wired like most people. Though she's sensitive, she is more sensitive to people's stories, not necessarily in the method of discovering

14

them. She's not always wrong, Solomon has learned plenty from her over time. Sometimes you have to push at awkward or uncomfortable moments, sometimes the world needs people like Bo to push the boundaries in order to encourage people to open up and share the story, but it's about choosing the right moments and Bo doesn't always get that right.

'You haven't asked *Joe* if you can film,' Solomon explains.

'I'll ask him when he arrives.'

'You can't ask him before his brother's funeral. It's insensitive.'

She looks around at the view and Solomon can see her brain ticking over.

'But maybe some of the funeral attendees will do an interview afterwards, tell us stories about Tom we didn't know, or get their opinion on how they think Joe's life will be from now on. Maybe Joe will want to talk to us. I want to get a sense of what his life is like now, or what it's going to be like.' She says all this while spinning around, seeing the view from 360 degrees.

'Pretty fucking lonely and miserable, I'd imagine,' Solomon snaps, losing his temper and getting out of the car.

She looks at him, taken aback, and calls after him. 'And after that we'll get you some *food*. So that you don't bite my head off.'

'Show some empathy, Bo.'

'I wouldn't be here if I didn't care.'

He glares at her, then having enough of the argument he senses he will lose he stretches his legs and looks around.

15

Gougane Barra lies to the west of Macroom in Co. Cork. Its Irish name *Guagán Barra*, meaning 'The Rock of Barra', derived from Saint Finbar, who built a monastery on an island in a nearby lake in the sixth century. Its secluded position meant St Finbar's Oratory was popular during the time of Penal Laws, for celebrating the illegal Catholic Mass. Nowadays, its stunning surroundings makes it popular for weddings. Solomon is unsure as to why Joe chose this chapel; he's sure Joe doesn't follow trends, nor does he go for romantic settings. The Toolin farm is as remote as you can imagine, and while it must be part of a parish, he's not sure which. He knows the Toolin twins were not religious men; unusual for their generation, but they're unusual men.

He may not feel it's right interviewing Joe on the day of his brother's funeral but he does have some of his own questions he'd like answering. Despite his frustration with Bo for overstepping boundaries, he always benefits from her doing so.

Solomon takes off on his own to record. Now and then Bo points out an area, an angle, or an item that she would like Rachel to capture, but mostly she leaves them to their own devices. This is what Solomon likes about working with Bo. Not unlike the Toolin twins, Bo, Solomon and Rachel understand how each member of the team prefers to work and they give each other the space to do that. Solomon feels a freedom on these jobs that is lacking in the other work he takes on purely to pay the bills. A winter spent

16

filming unusual body parts for a TV show *Grotesque Bodies*, followed by summer shooting at a reality fat fit club that sucked the life from him. He is grateful for these documentaries with Bo, for her curiosity. What irritates him about her are the very skill sets that help set him free from his regular day-jobs.

An hour into their filming, the funeral car arrives, closely followed by Joe, eighty years old, behind the wheel of the Land Rover. Joe climbs out of the jeep, wearing the same dark brown suit, sweater and shirt that they've seen on him hundreds of times. Instead of his Wellington boots he wears a pair of shoes. Even on this sunny day he wears what he'd wear in the depths of winter, perhaps a hidden layer less. A tweed cap covers his head.

Bo goes to him immediately. Rachel and Solomon follow.

'Joe,' Bo says, reaching out to him and shaking his hand. A hug would have been too much for him, not being comfortable with physical affection. 'I'm so sorry for your loss.'

'You didn't have to come,' he says, surprised, looking around at the three of them. 'Weren't you in America when I rang you?' he asks, as if they were on another planet.

'Yes, but we came home straight away to be here for you. Could we film, Joe? Would that be okay? People who watched your story would like to know how you're doing.'

Solomon tenses up at Bo's nerve but she also amuses him, he finds her gutsiness, her honesty, remarkable and rare.

'Ara go on,' says Joe, waving his hand dismissively as if it makes no difference to him either way.

'Can we talk to you afterwards, Joe? Is there a gathering planned? Tea, sandwiches, that kind of thing?'

'There's the graveyard and that's it. No fuss, no fuss. Back to business, I'm working for two now, aren't I?'

Joe's eyes are sad and tired with dark circles. The coffin is removed from the car and is placed on a trolley by the pallbearers. Including the film crew, there are a total of nine people in the church.

The funeral is short and to the point, the eulogy read by the priest, who mentions Tom's work ethic, his love for his land, his long-departed parents and his close relationship with his brother. The only movement the stoic Joe makes is to remove his cap when Tom's coffin is lowered into the ground at the graveyard. After that, he pops it back on his head, and walks to his jeep. In his head, Solomon can almost hear him say, 'That's that.'

After the burial, Bo interviews Bridget the housekeeper, though it's a title that's used loosely as she merely delivers food and dusts the cobwebs from their damp home. She's afraid to look at the camera in case it explodes in her face, looking defensive as though every question is an accusation. Local garda Jimmy, the Toolin twins' animal feed supplier and a neighbouring farmer whose sheep share the mountainous land with theirs, all refuse an interview.

The Toolin farm is a thirty-minute drive, far from anything, deep in the heart of the mountainside.

'Are there books in the Toolin house?' Bo asks out of nowhere. She does that often, blurts out random questions and thoughts as she slots the various pieces of information that come from different places together in her head to tell one clear story.

'I've no idea,' Solomon says, looking at Rachel. Rachel would have a better visual image and memory than any of them.

Rachel thinks about it, re-runs her shot-list in her head. 'Not in the kitchen.' She's silent while she runs through the house. 'Not in the bedroom. Not on open shelves, anyway. They have bedside lockers, could be in there.'

'But nowhere else.'

'No,' Rachel says, certain.

'Why do you ask?' Solomon asks.

'Bridget. She said that Tom was an 'avid reader'.' Bo scrunches her face up. 'I wouldn't peg him as a reader.'

'I don't think you can tell if someone's a reader or not by looking at them.'

'Readers definitely always wear glasses,' Rachel jokes.

'Tom never mentioned books. We lived their entire schedule with them for a year. I never saw him read, even hold a book. They didn't read newspapers, neither of them. They listened to the radio. Weather reports, sports and *sometimes* the news. Then they'd go to bed. Nothing about reading.'

'Maybe Bridget made it up. She was very nervous about being on camera,' Solomon says.

'She was very detailed about buying books for him at second-hand shops and charity sales. I believe she bought the books, I just can't figure out why we never saw one book in the house and neither of them reading. That's something I would have wanted to know about. What did Tom like to read? Why? And if he did, was it a secret?'

'I don't know,' Solomon says, yawning, never really hung up on the minor details that Bo dissects, particularly now, as the hunger and tiredness kick in again. 'People say odd things when they've a camera pointed at their face. What do you think, Rachel?'

Rachel is silent for a moment, giving it more clout than Solomon did. 'Well he's not reading anything now,' she says.

★　★　★

They arrive at the Toolin farmhouse and are more than familiar with the land; they spent many dark mornings and nights, in torrential rain, traipsing over this treacherous land. The brothers had separated the work. As hill sheep farmers, they had split their responsibilities from the beginning and stuck to that. It was a lot of work for little income, but they had each stuck to their designated roles since their father died.

'Tell us what happened, Joe,' Bo says gently.

Bo and Joe sit in the kitchen of the farmhouse on the only two chairs at the plastic table. It's the main room of the house and contains an old electric cooker, the four hobs the only part of it in use. It's cold and damp, even in this weather. There is one socket on the wall with an extension lead feeding everything in the kitchen: the electric cooker, the radio, the kettle, and the electric heater. An accident waiting to happen. The hum of the heater, Solomon's sound enemy. The room — in fact the entire house — smells of dog because of the two border collies that live with them. Mossie and Ring, named after Mossie O'Riordan and Christy Ring who were instrumental in Cork's victory in the All-Ireland Hurling final in 1952, one of the few times the boys travelled to Dublin with their father, one of the only interests they have outside of farming.

Joe sits in a wooden chair, quiet, elbows on the armrest and hands clasped at his stomach. 'It was Monday. Bridget had dropped by with the food. Tom was to put it away. I went off. I came in for my tea and found him here on the floor. I knew right away that he was gone.'

'What did you do?'

'I put the food away. He hadn't done that yet, so it was early enough when he died. Must have been soon after I left. Heart attack. Then I made a call . . . ' He nods at the phone on the wall.

'You put the food away first?' Bo asks.

'I did.'

'Who did you call?'

'Jimmy. At the station.'

'Do you remember what you said?'

'I don't know. 'Tom's dead', I suppose.'

Silence.

Joe remembers that he's on camera, remembers the advice Bo gave him three years ago to keep talking so it's him that's telling the story. 'Jimmy said he'd have to ring the ambulance anyway, even though I knew there was no bringing him back. He came by himself then. We had a cuppa while we waited.'

'While Tom was on the floor?'

'Sure where would I move him?'

'Nowhere, I suppose,' Bo says, a faint smile on her lips. 'Did you say anything to Tom? While you were waiting for Jimmy and the ambulance.'

'Say anything to him?' he says, as if she's mad. 'Sure he was dead! Dead as dead can be. What would I be sayin' something for?'

'Maybe a goodbye or something. Sometimes people do that.'

'Ah,' he says dismissively, looking away, thinking of something else. Maybe of the goodbye he could have had, maybe of the goodbyes he'd already had, maybe of the ewes that needed to be milked, the paperwork that needed to be filled.

'Why did you choose the church today?'

'That's where Mammy and Daddy were married,' he says.

'Did Tom want his funeral to be held there?'

'He never said.'

'You never talked about your plans? What you'd like?'

'No. We knew we'd be buried with Mammy and Daddy at the plot. Bridget mentioned the chapel. It was a grand idea.'

'Will you be all right, Joe?' Bo asks, gently, her concern genuine.

'I'll have to be, won't I?' He gives a rare smile, a shy one, and he looks like a little boy.

'Do you think you'll get some help around here?'

'Jimmy's son. It's been arranged. He'll do some things when I need him. Lifting, the heavy work. Market days.'

'And what about Tom's duties?'

'I'll have to do them, won't I?' He shifts in his chair. 'No one else left to be doing it.'

Both Joe and Tom were always amused by Bo's questions. She asked questions that had obvious answers; they couldn't understand why she questioned things so much, analysed everything, when to them that was that, all the time. Why question something when the solution was obvious? Why even try to find another solution when one would do?

'You'll have to talk to Bridget. Give her your shopping list. Cook,' Bo reminds him.

He looks annoyed at that. Domesticity was never something he enjoyed, that was Tom's territory, not that Tom enjoyed it either, he just knew if he was waiting for his brother to feed him, he'd die of starvation.

'Did Tom like reading?' she asks.

'Ha?' he asks her, confused. 'I don't think Tom ever read a book in his life. Not since school, anyway. Maybe the sports pages when Bridget brought the paper.'

Solomon can sense Bo's excitement from where he stands, she straightens her back, ready to dive into what's niggling at her.

'When you put away the shopping on Monday,

was there anything unusual in the bags?'

'No.'

Understanding Joe's grasp of the English language, she rephrases, 'Was there anything different?'

He looks at her then, as if deciding something. 'There was too much food, for a start.'

'Too much?'

'Two pans of bread. Two ham and cheese, sure I can't remember what else.'

'Any books?'

He looks at her again. The same stare. Interest piqued. 'One.'

'Can I see it?'

He stands and gets a paperback from a kitchen drawer. 'There you go. I was going to give it to Bridget — thought it was hers, and the extras too.'

Bo studies it. A well-thumbed crime novel that Bridget had picked up from somewhere. She opens the inside hoping for an inscription but there's nothing. 'You don't think Tom asked for this?'

'Sure why would he? And if he did it wasn't just his heart that there was something wrong with.' He says this to the camera and chuckles.

Bo hangs on to the book. 'Going back to Tom's duties. What are the duties you have on the farm now?'

'Same as usual.' He thinks about it as if for the first time, all the things that Tom did during his day that he never thought about, or the things they used to discuss in the evening. 'He saw to the well by the bat house. I haven't been there

24

for years. I'll have to keep an eye on that, I suppose.'

'You never mentioned the bat house before,' Bo says. 'Can you take us there?'

★ ★ ★

The four of them and one of the loyal sheepdogs get into Joe's jeep. He drives them across the land, on dirt tracks that feel dangerous now, never mind during the winter on those stormy days or icy mornings. An eighty-year-old cannot do this alone, two eighty-year-olds were barely managing it. Bo hopes that Jimmy's son is an able-bodied young man who does more than Joe asks, because Joe's not a man to ask for help.

A rusted railing stops them in their tracks. Solomon beats Joe to it and jumps out of the jeep to push it open. He runs to catch up with them. Joe parks in a clearing by the forest, Solomon collects his equipment. They must walk up a trail the rest of the way. The dog, Mossie, races up ahead of them.

'Bad land, we could never do nothing with it, but we kept it nonetheless,' Joe tells them. 'In the thirties, Da planted Sitka spruce and lodgepole pine. Thrive in bad soils, good with strong winds. About twenty acres. You can see Gougane Barra Forest Park from up here.'

They walk through the trails and come to a clearing with a shed that was once painted white but now is faded, beaten away by time, and reveals the dull concrete beneath. The windows have been boarded up. Even on this beautiful day it's bleak, the austere outbuilding at odds with the beautiful surroundings.

'That's the bat house,' Joe explains. 'Hundreds of them in there. We used to play in there as boys,' he chuckles. 'We'd dare each other to go inside, lock the door and count for as long as we could.'

'When is the last time you were here?' Bo asks.

'Ah. Twenty years. More.'

'How often would Tom check this area?' Bo asks.

'Once, twice a week, to make sure the well wasn't contaminated. It's over there, behind the shed.'

'If you can't make money from this land, why didn't you sell it?'

'After Da died, the land was up for sale. Some Dublin lad wanted to build a house up here but couldn't do anything with that bat house. Environmental people' — he throws his chin up in the air to note his annoyance — 'they said the bats were rare. Couldn't knock down the shed or build around it because it would ruin their flight path, so that was that. Took it off the market then. Mossie!' Joe calls for his dog, who's disappeared from view.

They cut filming. Rachel moves close to the bat house, presses her face up to the windows to see in through the cracks in the wood. Bo notices Solomon walk away, equipment in hand, and head towards the forest. She hopes he's heard something interesting to record and so lets him go. Even if he hasn't, she knows she's gotten him and Rachel up early and driven them here with no food, and they can't function without it, unlike her, and she's starting to sense their irritation. She lets him go, for a few moments on his own.

'Where's the well?'

'Up there, beyond the bat house.'

'Would you mind if we filmed you checking the well?' she asks.

He gives her that same grunt that she recognises as signalling he'll do whatever she wants, he doesn't care, no matter how odd he regards her.

While Rachel and Joe talk bats — Rachel can hold a conversation about just about anything — Bo takes a little wander, around the back of the bat house. There's a cottage behind it, run-down, the outside in the same condition as the bat house, the white paint almost completely gone and the grey concrete dreary amidst all the green. Mossie wanders around in front of the cottage sniffing the ground.

'Who lived here?' Bo calls.

'Ha?' he shouts, unable to hear her.

She studies the cottage. This building has windows. Clean windows.

Joe and Rachel follow her and turn the corner into the path of the cottage.

'Who lived here?' Bo repeats.

'My da's aunt. Long time ago. She moved out, the bats moved in.' He chuckles again. He closes his eyes while he tries to think of her name. 'Kitty. We tormented the woman. She used to hit us with a wooden spoon.'

Bo moves away slightly, closer to the cottage,

27

she studies the area. This house has a vegetable patch beside it, some fruit growing too. There are wildflowers sitting in a tall glass in one of the windows.

'Joe,' Bo says. 'Who lives here now?'

'Nobody. Bats maybe,' he jokes.

'But look.'

He looks. He takes in all that she has already absorbed. The fruit and vegetable garden, the cottage, the windows that are gleaming, the door painted green, fresher paint than anything else in the vicinity. He's genuinely confused. She walks around the back. She finds a goat, two chickens wandering around.

Heart pounding, she calls out. 'Somebody is living in there, Joe.'

'Intruders? On my land?' he says angrily, an emotion she has never seen from Joe Toolin or his brother in all her time with them.

Hands in thick fists by his side, he charges towards the cottage, as fast as he can, and she tries to stop him. Mossie follows him.

'Wait, Joe, wait! Let me get Solomon! Solomon!' she yells, not wanting to alert the person inside the cottage, but having no choice. 'Rachel, film this.' Rachel is already on the case.

But Joe doesn't care about her documentary and places his hand on the door knob. He's about to push open the door but stops himself — he's a gentleman, after all. He knocks instead.

Bo looks in the direction of the forest where Solomon disappeared, then back to the cottage. She could kill Solomon right now, she shouldn't have let him wander off, it was unprofessional of

28

him. She let him leave because she knew he was famished, because as his girlfriend she knows how he becomes. Grumpy, unfocused, ratty. Again, one of the frustrating parts of being romantically linked with a colleague is actually caring when your decisions mean they go hungry. The sound will have to be compromised. At least they'll have a visual, they can add sound in after.

'Careful, Joe,' Rachel says. 'We don't know who's in there.'

There's no answer at the cottage and so Joe pushes open the door and steps inside. Rachel is behind him, and Bo hurries after.

'What the . . . ' Joe stands in the centre of the room, looking around, scratching his head.

Bo quickly points out singular items she wants Rachel to capture.

It's a one-roomed cottage. There's a single bed by one wall, with a view through one of the small windows beside the vegetable patch. On the other side there's a natural fire, a cooker, not too dissimilar to the one in Joe's farmhouse, and an armchair beside shelves of books. The four shelves have been filled to the brim and stacks of books are piled neatly on the floor beside it.

'Books,' Bo says aloud, wonderingly.

There are a half-dozen sheepskin rugs on the floor, no doubt to warm the cold stone floor during the desperate winters in a house with no obvious heating other than the fire. There's sheepskin across the bed, sheepskin on the armchair. A small radio sits alone on a side table.

It has a distinctly feminine feel. Bo's not

exactly sure why she feels this. She knows it's biased to base this on the glass of flowers; there's no scent but it feels feminine, not the dirty rustic feel of Tom and Joe's farmhouse. This feels different. Cared for, lived in, and there's a pink cardigan folded over the top rail of a chair. She nudges Rachel.

'Got it already,' she says, the sweat pumping from her forehead.

'Keep filming, I'll be back in a minute,' Bo says and runs out of the cottage towards the forest.

'Solomon!' she yells at the top of her voice, knowing there are no neighbours around to disturb. She returns to the clearing in front of the bat house, sees him a short way down the hill in the forest, just standing there, looking at something, as though he's in a trance. His sound bag is on the ground a few feet away from him, his boom mic leaning up against the tree. The fact that he's not even working tips her over the edge.

'Solomon!' she yells, and he finally looks at her. 'We found a cottage! Someone lives there! Equipment, hurry, move, now!' She's not sure if the words she has used make sense or if they're in the right order, she needs him to move, she needs sound, she needs to capture the story.

But what Bo hears in response is a sound unlike anything she's heard before.

3

The sound is like a squawk, from a bird, or something not human, but it comes from a human, from the woman standing at the tree.

Bo runs down into the forest and the blonde woman's basket goes flying up in the air, its contents fall out on to the forest floor and her eyes are wide in terror.

'It's okay,' Solomon says, hands out wanting to calm her, standing between Bo and the stranger like he's trying to tame a wild horse. 'We're not going to hurt you.'

'Who is that?' Bo calls.

'Just stay there, Bo,' Solomon says, annoyed, without turning.

Of course she ignores him and comes closer. The young woman makes a sound again, another unusual, kind of chirping sound, if a chirp could ever seem like a bark. It's directed at Bo.

Bo is gobsmacked, but a smile crawls to her face with fascination.

'I think she wants you to back off,' Solomon says to her.

'Okay, Doctor Doolittle, but I haven't done anything wrong,' she says, annoyed at being told what to do. 'So I'm not leaving.'

'Well then just don't come any closer,' Solomon says.

'Sol!' she says, looking at him with shock.

'Hey, hey, it's okay!' he says to the girl, slowly moving a little closer, getting on his hands and knees to pick up the flowers and herbs from the ground. He places them in her basket and holds it out to her. She stops her chirping but is clearly in distress, looking from Solomon to Bo, eyes wide and fearful.

'My name is Bo Healy. I'm a filmmaker and we're here with Joe Toolin's permission,' she holds out her hand.

The blonde woman looks at her hand and makes a series of more distressed sounds, none of them words.

'Oh my God,' Bo looks at Solomon, wide-eyed, taking out her phone and calling Rachel. 'Rachel, come up to the clearing, quickly. I need the camera.' She hangs up. 'Record this,' she mouths to Solomon, signalling his equipment with her eyes, afraid to move the rest of her body.

The young woman is firing off one bizarre sound after the next and it is the strangest thing Solomon has ever witnessed. It doesn't sound like it's coming from her voice box, it's like a recording. He's so stunned and fascinated he can't stop watching her, he looks for wires and there are none. This is real.

He takes a few steps in the direction of his audio bag.

Rachel appears through the trees, rushing with her camera in her hands, closely followed by Joe.

'What the hell is going on down there?' Rachel shouts, coming to an abrupt halt as she sees with her own eyes.

The young woman turns to Rachel and starts making the sound of a car alarm. Solomon looks at what's happening from her perspective, surrounded by three people, strangers in the forest, she must feel completely trapped. He can't bring himself to record this. It's not right.

Bo senses his hesitancy and sighs. 'Oh, for God's sake,' she snaps. She does what she should have done at the outset had she thought of it at the time, and films the unfolding scene with her phone.

Joe joins them.

The blonde woman stops making her sounds, for a moment she looks at Joe and she seems relieved.

'Who are you?' Joe shouts, half hidden by a tree. The fear is obvious in his voice. 'What are you doing on my land?'

She panics again, backing away through the trees.

Solomon watches them all. Bo is filming on her phone, Rachel pointing the camera at her, Joe a fierce face on him.

Solomon is exhausted, he needs to eat.

'Stop!' he yells and everybody goes silent. 'You're frightening her. Everybody step away. Let her go.'

She stares at him.

'You're free to go.'

She keeps looking at him. Those green eyes on him.

'I don't think she understands,' Bo says, still filming.

'Of course she understands,' Solomon snaps.

'I don't think she can speak . . . words. What's your name?' Bo asks.

The young woman ignores the question and continues to look at Solomon.

'Her name is Laura,' he says.

Mossie suddenly comes racing from the direction of the bat house, towards the forest, he's barking manically, protecting his land from the intruder. But instead of stopping by Joe he continues into the forest and heads straight for Laura.

'Whoa, whoa, whoa, call him off her, Joe,' Solomon says fearfully, afraid he'll take a chunk out of her.

But Mossie stops right at her feet, circles her excitedly, jumping up and down for her attention, licking her hand.

She rubs him — clearly the two of them are no strangers — as she nervously keeps her eye on everyone around her. She holds her hand out to Solomon and he looks at her, confused, thinking she wants to hold his hand. He reaches out his hand and then she smiles and looks down at the basket.

'The basket, Sol,' Bo says.

Embarrassed, he hands it to her.

Laura sets off with Mossie in tow, trying to avoid everyone. She is tentative at first. As she passes Bo, she growls, a perfect imitation of a dog growl so real it sounds like a recording, or as though it has come from Mossie. Laura examines Joe carefully and as soon as she's clear of them she runs up through the forest, past the bat house in the direction of the cottage.

'Did you get that?' Bo asks Rachel.

'Yep,' she removes the camera from her shoulder, and wipes the perspiration from her forehead. 'I got the blonde woman barking at you.'

'Where did she go?' Solomon asks.

'There's a cottage around the back of the bat house,' Rachel explains. Bo is too busy reviewing her video footage to see if she captured the moment.

'Do you know her?' Solomon asks Joe, completely confused as to what happened but feeling the adrenaline running through his body and a light tremble within him.

'She's trespassing on private property,' he huffs, the anger steaming off him.

'Do you think Tom knew about her?' Bo asks.

That question stumps him. His face goes from certainty, to confusion, to anger, betrayal, to disbelief once again. Then he's sad. If his brother did know about this young woman living in the cottage on their land, then he was keeping it from him. The brothers with no secrets from each other, it turns out, had one very big one.

4

'There's only one way of finding the answers,' Bo says, rolling up the sleeves of her black blouse to reveal her bronzed skin, as the sun continues to beat down overhead. 'We have to talk to the girl.'

'She's not a girl. She's a woman, and her name is Laura,' Solomon says, not sure where the anger is coming from. 'And I seriously doubt she'll want to talk to us now after we scared the shit out of her.'

'I didn't know she was . . . that she had a . . . *disability*,' Bo defends herself.

'Disability?' Solomon splutters.

'Oh, come on, what's the PC term?' Bo searches. 'Developmentally delayed, developmentally disabled, unsophisticated. Any of those please you? You know what I mean, I didn't realise.'

'Well, she ain't exactly normal,' Rachel says, sitting down on a rock, exhausted and sweating.

'Whatever the word for her, there's clearly something *wrong* with her, Solomon,' Bo says, pushing her hair off her face and redoing the short ponytail in her hair, the excitement bursting from her. 'If I'd known that, I would have approached her differently. Did you two talk? Apart from her telling you her name. You were there a while.'

'I think what happens from here is Joe's decision. It's his land,' Solomon says, ignoring Bo's interview, his stomach grumbling.

Bo throws him an annoyed look.

Joe shuffles around, clearly very uncomfortable with this chain of events. Joe likes routine, for everything to remain the same. Already his day has been very stressful and emotional. 'I want Mossie back,' he says finally. 'And she shouldn't be living on my land.'

'Squatters laws are tricky,' Rachel says. 'Friend of mine went through it. You have to get a court order to remove them.'

'Did your friends get rid of the squatter?' Solomon asks.

'My friend was the squatter,' Rachel replies.

Despite his frustration with what's going on, Solomon smirks.

'She has no right keeping my dog. I'm getting Mossie,' Joe says, adjusting his cap and marching off toward the cottage.

'Follow him,' Bo says quickly, picking up Rachel's camera and handing it to her, ignoring the exhausted glare. But as she's doing that Joe runs out of steam.

'Maybe it's better a woman talks to her.'

'Don't look at me,' Rachel warns Bo.

Apart from his mother, Bo, Rachel and Bridget, Joe hasn't been around many women, and has rarely spoken to a woman for most of his life. Rachel is easy with all people but it took him some adjustments to get used to her, particularly as she's not the kind of woman he's used to; a woman married to another woman was a fact that boggled his mind on learning it. Joe doesn't consider Bridget a woman, he doesn't really consider her at all; and Bo is still a cause for some awkwardness because of her own social abilities, or lack thereof. Having to talk to another new woman would flummox him. Especially one so odd, who requires care, thought and understanding. The four go to the cottage, their movements less charged and aggressive than before.

Bo knocks on the door, while Rachel and Solomon wait outside.

'What do you think?' Solomon asks Rachel.

'I'm fucking starving.'

'Me too,' Solomon rubs his face tiredly. 'I can't think straight.'

They watch as she knocks again.

'If Bo was looking for a new story, then she sure as fuck found one. This is a whole new brand of crazy,' Rachel says.

'She won't agree to an interview,' Solomon says, watching the door.

'You know Bo.'

He does. Bo has a way of convincing people who are so sure about not wanting to appear on camera into eventually speaking with her. When she really wants them, that is; the three interviews at the graveyard weren't important so she hadn't pursued them. Solomon and Rachel aren't usually this listless when it comes to a project, but Bo's typical filming style has severely

38

altered today. She's jumpy, grabbing at things, obviously without a plan.

Laura appears at the window but refuses to open the door.

'Tell her I want Mossie,' Joe says loudly, fidgeting, his hands in his pockets. He's uncomfortable. It's been an emotional day, having to bury his soulmate. A day spent out of his comfort zone, a break in his routine that has gone unchanged for over fifty years. His world has turned upside down. It's taken its toll and he wants his dog and to get back to the safety of his farmhouse.

'Please open the door, we just want to talk,' Bo says.

Laura stares at Solomon from the window.

Then everyone looks at Solomon.

'Tell her,' Bo says to him.

'What?'

'She's looking at you to see if it's okay. Tell her that we only want to talk.'

'Joe wants the dog,' Solomon says honestly, and Rachel chuckles.

Laura disappears from the window.

'Smooth,' Rachel smirks. The two are now delirious from the lack of food.

Joe is about to bang on the door when it opens. Mossie runs out and Laura closes the door again and locks it.

Joe storms off while an excited Mossie dances around him, almost tripping him.

'I'll ring Jimmy,' Joe grumbles as he passes. 'He'll sort her out.'

'Wait, Joe,' Bo calls after him.

'Let it go,' Rachel snaps. 'I'm starving. Let's

head over to the hotel. *Eat.* Actual food. I need to call Susie. Then you can make a plan. I'm serious.'

Rachel rarely loses her temper. The only time she flares up is when something is disturbing her shot — people in the background making faces, or Solomon's mic boom appearing in the frame — but when she does lose her temper everyone knows she means it. Bo knows she's pushed them too far.

She gives in, for now.

★ ★ ★

Back at Gougane Barra Hotel, Solomon and Rachel dig into their dinners, not uttering a word, while Bo thinks aloud.

'Tom must have known about this girl, right? He was the one who checked that area, that was part of his responsibility, checking the well a few times a week. You can't check the well without noticing the cottage. Or the vegetable plot, or the goat and chickens. It would be impossible. And there's the extra items of food on the shopping list, the bookshelves and the book from Bridget. Plus, Mossie knows her, so Tom must have brought him to visit her.'

'He's a dog,' Solomon speaks for the first time since he started eating ten minutes ago. 'Dogs wander. He could have met her himself.'

'Good point.'

'Met her,' Rachel says. 'Do dogs *meet* people? I guess they meet people who speak dog,' she jokes, then stops laughing when the others don't

40

join in; Bo because she's not listening, Solomon because he's sensitive about mocking Laura. 'Whatever. I'm going to call Susie.' Rachel takes her plate of food with her to another table.

'What is that thing she was doing? The noises?' Bo asks Solomon. 'Is it a Tourette's thing? She growled and barked and chirped.'

'As far as I know, people with Tourette's don't bark at people,' Solomon says, licking the sticky sauce from his fingers before taking a bite of his pork ribs.

The sauce is all over his face. Bo looks at him in disgust, not understanding his absolute inability to function without food. She stops picking at her green salad.

'You have your food now, why are you still snapping at me?'

'I don't think you handled today well.'

'I think you've been jet-lagged, moody and irritable all day,' she says. 'Extra sensitive — which, for you, is saying a lot.'

'You scared Laura.'

'*I* scared Laura,' she repeats, as she always does, as if saying the words again will help her to process them. She does the same during interviews with interviewees' responses. It can be unsettling for them, as though she doesn't believe them, but really it's her trying to grasp what they've just said.

'You could tell she was frightened. You could see a young woman, surrounded by four people in a forest. Three of us dressed in black for a funeral, like we're ninjas. She was terrified, and you were filming.'

41

That set-up seems to occur to her suddenly. 'Shit.'

'Yes, shit.' He sucks his fingers again and studies her. 'What's going on?'

'What we saw today was remarkable. What that girl did — '

'Laura.'

'What *Laura* did, those sounds she made, it was like magic. And I don't believe in magic. I've never heard anything like that before.'

'Me neither.'

'I got excited.'

'You got greedy.'

Silence.

He finishes his rib, watches the news on the TV in the corner.

'You know everyone keeps asking me what I've got coming out next,' she says.

'Yeah, they're asking me too.'

'I've got nothing. Nothing like *The Toolin Twins*. All these awards we're getting — people are interested in my work now, I have to be able to follow it up.'

He's known she's been feeling the pressure, and he's glad she's finally admitting it.

'You should be happy you made *one* thing that people like. Some people never get that. The reason you were successful in the first place is because you took your time. You found the right story, you were patient. You listened. Today was a mess, Bo. You were rushing around like a headless chicken. People would rather see something authentic and worthy, than something that's been thrown together.'

42

'Is that why you're doing *Fat Fit Club* and *Grotesque Bodies?*'

The anger bubbles inside him as he tries to remain calm. 'We're talking about you, not me.'

'I'm *under pressure*, Solomon.'

'Don't be.'

'You can't tell someone not to feel pressure.'

'I just did.'

'Solomon . . . ' She doesn't know whether to laugh or be angry.

'You lost yourself in the forest,' he says. He hadn't planned on saying it, it just popped out.

She studies him. 'Who are you talking to? Me, or yourself?'

'You, obviously,' he says, then throws the rib down, it makes a louder sound than he intended, as the bone hits the ceramic plate, and he starts a new one.

Bo folds her arms, studying him for a moment. He doesn't look at her, doesn't say a word.

'We both saw something fascinating in the forest. I jumped into action, you . . . froze.'

'I didn't freeze.'

'What were you doing there, all that time, while I was at the cottage? Was she there the entire time?'

'Fuck off, Bo.'

'Well, it's a valid question, isn't it?'

'Yes. We had sex. In the two minutes I was away from you, we had sex. Up against the tree.'

'That's not what I fucking mean and you know it.'

Wasn't it?

'I'm trying to figure her out and you're not giving me anything. You must have had a conversation but you keep ignoring the question. She told you her name. You were alone with her before I got there, I want to know what you talked about . . . '

He ignores her; the desire to yell at the top of his lungs in front of everybody is too great. He buries the anger, buries it, buries it deep, until a simmer is all that remains. It's as much as he can manage. He looks at Sky News but doesn't see it.

Bo eventually leaves the table, and the room.

He could think about what Bo said, analyse it, understand it, look within himself for the answers. He could think about what he said and why, he could think about all of it. But he's jet-lagged, hungry and pissed off, so instead he concentrates on the news on the TV, starting to hear the words coming from the presenter's mouth, starting to see the words that scroll by at the bottom of the screen. When he finishes his last rib, he sucks his fingers dry of the sticky sauce and leans back in his chair, feeling bloated and satisfied.

'Happy now?' Rachel calls across the empty restaurant.

'A night's sleep and I'll be grand.' He yawns and stretches. 'How's Susie?'

'A bit pissed off. Weather's too hot. She can't sleep. Feet and ankles are swollen up. Baby has a foot in her ribs. Think we're going home tomorrow?'

Solomon takes a toothpick out of its packet

and picks at the meat between his front teeth. 'Hope so.'

He does want to go home, he knows that much is true. Because he feels spooked. Because he did lose himself in that forest. And Bo saw it happen. And just like Joe wanted to go back to his farmhouse, Solomon wants to return to Dublin, to the *Grotesque Bodies* show that he despises, to his apartment that constantly smells of curried fish wafting up from his neighbours. He wants normality. He wants to go where he's used to not thinking about how he's feeling, where no confusion or analysis is necessary, where he's not drawn to people he knows he shouldn't be, or to doing things he knows he shouldn't do.

'Are you asleep? Because your eyes are open,' Rachel says, waving a rib across his eyeline, sending sauce flying on the table and floor. 'Fuck.'

Bo comes running into the bar, with *that* look on her face, and her phone in her hand.

'That was Jimmy — the garda we met earlier. He's at the Toolin farm. Joe called him to go talk to that girl, but his car hit Mossie on the way up the track. The girl took Mossie into her cottage and she's doing that crazy voice thing. She's locked herself in and won't let anyone near her or let anyone look at Mossie.'

Solomon looks at her in a 'so what?' kind of way. It's all he can summon up, but inside his heart is beating wildly.

Bo fixes him with an intriguing look. 'She's asking for you, Sol.'

5

Jimmy is standing by his patrol car, doors open, garda radio on, car directed straight towards the trees at the bat house. It's still daylight on this summer evening.

He lifts his arms in an apologetic way as they approach. 'Mossie was running around the car, I didn't see him.'

'Where's the girl now?' Bo asks.

'She grabbed the dog, carried it to the cottage, and now she won't come out or let anyone in. She's in a hysterical state. Joe said to call you.'

He looks as stunned as they had been when they first witnessed Laura's vocal outburst.

'She asked for Solomon?' Bo asks, eager to move things along.

'She asked for Tom first. Kept demanding I get him, that he could tell me who she is. I told her that he was dead and she went even more doolally. Then she mentioned Solomon.'

They were in the forest, both unable to break their gaze.

'*Hi,' he said gently.*

'*Hi,' she said softly.*

'*I'm Solomon.'*

She'd smiled. 'Laura.'

Bo is looking at him in that same uncertain way.

'I told her my name before we had sex,' he snaps. Jimmy prickles, Bo glares at him.

'Are you going to get her?' she asks.

'Not if he's going to arrest her.'

'I've nothing to arrest her for. I need to talk to her, find out who she is and why she's on Joe's property. If she's a squatter, those laws are complicated, and if Tom gave her permission, there's not much we can do. I'm only here to put Joe's mind at ease. And I went and hit the feckin' dog,' he says guiltily.

'So what do you want me to do?' Solomon asks, feeling the pressure build.

'Go to the cottage and see what she wants,' Bo says.

'Okay, Jesus,' he curses, running his fingers through his hair, retying it in a knot on the top of his head. He walks up the trail to the cottage; the other two follow him but stay close to the bat house when he goes to the cottage.

Solomon's heart pounds as he approaches the door and he has no idea why. He wipes his clammy hands on his jeans, and prepares to knock but before he even lifts his hand, the door opens. He can't see her, assumes she's behind the door and so he steps inside. As soon as he's in, the door closes. She locks the door and stands with her back to it, as if to reinforce it.

'Hi,' he says, shoving his hands into his pockets.

'He's by the fire,' Laura says, eyes barely able to settle on him. She seems nervous, worried.

Even though she introduced herself earlier, Solomon is almost surprised to hear her speak. In the woods she had a wild girl feeling about her; here in her home she seems more real.

Mossie is lying on his side on a sheepskin rug before the log-burning stove, his chest rising and falling with his slow breaths. His eyes are open, though he seems unaware of what's going on around him. The fire blazes beside him, a bowl of water and a bowl of food sit untouched by his head.

'He's not eating or drinking anything,' she says, getting on the floor beside Mossie, arms over him, protecting him.

Solomon should be looking at the dog but he can't take his eyes off her. She looks up at him, lost, worried, beautiful enchanting green eyes.

'Is he bleeding?' He goes to Mossie and slides beside him, opposite Laura, the closest they've been. 'Hiya, boy.' He places a hand on his fur and gently rubs.

Mossie looks at him, the pain obvious from his eyes. He whimpers.

Laura echoes Mossie's whimper in an astonishing likeness that forces Solomon to study her again. 'He's not bleeding. I don't know where his pain is, but he can't stand.'

'He should see a vet.'

She looks at him. 'Will you take him?'

'Me? Sure, but we could ask Joe, seeing as he's his dog.' And then, at the look on her face, he adds, 'Too.'

'Joe doesn't like me,' she says. 'None of them like me.'

'That's not true. Joe isn't used to change, that's all. Change makes some people angry.'

'Change with the change,' she says, but her voice has drastically altered. It's lower, deeper, Northern England, someone else's.

'Excuse me?'

'Gaga. My grandmother. That's what she used to say.'

'Oh. Right. Will you come with me to the vet?' he asks. He wants her to come with him.

'No. No. I stay here.'

It is a general statement. Not, I *will* stay here. But I stay here. Always.

Her clear skin is illuminated by the firelight. It's so calm and serene in this room, despite Mossie's struggle to survive and Laura's quiet panic.

She strokes Mossie's belly, which moves up and down slowly.

'When is the last time you left the mountain?' he asks.

She hides her face behind her hair, uncomfortable with the question.

'How long have you lived here?' he asks.

She takes a while to answer the question. 'Since I was sixteen. Ten years ago,' she replies, stroking Mossie.

'You haven't left since then?'

She shakes her head. 'I've had no reason to.'

He's staggered by this. 'Well, you have one now. Mossie would probably prefer it if you came with him,' he says.

And as if in agreement Mossie breathes out, his body shuddering.

49

Bo is outside with Jimmy, pacing, making awkward conversation, watching the flickering fire in the windows, the scent of chimney smoke pumping from the cottage.

'Interesting Joe never noticed the smoke.' She looks up at the plume of smoke rising from the chimney.

Jimmy looks up, 'I suppose farms are always burning something or other.'

Bo nods, good point. 'So you don't know who this girl is?'

'I've never seen her before,' he shakes his head. 'And I'd know everyone around here. In a rural town like ours with a population of a few hundred, all spread around the mountains. It's a mystery. My wife reckons she's a tourist, not from around here, one of those hikers who stumbled across the cottage and stayed. We get a lot of them. Over the years a few have stayed. They fall in love with the place, or someone in the place, decide to put down roots here. She might not be here very long.'

Bo ponders that but his wife's conclusion does nothing to quell Bo's curiosity, only further fuels her multiplying questions. Why would Tom lie about renting the cottage? Was it for his own financial gain? She doubted that. She filmed on this mountain three years ago and Tom never brought them here, never even mentioned it. She guesses the girl has been there at least that long or they would have filmed here. 'Why the secret?' she asks, confused.

Jimmy looks thoughtful, but doesn't reply.

The door to the cottage opens and Solomon appears. He fills the tiny doorframe with his physique. The firelight is behind him, he is a dark large shadow. He looks like a hero, carrying a dog from a blazing fire.

Bo smiles at the image.

Solomon turns and speaks to the girl behind him, encourages her to come outside.

'Come on, Laura, it's okay.' And there's something in the way that he says that, or looks as he says that, that causes Bo's smile to freeze.

And then the girl appears, in a belted checked shirt-dress, with Converse and a chunky cardigan over it, her long blonde hair falling over her shoulders.

'We're going to take Mossie to the vet,' Solomon tells them. 'Where do we go?'

'Patrick Murphy, in the main street. Surgery will be closed now, but I'll give him a call,' Jimmy says, studying Laura. 'Hello, Laura,' he says kindly, wanting to make up for his earlier approach.

Laura stares down at her Converses. She looks terrified. She reaches out and holds on to Solomon's arm. She grips him so tightly, he can feel her body shaking.

'We should go quickly, Garda.' Solomon starts to move. 'Mossie isn't doing very well. I'm sure Joe would want him seen to first before anything else.'

'Right so,' Jimmy says, stepping back. 'Laura, we can arrange to have an informal chat over the next few days. This lad can be here with you if you like.'

Head down, Laura continues to cling to Solomon's arm, another protective hand on Mossie. She makes a sound that appears to be the crackle of a dispatch radio.

Jimmy frowns.

'We can arrange a time for you and Laura to talk,' Bo says to him, walking along with Laura and Solomon. 'And perhaps you'll agree to do the interview?' She'd asked him to talk about finding Joe at the house when Tom was lying dead on the ground, she wanted to hear the peculiar scene explained by someone else. Now is a good time to negotiate. She'll help him speak with Laura if he speaks with her.

Laura stops walking.

'Come on,' Solomon calls to her, gently, in a tone of voice that Bo has never heard him use with her, or with anyone for that matter.

Laura just stares at Bo, which puts Solomon in an incredibly difficult position, but this is getting ridiculous now. He's exhausted, he wants to sleep. Mossie is getting heavier in his arms.

'Jimmy, would you mind driving Bo to our hotel, please?' He avoids Bo's eye as he asks. 'I'll meet you there later, Bo.'

Her mouth falls open.

'You told me to help,' he snaps, following the trail that leads to their parked car, adjusting the dog in his arms. 'I'm helping.'

Laura sits in the back of the car with Mossie. The dog lies across the seat, his head on her lap. Bo gets into the garda car, a scowl on her face. It would be a funny sight if Solomon were capable of being remotely amused by what is happening.

'Thank you, Solomon,' Laura says, so quietly that Solomon's body immediately relaxes and the anger leaves him.

'You're welcome.'

★   ★   ★

Laura is quiet in the car, whimpering occasionally along with Mossie in what he guesses is a show of support. He turns the radio on, lowers it, then decides against it and turns it off. The vet is thirty minutes away.

'Why was the garda there?' she asks.

'Joe called him. He wanted to find out who you are and figure out why you're living there.'

'Have I done something wrong?'

'I don't know, you tell me,' he laughs. She doesn't and he gets serious again. 'You are living in a cottage on Joe's land, without his knowledge, that's . . . well, it's illegal.'

Her eyes widen. 'But Tom told me I could.'

'Well, that's okay then, that's all you need to tell them.' He pauses. 'Do you have that agreement on paper? A lease?'

She shakes her head.

He clears his throat, she copies him, which is quite off-putting, but her innocent face suggests no malice, nor any sign that she's even aware of what she did.

'Were you paying him rent?'

'No.'

'Right. So you asked him if you could live there and he said you could.'

'No. Gaga asked him.'

'Your grandmother? Could she support you on that?' he asks.

'No.' She looks down at Mossie and strokes him. She kisses his head and nuzzles into him. 'Not from where she is.'

Mossie whimpers and closes his eyes.

'Is it true that Tom is dead?' she asks.

'Yes,' he says, watching her in the mirror. 'Sorry. He had a heart attack on Thursday.'

'Thursday,' she says quietly.

They park in the main street and knock on the surgery door. There's no answer but the front door to the attached house opens and a man appears, wiping his mouth with a napkin, the smell of a home roast drifts out the door to them.

'Oh hello, hi,' he says. 'Jimmy called me. Emergency, is it?' he asks, seeing Mossie in Solomon's arms. 'Come in, come in.'

Solomon sits outside the surgery while Laura goes inside. He leans his elbows on his thighs and rests his head in his hands. His head is spinning, the ground is moving from the jet lag.

When the surgery door opens, Laura appears with tears rolling down her cheeks. She sits beside Solomon, without a word.

'Come here,' he whispers, wrapping his arm around her shoulders and pulling her to him. Another loss in her week. He doesn't know how long they stay like that, but he would happily remain that way if the vet wasn't standing at the open door patiently waiting for them to gather themselves and leave so he can to return to his family after a long day.

'Sorry.' Solomon removes his arm from around Laura's shoulders. 'Let's go.'

★ ★ ★

Outside in the now dark night, music drifts from the local pub.

'I could really do with a pint,' he says. 'Want to join me?'

A fire-escape door opens at the side of the bar and a bottle goes flying outside and lands in a recycling skip, smashing against the others inside.

Laura mimics the smashing sound.

He laughs. 'I'll take that as a yes.'

They sit outside the pub, at one of the wooden picnic tables, around the corner from the gang of smokers. When Solomon pulled the door open, and all the heads turned to stare at the two strangers, Laura quickly backed away. Solomon was relieved to not have to sit inside and be examined by the locals. Now she sits with a glass of water, while he drinks a pint of Guinness.

'Never drink?' he asks.

She shakes her head, the movement causing the ice to clink against the glass. She imitates the sound of the ice perfectly. It's something Solomon still can't wrap his head around, though he's unsure of how to broach the subject; it's as though she doesn't even notice.

'Are you okay?' he asks. 'Tom and Mossie — that's a lot to lose in one week.'

'One day,' she says. 'I only learned about Tom tonight.'

'Sorry you had to hear it that way,' Solomon says softly, thinking of how Jimmy had blurted it out.

'Tom used to bring the shopping on Thursdays. When he didn't come, I knew something was wrong, but I had no one to ask. I thought Joe was Tom today in the forest. I've never seen him before. They're identical. But he was so angry. I'd never seen Tom so angry.'

'You've lived there for ten years and you've never seen Joe?'

She shakes her head. 'Tom wouldn't allow it.'

He's about to ask why, but stops himself. 'Joe's grieving, he's usually more accommodating. Give him time.'

She sips her water, concerned.

'So you haven't eaten anything since Thursday,' Solomon suddenly realises.

'I have the fruit-and-veg patch, the eggs. I bake my own bread. I have enough but Tom likes . . . liked . . . to supply some extras. I was foraging when I saw you.' She smiles shyly at him as she remembers how they met. He smiles too and then laughs at himself for his schoolboy feelings.

'Jesus, let me get you some food. What do you want, burger and chips? I'll get some for me too.' He stands and looks across the road to the chipper. 'It's been a whole two hours since I ate.'

She smiles.

He expects her to mill into her food, but she doesn't. Everything about her is calm and slow. She delicately picks at the chips with her long elegant fingers, occasionally studying one before she takes a bite.

'You don't like them?'

'I don't think there's any potato in it,' she says, dropping it to the greasy paper and giving up. 'I don't eat this kind of food.'

'Unlike Tom.'

Her eyes widen. 'I always told him to fix his diet. He wouldn't listen.' She looks sad again as the news of his death and her loss sinks in further.

'Joe and Tom aren't the types to listen to anybody,' Solomon senses her blaming herself.

'He once told me he had a ham sandwich for dinner and I gave him such a lecture about it when he came back the next week he was so proud to tell me he'd had a banana sandwich that day instead. He thought the fruit would be healthier.'

They both laugh.

'Perhaps I was wrong,' Solomon says gently, 'he did listen to somebody.'

'Thanks,' she says.

'How did your grandmother know Tom?' Solomon asks.

'You ask a lot of questions.'

He thinks about it. 'I do. It's how I make conversation. How do you make conversation?' he asks and they both laugh.

'I don't. Apart from Tom I never have anybody to talk to. Not people, anyway.' Somebody at the table around the corner stands, pushing aside the bench, which screeches against the ground. She imitates the sound. Once, twice, until she gets it right. The bar girl clearing the table beside them gives her a funny look.

'I have fine conversations with myself,' Laura continues, not noticing the look or not caring. 'And with Mossie and Ring. And inanimate objects.'

'You wouldn't be alone in that.' He smiles, watching her, completely intrigued.

She makes a new sound, one that makes him laugh. It sounds like a phone vibrating.

'What is that?' he asks.

'What?' She frowns.

And then suddenly he hears the sound again and it's not coming from Laura's lips, though he has to study her closely. He feels his phone vibrating in his pocket.

'Oh.' He reaches into his pocket and takes out his phone.

Five missed calls from Bo, followed by three messages of varying desperation.

He puts it face down on the table, ignoring it.

'How did you know Tom?'

'More questions.'

'Because I find you intriguing.'

'I find you intriguing.'

'Ask me something then.' He smiles.

'Some people learn about people in other ways.' Her eyes sear into him so much his heart pounds.

'Okay.' He clears his throat and she imitates the sound perfectly again. 'We — me, Bo and Rachel — made a documentary about Joe and Tom. We spent a year with them, watching their every move, or at least that's what we thought. You seemed to elude us. My experience of Joe and Tom is that they had no contact with

58

anybody at all, apart from suppliers and customers, and even then it was rare for it to be human contact. It was just them, every day, all their lives. I'm not sure how Tom would have met your grandmother.'

'She met him through my mum, who brought them food and provisions. She cleaned their house.'

'Bridget's your mother?'

'Before Bridget.'

'How long ago are we talking?' Solomon asks, leaning in to her, enthralled, whether she's spinning bullshit or not. He happens to think it's the truth. He wants to think it's the truth.

'Twenty-six years ago,' she says. 'Or a little bit more than that.'

He looks at her, slowly processing. Laura is twenty-six years old. Tom did her grandmother a favour. Her mother was a housekeeper at their house twenty-six years ago.

'Tom was your dad,' he says in a low voice.

Despite knowing this, him saying it aloud seems to unsettle her and she looks around, imitating the clink of glasses, the smash of bottles in the recycling bin, the cracking ice. All sounds overflowing and overlapping each other as a sign of her distress.

He's so shocked that his summation is true. He places his hand over hers. 'I'm even more sorry you had to learn about his death like that.'

She imitates the sound of him clearing his throat, even though he hasn't made the sound; she has linked it to his feeling of awkwardness, is perhaps telling him she feels uncomfortable, is trying to show him how she feels, connect it to those moments when he feels like that. Perhaps there is a language in her mimicry. Perhaps he's losing his mind completely, investing such time and belief in someone that Bo considered unsophisticated, or developmentally delayed. But there doesn't seem to be anything unsophisticated about the woman who sits before him right now. If anything she operates and communicates on more levels and layers than he's ever experienced.

'Laura, why did you ask for me tonight?'

She looks at him, those bewitching green eyes. 'Because, apart from Tom, you're the only person I know.'

Solomon has never ever been the only person that someone knows. It seems to him to be an odd thing, but a beautifully intimate thing. And something that isn't to be taken lightly. It's something that carries huge responsibility. Something to cherish.

6

The following morning the film crew are in Joe's kitchen. Joe is sitting silently in his chair. Ring is by his feet, mourning the loss of his friend.

Bo has revealed to him, as gently as she could, that Laura is Tom's daughter. He hasn't said a word, made absolutely no comment whatsoever. He's lost in his head, perhaps running through all the conversations, all the moments he could have missed this information, the moments he was possibly deceived, wondering how Tom could have lived a life he never knew about.

It breaks Solomon's heart; he can't even watch him. He holds the boom mic in the air, looking away, out of respect, trying to give Joe as much privacy in this moment as he can, despite three people invading his home and a camera pointed at his face. Of course Solomon was against revealing this news to Joe on camera, but the producer has the final say.

'Laura's mother, Isabel, was your housekeeper over twenty-six years ago.'

He looks at Bo then, coming alive. 'Isabel?' he barks.

'Yes, do you remember her?'

He thinks back. 'She wasn't with us very long.'

Silence, his brain ticks over, sliding through the memory files.

'Do you recall Tom and Isabel being particularly close?'

'No.' Silence. 'No.' Again. 'Well, he'd . . . ' He clears his throat. 'You know, he'd do the same as with Bridget: pay her for the cleaning and the provisions. I'd be out on the land. I'd not much to do with that.'

'So you'd no idea about a love affair between them?'

It's as though that expression occurs to him for the first time. The only way for Tom to have become a father was to have had a love affair. Something they both had said they'd never had. Two virgins at seventy-seven years old.

'This girl is sure about that?'

'After Isabel died, her grandmother revealed to her that Tom was her father. Laura's grandmother, who was ailing herself, made an arrangement with Tom for Laura to live at the cottage.'

'He knew about her then,' Joe says, as if that's been the burning question the whole time but he was afraid to ask.

'Tom only learned she was his daughter after Isabel's death, ten years ago. The cottage was modernised as much as was possible, by Tom, though there's no electricity or hot running water. Laura has been living there alone ever since.' Bo consults her notes. 'Laura's grandmother Hattie Murphy reverted to her maiden name Button after her husband's death. Isabel changed her name too, and so Laura calls herself Laura Button. Hattie died nine years ago, six months after Laura moved to the cottage.'

Joe nods. 'So she's on her own then.'

'She is.'

He ponders that. 'She'll be expecting his share then, I suppose.'

Solomon looks at him.

'His share of . . . '

'The land. Tom made a will. She's not in it. If that's what she's looking for.'

The infamous Irish hunger for land rises in him.

'Laura hasn't mentioned anything about wanting a share of the land. Not to us.'

Joe is agitated; Bo's comments don't do much to calm him. It's as though he's readying himself for a fight. His land, his farm is his life, it's all he has ever known his entire life. He's not going to give any of it up for his brother's lie.

'Perhaps Tom had planned to talk to you about her,' Bo says.

'Well, he didn't,' he says with a nervous, angry laugh. 'Never said a word.' Silence. 'Never said a word.'

Bo gives him a moment.

'Knowing what you know now, will you allow Laura to continue living at the cottage?'

He doesn't respond. He seems lost in his head.

'Would you like to start a relationship with her?' she asks gently.

Silence. Joe is completely still though his mind is most likely not.

Bo looks at Solomon uncertain as to how to proceed.

'Perhaps a relationship is too much for you to think about now. Perhaps it would be simpler to consider whether you will continue to support her, as Tom did?'

His hands grip the armrests, Solomon watches the colour drain from his knuckles.

'Joe,' Bo says gently, leaning forward. 'You know this means that you're not alone. You have family. You're Laura's uncle.'

Joe stands up from the chair then, fiddling with the microphone on his lapel. His hands are shaking and he's clearly upset, becoming irritated by the film crew's presence now, as if they have brought this nuisance into his life.

'That's that,' he says, dropping the mic to the thin cushion on the wooden chair. 'That's that now.'

It's the first time he has walked out on them.

★　★　★

The crew move to Laura's cottage. Laura sits in her armchair, the same checked shirt-dress tied at the waist with a belt, and a tattered pair of Converse. Her long hair has been recently washed and is drying, there isn't a stitch of make-up on her clear, beautiful skin.

The camera is off, Rachel is outside with the gear, on the phone to Susie. The day is drizzly, unlike yesterday's heatwave, and Solomon wonders how she survives in this place in the depths of winter when even his modern Dublin

64

city apartment feels depressing. As Bo talks, Laura watches Solomon. With Bo in the room, this makes it somewhat awkward for him. He clears his throat.

Laura mimics him.

He shakes his head and smiles.

Bo misses what passes between them as she prepares for her conversation. 'So, bearing in mind we don't know how much of an assistance Joe will be to you, moving forward, we'd like, Solomon and I . . . '

He closes his eyes as she mentions him. It's a ploy to build Laura's trust by portraying herself as an ally to Solomon and therefore an ally to Laura. Technically, it's true; she is, after all, his girlfriend. But it still feels like a ploy.

'We'd like to make a suggestion. We'd like to offer to help you. I feel you and I got off to a wrong start — and let me explain why. I apologise profusely for how I behaved when I first met you. I got excited.' Bo places her hand on her heart as she speaks completely honestly, meaning every word. 'I'm a documentary maker. A couple of years ago, I followed your father and uncle for a year.'

Solomon notices how Laura flinches at that, as if equally uncomfortable with the truth as Joe is.

'They are, were, fascinating people and their story spread all over the world. Aired in twenty countries, I have it here. This is an iPad; if you do this . . . ' She swipes carefully, looking at Laura then back to the iPad to see if she understands.

Laura mimics the iPad clicking sounds.

'Then you press this to watch it.' Bo touches the screen and the film starts playing.

She allows Laura to watch it for a moment.

'I'd love to make a documentary about you. We'd love to film you here at the cottage, get a sense of who you are and how you live your life.'

Laura looks at Solomon. He's about to clear his throat but stops himself. Laura does it instead, sounding like him. Bo still doesn't notice.

'There is a fee, but it's small. I have the terms here.'

Bo takes a page from her folder and hands it to her.

Laura looks at the page blankly.

'I'll leave this with you, for you to decide.'

Bo looks at the piece of paper, wondering if she should explain it any further, or if doing so would seem patronising. With Solomon standing behind her shoulder, judging her, maybe not deliberately but she feels the judgement, this cold air that comes from him when she does or says something. She does appreciate that he has a better way with negotiating certain situations but she also wants the freedom to be able to act as she deems appropriate, without fearing or dreading the feedback, the sensing the disapproval and disappointment. Of always letting him down. Of having to check herself. She doesn't want any more cold air between them, but mostly she doesn't like to have to second-guess herself at a job that she knows she's more than capable of doing. In ways, it was easier when their relationship was platonic. She cared more about what he thought, rather than what he thinks of her.

She's sitting on the edge of her chair, too much in Laura's space. She pushes herself back and tries to appear relaxed, waits for a positive answer.

Laura is watching the first few minutes of video of her father and uncle on the iPad.

'I don't think that I'd like people to know about me,' Laura says and Solomon is surprised by his relief.

He would never consider their documentaries exploitive, but he's proud of Laura for sticking to what feels right to her, not being swayed by attention and fame as so many people are. Rarely does Bo have to convince anybody to say anything on camera, she dangles a camera in front of them and they jump to attention, ready for their five minutes of fame. He likes that Laura is different. She's normal. She's a normal person who appreciates her anonymity, who values privacy. That, and something else.

'You don't have to share anything with us that you don't want,' Bo says. 'Joe and Tom allowed us to follow them and see how they lived and communicated with each other but I don't think they felt we crossed any boundaries. We had a very well understood agreement, that as soon as they felt uncomfortable, we'd stop filming.'

Like this morning, in Joe's kitchen. It made Bo feel unwell, as though she'd had a falling out with a friend.

Laura looks relieved. 'I like to be by myself. I don't want — ' she looks at the iPad, and newspaper articles and magazine reviews on the table, 'I don't want all of that.'

She pulls the sleeves of her cardigan over her wrists and scrunches them between her fingers, and hugs herself, as if she's cold.

'Understood,' Solomon says and looks at Bo, an air of finality to it. 'We respect your decision. But before we go, we brought you some things.'

Solomon carries the shopping bags over to her and places them on the floor beside her. He'd probably gone overboard but he didn't want her to be left with nothing, especially if Bridget sides with Joe and doesn't continue to provide for Laura. He'd run across to the local tourist shop, bought as many blankets, T-shirts, jumpers as he could. He couldn't imagine how cold it got in here, wind whistling through the holes in the walls, the old windows, while bats are flying metres from her door.

Bo hadn't commented on his purchases. She'd stayed in the car checking emails, while he'd filled the boot with shopping bags. It's only now that Bo looks at the amount he places down, takes them in, and looks at him in surprise. He's embarrassed but she's impressed by his effort. In Bo's opinion, it could go a long way to convincing Laura to work with them.

'I thought it could get very cold up here,' Solomon explains, awkwardly, faffing his hands over the tops of the bags and muttering about their contents.

Bo smiles, trying to hold in her laugh at her boyfriend's discomfort.

'Thank you so much for all of these things,'

Laura says, peering in the bags, then addressing Solomon. 'It's far too much. I don't think I could eat all of this on my own.'

'Well, there's three people here who'd love to help you,' Bo jokes casually, still pushing, always pushing.

'I'll have to give them all back to you,' she says to Solomon and then to Bo. 'I can't do your documentary.'

'They're for you,' Solomon says firmly, 'whether you do it or not.'

'Yes, yes, keep them,' Bo says, distracted.

While Solomon is getting ready to leave, doing the thing where he doesn't want to push, doesn't want to be seen as being rude, in the way, Bo prepares. That part of it never bothers Bo, it's a momentary awkwardness in an overall larger picture. Bo feels it in her gut that she can't let Laura go. She's a fascinating, beautiful, interesting, ferociously intriguing girl, none of which she has seen the likes of before. Not only has she a personal life that is ripe for storytelling but a unique characteristic which is visually splendid. The girl is perfect. While Solomon says his goodbye to Laura, Bo lags behind, taking her time tidying her paperwork up. Placing the newspaper photocopies in a neat pile, running through her head what she can say next.

'You go ahead, Sol, I'll be out in a minute,' Bo says, placing her folder in her bag, slowly.

Solomon leaves, and closes the door behind him.

Dark disapproving boyfriend gone.

Bo looks up at Laura and the girl looks so

forlorn, as though she's about to start crying.

'What's wrong?' Bo asks, surprised.

'Nothing, I . . . nothing,' she says, a little breathlessly. She stands up and moves across the room, to her kitchenette. She pours herself a cup of water and drinks it down in one.

She's a peculiar girl. Bo wants to know everything about her. She wants to see the world from her eyes, walk in her shoes, she needs Laura to say yes. She cannot lose her. Bo knows that she is passionate about her work, that it borders on obsessed, but that's what it takes for her to fully understand her subject. She has to absorb herself in his or her life, she *wants* to do that. Bo was searching for something new after *The Toolin Twins*, and here it is, the natural birth of a new story has quite literally emerged from the first story. It's perfect, it's right, it has potential to be even better than *The Toolin Twins*. It's Bo's job to make other people see what she sees, to feel what she feels. She must make Laura see that.

'Laura,' she says gently. 'I respect your decision not to take part, but I want to make sure you are seeing the whole picture. I want to help you think this through. This week has obviously been a big week for you, a time of huge change in your life, with the passing of your dad.'

Laura looks down, her long eyelashes brush her cheekbones. Bo notes the reaction when she refers to Tom as her dad, to Joe as her uncle, she needs to be careful when using it. They're not terms Laura is comfortable with and she wants to know why. *Why, why, why!* It seems that this girl is built entirely on secrets; created on one, born on one, reared on one, exists on one. Bo wants to break the chain.

'It's a new beginning for you. Your life is moving on. There is uncertainty as to whether Joe will allow you to live here, and if he does, uncertainty as to whether he will assist you in living the life you have been living for the past ten years. I don't know if Joe will take on Tom's role of acting as an intermediary with Bridget for you, getting your provisions, and paying for them, because I assume Tom covered the costs?'

She nods.

'If Joe doesn't, how will you get to the shops with no car? Do you have money? Can you pay for food? Tom, as helpful as he was to you, really did leave you in a very vulnerable situation.' She leads into the next sentence gently. 'There isn't a mention of you in Tom's will. He has left his share to Joe. Perhaps he intended on discussing your presence here with Joe, but he never did.'

She leaves that to sink in with Laura, who has now reached out to grip the back of the chair tightly. Her eyes dart around the room, deep in thought, everything that has been her world possibly dissolving right in front of her.

'If you take part in this documentary, we can help you. The three of us will be here, we can bring you whatever you need. We can even help you get set up somewhere else if that's what you want. Whatever you want, we can help you. You're not alone. You'll have me, Rachel and of course . . . you'll have Solomon, who I can tell is so fond of you,' Bo adds, with a smile.

71

7

'She's in!' Bo sings, from the trail, making her way to where Solomon and Rachel are waiting by the car.

'What?' Rachel says, looking at Solomon. 'He just said she's out.'

'Well it's happening now!' Bo raises her hand in the air for a high-five. They both stare at her.

'Ah, come on, don't leave me hanging.'

Rachel high-fives her, with a surprised laugh. 'You are unbelievable. You truly are a piece of work.'

Bo raises her eyebrows, enjoying the praise, hand still in the air and waiting for Solomon.

He folds his arms. 'I'm not high-fiving anything until you tell me how you changed her mind.'

Bo drops her hand and rolls her eyes. 'Would you ask another producer that question? Or just me? Because I would like to have the same respect from you as you would give to somebody else, don't you think that's fair?'

'If I was in the room with a producer who got a clear no, and then I left, and he got a yes, then yes, I would ask him.'

'Why is the producer immediately a *him?*' Bo asks.

'Or her. Who gives a fuck? What did you do to make her say yes?'

'Okay guys, before you both go off on one, can we first get some of the logistics straight,' Rachel grabs their attention. 'I really have to get home to Susie — we have an anatomy scan on Friday, I will not miss it,' she says, fully serious. 'I need to know what's happening. Is there a plan?'

Bo looks at both of them, her eyes wide in shock. 'Guys,' she says, exasperated. 'Can we quit the moaning for a second and embrace, truly acknowledge the fact that we have the subject of a new documentary, *confirmed.* Can we not ruin the moment right now with a thousand questions, and celebrate?' She looks at both of them. 'We're ready to go again. Whoo! Come on!' she tries to jazz them up until they eventually cave in and celebrate with her, in a group hug, Rachel and Solomon momentarily hiding their reservations.

'Congratulations you relentless little shit,' Solomon says, kissing her.

She laughs. 'Thank you! Finally, the recognition I deserve.'

'So . . . ' Rachel says.

'I know, I know, *Susie,*' Bo says thinking it through. 'Of course you need to get back to her. My feeling is that all the signs are pointing to filming now,' Bo says. 'The weather, for a start. We've been here in winter, it's murky, it's complicated. Rachel, you slipped on your ass more times than I care to remember and, while it was hilariously funny, it was dangerous — as you pointed out.'

Solomon chuckles.

'And while I want to film what it's like for Laura living here in all seasons, because I think that's important, I want to get the principal stuff done now. I want to show people how we found her. Sleeping Beauty in her hidden cottage in the forest. I want the colour, I want light, I want these sounds,' she says, seeing it all. 'It's a summer vibe. Thirdly, if we leave it too long, there's a chance Laura will change her mind. I want her immediate thoughts, wishes, dreams, not something she's figured out a few months down the road. Her life has changed *now* — bam! We need to follow her now, when she's right on the cusp. And finally, I don't know how long Joe is going to allow her to live here. If we leave he may just kick her out of the cottage, if we're here he might be more likely to allow her to stay.

'So, bearing that all in mind, we go home today, gather ourselves, I'll prepare the paperwork, Rachel you gather the equipment, and we'll return Sunday evening. We begin filming here on Monday for a two-week shoot, tops.'

They all agree.

'Rachel I know that Susie's due date is three weeks away, if for whatever reason you have to leave . . . ' Bo says, starting to think of replacement camera people she's worked with. 'I could call Andy and see if — '

'Andy's a dickhead, his filming is deeply inferior to mine. Don't replace me with Andy. It

74

would be an insult. Don't replace me with anyone,' Rachel says firmly. 'This is a story,' Rachel says, pointing up the mountain to the cottage. 'I want to work on this.'

At Rachel's show of support, Solomon feels goosebumps rise on his skin. He's never heard her so enthusiastic, nor has he felt this way about a project before. They are all eager to begin, hankering to dive into discovering Laura's story. Buzzing with excitement Bo returns to the cottage to discuss the filming schedule with Laura, however, she emerges moments later with less energy.

'She's changed her mind,' Solomon guesses, feeling his stomach drop.

'Not quite. She's panicking. She's doing the noise thing. She wants you, Sol. Again.'

★ ★ ★

Solomon closes the door to the cottage. Laura is standing, pacing the small area between her bed, the kitchenette and the living area.

'Hi,' he says.

She mimics a sound and he doesn't know what it is until he closes the door and it is exactly the sound she has just made. The latch closing. Her sounds may be things she desires to happen, Solomon adds this observation to his list of studies.

'I thought it would be starting tomorrow,' she says, nervously twisting her fingers.

'The documentary?'

'Yes.'

'No, I'm sorry. It can't happen instantly. We have to go home, and prepare for the shoot but there's no need to worry, we'll be back on Monday for two weeks.'

'When are you leaving?' she asks, pacing the room.

'Today,' he says. 'Laura what's wrong?'

'If you go, I'll be here alone.'

She starts to make noises, agitated. Bird sounds, distressed.

'It's only five days. You're always here alone.'

'Joe doesn't want me here.'

'We don't know that Joe doesn't want you here,' Solomon says. 'He's in shock, it will take him a bit of time.'

'But what if he comes over here, when you're gone, and wants me to leave. What if the garda comes back? What will I do? Where will I go? I don't know anyone. I don't have anyone.'

'You can call me, if that happens. Here,' he roots around in his pockets for a pen and paper. 'I'll give you my number.'

'How will I call you? I don't have a phone.'

He stalls, the pen hovering over the page.

'Please stay. I'd like to film tomorrow,' she says, swallowing nervously. 'If this is going to happen, it has to happen tomorrow,' she says, trying to toughen up.

'We can't film tomorrow, Laura,' he says gently. 'Look, it's okay. Please calm down. I have to get to my mam's this weekend. She's seventy. She lives in Galway, I can't miss it. Rachel, the one with the camera, her wife is pregnant, she has to get home to her, and Bo, she's the director, producer, she's got a lot of work to do for next week, planning, paperwork, a lecture, that kind of thing. We need more equipment, there's paperwork to be done, permission to be granted, there's no way we could start tomorrow.'

'Can I go with you?' she asks.

He stares at her in shock, unable to think of how to reply. 'You want to . . . '

'Can I stay with you? I can't stay here any more. It's all been changed. I have to . . . change with the changes.'

She's panicking, her mind working overtime.

'Relax, Laura, it's okay, everything's okay, nothing's changed.' He goes to her, holds her by her arms, gently, tries to get her to look at him. His heart is pounding; just feeling her is sending him into a spin. She looks at him and those grassy eyes probe into him, into his very soul.

'My dad's dead,' she looks at him, eyes piercing. 'My dad is dead. And I never even called him dad. I never even knew if he knew that I was his daughter. We never even . . . ' The tears spill down her cheeks.

'Oh, come here,' he whispers, wrapping his arms around her and pulling her close to him so that her head is against his chest and she is completely enveloped in his love and care.

'How can a place be a home if no one wants you there?' she asks through her tears. 'This is not a home.'

He can't answer that.

He's the only person she knows. He can't leave her here.

'What. The. Fuck,' Bo says, sitting up, as Solomon walks towards her and Rachel with bags in his hands, closely followed by Laura.

'She's coming with us,' he says, avoiding Bo's stare, as he puts the bags in the boot of the car.

'What?' Bo joins him.

'She's scared here. She doesn't want to wait on her own until we get back. I wonder who scared the shit out of her, Bo,' he says through his teeth at her, the veins pulsating in his neck. He's really angry.

'But — you have to go to your parents' house.'

'Yes, and I'll have to take her with me. She won't go with you to Dublin,' he mutters, trying to slot her shopping bags and suitcase into the boot among their recording equipment.

He waits for Bo to tell him no way, this is ridiculous, she is not allowing her boyfriend to travel with a young, beautiful strange woman to his family party, but instead when he looks up, she's grinning broadly.

'Laura,' she calls, holding two thumbs up. 'This is the best news. The *best*.'

8

'Snow White!' Bo announces, slamming her beer bottle down on the table in the hotel bar, more loudly than she'd intended.

Rachel laughs. Solomon shakes his head and reaches for the bowl of peanuts.

'Seriously, she's like a real-life Snow White,' she says excitedly. 'I could definitely pitch that. Lives in the forest, sings to the fucking animals.'

Solomon and Rachel can't help but laugh at that, and at Bo's intensity. Bo's tipsy, her eyes are shining, her cheeks are rosy as they discuss plans for the documentary. Instead of going home, Bo managed to talk Rachel into staying for two more days. They'll stay at the hotel in Gougane Barra for two nights, film during the day at the cottage, go their separate ways for the weekend, return to Cork on Sunday night. She can't help herself and her excitement is contagious, both Solomon and Rachel find it impossible to say no. Laura is upstairs in her bedroom, a connecting room to theirs, which they'd filmed her entering. Bo had filmed everything. Laura's first baby-steps into the big bad world, not that there had been anything dramatic to capture. Laura hadn't been raised by wolves, she knew how to handle herself. Everything remained inside of her, contained. Rachel captured Laura sitting in the car, for the first time in ten years, the cottage disappearing in the background behind the bat house. Laura didn't look back, though she mimicked the engine starting up. When Laura left the Toolin property her face never changed. She quietly, slowly absorbed everything around her; it was calming to watch, as hypnotic as watching a new born baby. And while everything seemed locked inside of her, her sounds seeped out and revealed a little about her.

'I feel like we have a child,' Bo had joked to Solomon, about the connecting room, before shuddering.

'If Laura is Snow White, who is the evil witch who locked her up?' Rachel asks.

'Her grandmother,' Solomon replies, his tongue feeling loose. Considering he'd been falling asleep all day, he's wide awake now. 'But not evil. If anything, well-intentioned.'

'All evil people think they're well-intentioned in some shape or form,' Bo says. 'Manson thought his murders would precipitate the apocalyptic race war . . . What about Rapunzel?'

'What about Mowgli?' Rachel jokes.

Bo ignores her. 'Trapped in a cottage, on the top of a mountain, cut off from the world. And she has long blonde hair and is beautiful,' she adds. 'Not that it should make a difference, but it does and we all know it.' She points a finger in both Solomon and Rachel's faces to prevent them from objecting, not that they were going to.

'I don't know why you're going for Disney movies,' Rachel says. 'Is it a commercial thing?'

'Because this feels fairytale-like. Laura has that ethereal feel, other-worldly, don't you think?'

Of course Solomon agrees, he's felt that all along and perhaps he was wrong, foolish even, to think that he was the only one who was affected by Laura.

'She talks to animals and birds,' Bo offers. 'That's quite Disney.'

'De Niro talked to the mirror,' Rachel suggests. 'Shirley Valentine to the wall.'

'Not quite the same thing,' Bo smiles.

'She doesn't talk to them, she imitates them,' Solomon explains. 'There's a difference.'

'The imitator. The imitatress.'

'Gendered titles, from a feminist such as yourself. You should be ashamed,' Rachel teases, signalling the barman for another round.

'Echoes of Laura.'

'Perfect,' Rachel says. 'For True Movies.'

'She mimics,' Solomon says, thinking aloud. 'She repeats things that she hasn't heard before, a few times, until she gets it right. Maybe it's to understand them. She makes distressed sounds when she feels endangered, like the barking, growling, car alarm sounds when we first met her. She associates those sounds with danger or defence.'

They're both hanging on to his analysis.

'Interesting,' Rachel nods along. 'I hadn't realised there was a language to it.'

'Hadn't you?' Solomon asks. It had seemed

81

clear to him. The sounds were all different. Sympathetic when whimpering with Mossie, defensive, on the attack when she was surrounded. Mimicking Solomon's throat-clearing when she recognises when he's uncomfortable or generally an uncomfortable situation. The sounds make sense to him. Entirely peculiar, but there seems to be a pattern to them.

'Laura's Language,' Bo says, continuing her search for a title.

'So she's a mimic,' Rachel says. 'Laura the Mimic.'

'That's deep,' Bo laughs.

'She doesn't mimic actions or movements. Just sounds,' Solomon says.

They both think about it.

'I mean she's not on all fours, growling like a dog, or running around the room and flapping her arms like a bird. She repeats sounds.'

'Good point.'

'Our friend the anthropologist,' Rachel says raising her new pint towards him.

'Anthropologist, now that's a good idea,' Bo says, reaching for her pen and paper. 'We need to speak to one of them about her.'

'There's a bird somewhere, that imitates sounds,' Solomon says, not listening to the two of them. 'I saw it on a nature programme a while ago.' He thinks hard, mind foggy from the jet lag and now alcohol.

'A parrot?' Rachel offers.

Bo giggles.

'No.'

'A budgie.'

'No, it imitates all sounds. Humans, machines, other birds, I saw it on a documentary.'

'Hmm,' Bo reaches for her phone. 'Bird that imitates sounds.'

She searches for a moment. Suddenly her phone starts playing loudly and as the customers turn to her again, she quickly apologises and lowers the volume.

'Sorry. This is it.'

They huddle around to watch a two-minute clip of David Attenborough and a bird that mimics the sounds of other birds, a chainsaw, a mobile phone, the shutter of a camera.

'That's exactly like Laura,' Rachel says, prodding the screen with her greasy salty peanut finger.

'It's called a lyrebird,' Bo says, deep in thought. 'Laura the Lyrebird.'

'The Lyrebird,' Rachel says.

'No,' Solomon shakes his head. 'Just Lyrebird.'

'Love it,' Bo grins. 'That's it. Congratulations, Solomon, your first title!'

Elated, they call it a night at midnight and return to their bedrooms.

'I thought you were tired,' Bo smiles as Solomon nuzzles into her neck, as she opens the door with a keycard. She misses a few times, her aim off. 'You're like a vampire, coming alive at night,' she giggles.

He nibbles at her neck, which reminds him of a bat, which reminds him of the bat house, which reminds him of Laura, who is in the room next door, which knocks him off course, which makes him loosen his grip on Bo. Thankfully, she doesn't notice as she finally gets the key in the door and pushes it open.

'I wonder if she's awake,' Bo whispers.

Laura close to his mind, Solomon pulls Bo close to him, kisses her.

'Wait,' Bo whispers. 'Let me listen.'

She pulls away and moves to the connecting door to Laura's room. She pushes her ear to the door and while she listens, Solomon starts undressing her.

'Sol,' she laughs. 'I'm trying to do research!'

He pulls her underwear from her foot and throws it over his shoulder. He starts at her ankle and kisses his way up her leg, licking the inside of her thigh.

'Never mind,' Bo gives up on her research and turns her back to the door.

In bed, Bo lets out moans of delight.

Solomon pulls her down to him, to kiss her, and as their lips lock, he hears the sounds of pleasure again. Bo's sounds. But they're not coming from Bo, they're coming from the connecting door. They both freeze.

Bo looks at Solomon. 'Oh my God,' she whispers.

Solomon looks at the connecting door. The light from the bathroom is illuminating the otherwise dark room. Though the door on their side is still closed, Laura must have opened her own connecting door and is listening at their door.

'Oh my God,' Bo repeats, getting off Solomon and pulling the bedclothes around her protectively.

'She can't see you,' he says.

'Sssh.'

Solomon's heart pounds, as if he's been caught doing something he shouldn't be. Even if Laura can't see them, he's sure she can hear them.

'I don't care, that's sick.'

'It's not sick.'

'For fuck sake, Solomon,' she hisses, disgusted with him.

They listen out but there's no further sound.

'What are you doing?' she hisses, watching him get out of bed.

He goes to the connecting door and pushes his ear to the cold wood. He imagines Laura right on the other side, doing the same thing. Her first night away from her cottage, perhaps they were wrong to leave her alone for a few hours. He hopes she's okay.

'Well?' she asks, as he gets back into bed.

'Nothing.'

'What if she's nuts, Sol?' she whispers.

'She's not nuts.'

'Like crazy psycho-killer nuts.'

'She's not.'

'How do you know that?'

'I don't . . . it was your idea to bring her here.'

'That's helpful.'

He sighs. 'Can't we at least finish?'

'No. That's freaked me right out.'

Solomon sighs, rests his arms behind his head and stares, feeling wide awake, at the ceiling. Bo lies on top of him, her leg across his body, so he can't even finish himself off, while she sleeps.

Fully awake now, and unsatisfied.

He throws the covers off and moves so that Bo will get off him.

'If you're going to wank in the toilet, you better be quiet or the Lyrebird will be repeating your every sound for the next two weeks on camera,' Bo warns, sleepily.

He rolls his eyes and gets back into bed, the mood completely killed.

At some stage he falls asleep listening to the sound of Laura listening to him.

9

Solomon wakes in the morning to an empty bed. The connecting door is open a fraction. He sits up and gets his bearings. He hears Bo's voice drifting out to him. Gentle but organisational.

'Joe has agreed that we can have access to the cottage for today so that we can film you there. We can see you go about your day, what you do, how you live, that kind of thing. And then I'll ask you a few questions about how you see the future, what you'd like to do with your life. So maybe think about those kinds of things.'

Silence.

'Do you have these answers now?'

Silence.

Solomon gets out of bed and pads naked across the room to the door. He peeks through the crack in the door and sees them, Laura sitting on the bed, the back of Bo's head.

'Okay, that's okay, you don't have to answer my questions now. But you do understand what we're planning?'

'I understand.'

'We'll film today and tomorrow, break for the

weekend, and then return on Monday. Is that okay with you?'

'I'm going to be with Solomon in Galway at the weekend.'

'Yes.'

Awkward silence.

'Last night, Laura . . . '

Silence.

Solomon closes his eyes and cringes, wishing Bo would just let it go. It was the first night in ten years that Laura had slept in a different bed, a different room. Everything was different. Bo's sounds had been new for Laura, mimicking them was her way of understanding, that was all, he wishes Bo could get that and leave it.

'Em, last night I heard you make a sound. While I was in bed.'

Laura makes the sound again, an exact replica of Bo's pleasured moans, as if she had recorded it and was playing it from her voice box.

Solomon bites his lip, tries not to laugh.

'Yes. That.' Bo is mortified.

'You want that in your film?'

Solomon peeks through the crack again, to get a look at Laura, he noticed the change in the tone of her voice. It's playful. She's playing with Bo. Bo, on the other hand, misses it.

'No!' she says, laughing nervously. 'You see *that*, what you heard, was private, a private moment between me and . . . ' Bo pauses, not wanting to mention Solomon.

'Sol,' Laura says, repeating the name exactly as Bo does. It's Bo's voice coming from Laura's mouth.

'Jesus. Yes.'

'Solomon's your boyfriend?'

'Yes.'

Solomon swallows, his heart pounding once again.

'Is that . . . okay?' Bo asks.

'Okay for who?'

'For you. Okay *with* you,' Bo replies, confused.

Laura clears her throat awkwardly but it's not her sound, it's Solomon's. She looks quickly in the direction of the door and he realises she knows he's been listening. He smiles and walks away, to the shower.

★   ★   ★

They spend Thursday filming Laura's home. After realising that, under observation, Laura had a tendency to freeze up and look at the camera, lost, Bo has come up with a plan to film her making vegetable soup. This is something that Laura is comfortable with. At first she is wary of their presence, self-conscious of their eyes and camera on her. Then, as she gets lost in what she's doing, she visibly relaxes. They stay back, trying not to be intrusive, though as unnatural as three people with recording equipment in a forest are. She mimics their sounds less as she moves around.

She tends to her fruit-and-vegetable patch, she forages for herbs; wild garlic is plentiful along the streams and shady areas, she picks the larger leaves and flower heads that have blossomed.

She doesn't speak very much, sometimes

hardly at all. Bo asks her to describe what she's found in the ground but then she stops, deciding that this is going to be one of those documentaries, much like *The Toolin Twins*, where their audio will have to be added to the visuals at a later date, when answers can come from direct questions. Laura is no narrator but she does mimic the bird-calls; the birds seem puzzled, or at least convinced by her authenticity from afar, and reply to her.

Bo is buzzing, this much is obvious. They all are. They work together as silently as possible, respecting Laura's need for that. Between filming, their chat is kept to a minimum, basic communication. Hand gestures, a word here and there. It is possibly the quietest day of Solomon's life, not just because he's had to stay quiet — he's used to that — but most of his days are spent listening to others. Despite filming on the same mountain as *The Toolin Twins*, there is a distinct difference between the feel, sounds and rhythms. What they've got here is a completely different documentary. This is lyrical, musical, even magical. The images of Laura working her way through the forest, her white-blonde hair and calm disposition, are stunning, unearthly. It brings Solomon back to that first moment he saw her, how she'd quite literally taken his breath away. He could watch her all day. He could listen to her all day. He does. And with her sound pack clipped on her clothes, the microphone on her T-shirt, he can practically hear every breath and heartbeat. Yet when he looks at her, when their eyes meet, there's nothing dainty about her. She's strong. She's firm. That mind of hers is solid.

Laura stands up from the forest floor and stretches her back. She looks up at the sky, breathes in and, as if remembering the crew are there, she turns around and lifts the basket into the air.

'What did you get?' Bo asks, delighted Laura is ready for conversation.

'Wild garlic, it's good for flavouring soups. Also good for coughs and the chest. I use it for a wild garlic, onion and potato soup. I've got mushrooms . . . ' She runs her long fingers over the array of mushrooms.

'How do you know these are safe?'

Laura laughs, her laugh is older than she appears. She makes a vomiting sound, one so real it plays with Rachel's gag reflex, yet she doesn't seem to notice her sound, it's as if a memory for her has come alive through her own sound, as an image would flash in somebody else's mind.

'Trial and error for the first few years,' Laura explains, then runs her hands over the food in the basket. 'These are pig nuts, also known as fairy potatoes. They're good roasted. Alexanders, they're like celery. Nettles, gorse blossom for blossom jelly and garlic mustard. It's a wild member of the cabbage family, good for marinating meat. I like this because you can eat all parts of the plant, roots, leaves, flowers and seeds. The root makes tasty garlic mustard root vinegar.'

'Okay, great, thanks.' Bo smiles happily.

Inside the cottage, she opens her cupboards to show them her collection of food that has been pickled, dried and canned. She preserves the fruits and vegetables that don't grow in the winter, when her diet would otherwise grow monotonous. That's when she really relies on what Tom gives her. *Gave* her. She pauses, checks herself, before continuing. She is confident, proud of her work on her food and she is happy to talk about it. Her sentences are short and limited, of course, but for her, to offer any information unprompted is a sign of her confidence, which grows throughout the filming day.

She makes her soup that she then offers to them to taste. Bo politely sips a spoonful. Solomon and Rachel finish their bowls.

It is late in the afternoon.

'What would you do next?' Bo asks, trying to move things along.

'I would usually be still out foraging,' Laura smiles politely, aware that time is of concern to Bo.

'Don't feel you have to rush everything on our account, I want to capture you as you'd normally be.'

'I wouldn't normally have served three people my soup,' she smiles, and to Solomon. 'That's the first time I've done that in ten years.'

'Four people,' Rachel says. 'Can I have seconds?'

Laura laughs. She likes Rachel, this is obvious. She is wary of Bo. With Solomon, everyone knows it's a sure thing.

Laura suggests cleaning her clothes, something Bo isn't interested in. She doesn't scrunch up her nose but it's a similar reaction.

'How about we film you reading?' Bo asks. 'Books are an important part of your life aren't they?'

'Of course, I read every day.'

'They're your connection to the world?'

'I'd say they are the only things that *aren't* my connection to the world,' Laura replies. 'They're entertainment, escape.'

'Yes,' Bo says, though she's too busy planning her next shot to process the answer. 'Where do you usually read?'

'In lots of places. In here. Outside.'

'Let's go outside, show us where you'd go.'

'It depends on the time of year, on the day, on the time of day, on the light,' she says. 'I walk around until I find somewhere that feels right.'

'Let's do that then,' Bo says, smiling and when Laura isn't looking, she steals a look at her watch. It's not that Bo isn't interested — she is, she can't have enough information — it's that time has never been her friend. There is too much to do, and not enough time to do it in. The aim is to do everything, quickly, so that she doesn't miss a thing, and of course in doing things so quickly all the time, she *is* missing things, as Solomon constantly warns her.

Solomon accompanies Laura to her bookshelf, which is overflowing. Books are piled up on the floor all around.

'Do you have a favourite one?' he asks.

She picks up one, an erotic romance *A Rock*

and a Hard Place, and shows it to him. She then makes the sound she heard from the previous night, Bo's sounds of pleasure. She is quiet enough so that Bo doesn't hear her. Solomon laughs and shakes his head.

'You're in love with her?' Laura asks.

He's so taken aback by the question he's not sure how to answer. He should know how to answer, but he can't bring himself to address it.

She mimics his awkward throat-clear.

'I'm surprised Bridget brought you that book,' he changes the subject.

'I've never met her but I was surprised too,' she laughs. 'There was a whole box of them. Second-hand, church sale. A virgin named Betty Rock and naughty Nathan the window cleaner. They get a lot of suds in a lot of places.'

They both laugh.

'No. This is my favourite. I've read it over fifty times.' She hands him a picture book.

'There's no words,' he flicks through it.

'Words are often over-rated,' she says.

'What's it about?'

'A tree that turns into a woman.'

'Just like Bo said,' Solomon says sarcastically, studying it. 'Your connection to the world.'

She laughs.

He looks at the cover. *Rooted*. 'What's it about?'

'There's a tree in a park. A busy city park. It's hundreds of years old and it watches people every day. Children playing with a ball, mothers walking their babies in prams, people jogging, couples arguing. Life. As time goes by, the more she absorbs the life around her, the more human the tree becomes. Her bark turns into skin, her leaves to hair, her branches to arms. She shrinks. Until one day she is no longer a tree, she's a beautiful young woman. She uproots her feet from the soil and she walks out of the park.'

'Interesting,' Solomon says, flicking through the pages.

'You can read it, if you like,' she offers it to him.

'Does she walk out of the park naked?' he asks. 'Nudity is a must in a book with pictures.'

'That's revealed on the pop-up page.' She smiles.

He laughs and studies her, curiously.

She looks up at him, not at all self-conscious under his greedy gaze. She doesn't seem to mind his attention, so he drinks her in a little more.

He takes a deep breath, lets it out slowly. 'Thanks for the book. I'll return it to you in the same condition. Actually, I have a book for you.' Solomon takes a paperback from his audio bag. 'Bridget brought it here on Thursday. I'm sure it's for you.'

Solomon had to hand it to Bo. As soon as Bridget mentioned that Tom was an avid reader, she'd known something was up. He wonders what else she can sense.

Laura takes the book from him, her energy completely changing. It's the last book she received from her father, even if he hadn't chosen it, even if he never gave it to her, even if he never touched it, or knew what it was. He'd asked for it for her. She hugs it close to her.

'Let's go,' Solomon says. 'So, how do you clean your clothes?' he asks as they pick up their gear and prepare to go outside.

'The dry cleaner's at the top of the mountain, beside the nightclub,' Laura says, seriously. 'But Bo didn't want to know about that.'

Solomon throws his head back and laughs heartily.

Laura takes a note of that beautiful sound, records it in her mind, replays it over and over.

10

At night it is astonishing just how dark Laura's world is, how isolated and secluded she is. What during the day seems remote yet peaceful, during the night seems menacing and cruel, as though she has been abandoned. She has nobody. Nobody. Ring, the surviving sheepdog, comes to her sometimes when he's not with Joe, perhaps feeling comfortable with her over their shared grief of Mossie and Tom. He is her only company, and the birds and creatures that move around her. She has become adept at sensing them before anyone else does, warning Rachel before she takes a step backwards and uncovers a dead badger, or a fallen bird's nest. Her senses are so finely tuned to the natural world around her, it seems to Solomon at least, that Lyrebird, as Bo has now taken to calling her, has almost disappeared. It feels to Solomon that Laura doesn't consider herself to be present in the environment and instead takes on the sounds, the essence, the life of everything around her, just like her favourite storybook. While the tree absorbs human life and becomes a young woman, this young woman absorbs nature and becomes a part of nature, or tries to.

'There should be a sequel,' he says referring to the story-book, as they stand together by a window of the cottage. Solomon can't fight his instinct to look outside every time he hears a sound, he feels responsible to guard her, which is ridiculous as Laura easily identifies every single sound each time he flinches, to put him at ease. He's not sure who's protecting whom. Rachel and Bo are sitting on the couch by the firelight, looking over footage they'd filmed that day. 'I want to know how this shoeless woman who used to be a tree gets on in the world. Does she become a hot-shot business woman in the corporate world and lose all her emotions? Turn into a robot? Or does she fall in love, get married and have five tree children, or . . . ' he laughs.

'What?'

'Never mind.'

'Tell me.'

'Or does she step out onto the road as soon as she leaves the park and get hit by a truck, because she couldn't see traffic from the park.' He smiles but Laura looks thoughtful.

'I think she just needs to find someone to trust and she would be okay.'

'Trust,' he says, unimpressed by the word. 'Did tree woman learn about trust in the park?'

'No,' she laughs. 'Well, maybe. She learned about humanity. You'll have to read it. But she doesn't need to have learned it from the park. Trust is the kind of thing you feel inside.'

'Ah. It's instinctual.'

'Yes.'

'Don't give away the ending now.'

'That's not part of the story.'

He stares at her, not caring that she sees him doing it. Her eyes glisten even in the dark, her lips so plump and soft he wants to kiss them more than anything. He's disturbed by how powerful the instinct is, sure he's never felt this way before. He looks away, clears his throat.

'Do you want to sleep here tonight?' he asks.

'Are you going to?'

'No,' he says quietly. 'I can't, Laura.'

'Oh, I know.' She gets flustered, but he can't really read her eyes in the darkness. 'I meant all of you. You're all welcome.'

'All of us in there?' he asks, looking around the cottage.

'No, you're right, we'll go to the hotel,' she says. 'I don't want to be here on my own.'

And to herself she adds, *any more*.

★ ★ ★

The following morning, they visit Laura's grandmother's house where she and her mother were raised. Far from the main road, twenty minutes from town, it is a remote bungalow away from prying eyes. Like so many homes in the rural area, you wouldn't see the small track leading to the house if you didn't know it was there. Even if you did happen upon it, it lacked enticement, and belied the warmth and love that lay within its boundaries. It hasn't been inhabited since Hattie's passing nine years previously and it shows. Despite not having been there for ten years, Laura guides them as though she were there yesterday, Bo talking to her delicately as they make their way, aware how fragile this moment is.

Bo parked on the main road, she wanted to capture Laura's reaction as she walked home for the first time in ten years. Just inside the entrance to the trail there is a gate, which Laura tells them her grandmother added shortly after her grandfather died, for protection.

'Do you know if your mother or grandmother wrote a will?' Bo asks, as they walk the long driveway through tall trees to the house.

Laura shakes her head. 'How would I know?'

'By asking your grandmother's solicitor, or the executor of her will.'

'Gaga didn't have showers, I doubt she had an executor.'

Rachel and Solomon look away from one another to avoid laughing aloud.

'If there was no executor, then an administrator would be appointed. An administrator would be next of kin. The reason I'm saying all of this is because you could be entitled to this land and property, Laura. If there's money in a bank somewhere, or investments or a pension, then that could be yours too. I can help you look into it, if you like.'

'Thank you.' She leaves a long silence. She stops and bends to pick a freesia, she twirls it around in her fingers. Rachel moves to capture Laura's shadowed silhouette in the path of the sunlight, the sun's harshness dims and then burns behind the trees as they move, like the light on a lighthouse.

Laura moves again, faster this time. 'Gaga didn't have anybody else. She was an only child. Her parents long gone. She was born in Leeds, she left school at fourteen, worked in a factory, sewing. She moved to Ireland to mind children for a family nearby, but she didn't stay with them for long. The summer she arrived, she met Granddad . . . ' She looks up at the house as it comes into view. She catches her breath.

Solomon gets ready to steady her. At any moment he will reach out, dive forward to catch her.

Silence.

Rachel moves behind her. Dips the camera low. Laura's view of the house.

Solomon wants to see her face, but he must stay behind the camera. He studies her, takes in everything about her. How her shoulders have risen, frozen, stiff. Her fingers have stopped twirling the freesia. It falls to the ground, lands beside her boot. He listens to her breathing in his headphones. Quick shallow breaths.

Solomon drags his eyes away from Laura to take in the view. The grass has grown so tall it reaches the windows of the bungalow. It's far from a fairytale: brown bricks, flat roof, front door and two windows either side. Nothing enchanting about it and yet, for Laura, it's a treasure trove of precious moments.

He expects her words to be as predictable as Bo's words when she lifted her first award: 'Gosh, it's heavy,' words he teased her about as soon as she'd returned with the first piece of crystal in her hand. She never said it after that, more eloquent, more trained, less surprised. He imagines Laura's gentle wonderment — 'It's shrunk, it's smaller than I imagined,' the usual words of an adult returned to a childhood place — but the sight of it brings her somewhere else, a surprising comment.

'Gaga wouldn't have left this for me,' Laura says firmly, 'Because there is no record of me. The only people who ever knew that I existed are dead.' She speeds up away from them and wanders through the long grasses towards the house. Rachel looks at Solomon in alarm.

'Did she just say nobody knew she was alive?' Rachel asks in a low voice, as they cut for a moment.

Bo nods, not at all surprised, but her pupils are large and dilated with excitement. 'I've been asking around the town and not one person I spoke to knew that Isabel Murphy or Isabel Button as she preferred to be called, had a baby. In fact they all found it laughable.'

Rachel frowns. 'So is she lying?'

Solomon looks at Rachel, at first angry at her disloyalty but then remembers Rachel is always rational and her question was a sensible one. He panics a little, at the thought that this woman he has grown so attached to, in his mind at least, could be concocting this entire story. He was completely sucked in. While everything spirals away from him, Bo rescues him, reins him in and says something to make him love her all the more.

'I've listened to everything that everyone has

had to say about this family, which believe me is a lot of crazy shit, and it's not that I don't believe them but I do believe every single word Laura's saying,' Bo says firmly. She hurries away to keep up with Laura.

Laura tries the handle on the front door but it's locked. She looks in the windows of the bungalow, every single one, pushing her face up to the dirty glass, hands blocking out the sunlight. The glass is so grimy you can barely see inside. She walks around the back of the house.

'Which was your bedroom?' Bo asks, appearing.

'This one.'

Inside is an iron bed, no mattress, a wardrobe stripped of its doors. The rest is empty, no trace of Laura's life. Solomon tries to read her face, tries to get the best angles, but Rachel looks at him annoyed, he's blocking the light, getting in her way, straying off course.

Finally, he places his equipment down. He unties his sweater from around his waist and wraps it around his arm and elbow.

The glass smashes. Bo, Rachel and Laura turn to him in surprise.

'Now it's open,' he says.

Laura grins at him.

★   ★   ★

'Tell us about living here, in whatever way you like,' Bo says as they settle down outside, after their walk around the mostly rat-infested bungalow. Bo finds a beautiful setting in the long

103

grass, the house and forest behind them. It's a warm summer day, it's heavy, as though a thunderstorm looms, and the sky is filled with fast-moving clouds that disappear quickly into the next parish, as if they know something that everything that's still doesn't. It looks great on camera. Laura sits on a stool, Bo before her, but off camera. And with the usual prompts to tell the interviewee to try to put the question in their answer for the ease and flow of the documentary, they begin.

'It hasn't changed at all,' Laura says closing her eyes and breathing in. 'It feels the same. When I close my eyes anyway.'

'How do you feel about seeing the house like this?'

Laura looks at the house as though it's a stranger to her. 'It's not how I remember. It was never immaculate, Gaga and Mum were house proud, but in a different way. There were always things everywhere: glass jars, collections of things in them, twine, buttons, herbs, stones, fabrics. Potions, lotions, emotions . . . ' She smiles as if remembering a private joke. 'That's what Gaga always said about the house. The three of us filled the house with potions, lotions and emotions.'

'Gaga and your mum — can I call her Gaga? — ran a dressmaking and alterations business. I spoke to people who live locally, they said it was a successful business, popular.'

Both last night and this morning, Bo had disappeared from the hotel to do 'research'. It had been left to Solomon to entertain Laura, they'd played cards until Bo returned at midnight, with the smell of beer on her breath and smoke on her clothes. Solomon had been disappointed when she'd returned. He'd wanted more time with Laura, listening to her sounds, her mimicking the sound of the cards shuffling, the ice in his glass melting to find a new place to settle. It was like music. Her company was relaxing, slow, nothing urgent or panicked. Time was no issue, it was as if it didn't exist. She'd no phone to check, no watch on her wrist. She was simply there, present in the now, the soft line of her mouth, the way her long hair brushed and tickled his arm as she reached across for the cards. Everything subtle was big. His heart had never felt so content yet fluttered so much at the same time. It is only when he is away from her that the guilt, the conflict, the comparison to Bo begins, the inner silent terror that leaves him feeling cold.

'They ran a successful business,' Laura agrees. 'They had a loyal base of customers that they made dresses for — weddings, communions, parties . . . With so many huge families here, there was always some occasion. I loved the dressmaking. They used me when they were pinning, they couldn't see movement on the mannequins. I used to love twirling around in them, pretending it was my wedding, or my birthday, and it would drive them crazy.' She smiles at the memory. 'When the dressmaking side died down, it was just alterations, and then Mum did some housekeeping for a few elderly people living alone, shopped for them, washed and ironed their clothes, whatever needed to be done. There were a lot of people in remote places, here. Most of their children moved to the cities for university or work. People stopped coming home. Work dried up for Gaga and Mum.'

'Did the customers come into the house?'

'No. The studio, there' — she points at the garage — 'was their workshop. They didn't like people coming to the house.'

'Why not?'

'They were private. They wanted to keep their business separate to the house.'

'They didn't want anybody to see you, did they?'

'No.'

'Why do you think that is?'

'Because they were private.'

'Do you mind putting the question in your ans — '

'They didn't want anybody to see me because they were private,' Laura snaps a little. It comes out harsh, not something they could use. Too aggressive, too defensive.

Bo leaves her to settle for a moment, pretending that she's checking the sound with Solomon.

'It's perfect.' He winks at Laura when Bo's back is turned. Rachel eyes him.

'I have two questions about that. One I'll ask you now, one I'll save for later. What do you think their desire for privacy meant to you at the time?'

Laura ponders that. 'I could see that they were

106

happy with each other's company. They talked and laughed all the time. They worked together, lived together, they'd stay up late, drinking and chatting, until the early hours. They always had something to do, a project, whether it was a dress, or a recipe. They liked planning, discussing, looking at a bigger picture. They were patient, they had long-term plans, so many going on at once because if they did that it meant that something was always happening, a project or an experiment was always coming to its end, like being given a gift. They would marinate beech leaves in vodka for months, they'd have bottles and bottles of it in the pantry,' she laughs. 'Then they'd have late nights drinking and dancing, singing and telling stories.'

It reminds Solomon of his family, no different.

'They didn't need anyone else,' she says softly, yet it doesn't sound as though she felt left out, merely that she recognised it was a glorious thing. 'They were enough company for each other. I think they had a kind of a love affair together. Just the two of them.'

This reminds Solomon of the Toolin twins. Perhaps Isabel and Tom had more in common than anyone thought.

'Would you sit up late into the night with them? Would you take part in these parties?' Bo asks, her eyes shining, loving the picture Laura is painting.

'Sometimes I would stay up late with them. Even when I wasn't supposed to be there, I was listening. It's not exactly a large house, as you can see, and they weren't exactly quiet.' She laughs, that beautiful musical laugh. She bites her lip and looks at Solomon.

He looks up at her from the grass, beautiful big blue eyes that glint, a strand of hair comes loose and it falls across his eyes, over his long black eyelashes. He looks down at his equipment, moves a dial one way then back again.

'Tell us some of the stories they told,' Bo asks.

'No,' Laura says pleasantly. 'That's between them.'

'But they're not here now,' Bo jokes, conspiratorially.

'Yes they are.' Laura closes her eyes and breathes in again.

Solomon smiles. He looks down at Rachel and sees her beaming, teary-eyed. Bo gives Laura a moment before continuing.

'You were home-schooled,' Bo prompts.

'Gaga was home-schooled too. Her dad thought it was a waste of time to have girls educated, so he'd forbidden her from going. Her mother taught her secretly at home. She did the same with me.'

'Do you regret missing out on the school experience?'

'No,' she laughs. 'I think a lot of people are missing out on the joys of home-schooling. I remember Gaga chasing a frog around the stream; she said that Mum's school dissected them, to teach students how they looked when they were dead. She wanted to show me how it lived.' She bites her bottom lip again and Solomon eyes that lip, before swallowing. 'She was a sight, running around after it. I couldn't think of a better way to spend an afternoon. I still know the anatomy of a frog.'

Bo laughs with her. Then. 'Did you know at the time that you werc a secret? That nobody knew you existed?'

'Yes, I knew. I always knew that I was a secret. They didn't trust people. They were wary. They said if we stuck together, we'd be okay.'

'What do you think they were protecting you from?'

'People.'

'Did people hurt them?'

Silence while Laura searches for a way to answer. 'Gaga and Mum were different people on their own. When the customers arrived, I'd hear their voiccs, sometimes watch from the window, and I'd barely recognise them. Thcy wouldn't laugh, they were robotic and to the point. There was nothing magical about them. They weren't funny like they were at home, singing and laughing. They were serious. Sombre. Like a guard went up. It wasn't just because it was a business; they protected themselves. They were wary of people.'

'Your mother dropped out of school when she was young. When she was fourteen. Do you know why?'

Solomon studies Bo then. He's positive that she knows something about it. He can see it in her. Her body has tightened, though she tries to appear relaxed, but she's got that bit between her teeth. Bo hadn't told Solomon anything about what she'd learned from the locals, he'd been tired when she returned, grumpy at having to leave Laura. He'd wanted to sleep immediately, while Bo was hyper, unable to relax, moving around the room, making noises that caused him to snap at her. He should have guessed at the time her behaviour was because she had learned something that would affect the documentary, but he was distracted. He is intrigued now, although his defences have gone up because Laura's have. He doesn't want Bo to keep digging, he feels ready to protect Laura, like he's on the wrong side. The effect is dizzying, disorientating.

Laura stiffens. 'Granddad died. Gaga needed Mum to help her out with the business. Granddad had been a labourer on a farm. They needed more income. So Mum left school and Gaga home-schooled her. They expanded the dressmaking and alterations business. They made medicines too. Natural remedies, which they sold at markets. Mum said children at school called them witches.'

'Did that hurt her?'

'No. Gaga and Mum laughed about it. They'd cackle when they were making their *potions*,' she smiles, remembering.

'Children can be cruel,' Bo says gently. 'What other things did children say to your mum?'

You don't have to answer, Solomon feels like saying. Rachel is looking down now at her shoes, occasionally checking the monitor, a sign she feels uncomfortable.

'Mum wasn't like most other people,' Laura says, thoughtfully, speaking slowly, choosing every word with great care. 'Gaga made the big

110

decisions. Mum was happy for Gaga to take the lead,' she says, diplomatically. 'Mum had her own way. If you ask me what some children used to say about her, then I'd say they called her slow. Mum told me that. But she wasn't *slow*. It's such a lazy word. She thought differently, had to learn things in another way, that's all.'

When Laura's body language starts to close up, Bo changes tack.

'How did you end up at the Toolin cottage?'

'My mum got sick, very sick, in 2005. We never saw doctors, Gaga and Mum didn't believe in their medicines, they preferred to make their own natural remedies and were rarely ill, but they knew that something was seriously wrong with Mum that their medicines wouldn't heal so they went to a doctor who referred them to hospital. She had colon cancer. She refused all hospital treatments, she said she would rather go naturally, the way she'd arrived. So me and Gaga nursed her.'

'How old were you?' Bo asks gently.

'I was fourteen when she was diagnosed, she died when I was fifteen.'

'I'm sorry,' Bo whispers and leaves a respectful silence.

A bird flies overhead, a fly nearby. Laura mimics them both, showing her distress, as she attempts to gather herself.

'So then it was you and Gaga here at the house. Tell me about those days.'

'It was difficult for Gaga, because she had to run the alterations business alone. I helped her but she was still training me, and there was only

111

so much I could do. She was having problems with her fingers, arthritis, her fingers were bending inward and she couldn't do it any more, certainly not as fast. There were less and less customers too. Mum's housekeeping money had helped to that point, but that wasn't something I could do.'

'Even at fifteen you wouldn't deal with customers? You couldn't step out into the world then?'

'How would Gaga explain me suddenly appearing?' Laura asks. 'She couldn't. She would try and think of ways, but it would upset her. It would make her anxious, nervous. She didn't want to lie. She worried about tying herself up in knots, forgetting her story. She was forgetting a lot of things by then. She felt that at fifteen I was still too vulnerable, I was still a child.'

'Where did her fear come from, Laura?'

Again that question, but this time Solomon feels it's valid. Even he wants to know. But Laura has closed up. Bo doesn't push.

'Did you ever ask who your dad was?'

Solomon studies her. Laura gazes down, her eyes gleaming green, as though reflecting the long grasses she is sitting among. He wants to run his finger down her cheek, her chin, her lips. He looks away.

'No.' And then, as if remembering Bo's instructions, she starts again. 'I never asked who my dad was,' she says gently. 'I never asked because it was never important. I knew that whoever he was it wouldn't make a difference. I had all the people I needed here.'

Rachel purses her lips, clearly moved.

'What about when your mother passed away?'

'I did wonder then, when Mum was gone, if I should have asked, because I felt like she was my only way of knowing. I suppose I can never know for sure, but I felt so strongly that Gaga wouldn't have told me. Mum had the opportunity to tell me and decided not to, I knew Gaga would respect her word. It might not make sense, but I didn't think about who he was very often. It wasn't important.'

She thinks for a moment.

'I thought about him when I saw Gaga getting older, when I started thinking about being alone. She seemed to get old so quickly. Her and Mum were a team. They only needed each other in the world, which was beautiful, but they *needed* each other. They fed off each other. When Mum died, it's like Gaga suddenly started to go too. And she knew it. That's why she started worrying for me. Trying to plan. She wasn't sleeping, I know it was playing on her mind all the time.'

'Did they not make a plan for you before she died?'

'I never asked.' Laura swallows. 'But Mum wasn't ever the one to make plans. Gaga made them, Mum helped see them through. I felt that Mum would have approved what happened in the end. I know it sounds odd, like we didn't communicate, but we did. We lived so close to each other, in one another's pockets, we didn't always talk about things, each of us knew how the other was feeling, we didn't need to always ask.' She looks at Bo, embarrassed, but trying to make her see.

113

'I understand,' Bo says, genuinely, though Solomon wonders if she does. Bo is a person who usually has to ask. 'So when did you find out about Tom being your dad?'

'When Gaga told me about her plan to move me to the cottage. She told me that Tom Toolin was my dad, that he had never known about me. She had met with him and he'd agreed I could live on his land. She told me that he had a twin brother who could never know. That was Tom's only request.'

'How did you feel about that?' Bo asks, and it's obvious from Bo's tone that she's disgusted on Laura's behalf.

'I was used to keeping a secret.' She offers a soft smile, but her eyes reveal a sadness.

Bo decides to manoeuvre away from the topic of Tom and her new life on the mountain. 'You lived here for sixteen years before moving to the cottage, did you ever want to get out of the house? Away from here?'

'We did, many times,' Laura says, lighting up. 'Before Mum got sick. We went on holidays to Dingle. I swam in Clogherhead, nearly drowned,' she laughs. 'We went to Donegal too. They both liked to fish. They'd catch the fish, gut them, cook them. Make fish oils.'

'So you *did* get out?' Bo asks, surprised.

'They didn't lock me in the house,' Laura smiles, delighted by Bo's surprise. 'The opposite happened. They let me be free. I could be who I wanted, without anyone judging, or anyone telling me what to do. I don't believe there were any sacrifices. There were appointments for the alterations, no drop-ins allowed, so we knew I could play wherever I liked until customers came. They came when I was inside doing my schoolwork.'

'But you never did exams.'

'Not state exams.'

'Because the state didn't recognise you.'

'They didn't know I'd been born,' Laura says simply. 'There's a difference. Mum gave birth to me here in the house. She didn't register my birth.'

'Why do you think she kept you a secret? Away from the world?'

Back to that question.

'Mum didn't keep me away from the world. I've been here all along, fully immersed in it,' Laura says firmly.

Bo takes a moment, slows it all down. 'So, I asked you a two-part question earlier: when you were younger, why did you think your mum and Gaga kept you a secret. You answered, but I want to ask you the second part. *Now*, as a grown woman, with Gaga and Mum gone, what is your opinion of why they kept you a secret? Has it changed?'

Laura doesn't shut down immediately as she had before. It's the way Bo has phrased it, she has pointed out that Laura is a grown woman, she's not a child any more, her mother and grandmother aren't here, she doesn't need to keep defending them or answer for them. She can give her own opinions now.

She growls, not at anyone in particular, just in general. A threatened kind of feeling. Then there's the sound of smashing glass. A walkie-talkie sound, static radio. It's unclear whether she notices she's made these sounds.

'At the time I felt they were happy, wary, but content. When I look back, I think they were scared.'

Bo is practically holding her breath.

'They were afraid that somebody would take me away from them. They were afraid they would be seen as unfit to care for a child. There were . . . rumours.' The glass breaking, the same radio static. 'People talked about them. They were witches, they were crazy. They let them make their dresses or alter their clothes but they didn't invite them to their parties or their weddings. They were outsiders.'

'Why was that?' Bo asks gently.

'Gaga said she never really fit in, from the moment she arrived. But she loved my granddad so she stayed, tried. But it got worse. The rumours got worse.'

'When?'

Laura thinks about it. 'When my granddad died,' she says, and she closes down.

And then, almost as if Laura wants to keep talking or she's tired of the questions that will inevitably come, she continues.

'Gaga's health suffered after Mum died. She didn't want me to be left alone. She wanted me in a safe place, that's what she kept saying. Sometimes she woke me up in the middle of the night to tell me and I knew she couldn't get it out of her head.' She pauses for a moment. 'I read once that nest-building is driven by a biological urge in pregnant animals to protect their offspring, or themselves, from danger. Nests are designed to hide eggs from predators, to shield them. I believe that's what Gaga and my mum did. The cottage she brought me to was her bird's nest. Away from danger, and next to my dad. She did the best she could.'

Silence.

'Why did you stay at the cottage? You're twenty-six years old now, Laura, you could have left a long time ago. At this adult age you wouldn't have had to worry about being taken away.'

Laura looks at Solomon. Bo registers this. Solomon's eyes don't leave Laura. He doesn't care, to break her gaze would be rude, after they've listened to her story. Besides, his pull to her is magnetic, not normal.

'I stayed there for the same reasons as my mum and Gaga did what they did. Because I was happy to stay. Because I was afraid to leave.'

'You're not afraid to leave now. Is it because Tom died? Is it because you're ready for change?' she asks question after question to help her along.

'Change happens all the time, even on the mountain. You have to change with change,' she says, her voice going deeper again, as she mimics Gaga. It's the first time Bo and Rachel have heard it and their eyes widen as it seems another person takes over her body. 'I was looking for what Gaga and Mum had with each other. Tom had it with Joe. You just need one person to trust.'

She raises her eyes to Solomon, whose heart is pounding so hard he's afraid his boom mic will pick it up.

11

On Saturday morning, the four sit together in the hotel restaurant for breakfast. Laura looks around, not exactly as a Martian would, but with the eyes of someone who hasn't been around this kind of social situation before, if ever.

'Good morning, are you ready to order breakfast?' a waitress asks.

She can't pronounce her R's, pronouncing them as a W sound instead.

Laura studies her, fascinated, her lips moving to make a W sound.

Solomon watches, hoping she won't make the sound aloud.

'Yes,' Rachel says loudly, ready to eat the leg of the table. She fires off her order first.

'So let me just read that back: two sausages, two eggs, two tomato, mushrooms, two rashers . . . the rashers are from Rafferty's, local farmer. They're excellent. Award-winning.'

'Washers,' Laura says suddenly, mimicking the waitress perfectly. She's not even looking at her, she's buttering her toast and speaking as though she doesn't notice the words are coming from her mouth. 'Weady . . . bweakfast.'

The waitress pauses her order-taking and stares at Laura.

Bo feels no sensitivity towards the waitress who thinks she's being mocked, just watches, amused and intrigued, as hungry for this scene as Rachel is for her double Irish breakfast. Solomon of course feels the sweat trickle down his back from the discomfort of the situation.

'Wafferty,' Laura says.

'She's not teasing you,' Solomon says awkwardly, and he can tell the others are surprised he's even addressed it.

The anger that flashed in the waitress's eyes calms as she looks at Laura differently. Then Solomon realises that she thinks something else of Laura, that there's something *wrong* with her.

'No, she's not . . . you know . . . She's learning. It's a new sound to her. She . . . ' he looks at Laura to explain her further, and she's looking at him, amused. As if the joke's on him.

'Okay, folks, if there's anything else you need, let me know. I'll get this to the kitchen really fast.' The waitress grins at Rachel.

Laura can't help herself, she mimics 'really' as 'weally', an exact copy of the waitress's voice, and Rachel looks to be in serious pain trying to keep her nervous laughter in.

'Stop,' Bo says quietly.

'I know, I can't, I'm sorry,' Rachel says seriously and then starts again, doing a Jekyll and Hyde as she goes from serious to laughter in an instant.

The waitress leaves the table, uncertain as to whether Laura is simple, or if she's being mocked.

'She's going to spit in your cappuccino,' Solomon says, buttering his toast.

'Why were you laughing?' Laura asks Rachel.

'I can't help it.' She wipes the sweat from her brow with a napkin. 'I do it at awkward moments. Have done since I was a kid. Funerals are the worst.'

Laura smiles. 'You laugh at funerals?'

'All the time.'

'Even at Tom's?'

Rachel looks at her sombrely. 'Yes.'

Solomon shakes his head. 'Unbelievable.'

'Why did you laugh?' Laura asks, wide-eyed with curiosity and not at all insulted that Rachel laughed during her dad's funeral.

'Bridget farted,' Rachel explains.

'Ah now, come on,' Solomon says, shaking his head.

'Rachel,' Bo says, disgusted.

'Laura asked me a question and I'm telling her the honest answer. I was right behind Bridget. When she got off her seat to kneel down, there it was, a little parp.' Rachel makes the sound.

Laura imitates Rachel's fart sound perfectly, which makes Rachel laugh even more. Bo and Solomon join in, against their better judgement.

'It's called rhotacism,' Solomon says when the laughter has died down. 'Or de-rhotacisation.'

'What is?' Bo asks, confused, searching through emails on her phone.

'The waitress's 'r' sound. I had it as a kid,' he says to Laura.

Bo looks up, surprised. 'You never told me that.'

121

Solomon shrugs, cheeks going pink with the memory. 'I had to go to a speech therapist till I was seven to sort it out. My brothers have never let me forget it, gave me a horrible time about it. To this day my brother Rory is still called Wawwy.'

'I was wondering why they always say that,' Bo laughs. 'I thought it was because he was the baby.'

'He was. He was my baby Wawwy,' Solomon says, and they laugh.

Suddenly a cappuccino machine fires up to steam the milk. Laura jumps at the sound, she looks around for the root of the sound while mimicking it.

'What is she doing?' Bo asks quietly.

'I'd say percolating,' Rachel replies.

'Wow,' Bo says, picking up her phone and recording.

The diners at the table beside them turn to stare, two kids watch Laura, open-mouthed.

'Don't stare,' their mother says calmly, quietly, all the while keeping a close eye on Laura over the rim of her teacup.

Solomon fights the urge to tell more people that there's nothing 'wrong' with Laura.

'It's the coffee machine,' Solomon says, reaching out and placing a hand on Laura's shoulder, to centre her, calm her.

She looks at him, pupils dilated, scared.

Solomon points behind the counter across the room. 'It's a coffee machine. They're steaming the milk for the latte or cappuccino.'

She watches it, imitates the sound again before

becoming comfortable with it and turning her attention to the table again. The children go back to playing on their computer games.

Laura zones in on them, imitating the beeps, the shooting. The little boy puts his game down and kneels up on his chair to peer over the top at her. She smiles at him and once spotted, he sits down quickly. Their mother orders them to switch the sound off.

The waitress brings their food to the table. The full Irish for Solomon and Rachel, a grapefruit for Bo, who doesn't acknowledge it as she taps away on her phone, and two boiled eggs for Laura.

'Thank you,' she says to the wary waitress.

There's silence as they dig into their food, then Laura looks at Rachel's plate, examines its content and mimics the waitress so perfectly, innocently and without any cynicism or sarcasm. 'Wafferty's Washers.'

The three of them crack up laughing.

* * *

'I really think I should go to Galway with you,' Bo says suddenly as they're checking out. Laura is helping Rachel carry the bags to the car and Solomon and Bo are alone at the desk.

'That's the first time I've ever heard you say that about going to my family,' he jokes lightly, though it is true. When Laura has left the hotel, he runs his hands through Bo's hair.

She smiles and looks up at him, arms around his waist. 'Your family hate me.'

'Hate is a very strong word,' he kisses her gently. 'My family *don't like* you.'

She laughs. 'You're supposed to lie and tell me they adore me.'

'Adore is a very strong word.'

They smile.

'I think we've got something special here, Solomon.'

'That's so romantic, Bo,' he mimics her dreamy tone, knowing she's talking about Laura and not their relationship.

She laughs again. 'I think we should be filming the Galway trip. This is Laura stepping into the world for the first time and we're missing it. Like this morning at breakfast, that stuff is priceless. She is sound-bite fucking heaven.'

'You know why we can't film,' he shrugs, pulling apart, annoyed by Bo's greediness all of a sudden. 'We're not ready. Rachel has to get home, you've got your fancy university lecture. The prodigal student returns.'

She groans. 'If it wasn't for the lecture I'd go with you.'

'I recall you booking this date specifically so you would miss my mam's birthday.'

'True.'

'Karma's a bitch.'

She laughs. 'I'm not good at all that family stuff. I'm from a socially repressed family of four. All that touchyfeely singing and dancing, and self-expression, makes me nervous.'

Solomon has three brothers and one sister, all of whom will be there this weekend, some with partners, wives, children. Then there are his

124

uncles, aunts and cousins, before you even count the crazy neighbours and random people who drop in because they hear music when they're passing. It's noisy, it's not easy if you're not used to it and Bo doesn't have the kind of easy-going nature that can take an entire weekend of banter. He feels equally uncomfortable in her suburban house. There's too much silence, watching of words, politeness. Solomon's family talk about everything, a lively debate encompassing politics, current affairs, sport and what's happening between the bedsheets of the house next door. His family deplore silence. Silence is used for dramatic effect in a story only. Words, music or song were created to eradicate silences.

But truth be told, Solomon doesn't mind in the slightest that Bo won't be joining them. In fact, it will be easier for him with her not there, or it would have been if Laura wasn't coming with him.

'I don't think Laura is going to be a completely changed person by Monday when it's time to film. She'll still be making those sounds,' he says.

'You think?'

'Yeah. It's part of who she is.'

'Maybe we can help her to see someone about it. Document her therapy or something,' Bo says, stepping back in producer mode. 'As part of her moving on. There's so many ways to approach this documentary, I really need to get my head straight.'

'Why would she want to lose her sounds?' Solomon asks.

125

Bo fixes him with a confused look.

Solomon hears Rachel returning and Bo gives him one final peck before stepping away.

'You wouldn't stay here with her?' she asks. 'Save all her new first times until I get back?'

Solomon's heartbeat hastens at that comment, trying to judge her tone. He has picked her up wrong; of course she doesn't mean that first for Laura, if in fact it would even be her first. But he's thought about it, a lot, and his conclusion is that she must be a virgin, she's been at the cottage since she was sixteen. And there wasn't anybody in her life before? She would have said so. He tries to hide what Bo's comment has done to him.

He clears his throat.

'I'm not missing my mam's seventieth birthday.' He steadies his voice. 'Laura can go with you to Dublin, if you really want. You can watch her progress for yourself.' As soon as he's said it he wants to take it back. His heart drums even louder in his chest as he awaits her answer, but the reverse psychology has worked. Bo looks alarmed, like a new mother at the prospect of being left alone with her baby for the first time.

'No, she's better with you. She prefers you.'

He shields his relief as she guards her terror. He wonders if she can see through him as easily as he sees through her.

★ ★ ★

Solomon drives Bo and Rachel to the train station. The initial plan had been for Bo and

126

Rachel to drive to Dublin while Solomon was to catch the bus to Galway, however it was agreed that a three-hour bus journey with Laura and a packed bus full of new sounds might not be the best way for her to travel. On the way to the train station, Rachel and Laura sit together getting along together amicably, their conversations simple and easy.

'You've just revealed yourself to be one big softy on this one,' Solomon teases as they unload the car, helping Rachel with her camera equipment. 'It must be impending motherhood that's doing it to you. Hormones.'

'Less of the big, if you don't mind,' Rachel says gruffly.

'Seriously. Laura likes you,' Solomon says.

'Yeah. She likes you more though,' Rachel says, fixing him with a knowing look. A warning look. 'Be good. See you Monday.'

12

'Mam. It's Solomon.'

'Hi, love, everything all right?'

'Yes. Fine . . . Em. I'm on my way to you and I'm bringing somebody with me.'

'Bo?' That wary tone, though of all the members of the family she tries to hide it the most, always trying to be respectful to the various other halves she has not taken a liking to.

'No, not Bo — she's really sorry, but she couldn't get out of that guest lecture she has. It's a big honour, and she can't miss it,' he explains, covering all angles, and doesn't know why he bothers, always apologising to other people on other people's behalf when none of those people ever care.

'Of course, of course, she's a busy woman.'

'It's not that she's too busy, it's just that it's important. Not to say that your birthday's not,' he backpedals.

'Solomon, love,' he hears the smile in her voice. 'Don't worry. You worry too much, you'll tie yourself up in knots. Who are you bringing? Can he stay in your room? I'm tight on space,' she lowers her voice. 'Maurice is after arriving with Fiona and his three children. God love him, a widower and all, but the three children. I've put them in the room that was supposed to be for Paddy and Moira, but Moira couldn't come. Her back again. Paddy's in with Jack and he's in a right huff — sure the two of them don't get along at all, but what else can I do?'

Solomon smiles. 'Don't worry about it. They should be grateful they're there at all. I can stay in Pat's.'

'You will not stay in Pat's when your bedroom and home are right here. I'll hear nothing of the sort.'

'He's a *she*, Mam. So that will make it difficult for you. If you insist on us staying she can stay in my room, I'll go on the couch.'

'No son of mine will sleep on the couch. Who is she, Solomon?'

'Laura. Laura Button. You don't know her. She's from Macroom. She's the subject of this new documentary we're doing. She's twenty-six. We're not, you know, together.'

Pause.

'I'll put her in Cara's room so.'

'No, Mam, you don't have to do that, really. She can have my room. I'll sleep on the couch. She's better in a room on her own.'

'No one is sleeping on the couch,' she says firmly. 'Particularly not my own son. I haven't planned this for a year to end up with people on couches.'

As the owner of an eight-bedroom guesthouse, Solomon's mother is a nurturer, a feeder, someone who insists on others' comfort almost to the point of their own discomfort. Always putting herself last. But as welcoming as she is, she's old-fashioned in her views: none of her children are allowed to share a room with girlfriends or boyfriends until they are married.

'When you meet her, you'll understand. She's different.'

'Is she now?'

'Not like that.' He smiles.

'We'll see,' she says easily, with a laugh that's trapped in her words. 'We'll see.'

Solomon ends the call and waits for Laura. They'll see, indeed. Laura is standing beside the roadwork traffic cones, where four men in high-vis jackets and jeans below the cracks of their arses attempt to work while she stands beside them mimicking the sound of the jackhammer.

When she sees that Solomon is off the phone, and content her mimicry has been perfected, she joins him.

'We're going to get in the car now and continue our drive to Galway, if there's anything else you'd like to stop and see or hear, feel free. In fact, do it as much as you like because the longer it takes us to get there, the longer it takes us to get there.'

She smiles. 'You're lucky to have your family, Sol,' she says in Bo's voice.

'Say it your way,' he says.

'Solomon,' she says, and he smiles.

Every time he connects with her he has to purposefully de-link himself. It happens a lot. Then just as he's in the process of untwining his

130

soul from hers, she mimics his awkward throat-clear and he laughs.

They return to the car that Solomon abandoned in an awkward position when she decided to flee the vehicle while stopped at red lights to explore the source of the jackhammer.

'What is a lyrebird?' she asks as they drive.

He looks at her quickly, then back to the road ahead of him.

'I heard Bo say it when she was on the phone. She found a lyrebird. Is that me?'

'Yes.'

'Why does she call me that?'

'It's the title of the documentary. A lyrebird is a bird that lives in Australia and is famous for mimicking sounds.' What he really wants to say, what he had planned to say, was, *It's one of the most beautiful and rare and the most intelligent of all the world's wild creatures.* He'd come across that in his research, he'd planned to tell her that, but now he can't get the words out. He'd spent a good deal of time reading up about the curious bird ever since Bo had decided on the name. It's the first time he has raised the issue of her mimicry, and he's too nervous that she may take offence to the comparison. There's been no sign so far of her acknowledging her own sounds, even as only moments ago a crowd had gathered around her to watch her mimicking the jackhammer.

'Look' — he searches through his phone, one hand on the steering wheel, one eye on the road. He hands her the short video of the bird that he came across on YouTube. He struggles to watch

131

her reaction as he drives, thinking Bo will be upset with him for not capturing this moment on camera. She smiles as the bird mimics other birds from the platform that it builds in the woods.

'Why does it do it?' she asks, which is a question that intrigues Solomon. He'd love to ask her the same thing.

'To attract a mate,' he explains.

Laura looks at him and those eyes almost make him crash into the car that has stopped at the lights in front of him. He clears his throat and brakes hard.

'The male lyrebirds sing during mating season. He builds a platform in the forest, like a mound, and he stands on it to sing. The females are attracted to the sound.'

'So I'm a male bird looking for a good time,' Laura says, scrunching her face up.

'We'll claim artistic licence.'

She watches the video of the bird some more and when he starts making the sounds of chainsaws, and then a camera shutter, she starts laughing, louder and larger than Solomon has ever heard her before.

'Whose idea was it to call me this?' she giggles, wiping her teared-up eyes.

'Mine,' he says, self-consciously, taking the phone from her.

'Mine,' she mimics him perfectly, then after a short silence where he's wondering what's going through her mind she says, 'You found me. You named me.'

He cringes at that.

Laura continues. 'I read a book about Native Americans believing that naming can help enrich a sense of identity. People's names can change throughout their lives the same way people do. They believe nicknames provide insight into not just the individual but how other people perceive that person. People become a double prism, instead of a one-way mirror.'

Solomon drinks every word in.

She makes the sound of a car beeping, which confuses him, until he hears an aggressive car honk behind him. The traffic lights had turned green while he was lost in her words. He quickly drives on as they turn amber again, leaving the angry driver behind.

'What I'm trying to say,' she smiles, 'is that I like it. I'm Lyrebird.'

13

'Oh Solomon, she's a beauty,' Solomon's mother, Marie, says breathily, greeting Solomon outside the house, as though he's brought his first-born home from the hospital. She hugs her son, eyes on Laura the whole time. It's almost as if she's astonished, or her breath has been stolen. 'My goodness, look at you!' She takes Laura's hands, no longer paying the slightest bit of notice to her son. 'Aren't you an angel? We'll have to take good care of you.' She pulls her close and wraps an arm around her shoulder.

Solomon carries the bags inside with his father, Finbar, who nudges his son so deeply in the ribs he drops the bag. Finbar laughs and hurries ahead of him.

'Where are we going with these, petal?' Finbar asks his wife.

'The orchid room for dear Laura,' she says.

'That's my room,' a head peeks out from the doorway of a room to the right-hand side. 'Hiya, bro.' An identical but older version of Solomon, Donal, steps out and hugs his brother and greets Laura.

'Hannah down the road will take you,' she

says. 'If you weren't on your own, Donal, we'd find somewhere else for you here, but that's how it is now.'

'Ouch,' Solomon laughs, punching his brother in the arm. She's punishing him for leaving the only woman everyone thought he'd marry.

Laura smiles, watching them with each other.

'Is Solomon in the orchid room too?' Donal asks innocently, and his mother throws him a look of pure evil that he sniggers at. Solomon busies himself with the bags and tries to usher Laura away from the conversation.

'Solomon is in his own bedroom,' Marie huffs, enjoying the teasing. 'Now, off with the lot of you. Laura, angel, I'll take you to your room. Don't be starting anything with him in there, Donal,' she warns them as they go into Solomon's room.

Donal laughs. 'Mam, I'm forty-two.'

'I don't care what age you are, you were always at poor Solomon. I know it was you who kicked him off the bunk bed.'

Donal's grin gets wider. 'Oh, the poor baby Solomon.'

'I wasn't the poor baby and you know it,' Solomon says, distracted, trying to catch Laura's eye to make sure she's okay with all this, concerned that going from no contact with people, to this, in a matter of days, must be affecting her.

'Wawwy,' Laura says, a perfect mimic of Solomon's childhood speech impediment, and Donal howls with laughter. He holds his hand up for a high-five, which Marie drags Laura away from before they see her laugh. A mother's job, in her opinion, is to be stern; if they ever saw her lose her composure then she would lose her power. Now they try to constantly egg her on and it's her little game to maintain that composure.

Laura is brought away to the new 'wing', which is an extension of two new bedrooms for the B & B after the children had left home, though Rory is the only remaining child and probably will be for the rest of his life, at the rate he's going.

After giving her a few minutes to settle in, Solomon knocks on Laura's door.

'Yes,' she says quietly, and he pushes the door open. She's sitting on the double bed, her bags untouched on the floor at her feet, looking around at the room.

'It's beautiful,' she says dreamily.

'Ah yes. The orchid room is Mam's favourite,' Solomon says, stepping inside. His mother putting her in this room says a lot. 'My sister Cara is a photographer. These are her photos on canvas. For some reason, she likes to photograph flowers. And stones. But they're in the stone room. Crazy Uncle Brian is in that room. Mam's not so keen on stones.'

She laughs. 'Your family is funny.'

'That's one word for them.' He clears his throat. 'So the festivities will begin in one hour. About all of Spiddal is about to burst in here, with a song to sing, an instrument to play, a story to tell, or a dance to dance. You are free to stay here, in safety.'

'I'd like to come.'

'Are you sure?' he asks, surprised.

'Will you sing?' she asks.

'Yes, everybody has to do a piece.'

'I want to hear you sing.'

'Be warned, they might force you to sing. I'll try to stop them but I can't promise you anything. They're a tough bunch and I have zero sway with them.'

'I'll hide in the back,' she says, and he laughs.

'Why are you laughing?'

'The idea of you hiding. Even in a room filled with people you'd stand out.'

She bites her lip at the compliment, which he didn't intend to sound so corny. He backs away to the door cringing internally.

She mimics his throat-clearing.

'Exactly,' he agrees. 'Awkward. Sorry for that. I'll give you time to freshen up, shower, whatever. Is thirty minutes okay?' For Bo, thirty minutes would be enough, she doesn't spend much time thinking about how she looks, she is naturally beautiful and throws everything together to look cool. Preppy. Brogues and turn-ups, thin cashmere sweaters and blazers like she should be going to Harvard, a J. Crew wet dream. But he's had girlfriends where thirty minutes wasn't even enough time to dry their hair.

She nods. 'Wait.' She looks nervous. 'Is it dressy? I don't really have anything fancy. I made some things but . . . they're not really right for here.'

'What you're wearing now is perfect. It's casual.'

She looks relieved and Solomon feels bad that this would have been a concern for her all this time. This is the kind of thing Bo would have done better.

★ ★ ★

'What's the deal with the blonde?' Donal asks, as Solomon steps out of the shower and finds him lying on the bed in his bedroom. Donal is scrolling through Solomon's phone.

'Go ahead, look through my personal stuff, why don't you.'

'Where's cow?'

'Bo is in Dublin. She was lecturing for film students at the university this afternoon. She couldn't get here on time.'

Donal sucks in air, but sarcastically. 'Bet she couldn't get out of that.'

'I told her not to even try. It's a big deal.'

'Sounds like it is.' Donal studies him.

Unhappy with his brother's gaze, he drops his towel from around his waist and holds his hands up in the air. 'Look no hands!'

'That's mature.'

'Yeah, well,' Solomon roots in his bag for a clean T-shirt. 'It's easier for me that she's not here,' he says, back turned, while he hears the click of Donal's phone. 'You lads make it hard for me.'

'We don't.' He angles the phone on Solomon's arse and takes another photo. 'We're looking out for you.'

'By calling her *cow*.'

138

He genuinely laughs at that. 'You said speak English to her.'

Bó is the Irish for cow, something Solomon's Irish-speaking family delight in calling her.

'You never give her a break.'

'It's only banter.'

'She doesn't have the same sense of humour.'

'Wrong. She doesn't have a sense of humour. And she barely sees us, so she doesn't have to put up with us often.'

'Please stop taking photos of my balls.'

'But they're so pretty. I'm going to send them to Mam. She can decorate a new room, call it the bollox room.'

Ashamed to find that childish joke funny, Solomon laughs.

'So, do you go to *Bo's* folks' place, parties, brunches, soirees and the like?' he asks putting on a posh Dublin accent.

'Sometimes. Not very often. Once. Me and Bo are better on our own. Away from our families.'

'Away from each other.'

'Come on.'

'Fine. Last question. Are you going to get married?'

'Are we going to get married?' He sighs. 'You sound like an old woman. Why the fuck do you care if I get married?'

'Man, I think your dick shrunk when I asked that. Look — ' He holds the camera up to show him. 'Before I asked the question.' He slides the image. 'After.'

Solomon chuckles. 'It's a fine thing, you asking me all these questions. Single man of forty-two. You should have been a priest.'

'Might have got more action,' Donal says and Solomon rolls his nose up in disgust.

Donal chuckles at his own joke.

'Seriously, I overhead a conversation between Mam and Dad about you being gay.'

'Shut up,' Donal says, pretending not to care but dropping the phone.

Solomon picks it up. Thirty-two photos of his own bollox on his phone.

Donal changes the subject. 'Mam said you were in Boston. How did that go?'

'The *Irish Globe* gave us an award.'

'Congratulations.'

'Thank you.'

'So you're happy.'

'I'm always happy.'

'So are you going to marry her?'

'Fuck off.'

'What's with the blonde?' he repeats his opening question.

'Laura.'

'What's with Laura?'

Solomon fills him in on Laura's background and her lyrebird qualities, everything he knows about her.

'Why wouldn't she go to Dublin with Bo?'

'Because she wanted to stay with me. I was the person who found her. She trusts me,' he shrugs. 'Go on, tell me it's weird.'

'It's not.'

Solomon searches his face for the sarcasm.

'Man, would you put your jocks on.' He throws a pillow at him.

'This is what you get for taking photos of my cock. I'm going to text it to you and you can stare at it all you like.'

The door opens and two more brothers squeeze through the doorway. 'Wahay!' they all cheer, bundling into the room with a six-pack of beer.

Solomon laughs and catches the boxers Donal throws at him.

'What's going on here?' his eldest brother Cormac asks, looking Solomon up and down. 'Nice bollox.'

'Your date is standing at the window of the orchid room imitating cuckoos,' his youngest brother Rory says, opening the bottle's cap with his teeth.

'Yeah. *And?*' Solomon tenses up. He slides his legs into his jeans and faces them all, ready to fight, ready to defend. Wouldn't be the first time he'd punched any of them in the face.

'*And*. She's hot,' Rory says with a grin, and passes him a bottle.

★　★　★

Going downstairs, Laura hears the sounds of the crowds and stalls a little in fear. The brothers notice but keep on going without a word, which Solomon appreciates. If it was Bo they would never have let her go, probably would have picked her up and carried her down over their heads themselves.

'It's okay, I promise,' Solomon says gently. He wants to place his hand on her waist, guide her,

141

he wants to take her hand. But he doesn't do any of those things. He looks down at her, seeing the light freckles on her nose through her long lashes. She did change her clothes after all, a dress that she must have made herself. A simple design, long sleeves, but short hemline. Different fabrics sewn together. When she moved to the Toolin cottage she obviously moved with the garage of fabrics.

'You'll stay with me?' she asks him, looking up.

He wants to move the hair that's fallen before her eyes.

They're standing so close on the stairs that she feels the heat from him. She wants to press her face against the skin she sees through the open buttons of his T-shirt. She wants to smell his skin, feel the heat on hers.

They stand there just looking at one another. He feels the intensity of her stare. He clears his throat.

'Of course I'll stay with you. If you promise to stay with me. I could get eaten alive down there.'

She smiles.

She reaches out and links arms with him, hugging his arm close to her body; she couldn't stop herself.

'You'll be fine,' he says softly, to the top of her head, so close his lips brush her hair and he smells her faint sweet perfume.

14

The connecting doors of the living room, the dining room, the den and the kitchen have been opened, along with those leading into the conservatory, creating a grand space for the party. The dining table is filled with food that Marie has prepared and that neighbours have brought with them. There are one hundred people squeezed into the ground floor of the house and already Finbar is centre stage and telling a special-edition story of how he met Marie. It's in English, especially for her family and friends who travelled from Dublin.

After his story he presents her with a wooden heart that he carved himself from a tree that fell during a storm. It's the tree he claims they shared their first kiss under, but Solomon guesses it's closer to being a tree that stood in the park they once walked in. Still, the sentiment remains the same. In the four chambers of the heart are four drawers, inside each drawer is an item that represents the four generations together.

There are tears in everybody's eyes, phones are in the air capturing the moment as Marie, who always sits on stage with Finbar as he acts, loses herself in an embrace. Marie is next to perform. Before having four children and opening her own guesthouse, Marie was a professional harpist who travelled the world, mostly the US, playing birthdays, weddings, stage shows. She played classical, traditional, whatever was required, but Celtic music is her personal favourite; it was thanks to the Celtic show that came to Galway that Finbar first laid eyes on her. This red-haired goddess behind an enormous harp, entrancing everybody. Not to take away from her talent, but Solomon and his siblings have been hearing the same routine their whole lives and, while not bored of it, the sheen certainly has come off. It's in seeing the delight on other people's faces as they hear her for the first time that reminds them of her skill to capture a crowd.

Marie starts to play 'Carolan's Dream' and instantly Laura, who has been sitting by Solomon's side in complete silence the whole time, sits up, utterly transfixed. Solomon smiles at her expression and sits back, arms folded, to watch Laura watch his mother.

His pocket vibrating makes him sit up and check his phone. Bo. He excuses himself, though no one even notices or cares, all eyes are on Marie, as he slips from the room into the kitchen.

'Hi,' he says, picking at the party food on the kitchen island.

'Hi,' her voice shouts, and he pulls the phone away from his ear as the hum of a crowd breaks into his serene surroundings. Pub noises.

'I thought you were working at home,' he says, trying to keep his voice down.

'What?' she yells.

'I thought you were working at home,' he says a little louder and somebody shushes him and closes the door. He opens the back door and steps outside to the garden. The scent of honeysuckles is strong, reminds him of a life spent playing outside, long hot bright summers, adventures in every corner of the garden.

'I was. I am. Research,' Bo shouts, and he can tell by her voice that she's had a few drinks. It doesn't take Bo many to get drunk. 'I'm meeting with an anprothologist,' she says, then she giggles. 'You know what I mean. Anyway, I was trying to find one, so I sent footage of Laura off. Jack loves her. He wants her to audition for *StarrQuest*, he thinks she'd be amazing. We can't let anyone know he's seen her because the judges aren't supposed to know the acts before they audition, but he thinks she's incredible. I know what you think of the show but I'm thinking of exposure for Laura, you know, what that would do for the documentary?'

Bo's breathless with excitement and she sounds like she's walking too. Down the longest noisiest busiest street there is in Dublin. Or perhaps she's pacing.

Solomon's blood boils. 'Hold on. Jack Starr wants Laura to audition for *StarrQuest?*'

'It could be great, if you think about it, Sol. We could film her entire journey. She wants a new start, how exciting would it be for her? He doesn't just want her to audition, he'd want her for the live shows. Definitely. But again, don't tell anyone, they're not supposed to say that in advance. Think about it, how exciting would it be for Laura?'

'I am thinking about it and I think it's a fucking disgrace that you're even thinking about it,' he practically spits down the phone.

She's silent for one, two, three . . . 'I should have known you'd piss all over the idea. I called you, *excited*, Sol. Why can't you ever be enthusiastic about the same things as me? Or at least share in my happiness about something. You always drag it down.'

'What are you doing drinking with Jack?' he demands. Jack is her ex-boyfriend of five years, the guy she dated and lived with before Solomon. A middle-aged has-been who was the famous lead singer in an American soft-rock duo that had a handful of hits. He moved to Ireland in the eighties, dated a string of models and has lived off his name ever since. Now he's a radio DJ, fronts a TV talent show that Solomon once worked on, a job for the money, not for the love, and drives Solomon crazy. Jack enjoys that he and Bo were together before Solomon, dropping one annoying and degrading comment after another to taunt him.

'I wasn't out drinking with him,' she defends herself. 'I emailed the footage of Laura, looking for an anthropologist — ' She gets the word right this time, careful to watch every syllable.

'Why the fuck would he know an anthropologist, Bo? He's a washed-up fucking crooner. This is bullshit — you rang him because I'm away and

146

you wanted to hook up.' He's not quite sure where the anger is coming from, where the jealousy has surged from. He knows he has a right to feel a little put out, but certainly not this much; he can't help himself though. It's guilt for how he's been feeling for Laura, added to the natural protective role he's taken on. It fires him up.

She squeals down the phone, her absolute fury and disgust at being accused, but he talks over her, neither of them listening to one another but catching the occasional insulting word and jumping on that. They go in circles. And finally they go silent.

'If Laura auditions, it would help interest and funding for the documentary,' she says, business-like.

'I thought you didn't need funding. I think it's a tacky idea. I don't see how this will help you as a serious documentary maker. I think it will undo all the good that you have done this year,' he says coldly, hopefully his iciness comes across, wondering if he should give it more punch.

She's silent and he's wondering if he's made her cry, which would be unusual for Bo, but when she speaks again she's as strong as before.

'As producer, I am keeping all options open. So there's a change of plan. I'm not going to Cork on Sunday, instead you'll need to bring Laura to Dublin for the audition. Happy birthday to your mother. Good night.'

Before he can speak, she ends the call.

★ ★ ★

Bo stares at the phone in her hand, the screensaver illuminated, a photo of her and Solomon holding an award for *The Toolin Twins*. Tears of frustration prick her eyes. She feels such loathing for her boyfriend right now, but mostly hurt. Irritated, frustrated, suffocated, stuck in a box. It is so predictable. She knew that he would act like this, that he would stomp all over this opportunity, but despite knowing it, she still went to him with her enthusiasm and still was hurt by his reaction. She does the same thing over and over again and expects different results, she's sure that's the definition of insanity.

She feels arms slide around her waist. She closes her eyes remembering that feeling, savouring it, then slithers away.

'Jack, stop,' she mumbles.

He looks at her. 'Phone call with Prince Charming didn't go well?'

She can't even lie, can't defend herself or him. She feels the weight of his stare on her. He always did that: staring at her until she said things she never planned on saying. Well, she's not giving in now.

Jack zips up his leather jacket and pulls down his cap as a crowd passing stare and whisper about him. 'He's in Galway with another woman, you're here with me. There's something wrong with you two.'

'We trust each other, Jack,' she says tiredly.

'Come back to me,' he says and she laughs.

'So you can cheat on me again?'

'I never cheated on you. I told you that. You're the only person I never cheated on.'

148

She gives him a suspicious look. She never really believed that. Her definition of cheating and his was always different. Jack in a club, surrounded by a crowd of near-naked young women fawning over him, wasn't technically cheating, but he never stopped them brushing up, touching up. Never stopped himself either.

'So what makes me so special?' she asks, cynically, feeling like it's a line.

'You shouldn't have to ask me that,' he replies. 'You should already know what makes you special. You should be told every day,' he says gently.

'He tells me all the time,' she says, her voice flat. 'Good night, Jack.'

He reaches out and runs his thumb down her chin, the way he always did. She smells the cigarette smoke from his fingers.

'You should quit smoking.'

'Would it bring you back to me?'

She rolls her eyes but her irritation with him disappears. 'Would that make you stop?'

He smiles. 'Get home safe, Bo Peep.'

She stands outside the pub alone, surrounded by a dozen smokers laughing and chatting, but alone. She thinks about what he said. When was the last time Sol praised her, or told her she was special? She can't remember. But it's been two years, that happens, doesn't it. Things go stale, that's natural. At least he's loyal, that she believes, or has always believed in the past. She never worried when he went out at night, came home late; he wasn't that kind of guy. All she can think of is the times he's talked her down, the times he's tried to change her mind, in that soothing voice that now feels patronising. But that's natural too, that's the result of working and living together. There is rarely a break from each other, things overlap, lines become blurred, they're doing well, she thinks. Perhaps they need more rules, more help on how to maintain their relationship while working together. No more talking the director and producer down, he wouldn't do it on any other job. But then, she knows herself that she often needs it. She runs head-first into things, Solomon helps her to see other angles. Angles that seem obvious as soon as he says them, but that weren't there for her at the time. They're a good team.

But it doesn't feel like it, sometimes, that's all, particularly now. She's sure that's natural too.

As for the *StarrQuest* idea, despite Solomon's reservations, which she had too, she still thinks it's a good idea. Like Laura said, sometimes you only need one person to trust. *StarrQuest* is Jack's show and despite everything they've been through, Bo trusts him.

★　★　★

Solomon swears and stuffs his phone in his pocket. It's still bright outside, the sky starting to darken as the summer evening closes in. He takes a deep breath, his mind fuming over what Bo has said to him. Bringing Laura to Dublin to enter *StarrQuest* seems like the tackiest, cheesiest fucking thing that Bo could come up with, but he can't flat-out refuse. All he can do is

150

tell Laura and see what she says. It's her life, not his. He has to stop getting so involved in other people's issues, he has to stop being so sensitive to every little happening around him. It's not his job to put out other people's fires, it's not his job to feel other people's problems, but he is that way, always has been. He can't help it. He was always the lad who tried to get couples back together if there was a misunderstanding and they broke up. He was always the lad to try to cool a drunken argument between mates on a night out. Any misunderstanding that has nothing to do with him, he tries to jump in and fix. The arbitrator. The counsellor. The peacekeeper. It stresses him more than the ones directly involved; he feels the anger, the hurt, the injustice those people should be feeling multiplied in himself. He knows he does it, realises now that he probably shouldn't, but he can't stop.

As the anger cools, so does his body heat. The sea breeze causes goosebumps to rise on his skin. He plans on hunting for a cigarette — he only smokes when he's highly strung, or drunk, and right now he's feeling a little of both — but suddenly he hears a sound from inside that stops him in his tracks and sends his heart racing.

'Carolan's Dream' is being played again, but he knows it's not his mother playing. Marie wouldn't play it twice on a night, never has before, can't see why she'd do it now. It's close to her version, but not quite. It's somebody else attempting it, but he can't pinpoint what's wrong. There are no wrong strings being hit, nothing out of tune, but there is something removed, and there is nobody remotely as talented as his mother on the harp who could attempt that. Not in that room. He moves as if in slow motion, as if he's standing on a camera as it tracks across the scene. He barely feels his feet move, his head is in the music, the music is in his head. He follows it as if it beckons him, as if it's a beacon, drawing him in. From the kitchen, the kitchen door leading to the session is open again and all he can see is the crowd. All eyes forward, mouths agape, heads shaking, eyes wide and some filled with the beauty of what they're hearing and seeing. He stands at the doorway and nobody notices him. He looks at the stage and there sits Laura on a stool, alone on the platform, her eyes closed, her mouth open, mimicking the sound of the Celtic harp.

Solomon's mother, who is standing beside the raised platform next to Finbar, turns to see Solomon. She rushes towards him, a look of what appears to be concern on her face, hands to her mouth.

'Oh, Solomon,' she whispers, wrapping her arm around his waist and pulling herself close to him. She turns to face Laura.

'Are you okay?' he asks, confused. For a moment he's afraid she's going to throw a diva tantrum that Laura is playing her song on her special night. It would be completely out of character, but he can't place her emotions.

She ignores him for a moment, caught in Laura's spell. Then she turns to him. 'I've never seen nor heard anyone like her in my life. She's magical.'

Solomon smiles, relieved. Proud. 'Now you get to hear how beautifully you play,' he says to her.

'Oh my,' she says, hands to her hot cheeks.

He glances around the faces of the crowd, everybody utterly captivated, experiencing something new and astonishing for the first time in their lives.

Perhaps he was unfair to Bo. Perhaps he was wrong. Perhaps Laura deserves an audience, and not just the kind that a documentary would provide. She needs a live audience, a real live reaction. Seeing her in person is visceral, it brings her and her skills alive. Perhaps, like the lyrebird, on a platform is exactly where she's meant to be.

15

As soon as Laura has finished mimicking 'Carolan's Dream', the crowd erupts in applause. They jump to their feet, hollering and whistling, shouting for more. Laura receives such a fright from the reception that she stands frozen on the spot, staring out at everyone.

'Rescue her, Solomon.' Marie grips his arm.

He runs up to the platform and takes her by the hand. Flesh on flesh, she looks at him in surprise. Thinking of his argument with Bo, he quickly lets go and she follows him. He tries to leave the stage but his brothers trap him, and everybody, family and neighbours, call for him to sing. He knows there'll be no getting off the stage until he's sung at least one song. Rory goes to Laura's aid and ushers her to her chair, which Solomon watches with uncertainty while he sets himself up with his guitar. Rory is in her ear, and she is leaning close to him to hear what he's saying. This sets his blood thumping again, but there's nothing he can do about it while he's on stage, nothing that he could ever do about it because he has no claim over her. Rory is the baby, twenty-eight years old and closer in age to

Laura than Solomon is. He's also single, permanently single, bringing home sweet girl after sweet girl for family occasions but never staying with them for longer than a few months. Rory can have his pick of just about anybody, and he chooses well, always beautiful, nice girls, taken by his charm. Cute, sweet, is what the girls call Rory, and he laps it up.

Solomon tightens his ponytail on the top of his head to Donal shouting 'Get a haircut!' to laughter, and then strums the guitar once to get their attention. Laura immediately looks up. Rory couldn't be less interested in Solomon about to sing his song for the hundredth time and thinks of ways to get her attention again.

'I wrote this song when I was seventeen years old, when a girl who shall remain nameless broke my heart.'

'Sarah Maguire!' Donal shouts, and they all laugh.

'You've all heard this before, apart from one person, who's very welcome here tonight, wasn't she wonderful, lads?'

They all cheer Laura.

'It's called 'Twenty Things That Make Me Happy . . .'.'

They collectively 'ahhhh'.

'' . . . And None of Them Are You',' he finishes the title and they cheer. They always do, it's the same every time. All part of the comfort of the gathering, everyone knowing their part, getting involved, playing their role. And despite knowing its title and even the lyrics, they laugh generously.

And he begins. It's an up-tempo song about the simple pleasures in life, how important they are, how happy they make him. So much more than the girl who broke his heart, now belittled to nothing in his life, exactly what he wanted to do when he was seventeen and angry and hurt after she'd cheated on him with a mate. She wasn't his first love, he'd had others, but back then Solomon fell in love easily and he was in love with being in love, a young romantic who wrote love songs for himself and rock songs for his band.

His aim had always been to be a rock star, his first backup plan to be a recording studio sound recordist, second, to be a sound man on tour. He'd settled on sound recordist for documentaries for his soul, reality TV lately for his rent. He still writes and plays his guitar, though less now that Bo is living with him as he has less time to himself and the paper-thin walls of his city apartment don't afford him the luxury of his awkward, often embarrassing ways of finding his way through a song.

The crowd join in as he lists them.

One: Fresh sheets on the bed.
Two: A good hair day.
Three: Finishing work when it's bright out-
   side.
Four: A day off on a sunny day.
Five: Post that isn't bills.
These are five things that make me happy
   — ooooh . . .

156

He stops playing and the crowd fills the silence
with:

And none of them are you.

They cheer themselves and laugh and he
continues.

Six: A bacon bap with tomato ketchup.
Seven: The smell of freshly cut grass.
Eight: Scarface and a pint.
Nine: Jackie's Army in Italia '90.
Ten: Finding money in my pocket.
These are ten things that make me happy,
    oooh . . .

He stops playing and the crowd responds with:

And none of them are you.

'SARAH!' Donal yells, which sends everyone
into hysterics.

Eleven: A favourite song on repeat.
Twelve: Catching the morning bus.
Thirteen: Popping bubble-wrap.
Fourteen: Mam's apple tart. [This gets a cheer.]
Fifteen: Matching socks.
These are fifteen things that make me happy,
    oooh . . .
AND NONE OF THEM ARE YOU.

Sixteen: Packie Bonner's save against Roma-
    nia. [More cheers.]

Seventeen: Breakfast in bed.
Eighteen: A shower, shit and a shave.
Nineteen: The first day of the holidays.
Twenty . . .

He strums the guitar speedily, drumming up the anticipation, so that everyone joins in on the final line:

. . . And kissing your best friend!

The lyrics had always been 'fucking' your best friend, which is what he had done to help himself at the time, but it didn't work of course, and he kept it clean for his parents' sake.

The crowd erupt with joy and as he leaves the stage, Cormac, his eldest brother, gets up to say a piece from *Dancing at Lughnasa* by Brian Friel.

As Solomon makes his way through the crowd, stopping to chat to people he hasn't seen in months, he reaches his place to find Laura gone. He searches around and catches Donal's eye. He points at the door towards the kitchen. Solomon can't get into the kitchen quick enough.

The kitchen holds party stragglers picking at the food during Cormac's performance. Cormac possesses that ability to clear the room, not because he's not good — he's great, no one delivers it better — but because he lacks timing. When everybody is about to lift the ceiling off, he does his piece, dark and quiet and sad, which is in direct contradiction to what everybody wants. He kills the atmosphere, lets the energy dip. He does the same in conversation, brings up something sombre when they're all laughing.

His sister Cara has also escaped their brother's moment. She notices Solomon looking around, senses his mood.

'Out there' — she points out the window — 'gone to show her the cuckoos, our cuckoo-fucking-expert.' She does Solomon the decency of not even laughing at that. Solomon controls himself, his pace, tries to control his heart rate as he makes his way through the growing crowd to the door that leads to the garden. Once at the door, he stalls, his hand on the handle.

And what is so wrong with Laura being outside with Rory? Apart from it driving Solomon insane, she's a twenty-six-year-old woman who can do what she likes. What's he going to do, break them up? Declare that they can't be together? He knows his brother well, knows exactly what he wants from Laura, what any man would want from any young beautiful woman they have a private moment with, but his brother is not a sexual predator. He won't be on top of Laura, pinning her down to the ground; she doesn't need rescuing.

Or maybe Laura knows exactly what Rory wants, maybe she wants it too. Ten years alone in a cottage without intimacy, would she want sex? Wouldn't that be natural? Solomon knows that he would. But does he owe it to Laura to protect her? It's not his job to mind her, or is it? Perhaps that's a job that he's given himself, placing

159

himself in a position of importance for his own ego. An argument that is reminiscent of childish brotherly fights: *I found her first. She's mine!* But Laura did choose him, he is the one she wanted to stay with, though not necessarily be wrapped in cotton wool by him. He's not exactly her knight in shining armour either, thinking some of the things he's been thinking. With a girlfriend. A girlfriend he just accused of trying to hook up with her ex. He was projecting. Bo would see right through him, if she hadn't already. Most girlfriends would never allow their boyfriends to go away on a trip with another woman, especially to a family occasion, especially a young beautiful single woman. Was she testing him, or did she have ridiculously high reserves of trust and loyalty? Or did she want him to do what he so wanted to do? Was she egging him on, daring him to end it? Do the thing that she can't do. Because if he didn't, would they ever break up? Were they going to be together for ever because neither of them had the balls to break up, because there wasn't a good enough reason to break up?

Things were never bad between him and Bo, but he didn't exactly know where they were headed. They were working together, tied together through that, living together more as a result of an accident than from anything deliberate or romantic. And who does he think he is, imagining he is even entitled to a chance with Laura, as if that's something that is there for his taking. Frustrated with himself for sitting on his high horse, he knows he's entirely to blame and has been trying to justify whatever occurred to him in the forest the day he met Laura.

'Jesus,' Cara interrupts his thoughts. 'If you don't go, I will.' Cara hands him her bottle of beer, moves him aside and goes outside to the garden. The chill hits Solomon, which goes straight to his brain, a wake-up call. He downs the remainder of her bottle, follows Cara into the dark night and the security beam comes to life, illuminating the garden. There's no sign of Rory and Laura.

There are three places to go. Through an archway into the labyrinth; manicured hedging that they used to get up to mischief in, the beach.

'He wouldn't bring her in there,' Cara says. She looks across the road to the beach, then back to the garden. By now Solomon's heart is racing.

'Up here,' Cara says, and they leave the manicured garden behind and climb the rugged wild land beside. No man's land. They weren't allowed to go there as children. Everyone knew about the children that were taken by the old witch woman who lived there, who couldn't have children of her own — Marie's own version of the Bogie man. It worked to a point. It wasn't until their teens that they started hanging out there. Cormac and Donal had taken the fourteen-year-old Irish college students there for drinking sessions during the night while they were away from their Dublin homes for three weeks in the summer to learn Irish. It was fairly tame stuff, drinking and smoking, kissing and whatever body parts they were lucky enough to get their hands on, but one night

Donal had broken his ankle, gone over it on a rock, so they had to alert their parents, and it was game over. The students' disappointed parents had come to collect them and, crying, the girls had shamefully returned to Dublin, the talk of the school year, the shame of the school, the stuff of legend. While Cormac and Donal spent the summer grounded, Marie had learned not to allow Irish college students to stay in her house until the children were older.

Solomon and Cara pick their way across the dark land, Cara leading the way.

'There you are,' she announces suddenly, and Solomon catches up.

Laura and Rory are sitting on a smooth flat rock, hidden from view of the house, with a perfect view of the beach. The moon is lighting the way, the sea crashes to the shore. Rory's arm is around Laura's shoulder. Solomon can't even speak, he feels his heart in his throat.

'She's cold,' Rory says, with a cheeky smile.

It was always Rory who had the ability to wind him up. Solomon never had much problem with the others — and when he did they were physical fights — but Rory always managed to get inside his head. Not being able to pronounce Rory's name had made him agitated with his youngest brother from the beginning, ever since he was born. He was bullied by the others for not being able to say it, and Rory used it to his advantage, trying to get under Solomon's skin in any way he could.

'It is cold out,' Cara says. 'No cuckoos around, though. Bit too late for that, isn't it?'

162

Rory bites his lip but it doesn't stop his smile. He looks from brother to sister, knowing he has agitated them both and enjoying the feeling. Or he's agitated one, and the other has come to his defence. He seems proud of himself.

'What are you two doing out here?' Rory asks.

'Taking photos,' Cara says.

'You don't have a camera.'

'Nope.' She holds her stare with her brother, annoyed with him too.

Rory shakes his head and laughs. 'Right, Laura, I think we should go inside. Turner and Hooch are worried about you.'

'Okay,' Laura says, looking at the three of them, worried by what she's seeing and making Solomon feel awful for causing her to feel that way.

'Any time you need me, when this fool is boring you, just call,' he grins and starts to make his way across the rocks to the house. Cara follows him.

'Are you okay?' Solomon asks, finally finding his voice.

'Yes.' She smiles, then she looks down. 'You were worried about me.'

'Yes,' he says awkwardly, embarrassed.

They're so close she feels his warm breath reach her skin through the cool air. She smells beer. It's dark but his face is half-lit by the lights of the house. Strong jaw, perfect nose. She wants to undo the topknot, run her hands through his hair. She wants to know what it feels like, see how it moves. She sees his Adam's apple move as he swallows.

'You didn't need to worry about me.'

She means that she has no interest in his brother, nothing like the way he makes her feel by merely being in his company, but she knows it has come out wrong. He looks hurt. As if he has understood her to mean that she doesn't want him to worry, because she doesn't *want* him. Her heart pounds. She wants to take it back immediately, explain it properly.

'Watch out on the rocks,' he says gently, turning to make his way to the house.

16

The following morning the house that's filled to the brim with people, every bedroom full, every couch being slept on despite Marie's planning, is completely silent. It was six a.m. when the party finally ended, and though Laura went to bed after her discussion with Solomon, so annoyed with herself for saying what she'd said, and him embarrassed for trying to be her knight in shining armour, he had stayed up for a few more hours, watching Rory, watching the stairs to make sure she was safe. Rory had given Solomon a wide berth — physically but not mentally, Rory never could avoid that. Whenever they would catch eyes he'd wink or give him a cheeky grin that was enough to send Solomon spiralling into a silent jealous rage. He'd gone to his room around two a.m. and then been kept awake by the singing and shouting downstairs, and by Donal, who collapsed on him somewhere around five a.m., snoring as soon as his head hit the pillow.

Solomon could quite gladly have stayed in bed all day, or taken off somewhere quiet with his guitar to play or to write: he feels something stirring in him. The feelings of inspiration are rare these days, but he knows he won't settle. He reckons Laura will more than likely rise early, and he doesn't want Rory to take her off anywhere again. He isn't planning to act like her bodyguard the entire time, but he certainly isn't about to let it be his baby brother who gets his paws on her.

He showers quickly and goes downstairs. Every single window of the house is open to air the stench of stale smoke and drink. Marie is sitting at the kitchen table in her dressing gown, with her neighbours, drinking Bloody Marys.

'Will you have a fry?' she asks, her voice tired. The festivities have taken it out of her.

'I'm grand, thanks, Mam. Have you lads not been home yet?' Solomon jokes, pouring milk into his cereal.

'Yes, but we came around again for round two, ding ding!' their neighbour Jim laughs, lifting his Bloody Mary. '*Sláinte.*' Despite his cheer, the mood is calm as they dissect the goings on of the night. 'Your Lyrebird is a real treasure,' he says.

'How did you know she's called Lyrebird?'

'She told us. Said you'd named her that. Not familiar myself, but sounds like a fascinating bird. Nowhere near as fascinating as the girl, though. My word, that's some set of organs on her.'

'A great set of organs all right,' Rory says suddenly, shuffling into the kitchen sleepily and scratching his head.

'She went across to the beach,' Marie says, watching Solomon closely, trying to hide her

166

knowing smile as he suddenly throws heaped spoons of cereal into his mouth in an effort to finish quickly and get outside to Laura.

'Mind if I — ' He stands up and dumps the cereal bowl in the sink.

'Go.' She smiles. 'But don't forget you promised your dad you'd go shooting today.'

★ ★ ★

Laura is standing at the water's edge in another of her interesting fashion concoctions. It looks like she's wearing a man's shirt, probably Tom's, but using her alteration skills she has adjusted it to fit as a dress, added clashing fabric of another shirt along the bottom for length, with a leather belt knotted around her waist, a pair of black Doc Martens with woollen socks pulled up to below her knee, which work on her long lean legs, and a denim jacket. Solomon doesn't know much about fashion, but he knows she's certainly not following any trends. Even so, she looks cool. She looks like the kind of woman he'd chat up in a bar, the kind of woman who'd turn his head. The kind of woman who could turn his heart.

Laura feels like she could stand at the water's edge for ever; it has been years since she has been near the sea, since her last family holiday with Gaga and Mum in Dingle. She could easily stay standing here, but that was the problem with Laura, she could stay anywhere she set her mind to, for ever. Full days spent in the forest, leaning against a tree trunk, gazing up through the leaves at the sky. An entire day, lost in her mind, in her memory, in her daydreams. But not any more; she has to stop this, she needs to change with the change, prepare for a new direction.

She closes her eyes and listens to the water lapping gently, she almost starts to sway with the relaxation. The seagulls sing overhead and she relishes the beauty and perfection of the moment. It's made even more perfect with the arrival of him. She smells him before she hears him.

'Hi, Solomon,' she says before he says anything, before she even turns around.

'Hi.' He laughs. 'Are you psychic too?'

'That would mean I know what's going to happen in the future,' she says, turning to look at him. 'I wish I knew that.' He's wearing a blue long-sleeved cotton top, with buttons open at the top. A few dark hairs on his chest peep out. The sides of his head are shaved short and tight, but the rest of his black waves and curls are tied up in a high ponytail. She's never seen a man with a ponytail before, but she likes it. He's still masculine, like a warrior, and it shows off his features, his high cheekbones, his strong jaw that is always covered in stubble. She wants to run her hands over it as he does when he's thinking, looking lost and intense.

'What was that?' he frowns.

'What?' she asks.

'That noise.'

She wasn't even aware she'd made one, but she'd been thinking of one. The sound of his fingers brushing his stubble, the motion he makes when he's thinking. She likes that sound.

'Would you really like to know what happens in the future?' he asks, standing beside her, looking out to sea.

'Sometimes I'm more interested in what happened in the past,' she admits. 'I think about conversations I've had, or have overheard, or even things that I haven't. I think them through, imagine how they could have gone, would have gone.'

'Like . . . ?'

'Like my mum and Tom. How they had this secret love affair, I imagine it — not, you know, all of it, but . . . .'

'I know what you mean,' he says, eager for her to continue.

'I think that was probably my flaw. Why I never left the mountain. I was so busy thinking about the past, I forgot to plan for my future.'

She feels his eyes searing into her and she looks away; she can't take their heat.

'What about you?' she asks.

'What about me? I've forgotten what we were talking about.' He's not joking. He's nervous.

'Future thinker or past thinker?'

'Future,' he says, certain. 'Since I was a kid, I lived in my head. I wanted to be a rock star, I always thought about my future, being older, leaving school, conquering the world with my music.'

She laughs. 'Was that your flaw?'

'No.' He looks at her again and her stomach flips. 'I think we have the same one.'

'What's that?'

'Not thinking about the present.'

As soon as he says it, everything feels so *now*. Like a spell has been cast between them, her body tingles from head to toe, feeling so alive yet faint. She has never felt this way around anyone before, in her rare experiences with people; even she knows this isn't normal. It's something special.

He looks away and breaks the spell. She tries to hide her disappointment.

'Everybody loved you last night,' he says, almost businesslike, matter-of-fact. She's lost him again, to whatever goes on inside his head when he gets that intense distant look. 'They think you've landed here from another planet. They've never seen such a gift.'

She smiles her thanks. 'It is your mother who is gifted.' She thinks of Marie, sitting at the harp, sitting so beautifully straight at the harp, and she hears the song before she realises she's making the sound again.

'Did you like being on stage?' he asks her, captivated.

She can tell he has something on his mind. Like last night when he was angry with her because he found her with his brother. She has never met someone like him who seems to have so much going on in their head that isn't spoken. It's all in his eyes and his forehead. The thoughts seem to take shape and move around in his brow, knots of thoughts. She wishes they'd break free of his skin so she could see what they are for herself. She wants to place her hands on his forehead and say *Stop*. Smooth it down, give him peace. Better yet, touch her lips to his frown. He's uncomfortable now, something has shifted in him so quickly, going from being relaxed to tense in a matter of a few seconds.

He rubs his jaw. She mimics the sound. She loves that sound. Suddenly the bubbling thoughts are gone and the beautiful straight teeth are grinning at her instead. That's better.

'That's what that sound was you made earlier,' he says, happy to have placed it, perhaps happy that it's his sound.

Laura would make that sound all day if it meant he'd smile at her like that all the time. But it wouldn't work, he'd grow tired of the sound, the spark would eventually wear off, she would have to keep finding new ones and this new world was ripe with new sounds for her. Sometimes too many; it was starting to give her a headache trying to process them all. She was eager at first to hear them, understand them, but then as they moved from Macroom to Galway the sounds intensified. Particularly last night. She felt exhausted by the interaction and she looks forward to returning to Cork. Wherever it is she'll be staying, at least she'll be spending time on the mountain, surrounded by familiar sounds.

Though no matter how many times people had sung their songs last night, the spark had never seemed to wear off them. She was hearing them for the first time and it was as though they were performing for the first time. Especially Solomon's performance. He had brought the room alive. Laura's heart had been in her throat the entire time at the sound of his singing voice, of the twenty things that made him so happy at seventeen.

Solomon's concern has returned and she senses something. 'The reason I ask whether you enjoyed performing last night is because Bo called me last night.'

Bo coming into their conversation has altered everything, the space widens between them. Who made that happen, her or him? She looks down at the sand, sees that her feet have moved from her footprints, as have his. They both have stepped away from each other.

'She had a change of plan,' he says, sounding strained, forced.

Laura's heart thuds, hoping Bo won't pull the plug on the documentary. She doesn't care in the slightest about it, but she needs it. It's the only bridge off her island. If she doesn't have them, she doesn't know what will become of her life.

'She wants us to go to Dublin tonight. She's lined up some interviews for the documentary there.'

Laura feels such relief that it's still going ahead that she doesn't care about not returning to her home. She tries to fight the grin from her face.

'And she has a friend' — his face darkens and his forehead bubbles — 'who has a TV talent show, *StarrQuest*. They would like you to go on the show.'

He seems so conflicted, she's unsure. The signal to understanding him is coming and going. He keeps talking while she tries to figure him out.

'Bo showed footage of you to these TV people. Remember the coffee machine at breakfast yesterday?'

Laura makes the sound instantly as she recalls it.

'Yeah, that one.' His smile is tight.

'They like that sound?' She makes the sound again, listening to herself more carefully to see what was so special about it.

'It's unique, Laura. Nobody else makes that sound. Nothing other than . . . the coffee machine.'

'Then that coffee machine would have a big chance of winning,' she says, trying to ease his discomfort.

He laughs loudly and her joke seems to do what was intended.

'I've heard about *StarrQuest*,' she says. 'I've read enough magazines to know who the winners are of every single reality TV show going, and heard about them and their songs on the radio. What do you think of me doing it?'

'I'll be honest . . . ' He puts his hands to his face.

She makes the stubble rubbing sound and he stops, stuffs his hands in the pockets of his jeans.

'When Bo told me about it last night, I was not happy. I thought it was a bad idea. But then I saw you perform, I saw the looks on people's faces. They were captivated. Maybe it's wrong to deprive people of that experience, this experience of you that I'm having. Maybe I didn't want to share you. But the documentary would have done that anyway. Maybe it's wrong to deprive you of that experience, of that adulation, that celebration of your skills.'

She feels her cheeks glow pink because of his words. He didn't want to share her. But she's confused. 'My skills?'

He's not sure how to broach the sounds that she makes. He's not even sure if she's aware she makes them half the time.

'Like what you did last night at the party. Did you enjoy it?'

She thinks of the serenity she felt in his parents' home. The calm as she recalled the harp strings, the shared energy in the atmosphere. The explosive reaction gave her a fright, but she wasn't expecting it. She felt alone, which she likes, but as though she was sharing being alone with others.

'Yes,' she says. 'I did like it.'

He takes this in. He seems surprised by the reaction, perhaps disappointed. She's confused. He's not making this easy for her. He's asking her to do something that she's not entirely sure he wants her to do.

'Why would you want me to do this show, exactly?' she asks.

'It's not my idea,' he says quickly. 'It's Bo's idea. Her reasoning is that it would be good for the documentary. If you have a profile, then it will help the success of the documentary.'

Laura cannot lose doing the documentary. Without the documentary crew, she has nobody, she needs to cling to them as she would a life raft.

'Doing the talent show to help the documentary seems like a great idea of Bo's,' she says.

He nods. 'I suppose it is.'

She smiles. 'You don't always like Bo's ideas.'

He looks relieved to be able to tell the truth. 'No, I don't. And, Laura, to be perfectly honest, I'm not sure about this one. This is completely your decision.'

'What do you think of this talent show?' she asks.

He screws his face up, squeezes his eyes shut while thinking about an answer. 'I used to work on it,' he says. 'Sound.'

'That's not an answer.'

'Nothing gets past you.' He smiles. 'It's a risk. You could do the audition and not get through to the next round. The crowd could love you, the crowd could for some unknown reason take a dislike to you. You could audition and be booed off the stage. You could audition and possibly win. If that happens, your life could go in a myriad of directions. It depends on what you want to do with your life.'

'And if I don't win?'

He thinks about it. 'You'll be forgotten almost immediately.'

She gives it careful thought. Directions, Laura thinks. Options. Different directions sound good because she can't go back. If she makes a fool of herself she'll be forgotten, that's not so bad. That's almost a perk.

'I'll do it,' she says firmly, to Solomon's surprise.

From one bridge to another.

That afternoon, when Solomon's brothers have risen from their beds and come to life, they make their way to a clay pigeon shooting range nearby. Competition is the name of the game and always has been between the siblings and their dad, Cara excluded; she chooses to stay home and catch up with her mother. A keen poker player, Finbar always has his eye on winning and has instilled this into his children. Every year they go hunting; pheasant, woodcock, pigeon, game, whatever is available, and the amount they hit is the mark of the man. As it's out of season for bird hunting, they have to settle for clay pigeon shooting, and already Finbar has devised a method of scorekeeping and rules.

Solomon and Laura plan to follow the others in Solomon's car, but as they are moving out, the car door opens and Rory jumps in. Solomon feels rage but buries it. Laura's eyes light up and she politely giggles away at the ridiculous jokes and stories Rory tells on the way in. Solomon tries to compose himself while ignoring most of the things his brother says, but he's unable to ignore how animated Laura has become in Rory's company.

Laura walks with Rory to the shooting range, which consists of a series of wooden cabins in a row. Solomon stays protectively beside her, though not too close. He's not sure whether she wants him to leave but he chooses to stay regardless. Five cabins, all holding groups of six, are full. A weekend of good summer weather has brought the groups out.

Laura is content to sit on the bench and watch them fight it out. To Solomon's irritation, Rory sits beside Laura. Solomon stands nearby feeling like a spare part, trying to hear their conversation. She likes him, he knows that much, and so as the game goes on he moves away, gives them space, feeling pushed out and resenting his brother, and himself, the whole time.

Solomon concentrates intently on hitting the clay pigeons while Rory talks behind him. He feels that Rory is doing it deliberately, a ploy to put him off his game, and then again realises the arrogance of that thought. Solomon misses the first clay.

'Shut the fuck up, lads,' he barks, and they quieten. Finbar shushes Rory, which pleases Solomon and he hits every one after that. Five in a row, but that's only a warm-up round. Rory is up next and Solomon is pleased to have the bench.

Laura holds her hand up for a high-five.

Solomon smiles and meets her hand, allowing his fingers to cave in and join with hers. She smiles at him. They let their hands fall down slowly, still linked. Then he thinks of Bo and wonders what the fuck he's doing and lets go.

Rory hits every single one.

'That's what you get for missing Christmas,' Finbar teases Solomon, who missed the Christmas hunt.

'Ah, don't be too hard on him,' Donal says, picking up the gun and taking his place. 'These award-winning documentary makers are jet-setters now.'

'It wasn't me getting the award, lads, it was Mouth to Mouth that was receiving it.' Solomon folds his arms and stands next to Laura. He thinks about sitting down but there's no room on her side, and he doesn't want to sit beside Rory, who's taken his place again.

'You were receiving mouth to mouth?' Donal asks before pulling the trigger.

Solomon explains to Laura: 'It's the name of Bo's production company. She sees documentaries as a way of breathing life into stories. Helping them come alive.'

Rory makes a vomiting sound.

'Grow up, Rory.'

'Wawwy,' Laura says, in Solomon's perfect impression of himself.

She's not teasing Solomon and hopes he doesn't feel that, but she's assessing the atmosphere between him and Rory and puts it down to that. A simple word explains how Solomon feels. Though Rory doesn't see it that way, neither do the others. The lads laugh thinking she's mocking him. Solomon folds his arms and looks into the distance. 'Come on, get a move on, we'll be here all day.'

Laura looks at him apologetically.

They each have a turn. Their dad is in joint lead with Rory, who always works best when he has somebody to show off in front of. Cormac is last. Intense Cormac who thinks too much before he takes a shot.

'Cara shoots better photos,' Solomon teases him.

Solomon likes it when Rory takes his turn because it frees the bench beside Laura. He thinks about sitting in Rory's place, but then thinks it might be petty, that perhaps they'll jeer him, they'll read too much into it. So he remains standing and Laura is more interested in watching his shots anyway. Rory never misses one. As the only son who still lives at home with his parents, he has more time to go hunting with his dad.

To everybody's amusement, Laura mimics the shotguns, the clay pigeon machine, the sound as they're released, the sound as they're hit. It's interesting to Solomon how quickly everybody gets used to her sounds, and they continue without turning to watch her after every sound. Now and then a sound will rouse a chuckle from one of them, a 'Good one, Laura!' from his dad, an impressed, surprised cry of delight, never of jest, and Solomon could kiss them all for this.

Rory is now in the lead. Finbar and Solomon are tied. Cormac and Donal are lagging behind. If Solomon gets six out of six, and his dad misses one, then he'll tie with Rory. He steps up to the mark. Places the shotgun on his shoulder.

'Good luck, Solomon,' Laura says, and this softens him.

Behind him, Rory picks up his own shotgun and motions for her to follow. She frowns, but stands quietly and follows him. He moves to the side, out of his family's eyeshot, but they're not watching him anyway because they're all facing the other way, watching Solomon. Rory points at something a little way away in the grass and

Laura smiles with delight. It's a beautiful hare. A silly thing that has wandered off and found itself on a dangerous battlefield. It leaps wildly, trying to find a way out, the shotguns going off around him from the five cabins. Laura smiles and watches it. She hasn't seen a hare for years, there were none up on the mountain, badgers and rats being the largest mammals, neither of which were something she wanted to see around her home.

While she's watching it, Rory raises the rifle to his shoulder. Takes aim.

'What are you doing?' she asks.

He fires immediately, causing the others to jump at the sound so close to them, that hasn't come from Solomon's gun.

Laura screams. Solomon gets a fright and his finger pulls the trigger. He misses the clay pigeon, not that he cares because he's so concerned about Laura. He turns around and sees her duck under the wooden rail onto the grass.

'What's she doing?' Donal asks.

'Laura, no!' he yells, putting down the gun and running after her.

'Get back here!' Finbar yells after him, as do the others, but he ignores them. People are firing all around them, Laura could be hit.

The owner spots them, yells for everyone to hold their fire but word doesn't reach them instantly, and a few shots are fired as both Laura and Solomon run across the field.

'Laura! Stop!' Solomon yells, angry that she has put herself in such danger. He reaches her and wraps his arm around her waist, pulling her towards him, tight to his body. She pushes his arm away, as she looks around the ground in a panic as though she's searching for something. He lets her go and watches her circling the area, trying to find something, making noises, sounds he can't decipher. Animal sounds, gunshot sounds.

'Laura what are you doing?' He's calmer now that everybody in the cabins has put down their guns, but they're all lining up at the rails to watch the spectacle. He doesn't want her to become a spectacle, part of a circus.

She circles the same patch in the field, eyes down, panicked, making sound after sound, almost in an effort to track it down.

'Laura,' he says calmly. 'I'll help you. What are you doing?'

He feels his brothers beside him. His dad. He looks at them confused, sees that Rory is hanging behind, looking guilty.

'What did you do?' he asks him, roughly.

Rory ignores him.

'He shot something,' Cormac says, annoyed with his baby brother. 'Rory, Jesus, you could have hit one of us. You don't fire from the cabin.'

'This isn't fucking *Platoon*,' Donal says.

'What did you shoot?' Solomon asks. 'Did you shoot a bird?'

'There aren't any fucking birds,' Rory says, annoyed that everyone is turning on him now. 'Why would a bird fly over here?'

'Ah, don't touch that, love,' Finbar says suddenly as he spins around to see her on her

181

knees, on the grass, beside a hare. A hare that has been shot but isn't yet dead. Laura sobs, tears gushing down her cheeks, as she mimics its dying sounds.

'Jesus,' Rory says, looking at her as if she's weird. 'It's only a fucking hare.'

'You can't kill fucking hares here,' his dad snaps at him, trying to keep his voice down with so many eyes on them. 'Christ, what are you thinking, you'll have us all banned, Rory.'

'He was showing off, that's what,' Cormac says, annoyed.

'We really should get back to the cabin,' Finbar says to Solomon, eyeing Laura worriedly, conscious of the stares they've attracted.

'I know.' Solomon rubs his eyes tiredly. 'Just give her a minute.'

He watches as Laura kneels next to the dying hare, mimicking its sounds, sobbing with such sadness. While the others might think she's crazy, he understands her pain, her loss.

The owner starts to walk towards them, a red, angry head on him.

Solomon goes to Laura, hunches down and puts his arm around her shoulder. 'It's gone now, come on let's go.'

He feels her body tremble as she slowly stands and looks around. At all the eyes on her. At the sniggering, at the frowns, at the raised camera phones. Even Rory won't meet her eye now, hanging back and starting to head to the cabin without them. She wipes her cheeks and tries to compose herself.

Rory is gone by the time they reach the cabin,

he's hitched a lift with somebody else. The mood ruined, they're a man down and the game is over, so they return to the house.

Marie and Cara look at them questioningly as they arrive home earlier than expected to shrugs and awkward grumbles. Solomon leads Laura upstairs to her bedroom, he stands at the doorway.

'Are you okay?'

She lies down on her bed, curls herself into a ball, continues crying. Solomon wants to lie alongside her, wrap his body around hers, protect her.

'Do you want to leave?' he asks.

'Yes please,' she says through a sob.

It's a quiet goodbye to Finbar and Marie. Marie gives her a gentle hug and tells her to mind herself, but Laura is silent, aside from a whispered thank you. She insists on sitting in the back seat of the car while Solomon drives to Dublin, and at first it's because she doesn't want to be near him, but then he sees her lie down, facing away from him. He plays the radio lightly, a Jack Starr song comes on the radio and though he usually turns it off, he turns it up a little.

'That's Jack Starr,' Solomon says to her. 'The lad who'll be judge on *StarrQuest*.'

She doesn't respond. He looks in the rear-view mirror and sees her back still turned to him. He turns the music down, eventually changes the station and then decides to turn it off completely. Occasionally she whimpers like the dying hare and the sound merges into Mossie's whimpers of a few days ago, on the same back seat as they headed to the vet.

He keeps the music off for the remainder of the journey as she deals with yet another loss in her life in the same week, in the only way she knows how.

⋆ ⋆ ⋆

Laura lies across the back seat of Solomon's car. Her head is pounding, a migraine that pulsates behind her eyes; her sinuses throb, as if the pain has been transferred and now she's feeling the pain from the organs that saw it. She can't make it go away; the best she can do is to close her eyes, fixate on the darkness.

The darkness flickers with images of her mother, Gaga, Tom; all the things she could have and maybe should have said to him. At the beginning, when she moved to the cottage, things between them had been awkward. He was less used to human company than she was. She was gentle with him, took some time to observe his ways; read when he wanted to stay with her longer, read when he wasn't in the mood to converse. As the years went by, he would often sit with her and eat a meal she'd cooked. She would spend extra time preparing a special meal on Thursdays in case he had time to stay. Sometimes they sat in complete silence, him in his head, her observing him, trying to pick out all the parts of her that she recognised in him. Sometimes they talked constantly throughout his visit, about nature, about sport, about something she'd read in a magazine or heard on the radio.

184

Despite her being the hidden one, she felt she was the one who provided him with more information about the world. His world was his farm, and while hers was the cottage, she listened to the radio, and she read, so she was always connected to what was happening. She just needed him to bring the batteries. She felt that he liked listening to her talk. Maybe he was picking the parts of himself from her too. He wasn't someone to laugh easily, he was simple-minded, good-natured, a good listener and a keen observer. They were alike that way. She thinks of the last time she saw him, disappearing through the trees with a wave, Mossie at his heels. He was going to return later to fix her window. It needed sealer. He'd walk around the cottage tapping things, banging things, kicking things. At first she felt he was rude, never able to focus on her, then she realised it was his way of helping her, of showing he cared. For so many years he was all she had and she loved him.

She thinks of Mossie, of Rory and the cheeky smile on his handsome face before he shot that hare. The sound it made as it went down. It was far away, and the gunshot echoed in her ears, but she was sure she heard it. The sound it made as it left the world.

Cruelty.

What is she doing in this world? Where is she going?

She knows that she has so much further to go than the distance she has come. She could always go back. Her bridge is wavering, a rope bridge at best, its fragile supports are close to snapping if they take any more weight. She thinks of Joe, who looked so like Tom she thought it was him. She hears his angry shouts, directed at her, the wrong tone coming from his mouth, and her eyes are forced open. She feels Solomon in her space, imagines that his eyes are on her, feels his body pressed up against hers on the clay pigeon field as he tried to pull her to safety, his strong arms around her waist. Even when he's not physically touching her, he has that presence in her life. His arm around her waist, pulling her away from danger.

She's not sure about where she's going, but she knows she can't go back.

17

It's evening by the time Solomon and Laura arrive in Dublin. She still hasn't spoken a word to him during the entire trip, despite him calling out to her a few times, softly checking to see if she's okay or if she'd like him to stop the car. He thinks she may be sleeping, because the sounds have stopped. If that's the case, he learns she makes no sounds in her sleep, and there's an intimacy in knowing that about her, in even wanting to know that about her. He's never felt he's wanted to know so much about a person before. He watches her again in the rear-view mirror and then sighs, and settles into his seat.

Solomon's apartment is on Grand Canal, a newly developed area among swanky office blocks. Beneath each apartment block is a hive of restaurants and cafés, so that the first summer months Solomon moved in, he sat on the balcony with a beer, listening to the conversations of strangers below his balcony. He used to listen to everything, was interested in everything, then one night when the drink-fuelled arguments began, he was stupid enough to go downstairs and try to intervene. Instead of peace, he received a black eye. Those conversations eventually grew irritating. Nothing that anybody said was of any interest to him: prattle, small-talk, gossip, nagging, awkward first dates, silent settled couples, raucous groups of friends. So he avoided the balcony, or he'd cough loudly, clear his throat, turn up his music to alert them to the fact somebody was above them who could hear.

And then he stopped hearing them. He doesn't know when it happened, but it occurred to him during the first week that Bo moved in. She couldn't sleep one night because of the talking outside. Then she couldn't concentrate on her paperwork during the day because of the noise from the wakeboarding in the water outside. And while he was telling her a story over lunch, he could see she wasn't listening.

'Did you hear that?' she'd gasped, before leaving their breakfast table to go to the balcony where she leaned over and tried to locate the source of the mystery phrase.

He hadn't noticed it happen, but he'd stopped hearing everything outside. And as far as he knew, the same had since happened to Bo. Things happen like that.

Laura sits up as soon as they enter the city, able to tell the difference in the light, the sound, and in the stop-start of the traffic. She stretches and looks around, and Solomon studies her face, the first time he's had a clear view of her for hours. If she was sleeping, she doesn't look like it; she looks wide awake, beautiful, innocently looking from one window to another, taking it all in. She's never been to a city. The lights and action disappear as they drive into the underground car park below the apartment block.

'My apartment's above,' Solomon explains, as she looks around in confusion.

He slams the car door shut and it reverberates around the echoing underground. Laura jumps, startled. Somebody in the distance throws a trash bag into the communal bin and bangs it closed. It echoes and she jumps again.

Solomon watches her from the corner of his eye, concerned about bringing her here. 'There's a hotel on the next block. The Marker. It's nice. Modern, fancy rooftop bar, you can see the whole city.' He couldn't afford to put her up, but perhaps Bo could find the funds. She should be able to for the subject of her documentary. 'You can stay there, if you like.'

'No,' she says quickly. 'I want to stay with you.'

'Okay no problem,' he says easily, warmth flooding through him.

He lifts the bags from the boot, and closes it more carefully than he had with the doors. The exit door opens, a heavy fire door that slams and reverberates through the space. High heels walk across the concrete, the car beside them lights up and beeps. Laura mimics it, stepping away from the car. The woman looks at her as she climbs into her car, a scowl on her face, as though Laura's sound has insulted her. She starts up the engine and Solomon moves Laura away quickly.

'Okay. Let's get you inside,' he says, lifting the bags and leading her to the exit.

Bo is standing at the front door of the apartment. Solomon and Laura should be arriving soon. She feels nervous and she's not sure why. That's a lie. She's pretty sure why, but she's trying to pretend that Solomon and Laura being together alone for two days without her is not a cause for concern. She wants to be the kind of girlfriend who doesn't worry about things like that. Jealousy is a killer, a destroyer. She was never a jealous person — not in relationships, she never felt threatened that way. Work is another matter; if someone makes a better documentary, if someone is doing better than her, she'll admit she feels the jealousy then. She uses that feeling to drive her to do better. But she's not sure what this feeling can do for a relationship. She doesn't know how to be better than Laura, nor does she want to be.

And she isn't feeling this way because of what Jack said to her last night. It wasn't him that triggered alarm bells about her and Solomon, planting seeds of doubt, whispers in her ear and then disappearing into the night. The feeling was already inside her. Laura has insisted on being with Solomon at every single turn. What girlfriend would allow it to happen? Not just allow it, encourage it. She's pushing Solomon towards Laura. And *that's* what has brought on this anxiety, this twisted feeling in her stomach: the fact that she knows that she's letting it happen. She's pretending she's not, because to admit otherwise would be callous, weird, unfeeling. She's seeing what's between them right in front of her and she's encouraging it, for the sake of her documentary. There. She's admitted it.

The lift moves into action, ascends to her floor. They won't be expecting her to be ready for them, at the door. She wants to see their faces, not the ones they prepare before walking into the apartment. She'll know if something's happened by looking at them. The doors open. Her stomach twists, cramps. Solomon steps out. He's alone. He gives her a wide warning look with his eyes, then turns back towards the lift.

'Come on, Laura, we're here.'

Bo moves to the left and peers in. Laura is huddled in the corner of the lift with her hands over her ears. She rises, one of her bags in her hand, looking as timid as a mouse. The knot in Bo's stomach clears immediately. She's ashamed by her relief, she's ashamed by the pleasure that seeing Laura in this state brings to her.

'She doesn't like lifts,' Solomon says, a little nervously.

'Hi, Laura,' she says gently. 'Welcome.'

Laura's thanks is barely a whisper as she steps into the flat.

'How was your trip?' she asks tentatively, as Laura looks around.

Solomon shakes his head for her not to ask, but it's too late.

Laura opens her mouth and a flow of sounds surges out, merged and meshed together, one running into another, like a badly mixed song.

Bo's eyes widen, not quite sure how to deal

191

with the cacophony of noise. It's negative noise, something happened, something that has upset her. Stunned, she watches as Solomon leads Laura to the small spare room, as though she's a fragile broken bird. And all the while Bo tries to decipher one sound from another but can't. Did she hear a gunshot?

Solomon, however, understands them all, he identifies each and every single one of them as she repeats them over and over, an insight into her confused mind, her hurt heart. Mossie's whimpers. An angry Joe. The fallen hare, the gunshot, a door banging, high heels on concrete, the beep of a car alarm, the sound of the exit door, the whoosh of the lift when he pressed the button. A police siren.

And in there, hidden amongst them, was the sound of Bo making love to Solomon.

Telltale sounds. A medley of all the sounds Laura doesn't like.

★ ★ ★

Dublin city is alive with new sounds for Laura. From the hundreds of people who swarmed out of the theatre down the block, dispersing as they found their cars or hailed taxis to different parts of the city and back to their lives. The taxi drivers gather under the balcony as a sudden rain shower takes over. Even the sound of the rain is different. It falls on concrete and the canal across the road. No leaves to delay its eventual fall to the ground, no soil to soak it up. A police siren in the distance, somebody shouting, a

192

group laughing . . . each sound sends her rushing to the bedroom window.

She is grateful the room is so small. She doesn't think she could deal with a large strange space. There is too much of it, she needs her own cocoon. It contains a single bed that's pushed up against the wall; on the other side of the wall is Solomon and Bo's bedroom. There's a rail full of his shirts and so the room smells of him. Bo has the wardrobe in their bedroom, he'd told her. He is good that way, continuing to talk when he knows she's unsettled. It's calming for her. His voice is soothing, soft. Especially his singing voice. She closes her eyes to hear him again at the party, to relive the moment, and she's barely placed herself back in the room when a sound from outside causes her to jump. It's a girl laughing with a friend. Her heart pounds.

In Toolin cottage there were always sounds. It was never silent, despite what the crew say about its peace. Laura was used to those sounds though. She remembers the first night staying there alone. She was sixteen years old, she had been so afraid. No mother, she had lost her some months before, and she and Gaga had said their tearful goodbyes. She was no longer asleep in the next room but knowing that she was not far away eased her pain and fear. When she had learned of Gaga's death six months later, she'd plummeted to an all-time low. She felt utterly alone, but her grandmother's death had strengthened the friendship between her and Tom. Tom had shared the news with her in his usual way, with little sensitivity. He seemed to learn this over time. Knowing that she was alone, he stayed a while longer on visits, offered to help out more, fixed things she didn't ask him to fix, took more care. Having Tom nearby to help her if she needed him in an emergency was vital too. Sometimes Tom fixed her toilet, provided paint, or nailed something together in the cottage, provided medicine, but she was mostly self-sufficient. She liked that feeling, thrived on it, but she felt safe knowing that the twins were nearby, even if Joe didn't know about her.

There was never a hug, never a kiss, never even a touch between her and Tom but most important of all he tethered her to a world she sometimes felt locked outside of.

'He's not to know,' was all Tom had ever said about the issue when she'd asked, and that's how it was.

It had been a long time since she'd remembered her first night alone in the cottage so vividly. She'd lain in bed, looking out the curtainless window at the black sky, feeling like she was being watched even though the only people around for miles were Joe and Tom. Despite the work Tom had done to improve the old cottage before her arrival, it was cold. She had wrapped herself in sheepskin, huddled down and listened to the sounds that were alien to her, trying to place each noise and understand her new world. Ten years later, twenty-six years old, and she is back to feeling how she'd felt the first night in the Toolin cottage.

★ ★ ★

'I feel like I'm in Cork, in the Toolin cottage,' Bo whispers, then giggles.

'Stop,' Solomon says gently, not wanting Laura to hear her laughing. 'An owl,' he whispers, trying to identify the sounds coming from Laura's room. He recalls being back in her cottage, standing at the window and flinching at each sound. She had identified each sound for him, to help calm him. Perhaps he should be in her room doing the same thing for her. He starts to listen out, not just to Laura, but to the sounds inside and outside his apartment. He hears things he never even noticed before.

They're both silent as they listen. Flat on their backs on the bed, staring up at the ceiling.

'Bat?' Bo says, recognising a sound.

'Some kind of bird.' He shrugs. 'That's a frog croaking,' he whispers, identifying the next one.

'Wow, rain on a roof,' she whispers, snuggling down. 'The wind?'

'Who knows,' he says, enjoying being here with Bo, their closeness. They're naked, the covers are around their waists on a clammy night that the rain has tried to clear, listening to the night sounds of a remote mountain. He feels magically transported to another place, just by closing his eyes. It's an intimate insight into what it would be like to lie with Laura in her cottage at night.

'This is so romantic, I feel like we're camping out,' Bo says, snuggling into him, her head under his armpit, her body fitting next to his. She lifts her thigh across his body, nestles close to him. 'Ever had sex under the stars?' She starts kissing his chest, and works her way down his torso, his pelvis.

But it dawns on him that this is not romantic. It's Laura, alone in a strange place, remembering the things about home that she misses, conjuring familiar sounds to chase away her loneliness. He tries to shake away the thoughts of her, he tries to stop hearing her and get lost in Bo. But he can't, because even when she's silent she's still in his head.

18

The documentary crew and Laura sit in the laboratory of David Kelly of the Irish Ornithology Society. Rachel examines the monitor beside her, a nicely lit set-up, birdcages in the background, scientific equipment placed strategically in the shot while Mr Kelly looks on feeling powerless. 'Well, okay, but it wouldn't ordinarily be there,' he says, a little flustered as Bo moves his bird posters from one wall to another to fit the frame better.

He's finally in situ with Bo off camera, seated and ready to begin the interview. Solomon is all set, boom mic extended over them both. Laura is over his left shoulder. Everyone is happy, apart from Solomon; it is a sound nightmare. Each time David Kelly speaks, a bird squawks. And if that wasn't bad enough, Laura mimics it.

Just as Rachel loses her temper when something interferes with her shot, Solomon's mood is severely altered when something affects his sound. While David Kelly looks at Laura, exasperated at having to begin his response again, Solomon doesn't feel the slightest agitation. He's just happy she's here with him, her sounds a reminder of her presence, which is rather miraculous when it comes to his temperament.

She looks at David, wide-eyed and innocent, as if she hasn't done anything at all.

Solomon felt before the interview even began that it was inappropriate to bring her here, he's not sure how much she should be listening to as others speak about her or about aspects of her. Who ever needs to know what people say about them behind their backs? He's shared this with Bo and while she agreed they don't have many options; Laura refuses to stay in the apartment alone. She wants to be with Solomon.

'Okay, Dr Kelly, please go again. Same question, same answer, please,' Bo says.

'Certainly. A lyrebird is a ground . . . '

'I'm sorry, could you begin without the 'certainly'.'

'My apologies, of course.' He leaves a silence. Rachel gives him the nod. Rolling. 'A lyrebird is a ground-dwelling Australian bird known for its — '

'Hold on . . . ' Bo interrupts. 'Sorry, guys. Too fast,' she stops him. And she's right. Dr Kelly is trying to get the words out before another bird, and Laura, squawks. 'A little slower — as you were before was perfect. Please continue.'

Headphones on. Rolling.

'A lyrebird is a ground-dwelling Australian bird that is famous for its — '

Squawwwwk. Bird.

Squawwwwk. Laura.

' . . . powerful mimicry,' he continues. 'It

makes its home in the densely timbered . . . '

Squawwwwk. Bird.

Squawwwwk. Laura.

' . . . mountains. Very few people *see* lyrebirds. Though they . . . '

Tap tap of a beak against the cage, which is mimicked by Laura.

Solomon looks at Bo with frustration. This is a mess. Even David Kelly is looking flustered, continuing to talk while it looks like he's being constantly prodded in the ribs by an invisible attacker.

'No,' Rachel says suddenly, interrupting the entire thing. Solomon removes his headphones and tries to hide his smile. 'This isn't good.'

'Maybe we should try somewhere else where there aren't birds,' Bo suggests perkily, keeping the energy up.

David Kelly sneaks a glimpse at his watch.

The boardroom is quiet. No traffic, no people, no phones, no hum of an air-conditioning unit. The elements are good for Solomon. There's lots of dark mahogany and Rachel has more work to do with lighting, but it works. There are birds in the frame, birds in glass containers, standing on branches. Only problem is, they're dead, and stuffed, which concerns Solomon.

Laura joins them. She looks at the glass case of birds. Solomon sees the confusion in her face, but she doesn't say anything. He places the headphones on. Laura's fingers run over the glass cabinet, trying to get to the birds inside and before David Kelly can even speak Laura's sounds begin again; the gunshot, the hare that fell, its whimpers, Mossie's dying sounds. A new sound, the computer gunshots from the little boy's computer game in the hotel a few days ago, as she links the two.

Dr Kelly stands up and looks at her. 'Goodness. That is *remarkable*.'

Laura looks up, sees everyone staring at her and her sounds stop. Her hand falls from the glass. 'How did they die?'

'Lie,' Solomon says through a cough to him.

'Oh. Um. Natural causes,' he says.

Laura frowns and looks at Solomon. She imitates the cough he has made, over and over until the word lie is clearly audible. Solomon sighs.

'Look, I think we should do this in your office. It's the best place,' Bo suddenly decides.

'You said you didn't like that room,' David Kelly says, like he's an offended child.

'Now it's perfect,' Bo says, picking up her things and moving everyone on again.

'I really should get going. I have a lecture . . . '

'Won't be much longer,' Bo says with a reassuring smile. 'And you get more time to spend with Lyrebird. Think of it as research.'

This idea appeals to Dr Kelly, he is so fascinated with this birdlike woman. He examines her as the others move the equipment, and chuckles nerdily to himself.

Laura stares back at him, looking him up and down in the same way as he did to her, then mimics his chuckle. He claps his hands with glee.

Finally, in Dr Kelly's office — a small room,

filled with paperwork, that is dominated by his desk — they sit down to do the interview.

'Dr Kelly,' Bo says smoothly, 'Could you please tell us about the male lyrebird please, specifically about its mimicry talents.'

'The male lyrebird is a popular forest entertainer, admired and liked by other singers. Much of the vocal power of the lyrebird is devoted to mimicry of the songs of other birds, but he is also a very efficient singer in his own right. Roughly one-third of his singing is original, one-third may be described as semi-original, based quite clearly on bush sounds, elaborated and combined into a harmonious and continuous melody; the remainder of the song is mimicry, pure and simple; mimicry that is so accurate it's impossible to distinguish between the genuine and the imitated. There appears to be no sound that is beyond the power of the lyrebird to reproduce.

'Lyrebirds are creatures of habit. They thrive on routine. The mating season begins in May and ends in August. At the beginning of the mating season the male lyrebird builds a number of display mounds and diligently woos the female with song and dance. His mate follows him wherever he goes and watches every performance from a prominent position. When a performance ends, they both search for food, but as soon as the male begins to sing, the female stops to hear her mate. Mate birds are seldom seen apart and their continued devotion to their offspring indicates a family spirit.'

Solomon smiles at this description. Bo's head turns quickly to look at him, and he looks away, pretending to twiddle with his audio.

'A pair of lyrebirds, having mated, select a nesting site. Neither will wander. They're monogamous creatures, once they've chosen; they do not change their mates and matehood involves each mated pair in life companionship.'

Solomon purses his lips to hide the growing smile on his face. He turns briefly to Laura and she's staring at him, green eyes gazing at him intently.

★ ★ ★

It's ten p.m. Early for Bo and Solomon to be in bed, even earlier to have already made love, but with Laura sharing the same tiny living space it's easier to say good night and for everybody to retreat to their rooms for privacy.

They had made love as silently as possible again, particularly after their experience in the hotel. Solomon seemed distracted, and that was okay; Bo was too, with formulating and planning of the documentary taking shape in her head. Now they both lie on their backs, staring at the ceiling and listening to Laura's nightly song. Bo enjoys this, she finds it relaxing. She twirls a strand of hair around her finger and closes her eyes.

'She's going through her day,' she whispers.

'That's the ATM,' Solomon says, smiling. 'She came with me while you and Rachel were finishing breakfast. She'd never seen one before.'

Laura beeps through the ATM. Cash is dispensed.

'I wish she'd dispense real cash,' Bo jokes. 'If this documentary ends up being as good as I think it is, she will.'

'She could probably help decipher people's codes, by memorising those sounds,' Solomon says. 'She could be hired by some secret government agency with skills like that.'

Bo chuckles quietly. 'Now *that* I want to film.' Pause to listen. 'It's like she's flicking through her memories of the day, like I do with the pictures on my phone.'

They listen some more. Relaxed. Calm. Peaceful.

Then they hear Solomon's laugh. A rare hearty laugh.

'Is that you?' She looks at him.

'Yeah,' he avoids her stare. 'Can't remember what was so funny,' he lies, remembering as they'd both clung to each other, unable to stop laughing, his stomach hurting, his eyes streaming. While he was getting dressed he thought Laura was cooking bacon, from the sounds coming from the kitchen, the beautiful sound of a sizzling pan, the fat as it popped and hissed. When he stepped out to the living room, Laura was standing alone in front of an empty fridge mimicking the sounds. Laura was hungry. He'd been so confused by the empty hobs, and kitchen table, then so disappointed, she couldn't stop laughing at the look on his face. When he'd realised what happened he'd joined in with her laughter.

When finished mimicking his laughter, Laura mimics his cough with the hidden word, 'Lie.'

Solomon cringes.

She contrasts this with the laugh. Back to the lie, then to the laugh. She does this a few times.

'She's trying to decide something,' Bo says, looking at him, her heart racing now that she has understood what Laura is doing. 'She's trying to figure you out.'

Laura mimics his laugh again.

'Sol,' Bo says, concern in her voice.

'Mmm?' He can't look at her. His heart is pounding in his chest, he hopes Bo can't feel it next to her, his entire body feels like it's thudding.

'Sol.'

Lie. His laugh. *Lie.* His laugh. Back and forth she goes.

He looks at her. He sits up finally, head in his hands. 'I know. Fuck.'

19

The following morning Laura is on the balcony, her hands cupped around a mug of tea. She's making whistling sounds.

'What's she doing?' Solomon asks, fresh out of the shower and joining Bo in the kitchen. He kisses her. He makes it his business to kiss her, no hiding it any more. Last night, he and Bo had decided that it was best he step back from Laura for the time being, try to allow Bo and Laura to bond. He has to work anyway, filming *Grotesque Bodies*, which requires he travel to Switzerland tomorrow for a few days to film an operation on a man they had been following for a year. And while he and Bo had decided it was healthier for Laura's sake and the sake of the documentary that he disappear for a while, Solomon knows it's also better for himself. He's losing himself, he doesn't like what he's becoming, somebody who thinks about another woman when he's in bed with his own girlfriend. It's not him. Not who he wants to be. He needs to withdraw from the situation.

'She's talking to the bird next door,' Bo replies. 'Want scrambled eggs and bacon?' she asks, placing a plate down in front of him. 'Laura made them. She keeps asking for things I've never heard of. Herbs and things.'

'You should bring her to the supermarket,' he says, trying not to look at Laura. 'She'd like that.'

'Yeah,' she says, uncertain of how she's going to manage the next four days with Laura on her own. She'd almost change her mind about Solomon's closeness to Laura if it meant he stayed.

Laura chirps on the balcony.

'What bird next door?' Solomon asks suddenly, digging in, enjoying the quality of cooking in their home since Laura has arrived.

'The kid next door has a bird in a cage, a budgie or something. Don't tell me you've never heard it.'

'What kid?' he asks.

She laughs and hits him playfully with a tea towel. Then she joins him with an espresso and a grapefruit and keeps her voice low.

'Do you want to sit with me while I brief her about the audition?'

'We talked about this last night,' he says, concentrating on his scrambled eggs, 'It's time for you to get to know her better. She needs to start trusting you too.' Laura made his breakfast, they're the tastiest scrambled eggs he's ever eaten. He practically licks the plate. He needs to get out of this apartment fast.

'Yes, I know, but you really are better at handling her.'

He looks up at her, sees her nervousness. 'You'll be fine. Don't think of it as 'briefing' her.

Talk to her as you would a friend.'

'Probably too early for a bottle of wine at eight a.m.,' she jokes, but her uncertainty is obvious.

He looks at Laura properly for the first time since he sat down. It had taken her a few days after the incident in Galway at the shooting range to come out of her shell again. They'd had fun, he'd enjoyed showing her new things, he'd enjoyed watching her, listening to her, hearing everyday sounds that he had long stopped hearing. The hiss of a bus as it pulled in at a stop, the whistle of the postman, the shutters being lifted on a shop beneath them, the rattle of the keys, a motorbike, the ring of a bicycle bell, high heels against the ground. Her sounds were endless and they flowed from her effortlessly, without her even noticing. Bo's fears about Laura's sounds disappearing over the weekend were in vain; if anything, they are more frequent. He'd had fun with Laura. He'd laughed more with her in a few days than he can remember having done in a long time. But then he kept catching himself feeling like that and he'd close up. Laura was right to question his character last night, what was he doing, who was he? One moment he was open with her, the next moment he'd shut down, hot and cold. For Laura's good, for him and Bo, he'd have to stay away.

Through the open sliding door, Laura's chirping drifts into the apartment.

'She's not talking to the bird, by the way,' Solomon says, washing the plates in the sink.

'Hmm?'

'You said she was talking to the bird.'

207

'Yeah. She is.'

'Are you serious?'

'Sounds like a full-blown convo to me.'

'No.' He laughs, but he feels the familiar agitation rising, or maybe it's heartburn, a burning in the centre of his chest. Is it that which causes him to pick at Bo, or is it Bo that causes the burning? He's not sure, but he knows the two are closely related.

'The bird thinks they're having a chat,' she says easily, picking up her phone to check her emails again.

'Well I don't know what the bird thinks. I only understand humans.' And not so heavily disguised in that statement is the accusation that she doesn't understand humans.

'Fine, Solomon, she's not having a conversation with the bird.' Bo laughs. 'You tell me what's going on. You seem to have so much more understanding of her than I do.'

She's not being sarcastic, or cynical, there's no judgement in her tone.

'Okay, we're going to have a 'conversation' like the one they're having now. Right now. Starting now.'

'You want me to whistle?' she giggles.

'You want me to whistle?' he repeats and giggles too, as much like her as he can.

She laughs.

He imitates her.

'Maybe I should chirp.'

'Maybe I should chirp.'

Her smile starts to fade. 'Okay, Sol, I get the idea.'

'Okay, Sol, I get the idea.'

'She's not having a conversation with the bird.'

'She's not having a conversation with the bird.'

'She's mimicking the bird.'

'She's mimicking the bird.'

She stops talking altogether.

Outside on the balcony, though neither of them can see her, Laura smiles into her mug of tea.

Solomon stares at Bo, waiting for her to speak again, feeling like a child deliberately annoying his brothers.

'My girlfriend Bo,' she begins slowly, thoughtfully, 'Is the hottest producer in the world.'

He repeats it, moving his chair closer to hers, drawing her closer, eyeball to eyeball. 'With the hottest tits.'

She laughs. 'I didn't say that.'

'I didn't say that.'

Happy, fun. Them at their best. And then Bo ruins it.

'I'm going to marry my girlfriend, Bo.'

He pauses. Stares at her, pulls away a little from her face to see her properly, to get the whole picture, to see if she's joking. Her smile is gone, as is his. The tension between them is heavy. Why did she have to say that? Ruin what was a good moment, make it so intense?

'Is that what you want?' he asks.

She studies his face, it's obviously not what he wants, he couldn't even say it, not even as part of a dumb game. It's actually not something she wanted. It wasn't the objective of this relationship. It had been once, with Jack, but she was

209

younger and liked a project, and that man was a project. The ironic thing is she probably could have walked down the aisle quicker with Jack than she ever could with Solomon. It's upsetting, not because she especially wanted it, but because it's clear that he doesn't. She's not sure if being with someone who doesn't want to marry her is an insult even if it's not what she wants. Double standards. She has a few more of them.

She can hear Solomon's argument without him saying a word, merely looking at her in a panic, skin shiny as though he's broken out in a nervous sweat. She can hear his argument loud and clear; in fact, she is using it against herself, but she'd said the sentence for him to repeat nonetheless, to test him, which was unfair really.

'Now, that's a conversation,' she says, standing up. 'You should go, you'll be late for work.'

On the balcony, Laura exhales slowly, overhearing the tail end of their conversation.

The bird in the cage on the balcony next to her chirps noisily, rattling around his cage, leaping from a swing to the floor, pecking at his food, pecking at the bars. A little boy sits on the balcony beside it, crashing red cars into each other, making sound effects of the cars and the crashes. Laura mimics his childish sounds.

The past two mornings she has enjoyed sitting on this balcony and thinking. At least she has all the noise with fresh air. It makes it easier to handle, it seems to blow the headache away.

Bo joins her on the balcony. Laura gives her a quick glance. Everything about Bo is precise, neat, tidy, perfect. Not a wrinkle or crinkle on her clothes, her skin is smooth and flawless, her eyes a chocolate brown, her olive skin blemish-free. Her short chestnut hair is always tied up in a high ponytail, though there's barely enough hair to form it, two front pieces of hair fall down and are tucked behind her ears. Her hair is always glossy. When she smiles and forms certain words, two deep dimples appear in her cheeks. She wears tightly cropped jeans and loafers, a polo T-shirt with the neck pulled up. The fabrics look expensive, everything is well made. A pearl necklace sits on her collarbone. She looks like she should be in a photoshoot for a yachting magazine. She never seems to fumble, be flustered or out of control. She always seems to Laura to know exactly where she's going. She feels to Laura to be the exact opposite of her.

'Making friends out here?' Bo asks.

Laura looks at her, feeling confused. She's been on the balcony alone.

'The . . . never mind.' Bo's smile fades and she concentrates on the laptop she has placed on the table. 'I brought this to show you *StarrQuest*. It's important that you go in there fully aware of what's going on — I don't want you to do it if you're not comfortable with any aspect of it.'

Butterflies battle in her belly at the mention. The audition is this afternoon.

'That's Jack,' Bo says, pointing to the screen, and the soft way that Bo says his name makes Laura glance up at her quickly.

'What?' Bo's cheeks pink.

'Nothing,' Laura says gently.

'I'll, um, get you some more green tea,' Bo

211

says, and hurries inside.

Laura concentrates on the screen. Bo has lined up a list of YouTube viewings for her. *StarrQuest* contestants have two minutes to showcase their talent. Incredible acrobats, singers, musicians, magicians, all kinds of talents she never knew existed.

Bo returns and places the mug of tea in front of her. It has practically been filled to the brim with boiling water, water drips from the side. Bo obviously isn't a regular tea-maker. Laura questions why she's seeking out her flaws, but she's never met someone so seemingly perfect before, so self-assured.

'What do you think?' she asks.

'The talent is incredible,' Laura says. 'I'd feel out of place joining their ranks.'

'Laura, you're more unique than all of them put together,' Bo says. 'And Jack Starr, the show's judge, has asked to see you himself.'

'And you trust him,' Laura says. It's not a question, she has heard how Bo has spoken his name. With warmth. Trust. Love.

Bo freezes a little. 'Do I . . . yeah, I mean, he's . . . he's a talent spotter. He's a musician too. He's very talented himself, more than people know. He plays the guitar, the piano, the harmonica. He's known for a handful of hit songs, but there's a lot more to him. He has so many songs that people have never heard. Better songs. He has a lot of experience and recognises talent in others, and he's looking for something truly unique.'

Twice Bo said 'unique'; is Laura being entered

212

because she's unique or talented? She's afraid to ask. She's not sure she wants to hear the answer. She clicks on another link to a video. The show changes people's lives, the deep-voiced male narrator announces dramatically. Does Laura want her life to change? Laura's life has already changed, she can't stop it. She's trying to keep up.

'What do you think I should do?' Laura asks.

Bo doesn't even take a second to think about it. 'Do it. Ultimately, it comes down to this: we can do the documentary without you taking part in *StarrQuest*, of course — this is not a documentary about a talent show — but I think you gaining a profile would not only add to the content of the documentary it would also help the documentary. You don't need to worry about things like that, but for me as the producer it makes it easier to sell. A successful documentary would give you more options, more directions where you can go with your life. That in itself is a gift. Opportunity, options. Which is what I know you're searching for right now.'

Laura nods. Bo seems to know her so well. She says all the right things at these moments when she's confused.

'Do it,' Bo says perkily, with a grin, and her energy is infectious. 'Go on an adventure. What have you got to lose?'

'Nothing.' Laura throws her hands up and smiles.

20

Solomon and Rachel arrive at the Slaughter House, the venue for *StarrQuest*'s live auditions, at noon.

'Lambs to the slaughter,' Rachel says, viewing it distastefully.

The venue is famous for hosting gigs with big-name acts; small and intimate, it previously served as a slaughterhouse and was renovated as a live venue. The audition process is different to most talent shows: there are no queues of auditionees snaking around railings for hours on end, instead everybody has already faced a panel of judges and has been selected for the live auditions. It's a selection process driven by entertainment requirements as much as seeking out raw talent. The format of *StarrQuest* is that during the live, one-hour show, ten contestants are given two minutes to perform. Jack Starr sits on a throne, the audience sits around the stage like it's a gladiator arena. After each two-minute performance, Jack hits a button to reveal either an enormous gold thumb up or a thumb down for 'execution'. The format was devised by Jack Starr and his production company, StarrGaze

— a throwback to his band days, when he was lead singer of the Starr Gazers. Last year, after a lengthy court battle, he won the right to resume using StarrGaze as the title of his production company, record company and talent agency, after an unhappy ex-band member raised his dishevelled head to fight him on it.

The *StarrQuest* franchise has been bought by twelve other countries around the world and is fronted by various presenters with Starr-like qualities and similar histories in entertainment. But the elusive US market still hasn't bitten, and it's a target he's chasing more vigorously now that *American Idol* has ended its run. As Ireland has become his second home, and the only English-speaking territory that has bought the format, he chooses to appear as a judge on the Irish show. Winners are signed up to his record label and entertainment agency, StarrGaze. It is his moment to shine before the next talent show music don comes along, and he's enjoying the revival of success almost twenty years after his debut album won Grammys and led him to tour all around the world. He's making money again, due to the show and the re-release of his debut album. He's enjoyed the return to playing live gigs, his first love, and tries to include as much of his new material as possible to an audience that has only come to hear their favourite hits. His wish is for his new material to chart; it's far better than anything he produced in his alcohol-and-drug-fuelled twenties, but his popularity on the show has not spilled into his music career. Since *StarrQuest* aired, he's released one song that failed to reach the top forty.

In the centre of the *StarrQuest* stage is a four-sided screen. A golden glove wavers midway during decision time before becoming a thumbs up or thumbs down. The twist in this is that the audience gets to take part. The audience is made up of those in the studio and people at home who can vote via the *StarrQuest* voting app. If the audience votes *Thumbs Up* when Jack has voted *Thumbs Down*, then they overrule his decision. If he votes *Thumbs Up*, he overrules an audience's *Thumbs Down*, the message being that any Yes rules the day. Since turning to Buddhism after his wild life cost him his marriage, his career, almost himself, he's tried to breathe positivity into everything he creates. Previous formats of the show saw eliminated contestants who'd received the executioner's thumbs down leave in a cage carried off by gladiators, but this was abandoned after the first season when viewers protested at the offensive image of a ninety-two-year-old mother of eleven, whose children and grandchildren were in the audience, being carted off after her rendition of 'Danny Boy', and a crying ten-year-old boy whose magic trick had failed had a panic attack when forced to enter the cage. The execution cage had, however, remained popular in a Middle Eastern version of the franchise.

Despite the featured acts having been auditioned and scheduled months and weeks in advance, Jack Starr has managed to put Laura on this weekend's live show. The producers have watched Bo's iPhone footage of Laura mimicking the coffee machine and some additional footage supplied on request, so they are aware of what she will deliver tonight. But first, a meeting in person, a sound check and run-through to be completely sure. They're not that trusting.

Security is heavy at the entrance. Michael, Jack's personal security, decides to deal with Solomon and Rachel himself.

'You can go through,' he says to Rachel, but he holds a hand out to stop Solomon. It's a good twenty years since Michael was winning awards for knocking people out in a ring, but the passing years have done nothing to reduce his enormous frame. He glares at Solomon, who rolls his eyes and hoists his sound equipment on to his shoulder.

'I'm here to work,' Solomon says, bored. He's tempted to add 'Big Mickey' — the name he went by in his boxing days in the States. There, it might have sounded cool, but not in Ireland.

'Funny, I remember your ass getting fired after I threw you out.' At six foot eight, the American towers above Solomon. He was Jack's tour manager back in the day and they've remained loyal to each other during this revival. Jack's honourable that way. Can't stay faithful to a woman, but never forgets a friend.

Ordinarily, Solomon couldn't care less if he wasn't allowed into the building. He would be happy to never set foot near Jack Starr again, and he is trying to detach himself from Laura, but he needs to gain access for the sake of the documentary. He tells himself it's for that, nothing to do with wanting to be near Laura.

Tomorrow he will be in Switzerland and he won't have to continue this battle in his head.

Laura and Bo are already inside. They've had most of the day together while he's been off filming *Grotesque Bodies*, as Paul Boyle prepares for his pending operation in Switzerland. Solomon thought he would enjoy being away from them both after such an intense few days, but instead he'd spent the entire day worrying about Laura. Short texts from Bo kept him informed, but her last text had been an angry *FFS she's a grown woman, stop it.* She hadn't responded to his reply. He had no idea where they'd spent the day, or what they'd done, couldn't even imagine the two of them doing anything together.

Rachel steps back outside to stand with Solomon. 'I think he's going to let you in, he just wants to let you stew for a while.'

'Fine with me,' Solomon says, placing his equipment down and leaning against the wall for what will no doubt be a long wait.

'Did you hear from Bo today?' Solomon asks Rachel.

'I did and I didn't,' Rachel says.

'What does that mean?'

'She called me a few times when I was at the scan, even though she knew I was at the scan. She left a message asking me to come meet her and Laura.'

'To film?'

'No, just to meet them.'

Rachel's face said it all. She was annoyed about being disturbed on her personal time.

218

Solomon liked the fact that Rachel could talk about Bo as she wished, regardless of the fact they were in a relationship. He liked that she felt comfortable with him enough to say what was on her mind, and they could say what they liked about their boss. Solomon didn't like to complain about Bo, but Rachel knew, she always knew, when he was bothered. What bothered Solomon about Bo was what bothered most people about Bo.

'Was Laura okay?' he asks, frowning at the news that Bo had called Rachel for assistance.

'I'm sure Laura was fine. It may have been Bo that was struggling.'

Solomon wonders why, in all the texts she'd sent him, Bo never once admitted that she needed him. He gave her plenty of opportunities. Though he couldn't have dropped work and rushed to be with her. But he would have.

The door opens and Bo finally appears, looking uncharacteristically flustered. Having Solomon and Jack in the same building — one ex-boyfriend, one current boyfriend who'd beaten up the ex-boyfriend and thus gotten himself fired and thrown out of the building — was never going to be an easy situation. But as soon as she sees Solomon and Rachel, the worry disappears from her face. 'Hi, guys,' she says, her relief clear, then it turns to confusion. 'What are you doing standing outside?'

'He won't let me in,' Solomon says, indicating Michael.

'She can go in,' Michael says, taking a bite out of an apple. The apple is invisible as his

219

enormous hand wraps around it, the bite he makes almost ends the apple.

'*She* has a name,' Rachel says.

'My apologies.' He dips his head. 'But asshole here, doesn't.'

'Apology accepted,' Rachel chuckles.

'Michael,' Bo says, 'Jack said it's okay for him to come in.'

'Well, Jack never told me that.'

'I bet,' Solomon says.

'Why won't he let you in, Solomon?' Laura says suddenly, and they all turn to see her behind Michael's enormous frame. Her eyes are wide and fearful.

'Laura,' Bo says, annoyed, as though speaking to a child, 'I told you to stay in the waiting room.'

'Asshole's not allowed in,' Michael explains to Laura, 'because last time I laid my eyes on this little girl, she was having a hissy fit. Had to carry her out kicking and screaming.'

'*She* punched quite well for a girl, I thought,' Rachel defends Solomon. 'I wasn't here, but I saw the bruises in the photos in the newspaper.'

Michael turns his attention to Rachel.

'She's not a fan of Big Mickeys,' Solomon says, and Rachel rolls her eyes.

'Jesus, none of us will be allowed in if you carry on like this. Let me sort it out,' Bo says, rooting through her bag for her phone.

'Bo, please tell Jack Starr thank you very much for the opportunity, but I won't go in there without Solomon,' Laura speaks up, polite but firm.

220

Solomon looks at her in surprise and doesn't attempt to hide his grin from Michael.

Laura's honour doesn't impress Michael, who has seen enough fame-hungry blonde beauties pass through these doors.

'It's okay, Laura, I'll call Jack,' Bo says quickly, moving away from them with the phone to her ear, which bothers Solomon because he wants to know what she's saying to her ex-boyfriend about him. Within five minutes, they're whisked inside by Bianca, a handler equipped with a clipboard and headset, who is now leading them through a network of corridors.

'Hey,' Rachel says to Laura, 'I didn't greet you properly out there.' She throws her hand up for a high-five, which Laura smiles at and meets.

'How's your baby?' Laura asks.

'Big and healthy,' Rachel says with a grin.

'Have a good morning?' Solomon asks, trying to be casual but studying Bo and Laura's faces for hints.

'Yes, great,' Bo replies, a little too clipped. 'We went to the supermarket, then for coffee and tea, then a walk around Stephen's Green. I showed her some great clothes stores in case she wants to, you know, know where to go.'

'Uh-huh,' Rachel nods, looking from one to the other.

'I called you,' Bo says to Rachel. 'To see if you'd like to join us.'

'Oh, really? I didn't see that,' Rachel fakes it. 'I was at the *scan*.'

'Of course!' Bo realises. 'I forgot. How did it go?'

'Great. Like I said, the nurse reckons it's a baby in there, so I'm happy,' Rachel replies.

Laura laughs.

'How did it go?' Solomon asks Laura, as Bo and Rachel walk ahead of them.

Laura looks amused, then opens her mouth and Bo's voice comes out. 'Perhaps we should just go back to the apartment.'

It's the way Laura says it — the tone, the clipped, agitated vibe she captures — that causes Solomon to throw his head back and laugh. He recognises the sound of Bo trying to be polite but at the same time extract herself quickly from a situation.

Bo turns self-consciously to study them both, then carries on walking.

'Oh no,' says Solomon. 'It wasn't that bad, was it?'

Laura opens her mouth and Bo speaks again. 'Can you maybe not do that here?'

Solomon's smile disappears.

'It's okay,' Laura says quickly, hand going to his arm. He's wearing a T-shirt, her skin touches his and something happens. A tingle rushes through both of them. She looks at his arm so that he knows she felt the same thing. 'I was doing it more than usual,' she explains. 'She makes me nervous.'

'I think perhaps the feeling is mutual,' Solomon says.

'I make her nervous?'

'You're different,' he says, really wanting to say that Bo probably feels threatened, particularly after hearing the way Laura mimicked his laugh, the way she always wants to be with him and

222

clearly and honestly doesn't trust anybody else. 'Sometimes people are nervous around different.'

She nods, understanding. 'Me too.'

'Are you nervous now?'

She nods again.

'You'll be okay,' he says.

'You'll stay?'

'I'll stay.' He taps his audio bag with his hand. 'I'm always listening.'

Bianca finally leads them into a dressing room with LYREBIRD on the door.

'So, Lyrebird, you're here,' Bianca says. 'In around fifteen minutes we'll take you to wardrobe, hair and make-up, then a sound check at around four.' She looks down at her clip-board. 'You're the last act of the show, so you'll be on stage at eight-fifty for your two-minute audition. You are . . . ' she consults her notes. 'An impressionist. Is that right?'

Everyone looks at Laura. Laura looks at Solomon.

'She's not exactly an impressionist,' Solomon explains. 'She mimics though.'

'Mimic,' she writes down. 'Cool. Are you her agent?'

'Yes,' he replies solemnly. 'Yes, I am.'

Laura giggles. Bo rolls her eyes. 'No, he's not. He's part of the documentary crew.'

Bianca looks at Solomon, clearly not liking him, heavily eyelined eyes narrowing. 'Cool.' But it sounds like it's anything but cool to Bianca. 'So the producers would like to know how many impressions, or whatever, you're going to do?'

She looks at Laura. Again, Laura looks at Solomon.

'We'll discuss that now,' he replies.

'Now?' her eyes widen, alarmed. 'Cool.' Then, 'I'll come back to you in fifteen minutes, okay?'

There's radio interference on her walkie-talkie.

Laura mimics the sound and then sits down. 'Cool,' she says, with Bianca's voice.

Bianca's eyes widen. Nobody has laughed, everybody in the room is used to it now. She leaves the weird people and goes next door to the twelve-year-old gymnast.

'I thought you were going to work with her on her audition this morning?' Solomon says to Bo in a low voice as they set up for an interview with Laura in her dressing room.

Bo gives him a thunderous look. 'Sol, at the butcher counter in the supermarket she made the sound of every single fucking dead animal that lay on the slab. Then she beeped every single food item on the conveyer belt as if she was a scanner. She confused the poor check-out woman so much, she wasn't sure what she scanned.'

Solomon snorts and laughs, attracting the attention of Laura and Rachel.

'It's not funny!' Bo says, her voice shrill. 'How is that funny?'

He continues laughing until she has no choice but to give in and smile.

★ ★ ★

'How are you feeling?' Bo asks Laura.

They're filming. Bo and Laura's relationship flows so much better when there's a camera between them.

224

'I feel fine,' Laura says. 'A little bit anxious.' Laura mimics last year's winner. A seventy-year-old folk singer and harmonica player. Rachel smirks.

'It looks exciting,' Laura says, as if she hasn't sounded like a mouth organ. 'I feel excited. Like it's the start of something new. I mean, this whole week has been new.'

'Do you know what you're going to do for your audition? Should you rehearse something? Plan a routine?'

Laura looks down at her fingers. 'I don't really plan it. It just . . . happens.'

'Do you remember the first time you discovered you had this incredible ability to mimic?'

Laura is silent for a moment. Solomon is almost waiting for her to say, *what ability?* It has seemed so much a part of her, something she's not conscious of. She thinks hard, eyes flicking left and right as they search. Then they stop and Solomon is sure she has remembered, as is Bo.

'No,' Laura says finally, avoiding all eye contact. She's a bad liar.

The disappointment is clear in Bo's voice. 'Right, so it's something you've always done?'

Another pause. 'Yes. For a long time.'

'From birth, perhaps?'

'I don't remember back that far.' She smiles.

'I don't expect you to,' says Bo, her tone neutral. 'What I mean is, do you think this . . . ability . . . '

Solomon would have said talent, gift. He's sure Bo still isn't seeing it that way. To her it's an

225

affliction. Interesting only for the purpose of a documentary. Still, it's a positive that she didn't say disability.

There's a knock on the door, a loud quick rap and Bianca enters.

'I'll take you to wardrobe now, Lyrebird.'

Solomon wants to tell Bianca that her name is Laura, not Lyrebird, which is clearly the 'act's' name but he stops himself. Detach, Solomon, detach.

Keeping their sound packs on, Laura and the crew follow Bianca to wardrobe where she will try on clothes before her hair and make-up.

As she makes her way down the corridor, she turns and looks at Solomon with uncertainty written all over her face. He winks at her in support and she smiles excitedly and continues.

'It's a bit tight in here, ladies,' the head stylist snaps as Rachel and her camera, then Bo, try to squeeze in after Laura. She's not lying, the room is filled with dozens of rails of clothes from one wall to the next, there is barely room to turn around.

'I'll wait outside. Rachel?' Bo says.

'Got it,' Rachel replies, understanding the tone of voice to mean 'capture everything'.

'Wow,' Laura says. She walks down the rails, her hand running along the fabric.

'I'm Caroline. I'll be styling you,' she says looking Laura up and down, scrutinising her body. 'This is Claire.'

Claire doesn't smile and doesn't speak. Claire is an assistant who has probably learned not to open her mouth unless asked to.

Laura grins. 'Mum and Gaga would love this. They were dressmakers.'

Caroline doesn't seem overly impressed. She has ten people to style, in a room with no windows, and very little time to do it in, and a frustrating production team who keep changing their mind and expecting her to be able to pick up the pieces. But Laura moves at a different pace to everybody that's come through the door and into Caroline's world. She closes her eyes and suddenly the room is filled with the sound of a sewing machine. It is rhythmic and soothing, like the constant chugging of a train, a sound you want to sway with.

Caroline's eyes fill. 'My goodness!' She places a hand across her stomach and another over her heart. 'You've just taken me right back. That's a Singer.'

Laura opens her eyes and smiles. 'Yes.'

'My mother used one of them,' Caroline says, her hard voice suddenly emotional, her face softening. 'I used to sit underneath the sewing table and listen to the sound all day, watching the lace float to the floor beside me.'

'I did too,' Laura says. 'I used to make clothes for my dolls from the scraps.'

'So did I!' Caroline says, the stress completely eliminated from her face.

Laura's not finished yet. There are new sounds, the sound of scissors clipping at fabric, the snip snip, and the tearing and ripping sound of fabric pulling apart, then back to the sewing machine, which rises and falls, quickens and slows as it turns corners, manoeuvres the fabric.

227

'Oh. My dear. My love. Let's get you into something beautiful, you magical creature,' Caroline says, completely swept away by what she has heard.

Fifteen minutes later, Laura steps out of the makeshift dressing room.

'Well?' Caroline looks at Rachel. Of course Rachel doesn't respond, but her camera does the work. What she sees is Laura as she's never seen her before, and Laura as she has never been before. Laura looks at their faces, uncertain, but with a shy smile. She likes it, she hopes others do.

Claire sets about accessorising Laura.

'Wait until hair and make-up get their hands on you. You'll be hot stuff,' Caroline says. 'I'm not sure about the shoes, though,' she adds. 'Your legs are shaking, you poor love.'

Laura seems relieved to take off the platforms.

'Gladiator flats,' Caroline says finally. 'You have that vibe. Greek, angelic, goddess. Tall enough to pull them off too.'

By the time Laura's hair and make-up are complete, the team have created this goddess in a very short white slip, midway up her long toned thighs. If she lifts her arms it travels up past her underwear. Her long blonde hair is tied in a tight knot on the top of her head, gold metallic gladiator flats snake their way up to her knees, and around her bicep is a gold clasp with an emerald stone. Her green eyes gleam.

Everybody is silenced as she stands there before them.

'That will get you Jack's thumbs up for sure,'

the make-up artist says.

'It will get more than his thumbs up,' Caroline says, and they all laugh before realising the camera is recording, then they quickly hush and disperse.

Solomon is waiting at the stage with Bo. He catches up with his former colleagues while he waits for Laura to arrive for the sound check and dress rehearsal. Laura enters the stage set with Bianca and is guided up the steps to the centre of the stage. Laura, unaware of all the hungry eyes on her, looks around as though she's landed on a new planet. The lighting, the empty audience seats surrounding the stage, the enormous screen above her head that will display her thumbs up or thumbs down. The gilded throne where Jack will sit and judge her.

Solomon has his back to the stage while in discussion with crew he hasn't seen since his fight with Jack, but he senses the change of air in the room. It may sound stupid, but he knows that she has walked in. He sees everyone look up, stop what they're doing, he sees the looks in their eyes, the change in their expression. His friend Ted stops midway through his story, completely distracted by what's on the stage.

'Whoa.'

Solomon's heart started beating faster the second he felt the change in the room. He clears his throat and readies himself. He turns.

'Jesus fucking Christ,' Ted says. 'That's the Lyrebird?'

'She wins,' Jason says in a sing-song voice as he passes the two men. Ted laughs.

229

Solomon clears his throat again awkwardly. He doesn't know where to look. If he lays his eyes on her again everyone will know, absolutely everyone will know how he feels. He can't cope with looking at her, he can't control himself, the sudden tremble he feels, the awkwardness, the downright unsophisticated urge to take her, and have her all to himself, do all the things most men in the room are fantasising about right now.

Bo watches him, he feels her eyes on him, and he turns away from the stage, busying himself with his audio equipment.

'What do you think?' she asks.

'About . . .'

'Laura.'

He looks up again as if he'd barely noticed her the first time. 'Yeah. She looks different.'

'Different?' she studies him. 'She's unrecognisable, Solomon. I mean, she's fucking incredible. Even *I* want to sleep with her, but you know . . .'

Solomon looks at her in surprise. 'What?'

'It's not what I was expecting . . .' Bo studies Laura again, analyses her.

'Yeah,' Solomon agrees. It's not what he was expecting either. Not at all.

While Laura is surrounded by suddenly over-helpful crew members, and Bo is busy again, he takes his time to really study her now. He can see Laura's nerves. She looks over at him, a question on her face. She's seeking comfort, confidence, encouragement, and yet he can't do anything. If he goes near her, everybody will know. She will know, Bo will know. He can't allow himself to take one step closer to her right now, under these lights and cameras, for everyone to see. He keeps his distance, he glances at her from afar, from the corner of his eye, grabbing stolen moments.

The floor manager takes her attention away and Rachel documents it all. Solomon jumps into action and hurries over, headphones on, the boom mic in his hand, trying to avoid Laura's gaze.

'Lyrebird, I'm Tommy.' The manager reaches out his hand and she shakes it. 'You're very welcome. I know this is nerve-racking, every single person on the show tonight is feeling exactly the same way. But there's no need, we're a nice bunch. I'm from Cork too. Us Corkonians stick together.'

She smiles and he and she have a little chat as he succeeds in calming her nerves.

'Your king and executioner sits up there on the throne. When you're performing, this is your main camera. That's Dave behind it.'

Dave waves comically and she laughs.

'This is your place to stand. Do you think you'll be moving around?'

Laura looks at Solomon for guidance, he quickly looks down at his audio bag, plays with the tuning.

'Well, we'll have a run-through and we'll see for ourselves,' Tommy says good-naturedly. No panic. Not yet. A few hours till they go live. 'That's what we're here for.'

He explains timing issues with her, where she stands for the ruling, where she walks to when she's finished. Finally, it's time for the run-through. Solomon, Bo and Rachel leave the stage, as does everybody else, while the lights and music dramatically leap into action. Laura looks around, jumping slightly at the dramatic music. The ten-second countdown before she begins, while the stage is bathed in red, and then it is bathed in green, time for her two minutes to begin. The timer on the clock on the screen above her head counts down the seconds she has to convince King Jack Starr whether she will go through to the next round of semi-finals.

Laura holds the microphone to her mouth and looks around. She doesn't say anything. Her breath is audible in the absolute silence.

Tommy stands at the edge of the stage, holds his hands up in a grand gesture. 'Say something, *anything*, doesn't matter what, we just need to hear you.'

Bo looks nervous, Solomon isn't sure if she's worried about Laura or about her own reputation. Rachel is biting her lip and looking down at the ground, an angry energy emanating from her. Solomon makes a note to ask her about it later.

They go through the ten-second countdown again.

Laura looks at Solomon and spends the full two minutes making the sound of the coffee machine. Solomon laughs so much Bo elbows him in the stomach, production staff glare at him, and he has to leave the studio because he can't help himself.

★ ★ ★

Hours later, when the live show has begun, while four people have had the thumbs up and five have had the thumbs down, Solomon, Rachel and Bo film Laura's nervous wait backstage. She can barely speak with the nerves. Bianca, her handler, doesn't leave her side and Laura, jumpy, imitates the sound of the walkie-talkie in Bianca's hand and just about everything Bianca does. Bianca ignores it as though it's not happening.

Bianca counts her down to her performance. 'We'll go to the studio in two minutes.'

Laura's breath catches and she moves away.

'I need to go to the bathroom.'

'Hold on, hold on, you can't go now,' Bianca says, alarm in her eyes, things no longer cool.

Solomon puts the boom mic down, and Rachel too stops filming.

'What are you doing?' Bo looks at them, confused.

Rachel refuses to answer. The camera is on the floor beside her, her arms are crossed, her eyes to the floor.

'Solomon?'

He takes Laura by the arm and leads her around the corner, out of earshot from everybody else, but still just in case, he moves his lips to her ear, so close that he feels his nose brush her hair, his lips brush her soft earlobe.

'You have the ability to take people somewhere else. Somewhere they can't see, but somewhere they can feel. If you don't know what to do, if nothing comes to you, close your eyes, and think of something that makes you happy. Think of

233

your mum and Gaga.'

'Okay,' she says, so quietly, he feels her breath on his cheek.

He breathes her in. 'You look beautiful.'

She smiles.

He moves away quickly, head down, eyes down, Bo and Rachel's eyes on him.

'You ready?' Bianca asks, the alarm still in her eyes. The message being: *you better be*.

'Yes,' Laura says.

'Cool.' She lifts her walkie-talkie to her mouth. 'Lyrebird on the move.'

Laura stands on the stage, the audience's welcoming applause dies down and it's silent.

'Hello there,' Jack says from his throne, subtly looking her up and down, and not so subtly liking what he sees.

'Hello,' Laura says into the microphone. Solomon couldn't be more proud, Rachel is biting down on her nails. Jack has been generous with their access so far, but they can't film while the show is airing live, they will have to get their footage from the show.

'What's your name, tell us about yourself.'

'I'm . . . Lau . . . Lyrebird,' she corrects herself, 'I'm twenty-six and I'm from Gougane Barra in Cork.'

There's a cheer from a section of the audience.

Jack big-ups the people from Cork in the house. He likes Lyrebird, you can tell. He is wearing his charming face.

'And tell me, what are you going to do for us tonight?'

Laura is silent. 'I'm not sure yet.'

The audience laugh. Laura doesn't. Jack does.

'Okay, good answer. Well, I hope you decide soon, your two minutes is about to start. Good luck, Lyrebird.'

The studio spotlights turn red and the entire stage is plunged into a blood-red light. The timer on the screen ticks down ten seconds. Then it goes green and Laura's two minutes begin.

For the first ten seconds she doesn't say anything, she doesn't utter one single sound. She's looking around, almost in shock, stunned, taking everything in. Ten seconds of silence on live TV is a long time. The audience start to turn on her, they start to titter.

Someone shouts, a male voice, deep and a heavy Dublin accent. 'Come on, Lyrebird!'

Startled, she jumps, and mimics exactly what was just said.

The audience laugh.

The sound from the darkness is so sudden and explosive in her ear that she mimics the audience's collective laughter straight away. Then there are gasps, and silence. She has their attention. She sees the red light of the TV camera before her, the rest of the studio is in darkness. Jack Starr is lit up in his throne like he's some kind of king. She thinks of last year's winner and suddenly the harmonica sound fills the ear to less laughter and more shocked gasps. She knows she can't do that for the next minute, she doesn't know all of the winner's song.

The lights on her face are hot, there's a heavy expectant air.

She thinks of what Solomon told her. She closes her eyes. Thinks of her dear mum who would never believe that she is here right now, her Gaga who sent her to the mountain for her own safety, thinking being away from the world was going to protect her forever, but now she's here for the whole world to see, their worst fear for her.

A buzzer suddenly sounds and she opens her eyes in surprise. The lights are on full, no more darkness from the audience and the green has plunged to red again.

She looks around, bewildered, thinking she's blown it. She didn't say anything. She has lost her chance. She has embarrassed Bo, even worse, Solomon. She lowers the microphone from her mouth. She waits to be ridiculed, to receive the gold thumbs down immediately. Her heart pounds, she feels mortified. There is no applause, the lights change from red to normal again and she can see the faces in the audience. She has no idea what she has done but the entire studio is silent, looking at her and each other in bafflement and surprise. Some even with admiration. What has she done?

She swallows and looks at Jack Starr, who's now talking, analysing her performance, but she can't focus on the meaning of his words. She hears them individually, but collectively they make no sense to her. Her heart is hammering. She feels mortified. Her chance to begin something new and she has failed so soon. The audience have ten seconds to place their vote, as do the people at home. As does Jack Starr.

The audience vote is revealed first. She readies herself to be strong, to lift her chin and take it.

To her utter surprise, the stage is bathed in gold as the audience gold thumbs up is revealed.

Then Jack's vote is next. A giant gold thumbs up appears on the screen above her, but of course she can't see this. She hears happy fast music, the stage is bathed in gold light and Tommy the floor manager is standing offstage gesturing wildly for her to go to him. She looks around awkwardly then leaves the stage.

She's through.

21

'That was incredible, fucking incredible,' Jack
Starr booms down the corridor after Laura.

They all turn around, camera included, and
Bo and Solomon move out of the shot.

Jack goes directly to Laura and places his
hands on her shoulders, looks at her square
on.

'Lyrebird, that was unbelievable . . . magical.
Are you sure you haven't got a tape recorder in
there?' He pretends to look into her mouth.
'Seriously . . . ' He tries to calm himself, he is
genuinely pumped. 'That was phenomenal. I
have never seen anything like that before, never
heard anything like that before. I don't think
anyone in the world has seen anything like that
before. I mean, of course we've heard it before,
but not all from one human mouth.' He laughs.
'All those sounds, water, wind, people, laughter,
you gotta give me the list of everything. I mean,
wow. We're going to make you a star!'

Laura's cheeks turn pink. Solomon's insides
cringe and, as if Jack has realised the cheesiness
of what he has said, in Solomon's company, he
looks uncertainly in Bo's direction.

'Cut,' Bo says, straight away.

'Let's talk in your dressing room,' he says, quietly. It seems the entire production team and all the contestants have lined the corridors to watch their exchange. They go to Laura's dressing room; Laura, Bo, Jack and his producer, Curtis. Solomon and Rachel tail behind but the door starts to close in their faces. Rachel doesn't care and backs away but Solomon pushes against the door. Jack's head pops around the corner, 'We don't need cameras or sound right now, thanks.' He winks and closes the door.

Rachel eyes Solomon. 'Easy,' she warns. She leans against the wall of the corridor, keeping her eye on Solomon.

'One of these days I'm going to drive my fist up his arsehole.'

Rachel raises an eyebrow. 'Some men would pay for that.'

He smiles. 'He probably has.'

'Nah. There's plenty of women that would do it to him for free,' Rachel responds. 'Anything to be famous.'

'You really hate it here, don't you?'

'I'm all for talent. Susan has a ten-year-old niece who plays Vivaldi's *Four Seasons* on the violin with her eyes closed. Incredible. But she plays at school feis's and family gatherings. No reason to put her on stage and put her through this kind of shit,' she says, lowering her voice as a twelve-year-old contortionist walks by with her parents, face full of TV make-up and her costume bag over her shoulder.

'I suppose they're proud. They want to show

239

the world. Share it.'

'That's the thing, people keep asking her parents, why won't they let her do more with her talent? Put her on a TV show or something. Why? Because she's good at something?' She shakes her head, bewildered. 'Why can't people just be really good at something? Why do they have to be *the best* at something? I mean, my feeling on it is . . . ' She searches for the words, really passionate about it now. 'There's *sharing* a gift, and there's . . . *diluting* a gift. You know? They already have her looking like Helen of fucking Troy. Who knows what they'll do with her next. But that's just my unpopular opinion. I don't watch this shit.' She sighs.

Solomon grumbles some sort of response and quickly pushes her words out of his head because he doesn't want to know what she thinks about Laura being part of the show. He doesn't want to think that she might be right, and that he is responsible for Laura taking part. So instead he dreams about all the ways he can hurt Jack Starr. Punching his lights out was what got him fired from working on the show two years ago. It was over some derogatory comment about Bo, one that Jack had said deliberately, to anger Solomon, and he'd risen to the bait. He'd been glad he'd done it, he still thinks of the moment his fist drove into Jack's cheek, though he'd been aiming for his nose. Still, the feel of bone and flesh and Jack's painful girly cry was enough to send him to sleep with good dreams of an evening. He wouldn't rule out doing it again but he'll bide his time. He'll have to make it count, he couldn't miss out on being present for Laura's journey.

★ ★ ★

'So guys, how amazing was that? Jesus!' Jack says, sitting on the dressing room table, perfectly framed by the bulb mirror. 'Laura, I wasn't blowing smoke up your ass for the cameras, I *meant* it.'

Curtis nods alongside him, also leaning against the counter, two hands holding on to the edge, staring down at his two feet out before him. He's a tall angular man, pointed nose, white-blond hair. He doesn't say much, or anything, lots of head-nodding, arm-folding and looking into space as he listens. He's just there, a dark force.

'You are incredible. And don't worry about the nerves, I get it, first night on the stage, it's daunting, everybody feels the same, we'll work with you on that for the next show, okay? We can't have thirty seconds of nothing next time round,' he laughs, showing his nerves from earlier.

Laura nods.

'My head is bursting with ideas right now for the semifinals. Curt, remind me to tell you about them later at the meeting,' he says, buzzing, chewing gum excitedly.

'Sure, Jack.' Curtis nods, never lifting his gaze from his shoes, which are navy blue suede with orange soles.

Jack talks for a moment about the staging, technical jargon about lights and screens and staging, so fast, so many words per minute, and Curtis nods along as though catching all of it. No problem, Jack, no problem.

Then Jack addresses Laura again. 'Let's make this the best damn show together, yeah?'

He stops talking abruptly and looks around at everyone as if trying to find the source of the sound. His eyes land on Laura.

She's mimicking the sound of his gum-chewing. Curtis looks up and frowns, thinking she's being disrespectful to the star of the show.

'No, Curtis, she, um . . . don't worry . . . she is . . . it happens. Spontaneously. It's not, she's not being . . . we can talk about it later,' Bo says awkwardly. 'We filmed with an anthropologist yesterday who explained what Laura does really well. If I could remember how he phrased it . . . Actually, Solomon explains it much better.'

Laura coughs 'liar', mimicking Solomon, then his hearty laugh.

Jack and Curtis stare at her.

'If this is spontaneous, then can you plan an act for the show?' Jack asks finally.

'Good question.' Curtis rubs his chin, staring at her intensely as though his stare will force a confession from her, as though she's an imposter who will now be revealed.

Laura makes the sound of Solomon scratching his chin, while she watches him. He pauses and eventually drops his hands briefly, not knowing what to do with them, before placing them on the counter again.

'Did you plan what you did tonight?' Jack asks.

'No,' Laura says quietly, sitting upright, trying

to find a comfortable position to sit in where her tiny dress isn't rising up her arse. She's still not really sure what she did tonight.

'Huh.' He looks at Curtis, smacking his gum. Jack's expression is unreadable, but of course Curtis seems to understand it.

Then Curtis' phone buzzes. He reads a message and his face changes in obvious shock, probably the first genuine look he's had since he entered the room. 'Jesus.' He looks at Jack.

'What?'

'One hundred thousand views on YouTube already, of Lyrebird.'

'What?' Jack jumps off the counter and grabs his phone. Scrolls down. 'It's been, what, thirty or forty minutes since we got off air?'

Curtis nods. Really nods. An engaged nod.

Jack taps away at his phone for a moment, then looks at Laura.

'Curt and I have a few things to discuss now but, Lyrebird, make sure they take good care of you, here, yeah? Tell me if you've any problems?'

Laura nods.

'Keep me in the loop,' Bo says, standing and going for her phone immediately, her shock and excitement obvious.

'As ever, Bo Peep.' He blows her a kiss and leaves with Curt.

Bo rolls her eyes but she grins. She takes a moment to compose herself and sits down beside Laura. 'So . . . ' Instantly, she's back to feeling how she's felt with Laura all day: unsure of what to do or say, completely uncomfortable and unable to fill the time or form sentences. It's not necessary, of course, for her and Laura to become best friends, she'd rather learn about her subjects when the camera is on, not off, and perhaps that's what makes her anxious and unsettled around Laura. Like a chain-smoker who doesn't know what to do with their hands without a cigarette, or a musician who feels naked on stage without their guitar, Bo wonders if she has lost the ability to connect with people when the camera is off, then wonders if she ever had that ability.

Another aspect of Laura that Bo is uncomfortable with, apart from her making the sound of every dead animal on the butcher counter, is Laura's watchful gaze. Bo hates the feeling of being observed and Laura seems to drink everything in, every single little thing. If Bo sighs, Laura can imitate it. She feels under the spotlight, claustrophobic. She is normally the observer, when with Laura she feels instead like the observed and she hates it, it causes her to look at herself too much.

Laura looks at her now, seeing deep into her soul. She should tell her about the YouTube hits, she should talk to her about where they go from here, formulate a plan, but those green eyes make her feel so uncomfortable. They saw Jack blow her a kiss, they looked at Bo questioningly. They saw Bo grinning, Bo pleased by his attention. They seem to see everything she doesn't want her to see, and nothing that she wants her to see.

'Why don't you go to wardrobe and get changed?' Bo says, instead.

22

Solomon, Bo and Laura are restless that night after her *StarrQuest* performance. It's as though they're all on a high following the reaction. Solomon and Bo sit at computers and at their phones reading out messages on social media about Laura's act. Laura curls up on the couch drinking one herbal tea after another, completely overwhelmed by the feedback from these strangers. By midnight there have been two hundred thousand views of Lyrebird's performance and she leads the entertainment news online with the same simple headline on each: LYREBIRD.

Overnight the story grows and grows, gathers speed and gains momentum. Solomon left for his flight to Switzerland before Laura had woken which sends her into a disorientated spin. The internet hits keep growing. Tucked up in the apartment with Bo, Laura watches from her quiet room as her world appears to change without anything happening to her at all.

In the days that follow, occasionally Laura suggests to Bo that they go out, but Bo is keen to keep her out of the public eye, becomes like a paranoid minder when they're in the open, looking over her shoulder, narrowing her eyes suspiciously at couples raising their phones for photos, or scowls at people sending texts because she thinks they're taking photographs. She's uptight, and Laura's not sure who Bo's protecting: her documentary or Laura. A few times a day Bo turns on the camera and tries to gain insight into how Laura is feeling about everything, but Laura hasn't experienced this new, changed life of hers — how could she when she's been stuck in the apartment day after day. All she knows of her supposedly changed life is what Bo reads to her — the messages on social media, the articles in the newspaper. It's all just other people's words.

They go for walks along the River Liffey where it's quiet, and on the third night Bo concedes more than accepts Laura's invitation to see the musical in the theatre across the road from the apartment, the one that Laura has been watching people spilling out of with beaming smiles since she arrived. But when Laura unknowingly makes sounds during the show, which leads to a heated discussion between a member of security and Bo, Bo quickly ushers Laura out before the interval.

'I'm sorry,' Laura says, pulling her cardigan around her shoulders as the evening breeze hits her. They return to the apartment, Laura feeling like a scolded child.

'It's fine,' Bo says, the stress in her voice saying otherwise. 'Do you want to get some sushi?' she asks, looking at the restaurant near their apartment. Laura would love some, but she can tell from

Bo's tone that she's had enough for the evening.

'No, it's okay.' Laura's stomach rumbles. Or maybe it's not her stomach that makes the sound. 'I'll get an early night.' Again. She's sure that Bo will take her laptop into her bedroom for the evening. She spends all of her time in there since Solomon has been away, as though she can't stand being alone with Laura.

Bo looks relieved.

Once inside the apartment, Bo does exactly as Laura expected.

'Good night,' Bo says, and closes her bedroom door softly.

Laura goes out onto the balcony and watches the world going by.

★ ★ ★

Five days after Laura's audition, Lyrebird's online viewings have reached one hundred million. The media can't get enough of her. They are hungry for more information about this mysterious person who has caught the world's interest. The tabloid headlines scream GONE VIRAL BIRD.

Bo's self-imposed captivity in the apartment ends when StarrGaze Entertainment steps in. They set up base for Laura at the Slaughter House, and for two straight days she does short interviews with the media who have flocked to speak with her, with fans who film her and give her messages, gifts, words of support.

Can she describe herself in five words?
Does she have a boyfriend?

Would she like to have children?

What does she think about the gender pay gap?

If she could be a food, what type of food would she be?

What's her favourite film?

What are the top ten songs on her playlist?

Twitter or Instagram?

If she were stranded on a desert island, what would be the one book she would bring?

What inspires her?

What are her favourite sounds?

Who are her favourite impersonators?

What are her views on the American presidential race?

Does she have any advice for young women?

What's the best advice anyone has ever given her?

What is the one question she's never been asked but would like to be asked?

While Laura is holed up for two days in the press office of the Slaughter House, with Bianca by her side, Bo and Jack begin to argue.

She hears them while sitting on the toilet lid between interviews, with her eyes closed and her legs tucked close to her body, anything to escape Bianca's constant tapping on her phone. She hears the buttons in her head, they roll together, getting faster and faster, like a ticking time bomb.

'Hello?' Somebody knocks on her door, and she realises she's been making the sound. She quietens.

'Jack,' Bo says suddenly, loud and angry,

which makes Laura's eyes fly open. Bo's voice drifts through the bathroom vent.

'Bo,' he says playfully, 'Good of you to visit me. As if your emails weren't enough over the past two days, it's nice to be abused in person.'

'Jack, keeping Lyrebird here for the past two days is one thing, but your crew *cannot* take her to Cork.'

A door slams. There's a pause.

'Of course we can. We need stock footage for the press and the show. It's the best way, unless you want Lyrebird going to Cork with every single member of the press who asks for an interview? No, I didn't think so. This is the best way of handling it.'

'But I already have that footage. It's exclusive to my documentary. In fact, for the past two days I have not even been able to proceed with that documentary because you've had full media control of Lyrebird.'

'That's because she's part of the show, Bo!' he says, exasperated. 'This isn't a trick. She signed a contract that said she would take part in promotional duties. You knew that, you read it.'

'It didn't say that I couldn't be involved,' she fumes.

'Come on, babe, you're the only person we've allowed filming access to Laura. You're getting all the behind-the-scenes stuff that everybody is begging for. Curt is already breaking my balls for allowing that — how much more do you want from me?'

'I am *not* your babe. Curt is *not* the director of StarrGaze Entertainment, *you* are. So grow a pair of fucking balls.'

There's a silence.

'Fucking balls. Hmm. I think I have them already, and I think you know that.'

Laura hears a light laugh from Bo and she smiles at their interaction.

When Bo speaks again she has mellowed. 'Jack, my documentary was never supposed to be a fly-on-the-wall documentary, not a reality show or a behind-the-scenes reveal. It will not be some *StarrQuest* spin-off. It's an in-depth look at her life. From the inside, not the outside, and if you won't let me talk to her, then I can't gauge how she's feeling.'

'You live with her,' he laughs. 'You can't gauge it from that?'

The toilet flushes beside Laura and she's annoyed she misses Bo's answer.

'I'll talk to Curt,' he says, 'if you go to dinner with me. This would be favourable to me seeing as the giving up smoking for your attention is really hard work.'

'Jack,' Bo laughs, 'you're impossible. I have a boyfriend, *remember*?'

'Ah yes, the long-haired Prince Charming with the bad temper. But isn't he away right now?'

'Jack . . . please . . . What I'm trying to say is that I make feature film documentaries. You are compromising my art — you of all people should understand that. How often have you had to fight for what you wanted in your music? I brought Laura to you. I need to be more present. You can't cut me out of this.'

The hand-drier blocks out the rest of what Bo

is saying and then Bianca bangs on the bathroom door, giving Laura the fright of her life. Her next interview is waiting. It's a game called *Come and Have a Go If You Think You're Hard Enough* for the *StarrQuest* spin-off show, *Execution or Freedom*. Apparently it involves the contestants smashing a half-dozen hard-boiled eggs against their foreheads. The loser will be the person who discovers they drew the uncooked egg . . . as it smashes and dribbles down their face.

Laura loses.

★　★　★

Laura won't appear in the semi-final until the following week. There is one more live audition show this weekend and then the following Monday will mark the start of a week of nightly semi-finals, where one of five acts who perform each night will go through to the final. The live audition show that followed Laura's drew twice as many viewers, thanks to Lyrebird's worldwide publicity, the viewing figures overtook the Nine O'Clock News, traditionally the most-viewed TV show on the network. However, the demand for Laura to remain in the public eye is clear, from both the media and from *StarrQuest*, who recognise that interest in Lyrebird means increasing viewing figures for the show. The crowd of fans gathering outside the studios grows daily; they camp out, hoping for a glimpse of Lyrebird. News stations and other media report on both Lyrebird and the public's growing obsession with Lyrebird, which grows because of the media's obsession. Each feeds the other. Requests pour in from the US, UK, Europe and Australia on a daily basis for an interview with Lyrebird, or an appearance of some sort. An offer comes from Japan for Lyrebird to promote a new soft drink. After lengthy negotiations, headed by Curtis, they collapse due to a fee disagreement.

There are also requests for Lyrebird to do private events, corporate events, charity events. Agents and agencies are vying to represent her, PR agencies want to help promote her. Lyrebird needs an agent, and she has one: in accordance with the contract Jack had her sign, she falls under the StarrGaze Entertainment agency, meaning Bo has unwittingly relinquished control of her subject.

Bo phones Solomon, who's still away filming *Grotesque Bodies*, and complains, 'I'm afraid all these ridiculous Lyrebird interviews will cheapen the documentary. I'm used to spending years on a project before displaying it to the world, taking my time, editing, researching, shaping it. But this is moving so fast. *I* was the one to find Lyrebird, *I* was the one to hear her personal story first, and I'm afraid it's going to get out before I get to tell the story. And please don't say I told you so, that's not what I need to hear right now.'

'Well then I've got nothing else to say,' he says, fuming.

She sighs, annoyed. Solomon's negativity is not helping, she delayed sharing her reservations with him until now for that very reason, but now she needs help, she needs somebody to talk it through with.

It's only been a week since the initial audition and Lyrebird frenzy is already at fever pitch. But how long will that last? By the time Bo's documentary is ready, Lyrebird could be old news. Worst-case scenario: there could be a Lyrebird hangover, in which case nobody would want to touch the story. Bo's afraid that, despite the fact she found Lyrebird first, she'll be last when it comes to telling the story. She hates that it feels like a race; she has never worked this way.

Bo feels the claws reaching in from all around, trying to tear off a piece of Lyrebird. And if this is how Bo's feeling, what must Lyrebird be feeling? She can't even begin to imagine. And since when has she been calling her Lyrebird?

As Bo fills Solomon in on what has been happening since he left, his anger grows. 'How is Laura?' he asks.

'She's fine,' Bo says. 'She's busy. I barely see her.'

'Does she know that she doesn't have to do anything she doesn't want to?'

'But she does, Sol — she signed a contract.' She keeps her voice low so that Laura doesn't hear her next door.

He goes silent for a moment. 'Is she happy, Bo?'

'How the fuck would I know?' she says, tiredly. 'She keeps everything to herself.'

'Her sounds,' he says, trying to keep calm. If he were there, he would automatically know. 'At night, what are her sounds like?'

'I haven't noticed. I've been so tired, I suppose I'm so used to them now, I've stopped hearing them.'

253

She manages to talk Solomon out of coming home. He can't simply walk out — they'd never hire him again. Besides, things have not reached crisis point here. She also tells him that she's sure Laura has an infatuation with him and it's best he stays away. This is not a lie.

Bo knows that nobody has even seen the best of Laura yet, there is so much more she has to give. She only hopes Laura can figure out how to harness it, and condense it all into a two-minute piece for live TV. It will work in Bo's favour if Laura performs well in the semi-final. If she can't work one-on-one with Laura, then the show can. She reaches for her phone to text Jack about some ideas for Laura's next performance.

As she settles down to sleep, her neighbour's new puppy starts to howl.

And like last night, Laura's soft gentle sad howls join in. Bo lied to Solomon about Laura's sounds; she couldn't have told him that. Anyway, wasn't it Solomon who'd told her that these sounds were merely mimicry, and not a conversation?

She turns off the light, wraps the covers tightly around her and covers her head with Solomon's pillow to block out the sounds.

23

Exactly one week since her first live performance, Solomon and Laura sit outside the
production office in the Slaughter House studio
on plastic chairs, their heads leaning against the
wall. He has just returned and they haven't yet
had a chance to talk. Solomon tries to steal
glimpses of Laura, to see how she's doing; he's
not sure he can trust Bo's instincts as to her
wellbeing.

'I feel like we're in trouble with the principal,'
Solomon says, looking at her, then realises Laura
might not have a clue what he's talking about,
seeing as she never went to school. 'Sorry,' he
says, 'Never mind.'

'Me understand joke,' she says in a Tarzan
accent. 'Lyrebird see TV. Lyrebird read books.'

He chuckles. 'Okay. Got it.'

People appear in the corridor from secret
rooms, glance down at her, whispering, 'That's
her,' then disappear again. Others make obvious
detours to walk past her, checking her out with
sidelong looks before realising that at the end of
the corridor is a dead end, and then are forced to
walk by her again.

'So, any news? Quiet week?' he jokes. She laughs.

He's missed her so much. Being away from her has felt like a torture, but a necessary one. Ever since he heard her imitate his laugh that night in bed, he knew he'd have to go away. He owed it to Bo. He owed it to Laura. Going away was the only way he could escape Laura's sounds at night. Listening to them felt like being invited into her heart, reading her diary, and he had no place being there — all the more so because he wanted to be there. The fascination that the world is experiencing with her now is exactly what Solomon had experienced in the woods that first day he met her. But he has a nervous feeling that, in the brief time since he left last Monday, so much has shifted. Nobody could have foreseen this level of attention, but StarrGaze should at least be able to handle it. He's wondering now who's handling it.

'How are you feeling about all of this?' Solomon asks as somebody sneakily grabs a photo of Laura, pretending they're texting, the phone aimed right in her direction. 'It's been a crazy week. We haven't had a chance to speak.'

'No. We haven't.' She mimics his awkward throat-clear and his chin-stubble scratch.

His week away hadn't achieved the hoped-for goal of helping him to forget her. At the very moment Solomon was trying to get away from her, get her out of his head, the universe started conspiring against him. All week she'd been the topic of every conversation: 'Did you see that girl?' Even Paul, star of *Grotesque Bodies*, the show he was in Switzerland for, had asked Solomon about her in the waiting room one day, off camera.

At first Solomon hadn't wanted to talk about her, but he soon discovered that pretending he had no idea who she was only led the other person to start telling him all about her, how she looked, how she wasted time before eventually blowing everyone away. So he'd changed his response, admitting that he had seen her, hoping that would end the conversation, but instead he found himself having to listen to conjectures about whether she had a recorder hidden away — and how she managed it when there was no hiding anything in that dress, huhuhuh.

Thankfully, nobody, fans or press, has yet figured out where Laura is living. When not at the studio meeting fans and being photographed, filmed, or being fitted for the next performance costume, Laura has been closeted away in the apartment. She has been photographed buying flowers on Grafton Street — a set-up photo op — and walking in Stephen's Green. In particular, feeding the ducks. *Lyrebird Feeds the Birds.* She'll be getting more than tuppence by the time she's finished on the show, one clever tabloid journalist pointed out. Lyrebird's earnings from potential reality shows, magazine shoots, interviews and performances has been totted up. If they knew how she really spent her days — sitting in the apartment with the TV off, or on the balcony watching the water, mimicking the bird in the cage on the balcony next door — he doesn't know whether they'd be fascinated or bored by her. She would have loved to pass the time by cooking, but unfortunately Bo isn't an eater, which makes the tension even heavier between them.

'I'm okay,' Laura replies. She makes a smacking sound, chewing gum in her mouth.

Solomon knows immediately she's referring to Jack. 'What about him?' he asks.

It's a relief to be with someone who gets what she means. Bo still doesn't understand most of what she is saying. She doesn't understand the connections. She thinks Laura is like a broken machine spurting out random sounds, she doesn't get the underlying links. Neither does Jack, or Bianca, or just about anyone else, with the exception of Rachel, but most of all Solomon. It's not complicated at all to Solomon, though Bo makes out he and Laura are speaking a secret language. It's no secret; he pays attention, that's all.

'Jack doesn't like you,' she tells him.

'Shocking, isn't it?'

She doesn't laugh. Her heart feels heavy. She knew that making this decision to join the show was hers to make, but the only reason she'd gone along with it was because she thought it would keep her with him. Instead, it has somehow led to him slipping away. She hasn't seen him all week, and he has felt so far away. Not one phone call.

She plaits the suede fringing at the hem of her dress, undoes it and starts again.

'You should be in there with them,' Solomon says. 'Bo and Jack are talking about you, planning things for you.'

'I'd rather be here,' she says bluntly. Then she changes the subject, hoping to lighten the mood. 'What were you filming this week?' She's trying to pretend that she's not angry with him for leaving her, pretend that she's not angry with herself for being angry with him. Bo is his girlfriend. Bo is. Not her. Bo is everything Laura is not, could never be, would never want to be.

'We were filming a man with ten-stone testicles.'

Her eyes widen and she starts laughing.

'I know it's funny, but it's sad. He could barely walk, those things swelled up and wouldn't stop. He didn't have a life — not until the operation this week. It will take a while but eventually he'll be able to walk, get a job, get trousers that fit him. Same as the woman with three breasts.'

'I think that's the show I should have been on.'

'There's nothing grotesque about your body,' he says, and though he tries to stop it, he feels his face burn. He leans his head against the wall, closes his eyes and wishes his face would cool down. 'I mean, there's nothing grotesque about *any* of their bodies. It's a stupid name. They're just different.'

'Hmm. I'm weird, though.'

'Laura . . . ' He looks at her but she won't meet his gaze. She's busy concentrating on the strings in her hands. 'You're not weird,' he says firmly.

'I read it in the papers. 'Lyrebird is mysterious, supernatural, unearthly, strange.' 'Lyrebird's freakish ability . . . ' They're all saying I'm weird.'

'Laura,' he says, so firmly he sounds angry.

259

She looks up at him in surprise. She stops twisting the strings around one another.

'Don't read that shit, you hear me?'

'Bo tells me I should read it.'

'*Never* read that shit. And if you do, never believe it. Not the good, not the bad. You are not weird.'

'Okay.'

He seems so angry, she remains silent for a moment, not knowing what to say. She can't help but observe how his neck has gotten wider, how his eyes darken and his eyebrows furrow, his forehead in an angry crease. His voice has deepened, there's a rough edge to it. He leans his head against the wall and looks up at the light, breathing in slowly, his nostrils flaring, his Adam's apple seeming larger than usual; perhaps it's the anger, perhaps it's the angle. Even his anger has sounds.

He looks at her suddenly.

'What?'

'Is that what I sound like?' he asks.

Laura isn't sure what sound she made, but she assumes so.

'I sound like a horse breathing after a race.'

She shrugs. There's something on her mind.

'Bo and I went to the theatre across from the apartment.'

He looks at her, surprised, he had no idea. 'That's good.'

'My idea to go. Stupid idea. We had to leave. The security man said my noises were distracting the actors. That they would assist me in sitting somewhere else.'

'Who was he?' Solomon asks, thinking he'll stand outside the theatre and wait for him to leave work.

'He was perfectly nice. He thought there was something *wrong* with me. I mean, obviously there *is* something wrong with me because we had to leave.' Her eyes fill and she looks away, hating that she's become upset in front of him, but she's had no one to share these thoughts with, no one but herself, and she's driving herself crazy. Talking to Bo is like talking to a non-absorbent sponge.

'Laura,' he says gently, taking her hand.

His touch is everything to her. It has the effect of bringing her alive again, her heart lifts from that stuck place.

'I'm sorry, I didn't know, Bo didn't tell me . . . ' He's so angry. At Bo. At the world. His hand grips hers tightly and then loosens, tight then loose, over and over, as though massaging her. 'Let me tell you about your gift, Laura. People always say they don't like to hear the sound of their own voice, did you know that? Usually, when people hear themselves, they cringe, or they're surprised that they sound the way they do. We hear ourselves differently. What you do — ' He stops as another person walks towards them. 'This is a dead end,' he says bluntly, and the young girl turns puce and returns the way she came. When she turns the corner there are chuckles and giggles from a group of girls. 'I think what you do is let people hear people and the world exactly as it is. No filters. And in this world, anything raw and

261

untouched is a fucking rarity. People like to hear you for the same reason people like to watch movies, or look at art, or listen to music. It's somebody's interpretation of the world, not their own, and you capture it just as it is. What you have is a gift. You're not weird — and don't ever let anyone tell you that.'

Laura's eyes fill and he wants to take her in his arms, but he can't because he knows that's wrong. She wants to lean into him, but she can't because of that shield that he sometimes puts up, raising it higher and lowering it like a privacy window in a limousine.

The door to the production office opens and Bo steps out. She sees them huddled together, Solomon holding Laura's hand.

Laura lets go.

'Jack wants you,' Bo says coldly.

'Do you want me to go in with you?' Solomon asks.

'No, it's private,' Jack replies, from over Bo's shoulder.

Laura enters the office alone while Solomon stares at the wall ahead of him, fighting the anger that is surging through him. He hears himself for the first time, sounding like a panting horse. He remembers the feel of skin and bone on his fist. Jack is glaring at him, daring him to do it again, egging him on, give him one excuse to throw him off the premises for good. Jack wants him to do it, and Solomon wants to do it. And he will, but he's biding his time.

'Didn't take you long to get back to hand-holding,' Bo says cattily, sitting in the chair

262

next to him and examining her phone as she speaks. 'So much for staying away.'

'She was upset.'

'So you comforted her. Appropriate.'

Solomon fights the urge to storm out. He sits through it.

'She told me about what happened at the musical.'

She looks at him, ready for another argument, but she doesn't have the energy. She rubs her eyes tiredly. 'She was imitating the orchestra, Sol. She kept trying to get the trombone right, over and over again. I didn't know what to do, so I took her out of there. I didn't want to tell you because you'd get mad and upset.'

'That's exactly what happened,' he fumes.

'And what good was that going to do, when you're away in another country?' she says gently. 'I handled it as best I could.'

'She was upset about it.'

'I told her that it wasn't her fault.' She sighs. 'She opens up to you more than me, you know that.'

They're silent. He calms down. He can't be mad at Bo. He's angry with himself for not being there.

'That was a fucking disaster meeting,' she says finally, putting her phone down and rubbing her face. 'Jack's talking about flying her to Australia in the next few days. Melbourne and maybe Sydney. He says he'll have her back by Monday for the semi-finals.'

'Australia? For a few days? That's ridiculous. She'll be exhausted,' Solomon says, sitting up.

This seems to occur to Bo for the first time. 'Why, what were you worried about?'

'We're not allowed to go. Some exclusivity deal with the magazine and TV show in Australia. They won't allow any media that's unrelated to *StarrQuest*. We're supposed to be making a documentary about her and he's taking her away from us, *again*.'

He feels that familiar overwhelming frustration when Bo displays cold selfishness. 'You're disgusting, Bo.' He stands up and walks away from her.

★　★　★

'How's my Lyrebird?' Jack asks, taking Laura by the arm and squeezing her tightly. He grins. 'What a fuckin' week we're having, right?'

She nods.

'Sorry for swearing, it feels wrong to swear around you. You're too angelic.' He helps her to her seat and goes to sit behind his desk. He watches her thoughtfully. 'You're not one, are you?'

'What?'

'An angel?'

'No.' She smiles.

He returns the smile and drums his fingers on the table.

She imitates the sound.

'You're right. I need a cigarette. Gave them up a week ago.'

'For Bo,' she says.

He looks at her in surprise, then he grins. 'I swear you don't miss a trick.'

She makes the gum-chewing sound.

264

'Good idea. Where's my gum?' While he searches his desk drawers, Laura studies the walls.

'You don't happen to know if I'm in with a chance, do you? With Bo?'

'Bo Peep?' she raises an eyebrow. 'She's with Solomon.'

'Yeah, her long-haired lover. She should leave that loser. Tell me, you live with them, are they happy?'

Laura growls at him, the same way Mossie did when he heard a sound in the trees that he couldn't identify.

'Okay, okay,' Jack pops a chewing gum in his mouth.

Laura turns her attention to the walls. Framed discs, awards, artists she recognises, others she doesn't, his own from his band, Jack Starr and the Starr Gazers.

'You like music?' he asks.

She nods. She makes the crackling sound of vinyl, like logs burning in a fire, that comfortable, cosy, memorable sound.

His eyes widen. 'Jesus. You listened to vinyl?'

'Mum and Gaga loved jazz. Billie Holiday, Miles Davis, Nina Simone, Louis Armstrong . . .' She hums the tune to 'I'm a Fool to Want You', but her humming is deep and gravelly, not the voice of a young woman. 'Gaga's favourite song,' she explains.

He shakes his head, in awe.

Uncomfortable under his gaze, she looks away.

'I'm guessing you've never been to Australia,' he says.

'No,' she smiles.

'Well, they want you. Boy, do they want you. Biggest talk show over there has invited you. There is no Australian creature, with the exception of the koala, more firmly established in the public regard than the lyrebird. But you couldn't be more different. The koala is a hundred popstars you could name, all quaint and approachable, but you are elusive, exclusive. Man, you coming along is . . . well, it's the best timing for us, for the show. We've been trying to get into the Australian market for a while and I think this gives us a way in. The networks wanted to see that we could stir up public interest, and now they have. One hundred million views . . . ' He checks his phone. 'One hundred and eleven million views.' He laughs. 'Anyway, you don't need to worry about any of that, you just get to go on a free trip. Go on the country's biggest chat show. Pose with a lyrebird for the press. Do a magazine shoot. Then fly home for Monday night's semi-final. What do you think?'

'It all sounds . . . incredible.' She grins, unable to believe it. 'Are the others coming?'

'What others?'

'The other contestants. I don't think most of them like me very much.'

'They're jealous.' He smiles. 'It's a competition, you blew them all out of the water. And no, they're not coming. This trip is all about you.'

She chews on her lip, concerned about this.

'Don't worry, they're all doing interviews too. They've probably done more, in fact, but you're getting all the coverage. If I were to ask any of them to come on this trip, they wouldn't think twice about leaving anyone else behind. It's a competition, Lyrebird. So, you need to get your passport details to Bianca so we can take care of your flights.'

'Oh . . . I don't have a passport.'

'That's okay,' he says encouragingly. 'We have a few days, we can organise one. The show has had to organise emergency passports before. The passport office are good that way. Fans of the show. All you have to do is give Bianca your birth certificate. Don't worry if it's in Cork, we can pick up a copy from the Dublin office.'

Laura stares at him, open-mouthed, not sure what to say. He takes it the wrong way.

He laughs. 'I told you not to worry, this show takes care of all your needs,' he holds his hands out grandly.

Laura swallows. 'No, it's not that . . . I don't have a birth certificate.'

His smile fades.

★   ★   ★

Bianca, Curtis and Jack sit in the office in what Laura understands to be a crisis meeting. Curtis and Jack watch Laura, Laura looks at Bianca as she reads from a list of paperwork required to attain a passport.

'Baptism record?'

'She already said no,' Jack says, the irritation creeping in.

'School records.'

'I was home-schooled.'

'Yeah, but state exams would have you on file.'

267

'I didn't sit state exams.'

'Okay, cool,' Bianca says, looking down at her printout from the passport office. 'A letter from someone who knows you from an early age attesting they believe you to be born in Ireland.' She looks up at Laura. They all do.

Jack laughs. 'Well, that should be easy. Know anyone who knows you were born?'

Curtis chuckles for Jack's benefit.

'No.' Laura's eyes fill. 'I'm sorry.'

'Okay, wait. Something's up here. You need to tell us what's going on,' Jack says gently, and Curtis sits up, all ears.

Part 2

A solitary creature, the lyrebird is a creature of the wild. It cannot, or will not, subsist in cleared and settled areas. While they're a tame and shy bird, many lyrebirds have been snared alive and are subjected to examination by experienced naturalists. The outcome is that the lyrebird mopes in captivity and quickly perishes.

Ambrose Pratt, *The Lore of the Lyrebird*

24

After sharing her story with Curtis and Jack, StarrGaze Entertainment book Laura for an interview on Ireland's biggest radio chat show, an in-depth interview which reveals exclusive never-talked-about details of her life in the Toolin cottage alone for ten years, and a discussion of her inability to get a passport. There follows a debate on air about how Laura or anybody in Laura's very unusual situation can receive a passport. Members of the public, officials, ring in with tips and advice and tell their own stories. Her local TD's constituency office vows to help her.

After an exhausting day, feeling utterly drained from sharing herself, her personal story, with strangers who dig at her soul, Laura returns to the apartment. She leans against the door, her eyes closed, her migraine reaching an all-time high.

'You just shared our exclusive with the entire fucking nation!'

Laura opens her eyes.

Bo is standing before her, hands on her hips. Laura has never seen her so angry.

'Is that a problem?' Laura looks nervously to Solomon, who has just stepped out of the bedroom to see what all the fuss is about.

This angers Bo even more, that Laura continuously turns to Solomon for support. She's using him as her get-out clause. Poor little mountain girl who can't make decisions for herself, when she's turned out to be far more savvy than any of them could have imagined.

'Of course it's a problem,' Bo snaps. 'You told me you were going on air to talk about a passport. Not to reveal *everything*.'

Laura looks at her in surprise.

'You're doing the documentary with *me*, remember? You're supposed to be telling *me* your story, and instead you're planning to travel to the other side of the world, and telling all to the rag-mags. Oh yes, I heard about that one too.'

Laura swallows nervously. She makes a sound.

'No, don't start that, Laura, seriously. Sometimes I think you start that shit to avoid the subject. We're adults. Start acting like one.'

'Bo,' Solomon cuts in. 'Stop it.'

Bo ignores him and continues: 'I found you, I brought you here, I got you the place on *StarrQuest*, you're staying with me, I'm feeding you, you're sleeping here — '

'Bo, stop — '

'No, don't interrupt me,' she raises her voice. 'The deal was that you share your story with us, not use us to get to bigger and better things.' She looks Laura up and down, at her clothes and the stack of magazines in her hand. 'I see you reading through these all day, I see you have a new wardrobe, designer sunglasses. You want to be famous Laura, is that what this is all about?'

'Bo! Shut up!' Solomon yells at the top of his voice, which frightens Laura but Bo doesn't even blink.

'Stay out of this, Sol — Laura should be no concern of yours,' she hisses. Which means so many things.

'No, that's right, she's yours and Jack's baby, isn't she? The two of you get to play God over somebody else's life. You accuse Laura of wanting glory? The two of you couldn't be worse.'

While they shout abuse at each other, Laura looks from one to the other in alarm. Her eyes fill with tears, her hands go to her ears at the awful sound, the venom, the anger and hatred emanating from two people who are supposed to love each other.

'Stop it!' she shrieks.

They both look at her. She's trembling. She looks directly at Bo.

'The show bought me these clothes. I have to return them when it's over. Bianca gave me these magazines. Every single one of them has asked me to do an interview or a photo-shoot. They wanted me to look through them to see. I said no to all of them but the one I said yes to are paying me. In case you haven't noticed, I have no money.' She says this, anger rising in her voice. 'I can't pay for my food because I have no money. I can't pay for my clothes because I have no money. I can't buy you anything or give you

273

anything in return for what you've done for me because I have no money.

'Aside from not having any money, I couldn't get a passport. I had no birth certificate. I had no baptism records, no school records, not even a letter from somebody who could attest to me being born in Ireland. I had to go on national radio to tell my personal story to get a passport,' she says, tears of frustration welling in her eyes. 'Do you know how humiliating that was? Do you think I *wanted* to do that? Apparently, the contract that you assisted me in signing states that I'm obligated to carry out all promotional duties that *StarrQuest* request of me. Australia is included in that, but you don't need to worry because it doesn't look as though I'll be able to get my hands on a passport because there is nobody in the world who is a witness to my birth or existence.

'Our agreement, Bo, was that you follow me while I try to move on with my life. And I took you up on that because I had no choice. You told me Joe didn't want me at the cottage any more, and as I had nowhere else to go, all I could do was follow you. You encouraged me to take part in this talent show because you said it would give me options. This is me, trying to make a choice, to make something for myself in the only way that I know how. I have no idea what I'm doing, but I trusted you.' This she says to Solomon and her voice breaks. Then returning to Bo, she says, 'You were supposed to follow me, but what I was really doing was following you. You were the only people I had to help me and you have no idea how much I appreciate everything you've done for me. I try to cook as much as possible to show you my thanks, I try to stay in my room, or on the balcony as much as possible to give you both your privacy. Bo, I really do try to stay out of your way. I'm doing what I can.'

Laura seems to make a decision because the tears dry and a determination appears on her face. 'Unfortunately, instead of trying to build something up, I am clearly breaking things down. I'm going to honour the documentary because I'm an honourable person and I am thankful to you, but I think the best thing for me to do is to get out of here. To leave you in peace. I don't want to cause you both any more trouble.' She looks at Solomon, her eyes filled. 'And I certainly don't want to come between you two.' She turns away and moves towards the door.

'Laura, you don't have to leave,' Solomon says, feeling the pain rising in his chest.

'Yes, I do,' she says quietly, closing the bedroom door behind her.

Solomon turns to Bo, thunder on his face.

'Go on, Solomon,' she says, teeth bared. 'You have a go at me one more time over something I've said or done and I'll scream bloody murder. She can't go anywhere anyway.' She lowers her voice. 'Where's she going to go?'

Solomon thinks about it. Bo is right. There is nowhere for Laura to go, which makes him feel hugely relieved, and sad for her at the same time. But he needs to get away from Bo quickly before he says or does something he'll regret. 'I'm out of here,' he says, grabbing his jacket. 'Because, right now, I cannot stand to look at you or be anywhere near you.'

'Good. The feeling's mutual.'

'I'm out of the documentary. I don't want anything to do with it,' he adds angrily, without thinking it through.

She pauses, then replies less confidently, 'Good.'

'It started as something beautiful, but you made it ugly.'

'Great, thanks.'

'You hear me, Bo?'

'Loud and clear, the verbal bullying again. I'm a terrible person, Solomon, you're a saint. Got it. Why don't you run away and leave everybody else to clean up the mess? Then you can get on your high horse as usual and blame everybody but yourself.'

'Go fuck yourself,' he says, grabbing his keys and banging the door behind him.

Left in silence, Bo sits on the couch, the adrenaline pumping. She bites the skin around her nails, her foot bouncing up and down, pretending she doesn't care about either of them. But she feels the sting around her nail and tastes blood and of course she cares. She's got everything riding on this documentary. Financing, promises to investors, her reputation. Her relationship. Everything.

Laura isn't even moving around in her bedroom, there's no sound of her packing her bags. Bo doubts she'll leave. What she said to Solomon was the truth: Laura has nowhere to go. As the minutes tick by in silence she calms down; perhaps she went at Laura too hard about the radio show. After all, how could Laura discuss not being able to get a passport if she didn't tell her entire story. It's not entirely Laura's fault, the situation has gotten out of control. It was badly managed but who could plan for this level of insanity?

There's a knock at the door. Bo gets up to answer, assuming it's Solomon, but as she reaches for the latch, she remembers him grabbing his keys.

She pauses. 'Who is it?'

'Bianca from *StarrQuest*. Somebody downstairs let me in.'

Bo pulls the door open. 'What are you doing here?'

'Hello to you too,' Bianca says. 'I'm here to collect Lyrebird. I've booked her a hotel.'

Bo stares at her, open-mouthed. 'But you can't take her away.'

Bianca frowns. 'I'm not taking her away, she called me. Hi,' she says looking past Bo.

Bo's mind races. She should call Sol, he would stop this from happening, but by the time she processes it, makes a decision to search for her phone, Laura is leaving with Bianca, her hands full of her bags of belongings.

Laura turns to Bo. 'I appreciate everything you've done for me. Thank you for letting me stay in your home, but you're right, Bo, I'm an adult and I don't need minding.'

Bo stares at her open-mouthed as Lyrebird flies away from her life.

In a city centre hotel, pacing the floor of the box bedroom, Laura's heart pounds with panic.

What has she done, what has she done? She's cut herself off from the people she truly needs. Yet despite the fear of what she's done, she knows it's the right thing. The atmosphere in the apartment is toxic. She had to get away from them, and wasn't it Solomon who was slowly cutting himself off from her? At first it was off and on, and then he disappeared and he cut the ties completely. She may have lived alone for most of her life but she can still read people.

The phone rings, giving her a fright.

'Hello.'

'It's Jane calling from reception, Ms Button, we have a man here named Solomon who wishes to see you. Should I send him up?'

Her heart pounds.

'Yes, thank you.' She can barely breathe.

She rushes to the bathroom and splashes water on her face. Her mind races as she thinks of what to say. How she will refuse to go back to the apartment. Or perhaps she won't refuse at all, maybe this is exactly what she wants. He's saved her again, he's going to take her from this hotel where she doesn't want to be anyway.

There's a knock at her door.

She doesn't trust herself being in the same room as him. What she's feeling for him is wrong. She puts the chain on the door before opening it.

Solomon's dark eyes sear into hers. She

swallows. He looks at the chain, hurt.

'I understand if you don't want to see me, I wouldn't blame you after what we've done. I want to apologise for everything. I'm sorry for what Bo said today, I'm sorry I asked you to enter *StarrQuest*, I'm sorry I left you this week, I'm sorry I took you from your home. I'm sorry about it all.'

Laura's heart pounds. She can barely think straight with all she's hearing.

'I don't blame you for leaving the apartment. You're right and I don't blame you if you never want to see either of us again.' He looks down. 'I just came here to say that I'm sorry. You're right that you'll be better off without us. The show will take care of you. There is so much out there for you.'

She feels his hand on hers, and she looks down and sees that he has reached through the gap in the door. His touch is soft and her body tingles. She feels a rush of adrenaline, and sweet sadness. She feels the ache of his goodbye. He's slipping away, she's watching it happen, and her heart pounds and pounds like a warning drum. She wanted him to take her from here. She wanted him to say that they wanted her back. Instead, he's letting her go.

'If you ever need me,' he says, embarrassed to suggest it after all that he feels he's done, 'I'm here. I'll always be here.'

Then before he's had time to finish his final word, his hand is gone and so is he, leaving Laura breathless and staring at an empty gap.

The pain in her head seems to shift to her

heart, her entire chest aches. She slides down the wall, pushes the door closed and sits on the floor until the room gets dark, feeling yet another great loss in her life.

What has she done?

25

Laura was wrong about Bo's luck. It goes from bad to worse for her documentary as the public gets behind Lyrebird. Before she knows what's happening, Laura has been granted an emergency passport to fly to Australia. Mouth to Mouth productions are absolutely not allowed to accompany her on the trip. After the revelation of Lyrebird's sad and solitary life, she is firmly in the nation's hearts. They want to help her get along as much as possible.

By Sunday evening, carrying a new small carry-on case, Laura boards a flight to Australia. She will arrive on Tuesday morning at 06.25. She will do interviews and a photoshoot on Tuesday, the big TV appearance on Wednesday, then will leave Australia on Thursday at 22.25, returning to Dublin on Saturday night at 11.20. Two days in Australia. She will be back in time for her semi-final performance on Monday.

Despite her early arrival, Laura has to begin work at twelve. The assumption is that she'll have had plenty of rest in first-class during her twenty-three-hour journey. In reality, she barely blinked, there was so much to take in, to process.

She'd never been at an airport before, nor on a plane, and once on the plane she kept mimicking the sounds — much to the air steward's frustration as she mimicked the ping of the call button. He stopped coming to her after the first four times, but then when she really needed him to help her with her tray, he wasn't there.

She's wide-eyed and alert on the way to her hotel. There is so much to see, she has been greeted at the airport by more photographers and reporters, then bundled into a black jeep. She's taken to the Langham Hotel, to a beautiful hotel suite. She soaks in a bath and is starting to nod off when Bianca phones to tell her the car is ready to take her to the photoshoot in the Dandenong Ranges.

Laura sits in the back seat of the car, quietly, no conversation between her and Bianca, but she's happy with that. There is so much of this new world to take in. The new accents, sounds, smells, the new look. Despite wanting to immerse herself in what feels like a new world, she can't help but feel detached. It's as though there is a piece of her missing, a piece that she has left at home. She's homesick. She's felt like this twice in her life: when she moved from her family home to the Toolin cottage and when she moved from that home to Dublin. She feels disconnected, like the same person but in the wrong place. It is a surreal feeling, while everybody carries on as normal around her.

Photo with Lyrebird, is all the schedule says, but what Laura discovers on arrival is that the destination for the photoshoot is an enchanting boutique wedding venue called Lyrebird Falls, set within the evergreen forest of the Dandenong Ranges on the edge of Melbourne.

A crew waits for her. She shakes so many hands and hears so many names that go out of her head immediately, she barely has a chance to look around before she is seated in a chair for hair and make-up. Everyone is friendly and chatty, everyone is dressed in black, but she can't help feeling disconnected, like she's there but on the outside, watching everybody. She can't get inside the moment.

They have all seen her audition on *StarrQuest*. They all ask her polite questions about her talent, where did she learn to do it, how did she learn to do it? She has no answers for them and they fall into a polite silence. Bianca tells her she should prepare some of these answers in her head, for future interviews. Laura mulls over all of these questions, never having had to analyse herself and her actions so much in her life. Why does she do the things that she does, why is she the person she is? Laura wonders why these things are in any way important to other people.

Despite the hair and make-up team being familiar with her audition piece, they are concerned with her spontaneous bursts. The stylist unzips a bag, Laura mimics it.

'Are you okay?'

She unfolds a fantastic rail that magically appears from a small bag, and begins to hang the clothes.

Laura mimics the sound of the hairspray.

'Do you need some water?'

'Are you rehearsing?'

What hasn't been explained in the multitude of print and social media that's been dedicated to Laura Lyrebird Button is that this 'gift' she has is completely and utterly natural. It is not contrived, concocted, conceived as part of an act. It is within her, part of her. It is her make-up, her function, her way to communicate, as others have their own ways. There is no talk of her spontaneity, her quirk, if you will. It's almost as though it isn't seen, it doesn't want to be seen, as though the only gifts these days that are taken seriously are those that come in packages, carefully wrapped, and well-presented to the world. She cannot turn it on and off like a tap, yet it's left to Laura to rein it in, when they knew what they were getting in the first place.

Not once did Solomon ask her to stop or ask her why she made one single sound. Not once. Laura's head spins and she aches for him.

She absorbs the new sounds, new accents, the increase in tone at the end of their sentences.

This evening is an appearance on the *Cory Cooke Show*. Jack will do an interview on the couch, also on is Will Smith, who's promoting his new movie. And then on the show is Lyrebird.

'What am I doing on the show?' Laura asks Bianca.

'Schedule says TBC,' she explains, looking up from the rail of clothes. She's holding dresses against her body, posing in the mirror.

'What does TBC mean?'

Bianca assesses her for a moment to see if

284

she's serious. 'To be confirmed. We'll find out later what they want you to do.'

An hour later, hair and make-up on, clothes to be decided next, a total of six outfits for six shots, but have eight just in case. The show have been in touch with Bianca and the arrangement is to have Lyrebird sitting in the front row in the studio. Jack will do his interview 'on the couch' and the camera will throw to her as Jack discusses Lyrebird and her impact on the show. She is lucky, it seems, to be sitting in the front row in this studio, on the *Cory Cooke Show*.

An hour later, when photos emerge of her at the airport and social media hype grows that Lyrebird is in Australia, the TV show call Bianca as Laura is finished in make-up. Laura's front-row position in the audience is to be increased to two questions from the host, Cory Cooke. Questions are TBC after the staff meeting. By the time her hair is complete, Lyrebird has been moved from the front row in the audience to now walking down the illustrious steps that only celebrities are allowed to walk down. This, Bianca tells her, is a great honour. Bianca seems to see Laura in a new light. What Lyrebird will do when she gets to the end of the steps is TBC.

Laura begins to relax when she is given a minute to step outside for fresh air before she puts on her first outfit. She hadn't felt uptight but the forest lets her fall into an even deeper relaxation. She'd almost forgotten how it felt to be in that state of relaxation, almost hypnotic, as she went about her days and chores with a feeling of harmony. Even in her most relaxed moments in Dublin, on the couch with a cup of tea, talking with Solomon, she was nowhere near that old feeling.

Laura closes her eyes and breathes in, loving the fresh air and the sound of new accents and birdcalls. When she turns around, she sees the hair and make-up team, the journalist and press photographer gathered at the door staring at her.

'What?' she asks, self-consciously. 'Did I ruin my hair?'

Wanda, the sweet make-up artist, looks at her with amusement, 'You sounded like a kookaburra.'

'Really?' Laura smiles.

'And a whipbird,' the hair stylist says.

'I don't even know what a whipbird is,' Laura smiles.

They join her on the verandah, while Bianca nervously watches the time. She was chosen to come on this trip with Lyrebird because of their closeness in age. Bianca is a year younger than Laura and this trip is a big promotion for her, but Laura can tell her handler is just as nervous as she is, despite trying to hide it with her cool and confident demeanour.

'There,' Wanda says, 'that's the kookaburra. Jane, what does a whipbird sound like?'

They all listen in silence.

'There,' Jane whispers. She looks at Laura. 'There.'

Laura closes her eyes and listens. She doesn't even notice herself attempting it but they all start laughing with utter joy.

'You are bloody amazing!' they cry, and they

point out as many other birds as they can, though their knowledge of birds isn't broad. Magpies and cockatoos — that's as far as they get in identifying sounds, but Laura doesn't need to know what they are, she enjoys hearing strange sounds anyway. Despite Bianca pointing out that they're now behind time, Laura appreciates everybody pausing in this moment with her.

'This is nice,' Jane lifts her face to the sky and closes her eyes. 'Sometimes it's nice to just . . . stop.'

The others nod in silent agreement, breathing in the fresh air, lapping up their moment of time out before it all kicks off again, more appointments, home to their families, or their salons, always on the go, always planning the next thing. At least now they can be in the now.

'You've come at the right time,' Grace explains. 'Lyrebirds mate in the depths of winter, the adult males start singing a half-hour before sunrise, singing for their lives,' she laughs.

'You know what the weird thing is,' Bianca says. 'You might not even be mimicking a real kookaburra.'

They all turn to Bianca.

'You could be mimicking a lyrebird mimicking a kookaburra.'

Which is quite an interesting thing to come from Bianca. Bianca seems to be surprised by herself. Laura and Bianca laugh as if sharing a private joke.

★ ★ ★

Dress number one on, Laura and the team go outside for the first shot. She feels everybody's curious eyes on her; the stylist's team, the press photographer, the magazine photographer and his assistant, Grace the journalist. She feels self-conscious under their gaze.

Despite June being midwinter in Australia, the lushness of the greenery is beautiful. The air is fresh, she's glad of that. After air-conditioned airplanes and the hotel room, she can fill her lungs now. She longs to take a walk, but the stylist doesn't want the shoes to get dirty. The shoes don't fit, they've been stuffed in the front with tissue. The dress is too loose and has been clamped down the back, making it difficult for her to bend. She can turn to look at the lyrebird, but not so much that the camera catches the clamps, she's warned.

While they're doing more touch-ups to her face and the photographer busies himself checking the light, she hears Bianca tell somebody over the phone that Lyrebird is going to be walking down the steps on the *Cory Cooke Show*. Great news. Everybody at the shoot is impressed. Lyrebird won't be sitting on the couch, she won't be in the front row. Whether she sits at all is TBC. Laura laughs to herself. They look at her as though she is peculiar, which makes her laugh again. They think she is being peculiar *now*?

The photographer has a quiet word with Laura. He takes her aside, makes a big deal of it, all intense and brooding. He's handsome, his T-shirt is tight around his biceps, his black jeans fall low on his hips revealing an impressive V-line and Laura wonders if he's wearing any underwear. Laura feels that he's flirting with her, even though he's just discussing the shots. It's in his face. In his lips and eyes. The thought of this, and no underpants, piques her interest until she realises he looks at everything that way, all around him, a squint, a purse of his lips, a hand through his hair. He flirts with everything he sees. She's feeling tired now. She had a bowl of seasonal fruits at the hotel, but perhaps it wasn't enough. She feels slightly faint, light-headed. All these people, so many quirks, so much to analyse and understand in order to work with them; it's draining. Bianca must be feeling the same because she sits quietly away from everybody, sipping a bottle of water.

Laura looks around the forest. 'Are we going to wait for a lyrebird to fly into shot . . . ?'

'We're bringing the lyrebird to us,' Grace says with a smile.

And they do. Just as they flew Laura to them, the actual lyrebird arrives in a cage, carried by a ranger who places the distressed bird down on the woodland floor. It looks like a guinea fowl with a long neck and impressive plumage. The photographer tells her where to stand, the soles of her shoes have been taped over so they won't get dirty, she's been warned not to 'scuff' them, they must be returned to the store by the evening. Everyone watches her expectantly.

Laura doesn't know what they're expecting will happen. Do they think she will suddenly start a conversation with the bird in a secret lyrebird language? It's a bird. A distressed bird that has been scooped from freedom to captivity, driven across the reserve and plonked beside a jet-lagged woman, and Laura knows that, despite her nickname, she's human, a human that does not possess superpowers to communicate with or understand feathered creatures. Nor does the actual lyrebird possess that quality, both of them are mere mimics. But everyone watches, excited, moved by the pairing of these two species.

The photographer won't allow the lyrebird out of the cage until he gets his light reading. The lyrebird is in distress. Laura mimics his sound, watching him. As soon as it is let out of its cage it hops behind a tree, instantly, for safety.

'I don't blame you,' Laura says aloud. She follows it, ignoring the calls that they can see the clamps lining the back of the dress that's two sizes too big for her. She kicks off her shoes and the stylist rushes to pick them up. She gets closer to the bird, and she stands still and watches it, getting a good look at it.

The bird mimics the whirr of the camera shutter. Laura smiles and hunches down. The photographer wants her to get closer, but she knows the bird will run away, it's what she would do. It's what she should do.

The photographer is down, hunkered down, trying to get a good angle. He's talking to her, telling her to turn her face this way and that, her chin this way and that. Open her fingers, close her fingers, rest her arm, relax her arm. Look at the lyrebird, look over the lyrebird. Pretend you're looking at the lyrebird but over its head, into the distance. You're squinting, close your eyes and open them on three. No sausage fingers, give a posh mouth, bend her knee, tilt her chin, no, not that way, the other way. Bond with the lyrebird.

If the photographer takes one step closer to her she'll run, she'll hide. She'll do what this funny little creature is doing.

She remembers at her house she went out playing. She was supposed to be home by lunch but she misjudged the time. She arrived at the house and a customer was there, a car in the driveway. Children were playing in the garden, waiting outside for their mother. Laura hadn't been so close to other children before. She'd read about them in books, seen them on the TV, watched them from car windows on trips out of Cork. She hid from them in the forest, so close she felt she was one of them but so far they never knew she existed. They'd played Pooh sticks in the stream and she'd even dared to throw her own stick in, pretending to be a part of the gang. The kids thought the stick had fallen from a tree. She planned her hiding adventures after that. Hikers and walkers, hunters and ramblers.

When Laura looks up she sees tears in the eyes of the make-up artist. The photographers are snapping happily. Laura's not sure what sound she made recalling her childhood, but her sounds had made them sad. It is only when the lyrebird imitates her sounds that she realises exactly what she sounded like; he relays the sound of children's joyous laughter. She looks at the lyrebird in surprise. He looks back at her.

They are both silent. She gazes deep into his

little eyes, wondering if perhaps they do have a connection, perhaps everyone is right, perhaps they can understand each other.

The photographer takes a step closer and the lyrebird scarpers. He lowers the camera, disappointed. Laura watches the bird, happy that he has escaped. She hopes he finds his mate. She longs for hers.

★ ★ ★

That evening at 9.42 p.m., after Jack's interview with Cory Cooke where he has discussed his past success, his dabble with drugs, his stint in rehab, his failed marriage and his climb to the top and unexpected success with *StarrQuest*, Cory Cooke announces his next guest: Lyrebird.

'Not since *Police Academy's* Man of Ten Thousand Noises, Michael Winslow, have we seen anyone like this. Dubbed Lyrebird, our next guest auditioned on talent show *StarrQuest* in Ireland and in one week has received two hundred million hits on YouTube. That's staggering.'

'It's two hundred and twenty now, actually,' Jack interrupts and the audience laughs.

'That's even better,' Cory joins in the laughter. 'Here she is — Lyrebird!'

The audience goes wild. Almost as much as they did for Will Smith.

She's wearing a striking red dress and it's so tight the stylist called it a bandage. Her lips are bright red and she's afraid to move them in case she smudges them, while her strappy shoes are so high she feels her ankles shake as she descends the famous steps. She pauses at the top, as she's been told, a small wave to the audience, to the people at home. Then she descends the steps that are usually only for the clobber of celebrities. She stops at the area she has been told to stand on, a piece of tape marking the ground, and she greets the host. She doesn't sit on the couch, or the front-row seat. Everything was confirmed to her thirty minutes before this moment.

'Welcome, Lyrebird, to the home of real lyrebirds.'

'Thank you.' She smiles.

'How was your flight?' he asks. 'I believe it was your first time on a plane?'

She makes the sound of the announcement bell, the call button for the air steward, the sound of the seatbelt clip.

The audience laughs.

'I believe you had a photoshoot with a lyrebird today. How was it, meeting the family?'

The audience laugh.

She makes the sound of the photographer's camera shutter, the kookaburra, the magpie, whipbirds and cockatoos.

The audience love it.

Then she makes the sound of a train. She didn't plan it, she just remembered it.

'Right!' Cory says with surprise and a laugh, 'Puffing Billy, the steam train! So we've spoken to Jack about the incredible reaction to your audition, what it's done for him and the show. I can't imagine what it's done for you. Are you glad that you entered the show, after the reaction you've received?'

'I am,' she says. 'It's been overwhelming, but everybody has been so kind and coming here' — she makes the sound of the seatbelt clip, the call button, the camera shutter — 'has been a fantastic experience. My life has utterly changed.'

'What are you hoping for from this experience? Your own show? TV work, stage work? What kind of career comes from this ability?'

She thinks about it. Too long for air time, because he follows it up: 'Why did you enter? Did you know of Jack? Were you a fan?'

'No.' She shakes her head and the audience laughs. Jack holds his head in faux comedy embarrassment.

'You wanted your life to change,' he says, trying to wrap it up, hoping for a good and swift end.

'My life had already changed,' she replies. 'My dad died. My uncle didn't want me to live on their land any more, my mother and grandmother passed away many years ago. I had no choice. I had to move with the change. I had to start my life.'

This seems to touch the host, and he fixes her with a more rooted look, a look that shows he's not only listening to the voices in his ear.

'Well, Lyrebird, on behalf of Australia, we wish you the best of luck and hope that your life soars.'

★   ★   ★

'That was flawless,' Jack says, hugging her backstage. 'You see how smooth that ran? By the time you're in the studio for the semi-finals, you'll be an old pro.'

Jack, Curtis, and the team all go for dinner. Jack wants Laura to meet some more people at the dinner, but she insists on going to her hotel. She needs sleep, she needs isolation, she needs to retreat. She doesn't know how Jack can stand to be around so many people all the time, always on. It exhausts her, giving all that energy away. She's so jet-lagged the ground is moving beneath her, as though she's on a boat.

She rushes to catch the elevator and is surprised when she sees Bianca inside.

'Are you not going out with the others?' Laura asks.

She closes her eyes and groans. 'I escaped. Do you ever feel if somebody asks one more thing of you, that you'll scream in their faces?'

Laura looks at her in surprise.

Bianca laughs. 'I don't mean you.'

'Oh good,' Laura says relieved, she was thinking her and Bianca were getting somewhere with their relationship today.

'I'm tired. And I don't like being around lots of people.'

Laura looks at her, confused. 'But you're *so* great at being around people.' Despite Bianca's aloofness, she has spent the day organising, greeting, arranging everything for Laura.

'For a time,' she says, 'then when they've sucked the energy from me, I have to recharge my batteries.'

Laura looks at her in shock. 'So I'm not the only one who feels that way.'

'No you're most definitely not,' Bianca says with a yawn. 'My mom says it's because I have empathy. I feel other people's energies and it drains me. But I think she's just being nice.' The elevator stops and the doors open. 'I think it's because I'm a bitch.'

The way she says it makes Laura laugh. Bianca giggles too as she steps out to her level. 'Night.'

★   ★   ★

Laura sits naked on the enormous hotel bed, stripped of the clothes she's been told to wear for her new life. The new clothes feel like a uniform, and the clothes she wore in her old life no longer feel appropriate.

She reaches into her bag for her schedule and the extra page Bianca had given her hours previously falls loose.

Interview with Cory Cooke.
Q1. Lyrebird, how was your trip to Australia? First time on a plane?
Lyrebird: airplane sounds. Seatbelt, call button.

Q2. How was it meeting a real lyrebird?
Lyrebird: kookaburra, camera shutter, magpie, cockatoo, whipbird.

Q3. Are you glad you entered the show?
Lyrebird: It's been overwhelming but everybody has been so kind and coming here has been a fantastic experience. My life has utterly changed.

She crumples up the page, feeling disgusted with herself. Like a performing monkey. Jack had pitched it to her as honing her skill, but it makes her think of the honing rod Gaga used to sharpen the carving knife for Sunday roasts. It always frightened her as a child, the sound, the image and the look on Gaga's face as she ran the blade over the steel rod — especially as she knew what everybody thought about Gaga.

The phone on the bedside rings and the intense pain returns to her head, behind her eyes. These migraines are getting worse. She ignores the phone, thinking it's StarrGaze with something else for her to do. She doesn't know or sense that it's Solomon, as his morning begins, desperate to know if she's okay. She climbs under the covers and buries her head with a pillow to block out the ringing. No more sounds.

She falls asleep, naked in her bed, to the sound of Gaga honing the knife, realigning the edge of the knife blade over and over again, and that intense look on her face.

26

The floor swirls beneath Laura's feet. She feels as though she's sitting on a boat. This time yesterday she was in Australia. Was it yesterday or the day before? How much time did she lose in the air? She's not sure. She knows it's Monday night, the day of the semi-final. Yesterday was spent in rehearsals. Days ago she was in winter, today it's summer. She can't remember. The storm is building, the waves getting choppier. She reaches out to the wall to steady herself. Somebody catches her hand.

Gloria, the choreographer on *StarrQuest*. She throws her an angry look. 'That's the set,' she hisses.

Of course. If Laura was to lean against it, the entire thing would have toppled. Or would it? Surely sets are made of stronger stuff than that? It's wallpapered, floral, to look like someone's living room — an old woman's living room, by the looks of it, as the act before her settles down into their routine. She's not sure what the old woman's living room has got to do with the act, but then she's not really focusing on what's going on. Of course it's not real, she has been surrounded by unreal things since she got here.

Fake rooms are only the start of it. Exposed wires, fake walls, exposed ceilings, the underbelly, the back doors, the behind-the-scenes of the glamorous television world. She's left hotels through kitchens, restaurants through fire exits, she's entered buildings through back doors surrounded by trash more often than front doors. She crawls along the in between, the edges, the behinds, to suddenly be placed up front and in the middle. The expectation of her is that she must move through the darkness to emerge shining. The floor moves beneath her again as the jet lag takes hold of her. She squeezes her eyes closed and takes a deep breath.

'Okay?' Bianca asks. Despite Bianca being given a few days off to recuperate after their Australian trip she chose to return after one day for this evening's performance, a gesture Laura hugely appreciates.

They are moments away from her live semi-final performance and they have left Laura until last so that she could rest. Apparently, it was Bianca's idea. It's allowed her a lie-down, while her head spun and her mind refused to shut down, going over and over everything that has happened to her over the past week. It would have been easier to keep moving. There's little rest she could get in a small dressing room on a TV set. The building is throbbing with nervous energy, from the contestants to the producers. The show is under the microscope, receiving worldwide attention since Laura's audition, and the pressure is on them to entertain the growing audience.

Nervous people have been telling Laura not to be nervous, panicked producers have been telling her not to panic. An exhausted host has been telling her she couldn't possibly be tired when at her age he was travelling the world, a different country every day, a new set every night. Laura thought about reminding him how that schedule worked out for him. Drink, drugs, divorce, destruction, despair before rehab, a quiet life and then a reality show reboot. Young people don't suffer jet lag, apparently, as if young people are impervious to the pain of those doling it out.

The ground shifts seismically beneath her again.

She breathes in slowly, out through her mouth. As soon as Laura boarded the plane to fly home, Bianca had handed her a 'script' for her next *StarrQuest* performance. It was considered that her rehearsed appearance on the *Cory Cooke Show* was such a success, and again a viral one, that they would help steer Laura's next performance in a different direction, a direction they could predict, expect, manage, control, plan for.

'You'll be grand. Everyone's tuning in to see you,' Tommy the floor manager says, patting her arm.

Laura smiles lightly, no energy to summon up anything more. 'I'm sure they're not. It's not that. It's the jet lag . . . '

'Ah sure you're too young to be jet-lagged,' he laughs.

Laura wonders if this is a line they've all been fed to keep her going, or if it's something they truly believe.

She hears the sound of water lapping, oars

300

hitting the side of the boat, and realises it's coming from her. A memory of a boat trip with Mam and Gaga. On Tahila Lake, County Kerry on a rare summer holiday, off-season so no one saw them. Always off-season. Gaga hated the water, she couldn't swim and sat on a nearby rock instead, knitting, but she helped with the gutting and cooking of the fish.

Tommy is watching her, a sad smile on his face.

'Are you okay?' Laura asks.

'Yes. Yes,' he shakes his head. 'My dad was a fisherman. I used to go out on the boat with him sometimes.' He goes to say more but stops. 'Anyway, you don't need to hear that . . . I'm sure people are always putting their stories on you. You took me back, that's all.'

The crowd applauds as the act finishes. Laura's heart pounds, her mouth is dry, her legs are trembling. She needs water. The crowd roar as they go to a commercial break, it feels like her chest rattles with the crowd's rumble. The adrenaline from the five-hundred-strong studio audience feeds her like electrical blue lines firing towards her heart and gut.

The dancers line up around her, stretching their legs up and back behind their earlobes. They pat each other on the backs, on the arses, good luck. The choreographer, Gloria, oversees the routine; she's dressed in black, heavy black eyeliner and the usual scowl on her face as she throws her eyes over everything and judges, calculates, appraises and adjudicates everything everyone says and does, not just how they dance.

She catches Laura looking at her and starts to give her last-minute orders. Her face is all screwed up, twisted, and Laura tries to pay attention but all she hears is the sound of a corkscrew being twisted open, until it pops.

Gloria frowns. Laura's not sure how to explain herself.

Tommy motions her forward. Laura's stomach lurches. Everyone looks at her in surprise as she realises the vomiting sound has come from her. That time when she was new to foraging and chose the wrong mushrooms. Tommy looks at her, eyes wide and alarmed, unsure if she's serious or not, but treating her as if she has actually physically vomited, so convincing was the retching sound. The last time she felt this nervous Solomon had helped her. She recalls the feel of his breath in her ear, his scent so close to her. He'd told her she was beautiful. His presence always calmed her and she longs for him to be here, but knows it was she who walked away from him. It's her fault he's not here.

'Are you okay? Water?'

His pupils are dilated. The panic, the fear, a live fucking show and the star has lost it.

'I'm fine,' Laura says shakily.

She follows him to the stage, and as soon as she takes the few steps upward the crowd erupts in applause and cheers. Laura smiles shyly at the reaction, feeling less alone. She waves and takes her place on the stage, standing on the white mark that's her opening spot. A woman in the front row grins, showing all her teeth, and gives her the thumbs up. Laura smiles. They're just people. Lots of people. More people in one room than she's met in her entire life, but it's never the people she's worried about — it's herself.

Tommy counts down to the return of the show. One minute. Dancers take their places, form their dramatic opening positions. Laura's heart thumps in her chest, so loudly she's sure the whole room can hear her. Suddenly the crowd explode with laughter and she realises that it was her making the heartbeat sound.

She looks at Jack and he's grinning. He winks. He looks exhausted as Harriet from make-up powders his face. He looks how Laura feels.

Laura stands in the centre of the enormous stage, the dancers getting in place, the cameras in position while Laura's VT plays.

'The last week has changed my life completely. I went from a very quiet life in Cork to suddenly everyone knowing my name.' Footage of her walking down Grafton Street, then a crowd chasing her. It's all sped up, as though it's an old Laurel and Hardy film. Posed, of course. Filmed yesterday — or was it this morning? And then they air the words she was unsure of saying. She had wished to phrase them differently and they had kindly allowed her to, but then they wanted one take to be said and done their way, for them to have. Naturally, that's the take they use, each sentence sharply edited, her face zoomed in on closer for each one and made more dramatic by a booming drum to emphasise the stakes.

'I don't want to go back to being who I was.' Boom.

'This is my one chance to shine.' Boom.
'The whole world is watching me.' Boom.
'I'll fight for my place in the final.' Boom.
'Watch out world.' Boom.
'The Lyrebird is coming.' Boom.

Laura cringes at the sound of her own voice. It sounds as empty as she had felt while saying it. She doesn't even like that girl. She doesn't like the girl they're trying to portray. Doesn't like the girls like her that are sitting at home, thinking about the one time in their lives that they will have to prove themselves. No such thing exists. Nothing so great ever hinges on one such moment.

Suddenly the music starts, she feels the beat in her chest, the lights go up, the crowd cheer. It's showtime.

She starts walking. She's on a treadmill, behind her on the large screen is footage of the woods. It's animated. And it moves so that she appears to be walking through the forest. Her long blonde hair is tied into two braids that sit on each shoulder tied with two girlish red ribbons. She's wearing a puffy-shouldered mini dress, a blue-and-white gingham apron and she holds a straw basket. She's not sure if she's supposed to be Dorothy from the *Wizard of Oz* or little Red Riding Hood. She didn't care much when they'd shown her the costume after she'd gotten off her flight from Australia.

She wears white pop socks and red Mary-Jane heels.

The music playing is 'If You Go Down to the Woods Today', but a kind of remixed dance version. She makes the sound of her high heels on the ground and the audience laughs. Realistically, she'd told Gloria and anyone who'd listen that her heels would not make such a sound on the earth floor, but they'd explained it was a heightened reality. Laura comes across a house in the woods, it's made from sweets. She eats some, licks some, making appropriate sounds and the crowd laugh. She makes a knocking sound on the door, the door opens and three sexy female pigs run out, chased by a male wolf. Laura peeks inside, she sees a handsome bear man — a topless male dancer. She tries out the three different men until she finds the one that's just right. She moves across the stage, making appropriate sound effects that she was told to make, slapstick comedy, ducking and diving in Laurel and Hardy mime, making sounds in all the right places. It is quite the production; wardrobe must have hired out every panto costume going.

After a dance routine where Laura awkwardly tries to keep up with the three sexy pigs, the three hunky bears and the others who are dressed as sexy woodland creatures, Laura ends up with the hunkiest bear of them all. He's just right. A red heart-shaped spotlight frames them.

StarrQuest special guest judge, drafted in for the semifinals, star of stage and screen with her own stage school, Lisa Logan is on her feet clapping, hoping she'll make it to the viral clip which will boost her flagging career. Laura steps on the thumb mark in the centre of the stage and waits for the judges' feedback.

'Lyrebird, hi,' Lisa says excitedly. 'Out of all the contestants tonight, I, like the rest of the world, was most excited to see what you'd deliver. I must admit, despite your obvious talent, I was confused as to how that would transfer into showbusiness — how can you make sounds viable? Relevant? How can sounds be commercial? But you've shown us tonight that it can be done. This is exactly the kind of cabaret/Vegas-style route that you should go down. You're young, you're sexy, you're talented. You have ended this show on a high. Whooo!' she screams, punching the air. The audience join in.

Lisa Logan gives Lyrebird a gold thumbs up.

Laura is surprised by her excitable reaction. They really see her doing *this* as a career? Does she even *want* to do this?

Silence for Jack's response.

'Lyrebird,' he rubs his stubble awkwardly, as if struggling with how to say it. 'That was awful.'

Boos from the crowd.

'No, seriously it was.' Over their booing and hissing he continues: 'It was awkward. It was . . . to be honest, it was embarrassing, I was cringing for you. You looked uncomfortable. You're not a dancer . . .'

'No, she *can't* dance,' Lisa interrupts, agreeing. 'But that was part of the comedy. It was *funny.*'

'I don't think she intended to be funny, did you, Lyrebird?'

They both look at her. Silence.

'I wanted it to be entertaining and hope the people in here and at home were entertained,' she says with a smile.

The crowd cheer.

'No, Lyrebird. I think your strength is in what we saw you doing in your audition. Organic, earthy performances. Moving performances, where you transport the audience somewhere else. This was all wrong. This was a circus.'

Boos.

'As you know, only one act can go through to the final. Every night this week until the final. Have you been good enough tonight? My advice, if you go through, is to stick to the heartfelt pieces. Lyrebird, you're in trouble. I hope the public give you another chance because I fear for your place in the final.'

27

Laura sits before Jack's desk after the show. She got through to the final. She did it. But she didn't feel the joy that she should be feeling. Jack looks exhausted, even worse without the make-up that he's removing with a baby wipe.

'How am I still awake?' he says into his hands, rubbing furiously. He smudges his mascara. Laura can't bring herself to tell him.

'How are you holding up?' Jack asks her. 'Probably doing a lot better than me, you're twenty years younger.'

'I'm exhausted,' she says.

He must hear the change of tone in her voice because he looks at her, drops the tissue.

'This is tough, isn't it?'

She nods, feeling drained.

'Yeah, believe me, I've been there. In your shoes. I was probably the same age as you when my album went to number one in fifty countries. Crazy.' He shakes his head. 'I didn't know what was going on. I didn't know — '

Curtis enters the room, and Jack sits up straighter. Curtis places a coffee down on the desk before Jack, then goes to his usual position at the side, like a shadow.

'Thanks, man.' Jack takes a sip and gets into business mode, giving her feedback as he has done for all the contestants seeking reassurance. Before and after the show, they gather around Jack at every opportunity eager for his attention and praise, and over the past two days out of sheer exhaustion Laura has stood back and watched, feeling as if they're all birds loitering at an outdoor restaurant feeding on scraps of food and leftovers. They watch and wait, ready to be thrown anything by Jack their way; a compliment, a word of advice, a tip or a thinly veiled warning or critique. They catch it and they peck, peck, peck, analysing it, clinging to it, wanting to be filled by him, but they never are. They can never be fed enough praise, analysis, or dissection of themselves and their talent from the master.

'Look, Lyrebird, don't worry about tonight, it's part of the show. Everyone has their ups and downs. It's good for you to have a journey, to show that you, like them, have a struggle. But the audience chose to save you. Look at poor Rose and Tony, their act was a disaster. She fell on her face, dressed as a hotdog.' He starts laughing, a smoker's chesty laugh. 'Did you see the ketchup . . . ?' He stops laughing when she doesn't join in.

'Tonight's performance was written for me by your show while I was in Australia,' Laura says to him, confused. 'I was told to learn it on the flight. I had one day to learn the dance.'

He sighs. 'Rehearsal time was short, I

understand, but believe me, the Australian trip was the chance of a lifetime. We debated it, but felt it was the best thing to do, and we needed you on the first semi-final show on the back of the *Cory Cooke Show* and before public interest waned. That trip was the trip of a lifetime, and any of the others would have chosen going there over a longer rehearsal.'

'The others won't even look at me.'

'They're jealous. Lyrebird, you're going to win this show and everyone knows it.'

Her mouth drops open. 'Jack, you said I was awkward. You said it was awful. You said I can't dance. You were embarrassed for me — cringing, in fact . . . '

'That was true,' he laughs. 'It was fucking awful.' He laughs alone. 'Oh, come on. Lighten up.'

'I didn't want to do that routine. I told you I wasn't a dancer. I told you it wasn't me. We sat right here, I told you I didn't like the script. You told me to do it.'

'Lyrebird.'

'My name is Laura!' She bangs her hand down on the table.

'Don't forget yourself, young lady,' Curtis warns. 'Don't get too big for your boots.'

'It's okay,' Jack says tiredly. 'It's just a show, that's what we do. I was the big bad judge who talked bad about the nation's sweetheart. You heard how the audience reacted, tomorrow they'll all be talking about it and they'll love you even more. Trust me, that's the way it goes. Do you know how many votes our *winner* received

310

last year? Sixty-five thousand. Do you know how many votes you received tonight to get through to the final?'

She shakes her head and hates herself for wanting to know.

'Three hundred and thirty thousand.'

She looks at them both in surprise, but not for the reason they expect. She's honoured, flattered, flabbergasted by the figures, but there's something else that stuns her.

'This is all a game to you,' she says, her voice soft.

Perhaps it's the softness that gets Jack the most. It gives him nothing to feel righteous or indignant over. She's not angry, she barely had time to register the fact before she said it. Her bubble burst. He saw it happen. He just looks at her, frozen.

'Okay, let's wrap this up,' Curtis says, standing up from propping against a table, as usual on the edges of the room. 'You can leave now,' he dismisses her, turning his back on her.

'There's one more thing,' Laura says, feeling hollow. 'It's about Bo. She's feeling cut out. I know I signed a contract with you, but I also had an agreement with her. Before you. She brought me to you and I have an obligation with her to fulfil. I'm not comfortable not doing as I promised.'

It could be just the jet lag, but she doesn't think so, she's almost certain she's thinking clearly. Things in her life are certainly tilted at the moment, something, lots of things, feel off and it's spreading. The Australian trip made her look at things differently, the show tonight reminded of what she had tried to push out of her mind but this meeting has cemented her view. Something is wrong here. Whatever happened between her and Bo, and Solomon, before her trip to Australia, she knows that one step towards straightening everything out would be to resume filming the documentary.

'The issue with Mouth to Mouth productions is not for you to discuss,' Curtis says. 'It's a contractual issue that's currently with our lawyers.'

'Lawyers?' Laura looks at Jack. 'But this could be all so much simpler than that. Just talk to Bo.' She feels the panic welling up inside her. She thought she was walking toward freedom but instead she stranded herself on an island.

'I need a moment alone with Jack now. You can leave,' Curtis says, moving so that he's beside Jack's desk, leaning over, almost like he's having a word in Jack's ear, as though he owns that ear.

Laura watches him, in shock, her heart pounding, wanting to interrupt, to make one more attempt with Jack.

He speaks as if she's not in the room. 'Alan Murphy wants to talk to you about not being able to do gigs while the show is on the air. He says he can't earn any money. It's in the contract, he signed it, I told him that, he can't have his cake and eat it, I need you to know what's going on in case he brings it up with you.'

'Jesus, this is the biggest platform in the world right now and he's complaining?' Jack asks, irritated, throwing the scrunched up baby wipe down on the desk.

Laura slowly stands and makes her way to the door, but before she leaves, she directs her words at Jack. 'It's Alan's niece's Holy Communion. His brother asked him to perform, the show won't let him do it. He's not being paid.'

Jack looks at Curtis. 'That true?'

'Well, I don't know the specifics. A gig's a gig.'

Jack looks at Laura, he considers her. 'Find out what it is exactly. If it's his niece's Holy Communion party then for fuck sake let him do it, Curtis.'

Laura nods her thanks, recognition of his humanity, and opens the door, feeling Curtis' eyes searing into her back.

Jack's not finished with her. 'Don't worry Lyrebird, I'll have a word with Bo. We'll sort this out. It's gone on long enough and you're right: if it stays with the lawyers, it will never be resolved.'

The relief she feels practically lifts her off her feet and carries her down the corridor, past greedy eyes, past raised camera phones, then past the powerful flashes that dare to invade the blacked-out windows of the SUV and threaten to penetrate to her soul.

She shudders, hoping it's their own reflections they capture.

28

After not being able to keep her eyes open all day, now Laura is wide awake. As Michael drives her to the hotel, she's dreading another night alone in a hotel room, wide awake, suffering from jet lag, feeling a loneliness that aches. When Solomon had visited her here the final time they'd seen each other, he'd held her hand and told her to contact him if she needed him. She needs him now, she has always needed him, but she couldn't bring herself to pick up the phone and throw his life out of balance again. She can't deny that in trying to right a wrong between her and Bo, she has also knowingly taken steps to seeing him again. She parted with them on the promise that she wouldn't get between them, as she was so obviously destroying them. She can't deny her selfishness in longing to see him, and her weakness in sending Jack into the ring to do her dirty work for her. The more time she is spending around people, the more she discovers of her own character failures. In the cottage she was generous, she was kind, she was positive. In this world new sides of her are emerging and she doesn't like it. She thought she was a better person than this.

She makes her way through the photographers who snap her as she returns to the hotel, and she stops to sign photographs of herself for the fans who are there night and day, and praise her shambolic performance. She collects her key from the desk.

'There's a man waiting for you at the bar,' the receptionist informs her. 'Mr Fallon.'

Her heart lifts. Solomon. She grins. 'Thank you.'

She practically runs through the lobby to the bar, and slowly circles the bar searching for the black-haired Solomon, seeking out the high knot on his head that stands above everybody else. But he's nowhere to be found. Confused, she heads back the way she came.

She feels hands on her waist. 'Hey!' a man says. 'Remember me?'

Rory.

Laura makes the sound of a gunshot. A fallen hare. A whimpering dying animal.

'Yeah.' Rory looks down, scratches his head awkwardly. 'I wanted to talk to you about that. I came here to apologise.' He looks genuinely sorry, embarrassed even. 'Can we talk? I know a good place.'

★   ★   ★

Rory and Laura sit opposite one another in Mulligans, a dark pub, as shut away from others as possible. They're in the quietest corner they can find because as soon as Laura entered everybody stared. Everybody knew who she was, from young to old, and if they didn't recognise her, they certainly knew her name and of her abilities. The first drink is on the house, as a welcome to Lyrebird. Rory orders a Guinness and Laura has a water. He doesn't comment on her choice, he's messed up so much with her that he's keen not to make any more mistakes. He'd called Solomon to apologise for what had happened at the shooting range, which had taken him a lot to do, especially to Solomon. He asked to speak to Laura but Solomon was adamant that he couldn't, too busy keeping her to himself, which angered Rory even more. His brother had a girlfriend already, yet was protecting this woman like he owned her. His brother was always like that. Private about things, he kept things to himself, never let Rory in. Things between them had always been stilted, awkward, there was no easy banter like there was with the others. Rory understood the others, who laughed at his humour and even if they didn't laugh, they understood it. Solomon never did. He took offence easily, he always passed judgement on Rory.

Rory was embarrassed about the entire shooting range debacle. With hindsight, he could see it was an asshole stupid thing to do, but at the time he'd felt so compelled to get Laura to notice him that he hadn't thought about the repercussions; about the danger, about the sheer psychotic way it would make him look. It was one thing messing up on his own, it was another to do it in front of his brothers and dad, not to mention in front of Laura.

Of course Solomon wouldn't accept his apology, kicking him when he already felt down, and he knew that he wouldn't pass his messages along to Laura. After he'd watched her audition on TV and the whole world was talking about her, he knew he had to come and see her himself. She wasn't hard to find, any newspaper could tell you her whereabouts, and as soon as he saw she was staying in a Dublin hotel he knew getting to her there without Solomon around was his best chance.

He studies Laura now. She's unusual, but the most beautiful kind of unusual. Exotic, in a Cork mountains way. He wonders what happened at the apartment, and what made her leave Solomon and Bo. But his brother's loss was his gain, that's the way it has always been.

First, an apology — not that he doesn't really mean it; he intends to show how much he means it in the most genuine way possible. Big eyes, he knows the trick. Girls love that shit.

★ ★ ★

Laura's head feels light as she sits in the pub with Rory. She's had two glasses of white wine and she's not used to its effects on her. She likes it, she could have more. She doesn't feel so confused any more, that pounding headache that arrived in Galway after Rory's gunshot, the one that throbbed right behind her eyes, is now gone. She doesn't think it ever left her, just intensified in moments of stress. It's fitting that her headache is gone, as Rory was the first to put it

317

there and now he is the one to take it away. Or the wine is, but either way, he's responsible. He's funny, she hasn't stopped laughing since he started talking. She genuinely believes that he's sorry for what he did, even if he is heightening his apology more than she believes is true. He's doing the flirty thing with his face that the photographer was doing, softening his eyes. It's not real but they seem to believe it works, whatever it is. Not that he should be sorry at all for what he did. She's not judge and jury, it was an incident that affected her deeply, but she doesn't think she has a higher authority over anyone and tells him so.

He's like his father. He tells long stories about mischievous nights out, stories of him and his brothers as teenagers. He seems to have spent more time stitching his brothers up than anything else, but he's gleeful about it. She likes to hear these stories, particularly the ones about Solomon, about what he was like when he was younger. She tries to limit her questions after she senses him tensing when she asks too many, so she chooses to sit back and listen, waiting for the next mention with hope. When Rory says something about Solomon's ex-girlfriends she tries not to sit up too much, or make her interest too obvious. What she learns is that the girls he dated were always edgy, weird; one girl he dated seriously for a few years went to art college and the family had attended her exhibition on feet. Hairy, yellow-nailed feet; then he laughs, and Laura isn't sure whether it is true or not.

'Why do you think he dated these girls?' Laura

318

asks, trying to sound disinterested.

'Because Solomon is so uninteresting himself,' he says, and there's a hardness in his voice.

Being with Rory, bizarrely, makes her feel connected to Solomon. They're alike, for a start. Rory's hair is short and tight, and he's shorter in height, his features are less defined, but he's like a miniature version of Solomon. He's mousier, more baby-faced, while Solomon is stronger, harder, has sharper edges, everything is more intense — his movement, his stance, especially his eyes. Rory's posture is casual, his eyes rarely rest on hers, they're always looking around. They sparkle, they have a glimmer, a playful shine that reveals his inner spark and his mischievous nature, but they don't settle on anything for too long, nor does his concentration. That makes him an interesting person to be around. He talks while looking at something else, usually the thing he's talking about, because most of what he says is about somebody who's near them. He does funny voices, pretends to do the voices of the couple sitting nearby. He makes up their conversation until Laura's stomach hurts so much from the laughter that she has to tell him to stop.

He's a carpenter, and while she pictures him in a romantic setting carving furniture, just as his dad had for Marie on her birthday, he says it's nothing like that.

'Mostly it's moving around building sites or businesses, doing exactly what they tell you to do, fulfilling a brief,' he says, bored. 'To be honest,' he gives her big eyes and leans in as if sharing a secret, 'I hate my job. The others don't know. I couldn't tell Dad, it would break his heart, I'm the only one who went into the same trade. All the others flew the coop. I'm the one that got left behind,' he admits, with a smile that doesn't reach his eyes.

Laura feels he's being honest, perhaps for the first time since they sat down. She feels she can identify with him in a way. Despite his confidence and his overflowing personality, he's lost in there.

He finishes his fourth bottle of beer and she can tell he's restless. She's so comfortable here, particularly after the two glasses of wine, and she'd gladly stay but he's fidgeting in his chair, which makes it hard for her to relax.

'Rory I'm sorry I can't buy you a drink, I haven't got a cent to my name.'

He looks surprised.

'I can't even get on a bus, even if I did have somewhere to go. I have nothing,' she says and realises as she says it how much this terrifies her. 'At least at the cottage I could live off the land, I could forage, I grew my own fruit and vegetables, I had a cupboard filled with preserved foods, pickled foods, dried fruits, enough to get me through the winter when the options were small. I could survive without Tom's supplies if I had to, but here, in the city, I can do nothing for myself.' The irony of being surrounded by everything you could ever dream of and wish for and none of it attainable.

Rory's eyes suddenly light up.

'That's where you're wrong, my dear Lyrebird. You are the most famous person in the world right now.' And though she tries to laugh this off as ridiculous, he is adamant. 'I'm going to show you how to forage *city-style.*'

Foraging in the city includes going into an exclusive club with a twenty-euro entrance fee and not having to pay anything at all because Rory presented Lyrebird to the security guards as if she was a ticket herself. Foraging in the club was finding the right people to talk to who would buy them drinks, and welcome them to their table.

At midnight, when Laura feels herself stumble when talking to a man who reaches out and grabs her arm and continues talking as if nothing happened, with his arm still on her, she snaps out of her bubble of contentment. Excusing herself and freeing herself from his grip, the ground swirls as she makes her way to the toilet. As she goes, everything seems to get louder, the thumping music is in her head, in her chest, bodies bump her, seem closer together than they were. She's aware of the lack of space when before she felt fine. Once inside the toilets, the music fades and becomes a mere thud in her chest. Her ears are blocked, like they felt on the plane, and need to pop. There is a long queue ahead of her. Things feel very far away, yet she is here. She feels like she is behind herself. Everything moves quickly, her eyes registering everything they fall upon. Girl's shoe, cut ankle, smudged tan, wet floor, sink, soggy tissues. The hand-drier fires up beside her and she jumps, startled, she holds her hands to her ears and looks down. At her own boots. Drink stains on her boots, splashes of beer and wine and who knows what. She closes her eyes. The hand-drier stops and she removes her hands and looks up. The girl in front of her is looking at her, she recognises her. Laura wonders if she should say something. The girl says something but the hand-drier fires up and Laura blocks her ears again.

'Rude stupid bitch,' she reads the girl's lips.

There's a constant stream of toilet doors unlocking and opening, clickety-clack of high heels wobbling on tiles, doors banging. Everyone's looking at her now. All eyes, wide eyes. The ground is swirling, Laura needs to reach out to hold something or she'll fall. She decides against the girl in front of her with the mahogany skin and the big boobs in the belly-exposing top. Turquoise belly-button piercing. Lip liner but no lipstick. She looks out for something to lean on, the sinks, but there's a line of girls fixing their make-up, with their phones in their hands, pointing at her. Flashes blind her. No one will help her, she's not sure if she's calling for help. Perhaps she should. They're viewing her through their screens as though she's not real, as though she's not flesh and blood right there in front of them. They're looking at her as if she's on the television.

At the cottage, at home with her mam and Gaga, Laura used to look at people on television, or in books, newspapers and magazines. Sometimes she wanted to really see people, really touch them. In this world, people have that luxury and all they want is to see each other through screens.

She hears the clicking of the doors locking, the

bangs, toilets flushing, the clickety-clack of high heels. The girls around her start laughing, throwing their heads back, loud, dirty laughs. Perhaps those sounds were from Laura's mouth. She's not sure, she's so dizzy. She's here but she doesn't feel like she's here. She holds a hand to her foggy head. She needs help, she reaches out to the mahogany girl, sees a snake tattoo on her wrist, black and spiralling up the girl's arm. Laura hisses in acknowledgement of it, and falls into her, but she pushes her away. Some girls jump in and shout 'Fight!'

Laura's confused, she doesn't want to fight, she just doesn't want to fall.

Then all of a sudden, she's in someone's arms, the person is pulling her away roughly. She doesn't want to fight, all the girls are laughing, phones up in the air, taking photos or filming. She's taken from the bathroom and down a corridor, she realises it's a man she doesn't know who's dragging her and she panics. Starts to fight him. Why would the girls laugh at this, why wouldn't they protect her? Defend her?

There's a glass in her face, she doesn't recognise the man. He's trying to make her drink it. She doesn't want it. There's no one else around, the music is so loud, she can barely hear what he's saying. She's heard about people drugging drinks. He's pushing it in her face and his arms are wrapped tightly around her. She doesn't want it. She knocks it out of his hand and it smashes on the floor. The anger on his face. Laura is confused. She's led along the corridor by the man, looking around but it's all a blur, she can barely focus on any one thing. She can't see, she can't hear, she can't think. She wants Solomon, she needs him, she can't think of anyone else.

Suddenly she's outside the club and the angry man leaves her there alone. He comes back to give her her coat and she realises he wasn't trying to abduct her or drug her. He's security. She's freezing and she puts her coat on. 'Sorry,' she says quietly, but he's not interested. His suit is wet, he disappears inside, telling her to wait there.

He returns with Rory, who's putting his jacket on, confused at first, but then when he sees her he grins. 'What did you get up to? They couldn't get me out of there fast enough.'

Laura's head spins, she needs to get away. She turns to leave and sees a crowd of people who are trying to get into the club. She tries to step aside to let them pass but they don't, they form a wall in front of her. She realises they have cameras, they're taking photos of her. She can't see the ground in front of her, she can barely see with all the flashes. She stumbles and falls to the ground. She doesn't feel any pain but it takes her a moment to gather herself. Rory is there, hands under her arms. She hears him laughing, and he pulls her up.

She doesn't think this is funny. He can't stop laughing.

She tries to walk straight but feels herself go the other way. Rory chuckles and grabs her tightly. She feels sick.

This is all wrong. They're in an alleyway, she

can't see through to the other side, which makes her feel claustrophobic. There is no space in this city. There are too many people. She retches.

'No, not here,' Rory says, not laughing now. 'Laura,' his tone is darker, warning, as they're completely surrounded by paparazzi. Laura is slipping from his grasp, her body and legs are practically like jelly. She's taller than him, he struggles to keep her up.

'Move back,' Rory shouts at the photographers.

They reach the main street and there's a crowd of people standing by, wondering what all the scuffle is about, waiting to see which celebrity is leaving the nightclub.

'Lyrebird, Lyrebird,' she hears from lips, all whispering around her like the wind blowing through the leaves on her mountain. But she's not on the mountain, she's here, camera phones pointed in her face. Autograph books and pens extended.

A group of boys start making cuckoo sounds. The sounds chase her down the road. Rory gets them to the first taxi they see in the nearby queue. Laura falls inside and leans her head back, eyes closed. Cameras bump against the glass of the car, continuing to take photographs of her. She closes her eyes, takes deep breaths, trying not to vomit as her head swirls.

'Where to?' the taxi driver asks, bewildered as his car is surrounded by photographers.

'Solomon,' Laura says, her eyes closed, head on the headrest.

The cameras bang against the window.

'Hey, where to?' the taxi man asks, agitated. 'Watch my bumper!' he yells to the photographers, lowering his window. They continue to bang against the side of his car, the taxi driver clambers out and confronts them. Cameras continue to flash as Lyrebird's taxi driver is involved in an altercation, Lyrebird passed out in the back seat.

'Fuck,' Rory says, as they sit in the back seat with no driver, completely surrounded. 'Fuck.'

'Solomon,' she says again, sleepily.

'Uh, no, not Solomon. Okay, Laura, new plan.' He shakes her, trying to wake her. He opens his door and goes around to her side. He pulls her out, tries to stand her up but now she's both exhausted and intoxicated. The cameras ignore the taxi driver's altercation and follow Laura and Rory.

'Hey! Where are you going?' the taxi driver yells.

'I'm not sitting there while you argue,' Rory yells back.

'This is because of you, who do you think you are?' The taxi driver yells a load of abuse at him as he half-carries, half-pulls Laura away. The taxis have all left the queue. 'I've missed a load of fares because of you!'

A taxi stops for them in the middle of the road. The light is out. There are people inside. A door opens. 'Get in.'

Rory looks in and recognises two guys from the club. He puts Laura in the front seat, trying to pull down her dress that's rising up her long lean legs; that's a tartan shirt, with black Doc

326

Martens, and walking socks beneath. He gets in the back, squishing in beside the two men.

'Where are you going?' one asks. Rory thinks his name is Niall, a property guy, or was that someone else? As he looks at him, he wonders if he met him in the club at all.

'Anywhere,' Rory says, blocking his face from the cameras pushed up against the glass.

The men laugh. The taxi drives off.

29

Laura wakes up in darkness. Her head, her throat, her eyes, everything aches. There's a buzzing sound, the familiar vibrating of a phone and she thinks of Solomon. She looks around and sees light coming from a shoe. The phone is vibrating inside a trainer. It buzzes one more time, then makes the sound of a flat battery before dying, the light gone. It's like witnessing another death. The dull headache that arrived in Galway and worsened in Dublin, but disappeared after her first two glasses of wine, has now returned and is worse than ever. It hurts for her to lift her head, gravity appears to have intensified and pulls her down. She's afraid, she doesn't know where she is and so she sits up. She's on a couch, next to a double bed. There's a figure over the covers and a shape beneath it.

She smells vomit, realises it's in her hair, and on her clothes and the smell brings her back instantly, like a flashback to her head over a toilet bowl, a dirty toilet bowl with shit still stuck on the side. Somebody is holding her hair out of the way. There's lots of laughter, girls beside her and around her. A voice close to her ear is telling her she will be okay. A kind voice. A female voice. She remembers Rory, the nightclub, the man who attacked her. Being brought outside. The camera flashes, the taxi, another taxi, feeling sick.

She doesn't remember this place that she's in. She doesn't remember getting here, how she got to this room or who she's with. She looks at the pair of Converse with the dead phone and she recognises it as Rory's. So he's here, quite possibly the person lying on the bed. He brought her here. She can't blame him for what happened, she can only blame herself. She's twenty-six years old and she should have known better. She's so ashamed of herself for losing control, for such irresponsibility, for allowing others to see her like that, she can't bring herself to wake Rory. She's still wearing her boots, she doesn't care about finding her jacket, she just wants to get out of there.

She stands up and steadies herself as her head swirls. She takes a moment for the dizziness to pass, takes long deep breaths as silently as possible so as not to stir the sleeping others. The room is hot and stuffy. It smells of alcohol and hot bodies, which turns her stomach. She steps over the shoes and bottles, falling over and catching herself on the wall. She bangs against the wall and hears somebody stir behind her, waking as if in fright. She doesn't look back, she keeps walking, she knows she needs to get out of there before they wake.

Out of the bedroom she finds herself in a corridor. She sees the main door. The next door

329

is the bathroom, then the front door. She passes an open-plan living and kitchen area, more bodies on floors and couches, a couple slowly kissing on the couch, his hand moving around inside her top as she makes soft breathy sounds.

She thinks of Solomon and Bo in the hotel when they were making love and she must have made a sound, given herself away, because suddenly the couple stop kissing and look up. A head pops out from the kitchen.

'What the fuck was that noise?' the girl asks.

'The bird,' the guy on the couch says.

'*Lyrebird*,' she says, giggling.

'Whatever. Hi,' he says and she thinks she recognises him. She remembers him from the nightclub. He was friendly, offering to buy her drinks, giving out to somebody for accidentally shoving her as he passed. Getting the barman's attention faster than the others. Whispering in her ear. Did he kiss her ear? Her neck? He's the one who held her arm tightly when she stumbled.

'I'm Gary, I'm an actor. Our premiere was tonight at the festival,' he says. She remembers being impressed, she'd never met an actor before. Not a professional one anyway, as it turned out.

'Gary, you little shit,' the girl says, hitting him, jumping up from the couch so quickly she knees him by mistake. He groans. 'You told her you were a fucking actor? Who are you, Leonardo DiCaprio?'

'I was only messing, babe, chill out.'

'Don't babe me,' she wallops him again, which

330

stirs the others, who are sleeping.

Her voice is familiar. Laura studies her, trying to pinpoint how she knows her. Then she remembers. In the toilet, her head literally in the toilet, trying to ignore the dried shit, hearing laughter, that girl's voice, looking up between retches to see a camera phone in their hands.

'Stop,' Laura had said, trying to block her face.

'Get out of here, Lisa,' another voice had said.

'It's going on Facebook,' she says, leaving the bathroom. 'Lyrebird, dirtbird,' she says, giggling.

Laura must have said this all out loud.

'Cara, you put photos of her puking on Facebook?' Gary asks. 'And you're giving out to me?'

'Are you okay?' a voice says from the kitchen. 'Do you want a cup of tea?'

Laura doesn't recognise her face, but she knows her voice instantly. It was the one that was in her ear. 'Ssh. Ssh. It's going to be okay.'

Laura knows she has repeated this because the girl is smiling. She has a friendly face, it's nice to see one. She holds a cup of tea out to her.

Laura shakes her head and keeps walking to the door. She should go into the bathroom to clean herself up, but she knows she must leave, she doesn't want Rory to wake up, she doesn't want to have to deal with talking about what happened.

She has no idea where she is, or where her bags are. She's in an apartment block somewhere. She heads for the fire escape and runs down five flights of stairs, thinking someone is chasing her, not hearing any footsteps but afraid to stop or look behind her in case they catch her. It's like a bad dream being played out and she's the one playing it out with an overactive imagination. She races downstairs, clinging to the rail, hand brushing the metal and feeling splinters from the chipped paint. She thinks she'll be stuck on that staircase forever, that it will never end, until finally she reaches the ground floor. She passes a wall of grey postboxes, all numbers no address, not that it would mean anything to her anyway. She bursts out on to the street, hoping to see somewhere familiar, one of the places she's been to with Solomon, Bo, or Rachel, but she doesn't recognise it. Across from her is an identical building, beside and all around her is the same.

A loud horn frightens her and she looks up in time to see the city tram headed straight for her. She jumps onto the path, her heart pounding as the driver shouts as he passes.

When she has calmed herself somewhat, she looks left and right, decides to go left in the direction of the tram, it must be bringing people somewhere. Somewhere is better than the unknown, that same thought pattern she's had since Bo and Solomon came into her life. *Follow them, they're going somewhere, somewhere is better than nowhere.* While she walks she thinks of the sound of the tram that almost stopped her heart. She doesn't hear herself mimicking it, though she hears its sound, like a song she can't get out of her head. But people are startled, jumping away, some laughing when she nears.

Perhaps she's not making a sound at all, perhaps it's the sight of her that is so shocking to them and the smell of her. The vomit in her hair, the dried vomit on her boots that she sees now for the first time. She looks a disgrace, she smells even worse. She attempts to tie back her hair, make her appearance neater, especially when a camera phone comes out of a bag. It's like a tidal effect, once one is out it gives others the permission, the confidence to do the same.

She feels the beat in her chest of last night's music, the people shouting, the broken glass, the muffled sounds that blend together into one noisy, disturbing cacophony. She holds her hands to her ears, to block it all out. The people staring at her, the phones are held up, the flashbulbs of the photographers, now she remembers. The photographers. Oh God, people will see her in the newspaper. Would they print such awful pictures? She thinks of Solomon, opening his morning paper. If he sees her, she will never look him in the eye again, such is her embarrassment.

She hears the rustle of his morning paper while Bo clicks away on her phone, everything for her on a screen, everything for him to be touched. Rustle, click, tram warning, smash of a glass. An angry taxi man, shouting at her. A rough hand on her arm. She remembers now. She'd thrown up in the taxi, he'd thrown them out. She'd kneeled on the roadside and vomited some more. The lads laughing. Blue Converses standing beside her, splashing the white tip with vomit. More laughter. A hand on her head now and then, an arm around her waist. Not being able to stand, being taken away, a girl, the nice girl asking the owner of the arm around her waist what he thinks he's doing. Rory telling the man with the hand around her waist to back off. What was he going to do to her? Her cheeks flame with the shame that she allowed herself to end up in that position.

Then the bathroom. The toilet bowl. The shit stain on the side. A warm blanket. A glass of water. Distant laughter and music.

She holds her hands over her ears, she sinks to the ground, trying to hide from the cameras. Her mum and Gaga were right to hide her, she's not able for all of this, she can't run anywhere. She wishes they'd hide her now.

As she thinks of them, the noises in her head start to calm. She can think more clearly, as the thoughts quieten she hears herself whimpering, crying, breathless, hiccups. She's sitting on the ground. A crowd gathers around her. Some people too polite to look directly at her but still they hover nearby. She looks up at the person standing beside her. A garda. A female one. Mam and Gaga said not to trust them. But this garda seems kind. She looks worried. She bends down, gets to her level and smiles, concern in her eyes. 'Want to come with me?'

She holds out her hand and Laura takes it. She has nowhere else to go. Somewhere is better than nowhere.

30

Laura sits in a corner of the room in the garda station, wrapped in a blanket. Between her hands she holds a mug of hot tea, which has helped to calm her. She waits for somebody to pick her up, she wouldn't give Solomon or Bo's name, she doesn't want them to see her like this, or know anything about what has happened. Her pride has been bruised. She wanted to prove that she could be okay without them and she failed.

The gardai work around her; opening and closing the hatch to stamp passport forms, and driving licences and whatever else people need. Lots of paperwork; the behind-the-scenes of keeping the law. She feels like she is in a safe area, no nasty robbers being dragged into the cells. If her mum and Gaga knew about this they would be terrified, their worst fears realised, but there's no sense of terror here, it's calm. Laura thinks of Gaga and hears the sound of the carving knife being sharpened. Not an appropriate sound to make in a police station; heads turn. Maybe that's why she does it, because she's not supposed to. The nerves have gotten to her, or she wants to rebel, she wants to be different, to be seen? These are all the questions Bo asked her when they were alone. Laura thinks about it now, in a way that she never has before, she's never had to analyse herself so much. She's not sure why she makes the sounds she makes, not always anyway, sometimes it makes perfect sense. But now, making knife-sharpening sounds in a police station, that's not smart. When she's relaxed on the mountain that makes sense, reading a book and a robin is building a nest above her. She can't help but join in with their sounds then.

'A robin,' the male garda says suddenly. 'I recognise that one.'

'Didn't know you knew anything about birds, Derek.'

'We have a family of them in our back garden.' He spins around in his chair to talk to his colleague. 'The daddy bird is vicious enough.'

'They're very territorial,' Laura says, remembering.

'That's it,' he says, dropping the pen to the table. 'Those robins would win in a fight against our dog any day. Daisy is terrified of them.'

'I'd say Daisy wouldn't win in a fight against anyone,' his colleague says, still rifling through papers. 'With a name like Daisy.'

The others laugh.

As everybody relaxes, the sound of their laughter triggers something. She feels the beat of the music from the nightclub, in her heart.

Rude stupid bitch. The girl had thought Laura was blocking her ears to avoid a conversation with her, when it was because the sound of the

336

hand-drier had given her a fright. It was all a misunderstanding.

Misophonia, Bo had explained to her one day. People with misophonia hate certain noises, termed trigger sounds, and respond with stress, anger, irritation and in extreme cases, violent rage. Laura hadn't felt that it applied to her, but perhaps Bo was right? She thinks of the moment again.

The girls laughing in the toilet, camera phones held up. The man with his hand around her waist, bringing her somewhere, saying ssh in her ear. The kind girl whispering ssh in her ear, holding her hair, rubbing her back.

No, Laura stops. She hadn't reacted violently, she had merely blocked her ears.

Hypersensitive to sounds, Bo had said to her another time.

The garda with the family of robins in his garden rolls over to her on his chair on wheels, he looks at her with a concerned fatherly face. 'If there's anything you need to share about last night, you can tell us.'

She swallows. She shudders, then shakes her head.

A garda she hasn't seen before arrives to start his shift and drops a tabloid newspaper down on the desk. Laura sees a photograph of herself on the front page. The headline reads DRUNK BIRD. She starts to panic. He's startled, had no idea the Lyrebird is in his station. The kind guard who found her covers up the newspaper and tries to calm her again.

Laura can barely hear her words through her

own panicked sounds; the airplane, Mossie's snarl, the bats at night, city sirens, camera shutter, the sound of the lyrebird's cage, the airplane seatbelt clicking, toilets flushing, high heels on tiles, the noisy hand-driers. Everything meshes in her head.

Despite the kindness from the gardai she should have known it wouldn't stay so peaceful for long. Somehow the press discover she's at the station. They're outside and waiting for her to appear. Bianca and Michael arrive. Michael stays outside, clearing a route for Laura to the blacked-out SUV. Laura didn't want to contact Solomon and Bo, Bianca had been the only person she could think of.

'Are you okay?' Bianca asks with concern as Laura is brought out to reception.

Laura whimpers, Mossie's dying sounds, the fallen hare.

'She's had a rough night,' the kind garda says. 'She needs a rest.'

'Is the girl pressing charges, is she in trouble?' Bianca asks.

'We haven't had anybody here pressing charges,' the garda says.

Bianca turns to Laura. 'There was a girl in the toilets of the nightclub, she says you pushed her, assaulted her. Curtis needs to know. They have to release a statement to the press.'

Laura swallows nervously trying to think. 'I didn't push anyone. I felt dizzy, I was trying to lean on her. I needed help, I was . . . am I in trouble?'

'No,' the garda says, annoyed. 'Nobody has

pressed any charges. You should believe us over the newspapers. You're going to take her somewhere safe, I hope?'

Laura makes sounds. She's nervous, flustered, trying to relive everything that happened so she can understand it.

Bianca eyes her cautiously. She's heard Laura's sounds before but nothing as distressed as this. They spill from her like the shaky breath and hiccups after a long cry. 'Are you okay, Laura?' she asks gently.

'It's our understanding that these sounds are normal for her?'

'Yes, but . . . ' Bianca looks really concerned.

'I'm fine,' Laura says. 'I just want to go . . . ' she almost said home. Home. She doesn't know where that is any more. Exhaustion sweeps over her.

'Okay, we'll get you somewhere comfortable and safe, don't worry. There are loads of photographers outside,' she adds, looking at Laura's appearance nervously. 'Here, you can wear these — ' She hands her her large sunglasses. Laura puts them on and immediately feels shielded from the world. 'And wear this — ' She takes off her fur gilet and hands it to Laura. Laura hesitates. This is a new Bianca.

'It's not real fur,' she says, as if that's the problem.

Laura finally puts it on, agreeing that, while it may not be the best look over a tartan shirt that was an oversized man's shirt that Tom gave to her, and which she accessorised with a belt, it does cover the stains. She thanks the guards and

339

faces the barrage of more photographers and a TV camera. At first she thinks it's Rachel behind the camera, and naturally expects to see Solomon standing by her side, feeling hopeful to see the intense look of concentration on his face as he listens to the sounds around him, but he's nowhere to be found and she realises it's a news station, the correspondent barking questions at her with an oversized mic thrust in her face. Bianca and Mickey walk her so fast it's all a blur around her. In the photos afterwards she looks like a different person. Her hair has been tied in a high topknot to hide the dried vomit, the fur gilet over the tartan shirt, the oversized sunglasses, the scuffed Doc Martens she's had since she was sixteen and the walking socks pulled up. She hits the fashion magazines as a new style icon. Fur and tartan, Doc Martens and woollen socks. Everybody loves the quirky Lyrebird look. She doesn't recognise herself when she sees the magazines. As the jeep drives off, Bianca throws a newspaper on to the seat beside Laura.

'This is the only one that made it to print on time. There'll be more stories tomorrow apparently?'

'She doesn't need to see that,' Michael says, protectively.

'Curtis told me to show her,' she says. Michael sets his mouth to a firm straight line. Laura looks down at the paper on the seat beside her.

DRUNK BIRD
LYREBIRD GOES CUCKOO

NIGHT OWL IS BIRD BRAINED AFTER NIGHT
OF HEAVY DRINKING

Her heart pounds, she feels sick. She lowers
the window for air, wondering why they are so
angry with her. She feels the waves emanating
from the pages of the paper and it terrifies her.

Bianca twists around in the front seat, Mickey
studies Laura in the rear-view mirror. Bianca
reaches back and grabs the newspapers, stuffs
them on the floor in front of her. But even
though Bianca took the papers away, Laura has
seen enough to remember for ever. Horrendous
images of herself, being propped up by Rory,
who's laughing while her hair flies across her
face. Her face, her legs, her feet are at all angles,
out of joint, some photos of her with her eyes
half-closed make her look drugged. Her eyes are
dead, her pupils so dilated they almost take over
the green. In some she's sprawled in a dirty alley,
lying on ground that's wet from spilled alcohol
or who knows what. Her face is bright white
from the force of the flash. She doesn't look
drunk and scared, she sees what they're talking
about, she's a liar because she's not an innocent
girl who doesn't drink and is connected to the
earth in ways that nobody else is, as they were
saying before. She looks out of control, she looks
like she's on drugs, she looks like someone she
wouldn't want to know. The papers are angry,
they feel duped.

Maybe she is. Maybe they're right.

She takes the papers from Bianca. The worst
tabloid of all procured photos from the girl at the

341

party where Lyrebird crashed out. It doesn't read as if she's being sick, as if she's scared, and wanted to go home. It looks as though she has injected herself with heroin. She can't close the pages, she can't stop looking at herself. She can't find herself in them. She can't reconcile the pictures with how she recalls feeling: afraid, confused, scared. But the look on this girl's face is smug, high, cocky.

'We're bringing you to the contestants' house for the final. We've checked you out of the hotel, there's too many press there. StarrGaze will put the semi-finalists up until after the show. So far it's just you. It will protect you from the press and it should protect you from them talking to the press, which some of them have done already.' She turns around. 'Watch out for Alice. She's a weapon. Her semi-final is tomorrow night, but their votes have been high and they're expected to go through.'

Instead of feeling concern over having to face Curtis, and live with Alice who has never been a fan of Laura's, she feels relief rush through her body that they're taking her somewhere. Another bridge, she's not stranded on her lonely island yet. Another home, another place for her to hide, another bridge for her to walk across while she heads into the absolute unknown. There's no going back now, none at all. Physically, she couldn't even get there.

The contestants' house is outside of Dublin in the Wicklow Mountains and she's happy to be surrounded by nature, by trees and mountains and space. She can barely enjoy the view, though, as she keeps looking at the photographs in the newspapers, at the stranger wearing her clothes. But at least looking at the trees helps her to breathe again.

When they reach the gates, photographers are outside and she faces more cameras banging against the window, which brings her back to last night. She hears herself making the sounds. Michael studies her in the mirror as they wait for the gates to open.

'We're nearly there,' he says gently.

The house is visible from the gates, which don't provide much privacy. All the curtains are open and Laura sees someone standing at the window, watching, before quickly moving away. She makes a note not to stand at a window.

She can't look at Simon, the production staff member that greets her. He'll be living with the contestants to tend to their every need. She wants to apologise to Michael, Bianca and Simon for bringing all this attention to the show, but she's too embarrassed to meet their eyes. She keeps Bianca's glasses on, she likes how much they shield her. She keeps her eyes down as they watch her walking up the stairs, Mickey helping her with her bags. Bianca tries to help her to settle in, and tells her that Curtis will visit tomorrow. Despite her lightness of tone, it sounds like a warning.

Laura turns the lights off, she closes the curtains, thankful her windows are looking out the back, to a view of the trees. A swing and a slide in the garden. She has a shower, feels clean at last, then climbs into bed, still sick from the alcohol, and mortified. She's hungry but doesn't want to go downstairs to see anybody. She lies in her new bed, curled in a ball, under the duvet, hiding. She sleeps.

31

'From anonymous mountain girl to internet superstar, it seems the pressure of her newfound fame is finally getting to *StarrQuest* favourite Lyrebird, as Laura Button's spokesperson confirms reports that she was involved in an incident in the toilet of a Dublin nightclub last night. Photographs in today's papers show her being carried out by nightclub security, who intervened in the incident, and who she then attacked by throwing a glass of water at him.'

The report jumps to video footage of Laura.

'Her audition made her famous around the world in a matter of weeks, but according to reports she was found wandering the streets of Dublin extremely distressed, and was taken to a police station for her own safety. She is now back in the custody of the show's producers and is staying at a *StarrQuest* private home for the finalist contestants.

'*StarrQuest* producers jumped to Lyrebird's defence today, releasing a lengthy statement calling for the nastiness to stop. Jack Starr has described Lyrebird as a gentle, kind, young woman who's had a challenging life. Laura was abandoned at a cottage by her grandmother at the age of sixteen after her mother died and she lived there for ten years, unknown to anyone apart from her father, who kept her existence a secret. Starr says Laura is finding it difficult to cope, and has been overwhelmed since her first audition. He says becoming the biggest star on the planet so fast is scary and unsettling, as Laura has discovered.

'Lyrebird has had more than fifteen minutes of fame and stands to make millions from book deals, endorsements and appearances. But fame comes at a price and it seems Laura Button's beginning to pay for it.'

Solomon stands up and throws the remote control against the wall over the fireplace. It crashes against the brickwork. The back falls off and the batteries scatter to the floor. Bo ducks and huddles even tighter in the corner of the couch. He looks at her, but neither of them say anything, he doesn't need to; Bo looks as guilty as he feels.

'We have to do something,' Solomon says, feeling and hearing the emotion in his voice. He can barely take this, sitting back and watching Laura being picked apart.

'I'm trying, Solomon,' Bo says, tears in her eyes.

'I've had enough of trying to talk to her through *StarrQuest*,' he paces the lounge, angrily. 'We have to get to her ourselves. Where is the contestants' house the news mentioned?'

'I have no idea,' Bo says, lost in thought, then she sits up with an idea. 'But the fansites will know.'

'I'm a friend of Laura Button's, I'm here to see her,' Solomon says to the security guard on the gates outside the contestants' house.

The guard laughs and approaches him with a clipboard. 'You and all the others.'

Solomon looks around. A dozen photographers and a camera crew watch him, at first with interest and then with amusement when his wish to pass is denied. Behind a rail are a handful of hardcore fans, sleeping bags lining the grass, a home-made banner that says We ♥ Lyrebird.

'Leave her alone,' one girl shouts across to him.

Anger rises in Solomon.

'If you could tell her that I'm here, then she'll tell you to let me in.'

Security looks him up and down. 'Why don't you go ahead and give her a call first? Tell her to call me and ask me to let you in.'

Solomon grinds his teeth. 'I can't call her. That's why I'm here.'

'Yeah. Well, I can't let you in. Your name needs to be on the list and you're not on the list, so I can't let you in.'

Solomon turns off the engine and gets out of the car.

'Sir, I'd advise you to stay in the car. There's no need to get out of your car.'

He's standing so close to the car door, Solomon can't open it. He pushes it a little harder. It hits the guard and he takes a backward step.

'Hey, what are you doing? I said get back in the car!'

'Then don't block my door! Don't block my door!' Solomon gets in his face as they both shout at each other.

A bored photographer takes a few photographs.

A second security guard appears from the hut. 'Barry?' he says, concerned.

'Great, hopefully you can help,' Solomon says, pushing his hair off his face and trying to compose himself in front of the crowd. 'I need to contact my friend Laura Button. I appreciate that I'm not on the list but if you call her, which will take one second of your time, then she will immediately let me in. Okay?'

'Who?' he asks, looking from his colleague to Solomon and back.

'The Lyrebird,' Barry says.

'It's actually Laura. Laura Button is her name,' Solomon gets het up again.

'Leave Lyrebird alone,' the fan shouts at him again. 'People like you aren't helping her!'

Solomon ignores her.

'So you know her real name, you read the news,' Barry says, unimpressed.

'Okay okay, let's keep it calm,' the second security guy says. 'There's no need to get upset.'

Solomon calms down, he likes this guy, he may see reason. 'Step this way with me.' He follows him, out of eyeshot of the crowd, into the security hut. Solomon feels he's been taken seriously. 'Now let me tell you how it works here,' he says calmly.

'I told him,' Barry interrupts, behind him.

'Barry,' he warns, and Barry leaves the hut swearing.

'We are given a list of people who are allowed to visit. It's a very strict list. If you want to visit somebody in the house you're supposed to contact the production office, who then alert us. We're not allowed to let any Tom, Dick or Harry just waltz in. And you're not even family. And it's ten o'clock at night. Too late for visitors.'

'I understand that, I appreciate that. And that's the way it should be, but I know that Laura wants to see me. I'm not on the list because she didn't know that I was able to visit, but I can and now if you let her know that I'm here, I promise you this won't be a waste of time.'

He looks at Solomon like he's trying to figure him out.

He picks up the phone and the relief floods through Solomon.

'Simon, it's Richie. I've got a visitor for Lyrebird. Yeah. He's here right now. Not on the list but he wants to see her.'

'Solomon Fallon,' Solomon says, realising he hasn't even asked him his name.

'Solomon Fallon,' he says down the phone. He listens. They wait. 'They're checking,' he says. He looks around as he waits a little longer.

Something's up. Solomon senses something amiss. He looks at the phone and realises that Richie isn't even on the phone. He hasn't made a real phone call, this is all a farce. When Solomon listens carefully he can hear the dial tone on the other end of the phone.

349

'This is bullshit. Fucking bullshit.' He swipes all the paperwork off the table and storms out and gets into his car. Barry outside salutes him, while Richie shrugs as if it was worth a try.

'Contact the production office,' Richie repeats firmly, tapping the hood of the car with his hand.

Solomon puts his foot down and drives away at top speed, his blood rushing, his heart racing with anger.

★　★　★

A knock on the door wakes Laura the following morning and Simon from StarrGaze Entertainment tells her that Curtis is here. She slips on a pair of jeans, a T-shirt and an oversized cardigan that she hugs around her body for protection. It's one that Solomon chose for her in Cork. She leaves her freshly washed hair down so she can hide her face and pads barefoot downstairs to the meeting room.

Curtis sits at the head of a dining table. The dining room faces the front of the house, Laura pauses at the door and looks at the window.

'Sit down,' he says.

'Can they see us?'

He looks out the window. 'You're worried about being seen now?' He stands up and closes the curtains anyway.

'Thanks,' she says quietly, nervously.

'StarrGaze has done a lot for you. We welcomed you, treated you well, gave you an international platform, flew you to Australia, paid for your clothes, hair, hotels. We haven't held back on anything.'

'I know and I truly — '

He continues as if she hasn't spoken. 'We are a family show. Our demographic from sixteen to thirty-four is over seventy per cent.' He maintains his hostile stare, as if to emphasise that she really needs to grasp this. 'We expect you to adhere to the contract you signed, which stipulates that you will not do anything to harm the good image and brand of *StarrQuest* and StarrGaze Entertainment.'

He doesn't let her get a word in edgeways.

'We've talked and we reached the decision that you can proceed with the remainder of the show. We will allow you to perform in the final.'

He leaves a long pause and Laura looks at him, eyes wide. It hadn't occurred to her that she might be removed from the show.

He looks as if he's waiting for something.

'Thank you,' she whispers, her throat catching, feeling like she's been given an extra life that she never even knew she needed.

'You're welcome,' he says sombrely. 'But you have an uphill struggle. You have a lot of people to convince, a lot of minds to change.'

Laura nods, her head racing.

He stands up and speaks as though his words have been learned, rehearsed, written for him. 'I recognise that your life has changed immensely. It's a lot to take on board. *StarrQuest* has a qualified therapist available to you, if you so wish. I advise you to speak with him. Would you like me to arrange an appointment?'

Laura thinks of sitting down with somebody

else from *StarrQuest* and having to explain herself. It wouldn't make anything better. It would make her relive it all over again and all she wants to do is forget it happened.

She shakes her head.

'If you change your mind, you should tell your handler. I suggest you don't talk to anyone before your performance. No media. And that's not a suggestion, it's a direct request on behalf of *StarrQuest*.'

'Okay.' She clears her throat. 'What about the documentary? Jack was going to speak with — '

'With Mouth to Mouth productions — yes, your relationship with them has ended.' He says this with an air of finality.

She feels tears rush to her eyes. It's confirmed. It's real. She is truly disconnected from Solomon and that breaks her heart, and she feels her face flush and her eyes become hot with tears. She's afraid to ask if it's because Bo and Solomon don't want her now as a result of Monday night's behaviour or if it's Curtis simply getting his way. Despite her loss she's relieved she can hide from Solomon, she's too embarrassed to face him now. She had tried to convince herself that he may not have seen the papers but she needs to be realistic, his brother is in the photographs, his family will all see them, his friends, his kind neighbours that she met at his mother's party. All those people who were so good to her will see what a mess she made of herself.

As Curtis leaves, he stalls, almost as if he's having second thoughts, a change of heart, if he had one. Laura's heart hammers as she waits for him to say that it's okay, she can see Solomon. Or she's out of the show.

'This story will run in a few days. I was given a copy in advance that you should see, to give you a chance to respond to it.'

He places a large brown envelope down on the table and he leaves.

She stares at the brown envelope, her heart pounding.

There's a knock on the door and she turns around. It opens but there's no one there. Then a face appears at the doorframe, but not a human face. It's Alan's ventriloquist doll, Mabel. Alan is nowhere in sight.

Mabel clears her throat.

'Hi, Mabel.' Laura smiles.

'Mabel wants to know if Lyrebird wants a cup of tea. Lyrebird hasn't eaten since she arrived yesterday I hear. Alan is making one.'

'Thank you, Mabel,' Laura smiles. 'You're very kind. You can call me Laura though.'

'Okay, Laura,' she says shyly, and Laura laughs. Even though Mabel doesn't blush, she's so lifelike and Alan is so good at moving her entire face that she seems real.

Alan then sticks his head around the doorframe. Laura likes Alan. He auditioned the same night as her. He's a nice man. A peculiar man. Forty years old and lives with his parents, he puts all his money into Mabel and his act. He has a kind heart and is hugely talented.

'Congratulations, Alan. I didn't know you'd gotten through, I missed the show last night.' She feels embarrassed for shutting out a night so

important to her fellow contestants, her selfishness breaking through again.

'Thank you. Feeling pretty rough today, Mabel
made me stay up and drink a bottle of Jameson
to celebrate.'

Laura laughs.

'Mabel told me she can call you Laura, does
that mean I can too?'

'Of course.'

He steps inside, almost tiptoes, as if he
shouldn't be here. He's like that everywhere, acts
as though he shouldn't be there, as if he's in
people's way, but as soon as Mabel is on his
arm, he becomes another man, witty, charming,
naughty even. He says things as Mabel that
Laura doesn't imagine Alan even thinks. He
brings nothing but joy to people.

'Just wanted to see if you're okay,' he says.

Her eyes fill and she looks away.

'Oh no, you've made her cry, you idiot,' Mabel
says.

Laura laughs.

'And you made her laugh,' Alan says to Mabel.

'What would you do without me?' Mabel says.

Laura wipes her eyes.

Alan sits down beside her.

'I'm so embarrassed, Alan. I can barely bring
myself to look anyone in the eye.'

'There's no need to be embarrassed. We've all
had nights like that.'

Laura looks at him.

'Well, I haven't. But Mabel has.'

Mabel gives him a slow look.

Laura laughs again.

354

'Look, we're all in this together. Some of the others . . .'

'Alice,' coughs Mabel.

' . . . see this as a competition. Us versus each other. But I don't. I'm in competition with myself. Always have been. It's up to me to be as good as I can be.'

'And me,' Mabel interrupts.

'And you, Mabel. It's life-changing stuff. I was recognised at the pharmacy yesterday. Buying a Ped Egg. Do you know what that is?'

She shakes her head.

'A file for calluses and dry skin on your feet.'

'Sexy,' Mabel says.

'Indeed,' Alan agrees. 'I signed my first autograph over a discussion about a Ped Egg.'

Laura laughs.

'I'm not getting it anywhere near as much as you and I'm struggling. You're a target for them. Two hundred million people want to know what you're going to do next.' He shrugs. 'So blow them away.'

'Thanks. The show's going to give me another chance.'

Alan looks at her in surprise. 'That's what Curtis — '

'Asshole,' Mabel interrupts.

' — was here to talk about?'

She nods.

He leans forward. He drops Mabel on the table and she actually says, 'Ow.'

'You do know that they'd be nothing without you. Just a crap Irish entertainment show that no one's ever heard of, if it wasn't for you?'

Laura is shocked to hear this.

'You've put them on the map. Because of you they've sold the format to twelve more territories and counting. If you dropped out now, they'd be nothing.'

'Speak for yourself,' Mabel says from the table, lying on her back staring at the ceiling.

Laura processes this.

'What's that?' He looks at the brown envelope.

'An article that's going to be in the paper tomorrow. Curtis gave it to me to read.'

'Don't read it,' Alan says.

'I should.'

'No, you shouldn't. You shouldn't read any of them ever again,' he says, not a hint of humour in him now. 'Don't poison yourself with that, Laura. You're the purest, most natural person I've ever met. I want you to win.'

She smiles. 'And I want you to win.'

They hold each other's look, and Laura appreciates the support so much. When it gets awkward, Mabel pipes up.

'And what the fuck about me?'

They both start laughing.

'Right, I'll get you a cup of tea. We might as well enjoy the silence before the next act arrives tonight. And I'll make some lunch. I can't cook, but ham and cheese sandwich okay?'

'Perfect, thank you.'

'I wouldn't eat it, if I were you,' Mabel whispers in her ear before they both leave. 'I think he's trying to poison me.'

Laura laughs as he leaves her alone in the dining room.

Feeling more confident, she stares at the envelope on the table. He's right, she needs to rise above it and she's feeling marginally stronger after their chat, but she still needs to know what people are thinking of her.

She slides the papers out of the envelope.

The opening page is a solicitor's letter, from the newspaper, stating that they are going to run with this story tomorrow. If there is anything that Laura Button would like to respond to, please do so by end of business.

She removes the letter and starts reading.

LIARBIRD? is the headline and the story is about how a garda in Gougane Barra believed that Laura's grandmother Hattie Button killed her husband. It was thought by the garda at the time that her fourteen-year-old daughter Isabel, who became Button after her father's death, was also involved. Garda Liam O'Grady died years ago, but his daughter has done an interview with the newspaper. She tells them how her poor father dedicated his life to trying to bring to justice those he believed responsible for the death of his friend, Sean Murphy. The deceased's wife was Hattie Button, an English-woman, who Sean met while she was minding children for a local family. Sean fell for her and they quickly married and had a daughter, but Hattie was unusual, she didn't venture to the town much or get involved, was always considered a social outcast. Yes, Sean liked a drink, but he was a hard-working farm labourer and a good man. When asked whether Sean was violent, as bruises and cuts, old and new, were found on his wife after his death, the garda's daughter says she doesn't know, and anyway it doesn't alter the fact that Hattie Button and her daughter killed Laura Button's grandfather Sean Murphy.

Laura feels sick.

Sean was found face down in a creek on their grounds. He had drowned in shallow water. There was alcohol in his system and a blunt-force trauma to the back of his head. Sheila says her father always believed Hattie was responsible for Sean's death, but he'd never been able to find proof that Hattie killed him. She took her daughter out of school and they became hermits, their only contact with the community was through the family business of dressmaking and alterations, which they needed to keep going. Garda O'Grady always stayed in Hattie's life, hoping he would catch her out eventually, but it was not to be. He went to his grave feeling he had failed his friend. Laura's mother was a simple woman, 'something not quite right with her', whatever she thinks about her role in Sean Murphy's death, the garda's daughter says it's shameful what 'Tom Toolin did to her, taking advantage of a sick woman. No wonder they hid the child.' Sheila is not surprised to learn of Lyrebird's violent behaviour in the nightclub. 'She's not as sweet as she makes herself out to be. She's a liarbird, not a lyrebird. A liar like her grandmother and mother.'

Laura can't breathe. She can't breathe. She can't make a sound. She reads it all over again, her precious Gaga and Mam being torn apart when they're dead and buried. Their secrets spilling out, dirty horrible lies that they tried so hard to contain; none of their spirit captured or known, the joy and the fun, the happiness that embraced that cottage, just these cold, ugly, dark, horrible lies.

It's Laura's fault. She brought this on them. She should have stayed hidden in the woods.

32

'I think she's in shock,' Selena, the opera singer, says. There's a smell of cigarette smoke off her, as she's just returned from the garden after having her hourly menthol cigarette that she thinks nobody notices her having.

The *StarrQuest* semi-finals are complete, everybody that has got through to the final is now in the house, the newest arrivals came late last night; Sparks, a nineteen-year-old magician, and Kevin, a young and hunky country and western singer. Despite the fact that only one of them could go through to the final, the votes had been split as the nation had fallen for both young men. Jack, in a moment of weakness, couldn't bring himself to choose one of them and instead sent them both through. It was a results show of tension and tears. As a consequence of his heart-felt decision there will be six acts in the final next weekend and all have a week living together and to prepare their final performances. Now the five other acts stand around Laura's bed, watching as she's curled into a foetal position, staring into space, completely unresponsive.

'She's definitely in shock,' Master Brendan of

the Alice and Brendan circus act says. 'If I'm finding this entire thing weird, imagine how she feels.'

'I'm loving it!' Kevin, the country and western singer, pipes up. After famously singing a song to a secret crush, admitting his love for her, he received five hundred thousand hits on YouTube. Heartfelt decisions aside, he was simply too popular an act for Jack to lose from the final. And he had moved the focus of his affections from his one true love to Alice, of Alice and Brendan the circus duo.

'Can she hear us?' Alice says loudly. 'Maybe she's had a stroke or a nervous breakdown and she can't hear us.'

'Of course she can hear us,' Alan says. 'She's choosing not to answer.'

'You fucking idiot,' Mabel says.

'Hey, you need to stop that,' Kevin defends his crush.

'And you need to get a sense of humour,' Ringmaster Brendan snaps at the country and western singer who fancies his contortionist partner who he's secretly had a crush on for years. They met when she was fourteen and he was twenty-four, and it always seemed wrong for him to tell her how he felt, as he knew her from when she was so young. But now she's twenty-two and he's thirty-two and it would be okay, if not for this country and western dimwit who is getting in his way.

'Have you noticed that she hasn't said anything?' Selena asks.

'I'm not fucking deaf,' Mabel says.

'I don't mean *talking*,' the singer says, addressing Mabel. They all see her as the extra member of the team, such is the presence she has in the house, and Alan seems entirely unable to control her. 'She's not making any of her sounds. She always makes her noises.'

They watch Laura, huddled in her bed, staring at the wall like she doesn't have the contestants of a TV show gathered around her. No sounds come from her at all. It is unusual, for her.

Alice is clearly delighted by this. Less competition for her.

'It's like a murder mystery,' Alice giggles. 'Which one of us stole the Lyrebird's lore? Well, it wasn't me.'

'It was them,' Alan says, looking at the newspapers surrounding her bed. He picks up the open tabloid with the article about Laura's mother and grandmother allegedly being responsible for Laura's grandfather's death. It had been published yesterday, on the final day of the *StarrQuest* semi-final, front page of a tabloid, LIARBIRD'S LAIR, and while Laura had been relatively silent since Alan's arrival four days ago, she had disappeared into this state after reading it. He's worried. He folds the paper up and tucks it under his arm, the anger building inside of him, intending to destroy it so she can't set eyes on it again. Another tabloid article reveals the inside story of how the infamous Laura-meets-a-lyrebird photoshoot took place in Melbourne, the superb lyrebird having been shockingly captured for the purpose of promotion. This is accompanied by a large photograph of Laura beside the caged bird which has animal and bird protectors shouting out in outrage.

'We should tell the producers,' says Sparks nervously.

'No,' Alan says quickly. 'We don't tell the producers. They're the ones who got her in this position. They'll put her on the show like this if they have to.'

'What about Bianca? She called by a few days ago to tell Laura to call some guy. She left a number but Laura barely even looked at it.'

'We only need her to speak to people who will help her,' Alan says, dismissing that. 'What about the therapist we've been told about?'

'Larry,' says Sparks. He got through on his amazing card tricks, but along the way he's developed a tremble in his fingers that he can't control. He had a three-hour therapy session with Larry this morning.

'Is he any good?' Selena asks.

'Show us your hands,' Mabel pipes up and Alan looks scornfully at her for the inappropriate remark.

'Sorry,' Alan says to Sparks on Mabel's behalf.

'It's okay,' Sparks says, forgetting momentarily that Mabel is Alan.

'You'll call the therapist for her?' Alan asks.

'Yeah.'

'Good man.'

'You can count on Sparks,' Mabel says as soon as Sparks has left the room. 'Steady as anything, is our Sparks.'

The others smile and shake their heads, not wanting to laugh.

Alan admonishes Mabel again.

Laura hears them. Of course she hears them. She's grateful that they care, but even more grateful when they finally leave her bedroom. She sits up when they're gone, feeling panicked. She hadn't noticed it, but they're right: she hasn't felt herself mimicking, or heard herself do it — not that she would always be aware of it, but she's certain they're correct. She hasn't made a sound. She hasn't been thinking about her past; no happy, sad or any kind of memories. She feels too numb to revisit a single moment of her life aside from the here and now, and now is nothing. Anything else is too painful. Her mind is completely devoid of memories, thoughts and feelings. Just here, now, this, nothing. Then the panic fades and a calm sweeps over her.

If she's silent, then perhaps the world will be silent with her. And she finds a great freedom in that.

33

Solomon's frustration is immense. They can't film the documentary on Lyrebird because of *StarrQuest*/StarrGaze Entertainment restrictions, which Bo's high-powered barrister father is working on. All contact is with StarrGaze Entertainment's team of lawyers, they can't reach Laura at all. Bo's father had asked them, do Mouth to Mouth productions wish to issue proceedings against Lyrebird?

Solomon had been delighted and relieved to hear Bo respond with a firm 'no'.

The entire situation is a mess and in reality he doesn't give a damn about the documentary, all he cares about is seeing Laura. He feels like an addict, he needs her, and the more he can't see her, the more people that say no, and slam doors, and hang up phones, the more he wants her. With filming halted on this season's *Grotesque Bodies* he has nothing else to do. He doesn't want to be at the apartment with Bo, sitting around as though they're waiting for something to happen. Their lives are on hold, which shows him how much of their lives hinges on this project. When it's gone, they have nothing. They talk only about

Laura. First about how fascinating she is, now about how to get her back. She is like the child that was taken away from them. And it was Bo's greed and both their naivety that caused that to happen. When Laura was with them, she tore them apart, now that she's gone, they're linked by her, but without her or talk of her they've got nothing, things have grown stale.

His priority this week has been to stay in Dublin and try to make contact with Laura, both through visiting the house and trying to contact her through Bianca, though Bianca's requests to Laura to call Solomon have failed. He's not sure whether to believe Bianca is passing on those messages at all. With the last of his attempts failed, he can no longer sit around the apartment with Bo feeling in limbo. Their work life in limbo, their relationship in limbo. His immediate plan is to drive to Galway to beat the shit out of Rory. He has been planning this for some time, since Tuesday morning when news of Laura's night out hit the newspapers alongside his baby brother's mischievous mug on almost every page. He has savoured the thoughts of what he will do to his brother and now he is ready.

The three-hour car journey does nothing to calm his anger, if anything it intensifies. He has time to dwell on all the photos in the press that keep floating to the murky surface each time Laura's name is mentioned. Laura falling all over the place. Rory laughing. *Laughing*.

It's Saturday. He calls Marie to casually ask if Rory's home. Rory works with his dad, they both still go home to Marie for their lunch. He's calm, he's just enquiring, he's sure she doesn't notice, he doesn't say anything about visiting, about being on the road on the way. But she knows him well. When he arrives at the house, his parents, plus brothers Cormac and Donal, are there, along with his sister Cara. The entire welcoming committee sitting at the kitchen table.

'What's going on?' he asks angrily.

Marie looks down at her hands, and then away, with guilt. Then she can't take his stare any more and crosses the kitchen to fill the kettle. Tea. Distraction.

'It's a Solomon anger-intervention,' Donal jokes, but Solomon isn't in the mood to laugh. He came here to kick the shit out of somebody, not use words. He's been waiting for this for days, far too long actually, and he's been sitting for hours, he has a lot of energy to dispel. He doesn't want it to go to waste.

'Where is he?' Solomon asks, not even bothering to disguise what he's come here to do.

'Let's talk first,' his dad says.

'Where is the little fucker?' he growls. 'Look at you all, you're like his bodyguards, always have been. That scared little shit has never had to face up to one of his messes, ever, in his whole life. And look at all the good your protection has done for him. Still at home with Mammy and Daddy, still getting a packed lunch every day. No disrespect, Mam, but he's a spoiled little shit. Always has been.'

Mam looks pained. 'He's so sorry about what happened, love. If you saw him — '

'Sorry?' Solomon laughs angrily. 'Good. Tell

me where he is so I can see for myself how sorry the little fucker is.'

Marie winces.

'Enough,' his dad says sternly.

'He's an idiot, Solomon,' Donal says diplomatically. 'We all know that. He messed up, but he didn't mean it. He'd no idea what he was doing.'

'Lads,' he calms himself and looks at them all, tries to make them understand. 'He *ruined* her life. On a global level, *destroyed* her reputation. She had *nothing*, lived on a mountain, knew no one, no one knew she existed and then suddenly everyone knew she existed. She had a chance . . .' The anger rises again and he fights hard to beat it. 'She'd never even had a drink before. Not one.'

Marie looks upset.

'He takes her out — to a *pub*. Then to a *club*. Some celebrity club, just so he could get in, using her as his ticket. Nothing to do with her, what she wanted — it was all for him. A free trip to Dublin for him, what can he get out of it? At no time did he call me. I would have helped. After being surrounded by photographers, she can barely *stand up*, and what does he do? He takes her to a *party*. He lets people take photos of her, throwing up, falling over, passing out. Where the fuck was he? He should have been watching her. She was his responsibility.'

This he says almost to himself. Laura was his responsibility and he knew that. He let her slip away, he let this happen. He will beat the shit out of Rory for his own irresponsibility.

'I can't listen to this,' Rory says suddenly, and Solomon spins around to come face to face with him. 'What era are you living in? She's a grown woman, Sol, she doesn't need minding.'

Solomon closes his fists. Picks a place on Rory's pretty face to hammer. Takes his time, enjoys the moment. He hears the chairs scrape as they're pushed against the kitchen tiles. His brothers and Cara standing, readying themselves. He senses them behind him.

'Rory,' his dad says. 'You were wrong and you know it. Admit it, apologise to Solomon and let's put this behind us. Be men now.'

'Why should I apologise to Solomon? What's he to Laura? It's Laura I should be talking to.'

'You're not going near her ever again,' Solomon growls.

'Neither are you, I'd say,' Rory says with a smile.

They stare each other out of it.

Rory looks at Solomon's fist. 'What are you going to do, hit me?' He smiles, a teasing smile. Solomon recalls him as a young boy, mocking his speech impediment. His stutter and his 'w's. He feels an uncontrollable anger, a hatred so strong he's worried about what he could do right now. He wants to hurt him but he thinks about the ways he can without ending him.

'Say sorry to Solomon *now*, Rory,' Marie says sharply and Solomon feels like he's a child again.

'I'm sorry,' Rory says finally. 'I really am. I had no idea she would get messy like that. The reason I didn't call you is because she said she didn't want me to.'

Solomon's heart pounds even faster. Everything Rory says is designed to drive Solomon's fist through Rory's face. Then Solomon would be wrong and everybody would run to Rory's aid.

'She has a name.'

'Lyrebird,' Rory rolls his eyes. 'Lyrebird said she didn't want me to call you.'

'Her name is Laura,' Solomon says through gritted teeth. 'You don't even know her fucking name.'

'I didn't know where to take her,' he continues his fake apology. 'She didn't want to go to the hotel, she couldn't go to your place, seeing as you'd had a falling out and she had to leave, so I thought I'd take up a few people on their kind offer to help. The girls at the party were looking after her, I thought she'd be in safe hands with them. I really didn't know.'

Rory's demeanour doesn't match his tone. Solomon feels his brothers near him, just behind him.

'Of course I'm sure we all know that this wouldn't be such an issue if Solomon wasn't jealous because I took *Laura* out for a drink.'

'Stop it,' Marie says.

'Shake hands,' Dad says.

Rory reaches out his hand, Solomon takes it. He wants to pull him in, head butt him. Break that fucking nose. Rory's grip is tight and strong for a little fella, but then Rory always had to resort to other tactics to survive in the family, to get attention, to be seen and heard. Being ganged up against like this is a big deal for him.

Even if he's not showing it right now, even though he's cool as a cucumber, his 'I don't care' attitude doesn't wash with Solomon. Solomon realises that this is the worst possible situation for Rory, the entire family forcing him to apologise to Solomon for something he knows he did wrong. Suddenly Solomon enjoys this knowledge, allowing Rory to think he's getting the better of him, when the reality is that Rory's weakness is showing. Solomon feels the tension release ever so slightly from his shoulders.

Perhaps Rory realises he's losing Solomon's anger, that Solomon is no longer the underdog, because he then scrapes the barrel.

'She's a great little ride though,' he says, to his mother's dismay and a yell from his dad.

Rory lets go of Solomon's hand. Solomon's throat is sticky and dry, his heart pounding manically, a tribal drum calling for war.

Then Solomon sees a fist arc through the air before making contact with Rory's face. Rory staggers. Surprisingly, it's not Solomon's fist, it's Cormac's. Big brother Cormac, the responsible one. They all look at him in shock at first and no one makes a move to help Rory, who's fallen to the floor, but then Cormac's high-pitched cries move them to action.

'I think I broke my fingers,' he squeals.

Rory sits up, holding his head, in agony. 'Who punches a forehead?'

Cara starts laughing at them all. She holds her camera up and takes photos.

★ ★ ★

371

Later that night, the brothers and Cara sit outside in the garden on the round garden furniture table, drinking bottles of beer. Marie is ignoring them all, giving them the silent treatment for their behaviour and their dad is supporting her by doing the same, though they all know he's dying to join them.

Cormac's hand is in a sling. Two fingers are broken and the mix of painkillers and alcohol has made him the entertainment of the night.

Rory sits away from Solomon, a lump the size of a quail's egg protruding from his forehead. The storm clouds have delivered rain but nothing has dried, the landscape is utterly drenched and so they perch on the dry spots for now. One thing is preying on Solomon's mind: did Rory sleep with Laura? He's almost sure that Rory made it up to get at him, which he succeeded in doing, but he can't get it out of his head. Thankfully, Cara comes to his aid.

'You know Rory, if you did sleep with Laura, you might have to answer some questions from the guards.'

'What?' Rory yelps. 'What are you on about?'

'There's such a thing as consent, probably not a word you're familiar with . . . '

Cara explains. 'It requires the woman saying yes. It's a real thing. Other men actually have sex with women who aren't locked out of their heads. Women who can see the faces of their lovers. Now I know it's not usually how you operate, but — '

'Shut the fuck up, Cara.'

She winks at Solomon. 'Seriously, we all saw

the photographs. The whole world saw them. She couldn't put one foot in front of the other. If you took her to that party and did what you said you did, then you could be in serious trouble.'

Rory looks at them all, ignoring Solomon. 'Oh, whatever. Of course I didn't sleep with her — she could barely remember her own name. She spent the entire night vomiting.'

The relief in Solomon is overwhelming, but his heart breaks for Laura, for what she went through alone.

'Rory was right about one thing though,' Cormac slurs.

'Here we go,' Donal smirks.

'Ah now, hear me out.'

They settle.

'It's clear to see that you are enamoured with this young woman, Solomon.' It takes him a few attempts to say *enamoured*, but he's intent on using it. 'And while Rory was wrong to do what he did, you wouldn't feel this angry if it wasn't for your feelings for her.'

'Cormac Fallon, Spiddal's Dr Phil,' Solomon laughs it off.

'He has a point,' Donal says.

'Pity she likes the wrong brother,' Rory pipes up, and receives a knock on the head from Cormac.

'Get off me, my head is pounding.'

'Then shut up,' Cormac says.

They chuckle, including Rory. This behaviour is so unlike their eldest brother.

'Bo,' Cormac continues, scrunching up his face. 'I'm not convinced on you and Bo.'

'I'm not convinced on you and Madeleine,'

Solomon says quickly, taking offence, then a slug of beer.

The others *oooh* and watch with interest.

'You're right,' Cormac says solemnly, which receives a chuckle of surprise. 'Sometimes I'm not convinced on me and Madeleine either.'

Rory picks up his phone and starts filming.

'Stop being a dick,' Cara says, slapping the back of his head. He drops the phone.

Cormac continues. 'Madeleine is . . . sometimes I don't even *like* Madeleine.'

They all laugh while Cormac attempts to stop them so he can finish.

'But . . . but . . . listen. She is often the most annoying person in the world. And I want to strangle her. Or leave her. But even in the worst of times — and we've had a lot, especially lately . . . this fucking menopause thing. If I could leave her until it's over, I would. I really would.'

They piss themselves laughing, but Cara shakes her head. 'Unbelievable.'

'But I couldn't. Because even when I don't like Madeleine, I fucking love Madeleine.'

Which is possibly the most twisted but romantic thing any of them has ever said about any of their partners.

'Anyway, where was I?' He tries to focus on Solomon, one eye closed to help. 'You and Bo. I don't think you're right together. You're not a good match.'

'With all due respect, Cormac — and I appreciate that you care for me,' Solomon says softly, 'Bo and I aren't for anybody else to think if we're right.'

'Of course!' Cormac throws his hands up and splashes his bottle contents. He reaches out and pokes his beer-drenched finger in Solomon's chest. 'But do *you* think you're right together? Solomon, this is life brother, there's no harm, or shame in admitting something's not working. Get out now while you can,' he waves his hand dismissively. 'I don't know what you're hanging on for.'

★ ★ ★

The next day, struggling with a mighty hangover, Solomon drives to Dublin thinking about everything Cormac and his siblings had said to him.

It had all made so much sense last night, he would break up with Bo. Cara had coached him on the right words, they'd spoken until the sun rose, but in the cold sober light of day, it terrifies him.

He turns on the radio to distract himself.

'And in entertainment news it is unclear whether Lyrebird will take to the stage in *StarrQuest's* live final. The contestant, whose real name is Laura Button, received two hundred and fifty million views on social media following her first audition, but last weekend she hit the headlines after a night out clubbing, leading to a media backlash. Jack Starr had this to say at a press conference with the finalists today.'

'We're very much hoping that Lyrebird will take part. It is of course up to her, and all of us at *StarrQuest* will give her the encouragement and support she needs.'

'And Lyrebird's fellow contestant Alan, from the popular act Alan and Mabel, had this to say . . . '

'Laura is doing great. She's fine. She's just emotionally, physically and mentally drained. It has been the most extraordinary roller coaster, for all of us, so I can't imagine how it's been for her. I think all she needed was a bit of R&R, being somewhere private, so she could get over what's happened to her, because what's happened to her has been unprecedented.'

'On Lyrebird's sensational night out that grabbed every front page across the world, Alan had this to say . . . '

'Laura got off a flight from Australia where she'd been for only two days, working an intense schedule, she then had to go straight into rehearsals for the semi-final, which she won, and she had a few drinks for the first time in her life. She was entitled to celebrate her success. She did nothing wrong in that nightclub, it was a misunderstanding, she needed support and help, and instead people took advantage. She learned some harsh lessons, but she has learned.'

'Will Lyrebird perform at the final?'

'I hope she does,' Alan says.

'Really? But she's your greatest competition. You two are the favourites.'

'She's the most genuinely lovely and naturally talented person I've ever met. I hope she goes up on that stage and proves to people why she got their attention in the first place, and I hope she wins.'

'Which just makes us all love the amazing Alan and Mabel even more. So has the Lyrebird lost her lore? Tune in to the *StarrQuest* final to see!'

Solomon drives the car across three lanes to pull into the hard shoulder to angry drivers' beeps. He puts on his hazards, lowers the window and breathes deeply. He has never wanted or needed somebody so much in his life.

34

When Laura chose to close her mouth, she closed all the doors around her. To her fellow contestants who she lived with, to Curtis, who she refused to see, and Bianca, who she refused to speak with, even to Solomon, who she couldn't bear seeing after her embarrassment, and to Bo, because under StarrGaze Entertainment's orders she's forbidden from speaking with any media for the foreseeable future.

Despite Bo's protestations, despite her attempts to change Jack's mind, sweetly and then through threats of solicitor's letters, nothing is working. Bo can barely get to Jack, Curtis is blocking everything and it seems the whole of *StarrQuest* is in a panic, faced with the worldwide spotlight — attention they had enjoyed when Lyrebird was attracting hundreds of millions of online views, but not now. The backlash has moved on from Lyrebird to focus on *StarrQuest* and StarrGaze Entertainment. They've been getting it from all sides: opinion pieces in the press and talk-show panels have debated whether the show failed its star. After all, wasn't Lyrebird their responsibility? Didn't they effectively allow this meltdown

378

to happen? Shouldn't they do more to screen their contestants: insist that they undergo psychiatric tests, provide therapy before, during and after the audition process and live show? Shouldn't talent shows have a greater responsibility for their contestants' welfare?

Jack Starr is doing interviews with CNN, Sky News and all around the world, explaining the close relationship he has with his contestants, that their welfare comes first at all times. 'Nobody could have anticipated the effects of Lyrebird's first audition, nobody could prepare for it. Nobody could ever know how that level of attention could affect a person. It was new to everyone and everyone was and is responsible: the show, the media, society, the public, even Lyrebird herself. It was unprecedented. Her talent is immense and I want to nurture it and her. Rest assured, that's what we're doing. This is entertainment. If there is no joy, what's the point? Lyrebird has been asked many times if she wants to proceed. Whether she chooses to continue with *StarrQuest* or not is purely her decision, there is no pressure on her from our side.'

'Jack, bearing in mind your own personal journey in the music business, should you not have been more prepared for the effects fame can have on an artist? Isn't that the whole point of having a mentor like you, someone with inside knowledge of the positive and negative effects of the industry?'

Jack stares at the journalist, almost like he's frozen, shocked. He doesn't know how to respond. Surprise, realisation, guilt, all pass over his face at once.

'Will Lyrebird take part in the final?'

Jack manages to compose himself. 'Lyrebird has a lot of supporters but she has a lot of critics. She will and should prove them wrong.'

Laura turns off the television in her bedroom and there's silence. She likes it in this room. It feels like a cocoon. Safe. Her curtains are drawn all day and night, it has a pale nude palette, nothing at all like her Cork retreat. Like the rest of the house, it's sparse, there's no feeling that anybody has lived here, that anybody owns it. The place has no identity, apart from the swing set and slide that stand abandoned in the garden. She likes its lack of identity. Cream and beige, a pale furry rug. She snuggles under her duvet and closes her eyes. She listens out for her sounds, but nothing comes.

Nothing at all.

Part 3

The first feathers to be shed by the male bird in the moult are the two fine, narrow, wire-like, lyre-shaped plumes which, when the tail is spread, project above the fan and are always maintained at an acute angle from the main plumes while the bird is displaying . . .

When the tail moult is complete, the male bird is hardly to be distinguished by a casual observer from the female for a period of several weeks. During this period the male bird keeps more or less in retirement. He disappears from his accustomed haunts and his singing is rarely to be heard . . . He never dances and seldom sings . . . Moreover, his general mien is sad and dejected. Close and prolonged study has induced the conclusion that the male Menura is an intensely proud and vain creature, who, when shorn of his magnificence, feels ashamed and disconsolate and is happiest in hiding.

Ambrose Pratt, *The Lore of the Lyrebird*

35

Bo sits alone in the silent apartment watching the clock. Solomon hasn't returned from his trip to Galway yet, he hasn't even phoned. She hasn't called him either. She's not sure if he's coming home today or tomorrow. She's not sure she cares. They've had so little to say to each other that's positive, lately, and it's clear to her that they've reached the end. This wasn't just a speedbump — those were designed to make you slow down, get your wits about you, process what's happening. No, this time they'd come up against an enormous stop sign, yelling at them to quit. No more moving forward.

She sits at the table, her head spinning, contemplating what's left of her life. Her documentary has fallen apart, she doesn't want to press charges against Laura as her dad was suggesting — that was never her intention. She needs to move on, that much she knows. But how can she move on? The embarrassment is not the worst thing that has come from this, though. Her reputation is a little tarnished, but that's not what's bothering her. It's that she can't bring herself to move on to the next story until she's finished telling this one. Despite whatever Solomon might think, her heart is in Lyrebird's story.

The phone rings and when she looks at the caller ID her heart leaps. Since they broke up and she embarked on a relationship with Solomon, Jack always managed to call her at her weakest moment; as if he could sense when she's at her most vulnerable, her most likely moment to let him in. Since this Lyrebird legal mess had begun, she had been praying for the return of those calls that she'd begged him to cease.

'Hello.'

'Hi,' Jack says, sounding defeated.

'I appreciate you finally calling me back,' she says unable to keep the anger from her tone.

He sighs. 'Bo Peep. Help.'

She's surprised by his tone. It's rare for him.

'It's been so crazy around here the past few days. Really stressful. I'm exhausted, Bo,' he says, and leaves a silence. 'I thought I'd learned from all my mistakes last time round. I thought I knew how to help an act. I thought I could stop what happened to me from happening to them. I thought . . . ' He sighs. 'I fucked up. I'm off my high horse now. Screw the lawyers. Screw it all. I need your help.'

'My help?'

'Lyrebird hasn't left her bedroom for days. She hasn't said a word to anyone, she hasn't made a sound. We have no final if we don't have her. We can't pressure her to go on, there's too much attention on us now. Everyone's watching. Watching for the show to fuck up, for her to fuck up. I mean, when did it stop being about the talent? And I can't say I blame her. I've been right where she is now.'

Bo is so surprised by this, she was expecting an argument.

'Bo, we need your help. You know her better than us. What should we do?'

'I gave you advice for the semi-final, I told you to go with a forest theme, I told you exactly what to do and you messed that up.'

'I know, I know, I'm sorry,' he says. 'We've fucked up on this. I prided myself on protecting the talent, not on this happening. You know she reminds me of me, right now, where I was when everything went black. This is all bringing me back there . . . ' He goes quiet. 'I mean, I'm not going to have a drink,' he says, sounding like he's trying to convince himself. 'I'm not. But I had a cigarette. I hope that doesn't spoil our chances,' he adds a weak joke, his heart not in it.

'Can we meet up?' Bo asks, sitting up, feeling all the energy that drained from her surging back at full force. She's worried about him, she's excited about being included. Contact at last.

'Please,' he sighs. 'We need all the help we can get. *I* need all the help I can get.'

'I'll do what I can,' Bo says, standing up and grabbing things, throwing them into her bag. 'But first, one little tip.'

'Go on.'

'Start by calling her Laura,' she says gently.

'Right. Got it,' he says.

36

Laura awakes with a start, her heart drumming and the sound of chirping loud in her ears. If she had a nightmare she doesn't remember it, but she feels the remaining panic in her heart and chest. Something scared her. She hears the other contestants downstairs talking and laughing, drinking after the latest drama, which has forced a contestant out of the show and caused another to join the house.

Country singer Kevin has been kicked out after *StarrQuest* discovered he once had a record deal that he is still signed to. It is against the rules for anybody to have a contract of any sort that would affect StarrGaze's rights over the act. The happiest person in the house is Brendan. But he doesn't know that when Kevin returned for the last time to pack his bags, Alice gave him a parting gift. In the bedroom next door to Laura's, the headboard was banging in time with Kevin's throaty groans of 'Sweet Jesus!' Then the two lovers discussed their magazine offers and plans to enter *Celebrity Big Brother*, before Kevin packed his cowboy hat and boots and left.

The twelve-year-old contortionist has taken

his place. She's outside now, practising for her pyro show, diving through loops of fire, while her mother and father look on, wearing tracksuits with her name and face on their backs.

Alice's tears soon dried and now she is in the hall, arguing with Brendan about her focus, or lack thereof. Wide awake now, Laura sits up and listens. He tells her she needs to focus on her career, on him and her. Alice is fed up with him and her, she needs a life beyond the act, this show has given her that. It's like a bullet through the heart for Brendan.

Throughout their argument, Laura hears the echo of chirping in her head. It hasn't come from her, she's sure of it. As far as she's aware, she still hasn't made a sound and she feels as though someone has drawn a curtain on her throat. She turns on the bedroom light and sits up, the room is wrapped in a warm orange glow.

Still, her chest pounds.

She breathes in and out slowly, trying to settle herself, confused by this feeling. For days now this room has been her haven. Through drawing the curtain on her voice, she has drawn a curtain on the world; for a while it helped her to feel safe, protected, at peace. Now she feels trapped, as though the walls are closing in on her. Where previously it seemed big and spacious, now it feels like there's not enough air to breathe. Like she's in a cage.

That thought sparks off the chirping again in her head and she realises where the sound is coming from. She throws off the covers and dresses quickly, peering outside. It's two a.m., the photographers don't stay all night, she'll be able to leave without being seen. She packs some things in a backpack, including the per diem, the allowance the show has given them each day. Getting out of here will be a problem; the house is in a remote area in Enniskerry, and though there is a village minutes away, it's not walkable, not at this hour. She would have to call a taxi and all the phones are downstairs. Alice and Brendan have moved away from where they were arguing. She opens her door and walks as quietly as she can down the hall, hoping to miss Alice, who seems to report her every move to the press.

She winces as the floor creaks underfoot. By the time she makes it downstairs, everybody seems to have gone to bed, getting ready for the final tomorrow night. She tiptoes into one of the lounges and is about to phone for a taxi when a figure appears at the door.

'Alan,' she says, getting a fright.

'Laura!' He sounds as surprised as she is. 'What are you doing?'

'Calling a taxi.'

'I'll drive you.'

'You don't even know where I'm going.'

He shrugs. 'Anywhere but here would be an attraction right now.'

She smiles at him sympathetically. 'What are you doing up so late?'

'Only time I get to practise. It's so crazy with everybody here in the day. Too many people keeping an eye on each other. I envy you sometimes, up there in your room.'

'Sorry.'

'Don't be.'

'I need to get out,' she explains.

'Are you coming back?'

'I want to,' she says honestly. She wants to honour everybody who has helped her. It's not their fault that it has all come to this point; the blame for that is all hers. But how can she take part in the show when she hasn't uttered a sound? She's heard the radio and TV reports that the Lyrebird has lost her lore.

Alan looks tired.

'You should sleep, Alan. You have a big night tomorrow.'

'I can't,' he says, rubbing his eyes. 'I've never been so nervous in my life,' he stammers. 'Mabel, on the other hand, is getting her beauty sleep. She needs it.'

Laura laughs. 'I meant what I said: I want you to win. You deserve it more than anyone.'

'I think we both deserve it more than anyone,' he says kindly.

They smile.

'Then if either of us win, we've both won already,' he says. 'Can I ask you something? Why are you taking part in this show? You're the last person I'd imagine being interested in this kind of life. Not that I'm being judgemental,' he stammers. 'If you saw where I'm coming from, you'd understand why I entered. I have nothing. I live with Mam and Dad. It's me and Mabel and . . . that's it. If I don't make it work, there's nothing else that I know how to do. I've tried everything else.' He shakes his head. 'I've failed at everything else. Mabel is all I have.'

Laura thinks about it. 'I think, Alan, the two of us have more in common than you could know. If I wasn't here right now, I can't think of anything else that I could do either, but I didn't know that being able to do the thing that I love to do, naturally, would make life so complicated.'

He smiles sadly. 'And we are the lucky ones. Imagine if we didn't know?'

Laura ponders that.

'I'll get my car keys.'

They leave the house unnoticed, though Laura wouldn't be surprised if reports of a secret affair between Alan and Laura were to emerge in the press. There's nothing Alice wouldn't do to jeopardise their positions in the competition. Laura is certain Alice was behind the leaked 'backstage altercation' between Lyrebird and the *StarrQuest* producer.

The drive to Dublin city is calm, there being no traffic on the roads at this hour.

'Is this the sound guy's place?' he asks, looking up at the block of apartments.

'Yes,' Laura replies. 'How did you know?'

'I've seen you with him,' he says. 'Mabel felt you had a thing going.'

Laura leans her head back against the headrest. 'Mabel's got it wrong. There was nothing between us.' She fights her tears from welling.

'I don't know, Mabel is pretty smart,' Alan says studying her. 'Bianca left his number for you to call him, you know.'

'I know,' she sighs. 'I couldn't. I was too embarrassed.'

'Laura you have to get over it. At my brother's wedding I got so drunk I gave his mother-in-law a lap dance. I don't even remember doing it. Saw the footage though. I ripped open my shirt. Popped every button. Almost took her eye out. If I can look her in the eye every Christmas, Easter and every family occasion, then you can.'

Laura giggles. 'Thanks Alan.'

He's reluctant to leave her at Solomon's apartment block, but Laura convinces him she's okay, fooling him by standing at the door and pretending to buzz his intercom. She watches him drive away, back to the contestants' house, no doubt practising his act with an invisible Mabel in the car.

As she stands beneath the balcony, she imagines she can hear Solomon's guitar playing. She hopes to be able to summon it herself, but there's nothing, the curtain is still drawn over her vocal cords. She looks up at the window of the bedroom she slept in with his rails of shirts and T-shirts. She loved the smell and feel of his things around her, his music equipment, his guitar in the corner of the room, his recording equipment. She thinks of Bo and Solomon making love and this twists her heart. She needs to stay away from him, move on. It's not their apartment that she's here to visit.

She hears the chirping in her head again, the sound that woke her from her nightmare. The restaurant beneath the apartments has left all the tables and chairs outside; they're stacked up in the corner against the glass. She gets an idea. She moves as quietly as possible, knowing how clearly she could hear everything outside when she was in the spare bedroom. She is more sensitive to sounds than most; Solomon is the only other person she's ever met who hears things as she does. His ears have been finely honed either from his music days, or his sound recording days, trained to listen for that something extra. She stacks the chairs four high and struggles to climb on them. Too wobbly and not high enough. She half lifts, half pulls a table closer to the balcony and removes some chairs from the stack and lifts them onto the table. Dragging the table has made a noise and she looks up to check the apartments. All lights are off, clear balconies, no heads hanging out the windows. She uses one chair to climb on to the table. She holds on to the café window while climbing on to the stacked chairs. She's high enough to reach the balcony, but it's incredibly wobbly under her weight. She takes a chance and leans over and grabs the rail. She holds on tight and places one foot on the floor of the balcony, another staying on the wobbling stack of chairs. Finally, she takes a deep breath and heaves her body to the balcony so that she is standing on the outside of the railing. As she pushes against the stack of chairs, they topple off the table and fall to the ground, which makes an enormous crash that reverberates around the canal. Heart pounding, she sees lights go on, hears windows open, and quickly climbs over the balcony rail and ducks down, back against the wall. She catches her breath and hopes nobody will see her, huddled in the dark. She may be safe now, but getting down will be impossible now that she's stupidly knocked over the stack of chairs.

She hears the chirping again and looks for the cage. The floor of the balcony is decorated with toy boxes, protecting the toys inside from the elements, the boy's mother using every available space in her small apartment for her child. Laura's ready to free the bird. After listening to his chirping for so long and watching him from Solomon and Bo's balcony, she still can't speak bird, but during her time mimicking the sounds she felt it was saying something. *I'm trapped. Get me out.* But her smile fades as she searches for the cage. It's gone.

She starts to cry, feeling useless, helpless, pathetic.

The lights suddenly go on in the apartment and she panics, knowing that to jump from the balcony to the table would be dangerous. The table would topple under her weight, she'd end up on the ground. Should she risk it?

The curtain slides open and a woman's face appears. When she sees Laura, she starts screaming. In Polish. Laura stands up and holds out her hands to calm her.

'It's okay,' Laura says, knowing the woman can't hear her, and even if she could, she might not understand English. 'Please . . . '

The lights in Solomon's apartment go on.

Laura panics. He can't find her here, not like this. The balcony door slides open and Solomon steps out sleepily. He's not wearing a top and his tracksuit bottoms sit dangerously low on his hips. Despite her panic, Laura can't help but take him in. He rubs his eyes as if he can't quite believe what he's seeing.

'Laura?'

She starts to cry again, feeling ridiculous, pathetic, mortified and relieved to see him again. All those feelings, all at the same time.

★ ★ ★

Solomon bangs on the door. He can hear Katja inside, screaming, and a child howling. She's not answering the door, but she sounds like she's talking to someone in the apartment. She's shrieking and crying, the little boy is crying. Others have stepped out of their apartments into the corridor and glare sleepily at Solomon as he bangs on the door, as if this is all his fault. He ignores them. His heart pounds, he needs to get inside.

'Katja!' Solomon raises his voice, ignoring the hushing and shushing from his neighbours.

At last she opens the door. Her terrified eyes are red raw, tears stream down her face, snot down her nose. A baby is in her arms crying, a little boy clinging to her leg, and she has a phone to her ear.

'I'm Solomon, your neighbour,' he says when the terrified expression gives way to confusion. They've never spoken, aside from a few quick hellos as they've passed each other in the hall, but nothing more than that, nothing friendlier than that.

'There's a burglar on the balcony,' she says to him, then returns to rapid fire Polish as she speaks down the phone. She leaves the door open and moves inside the apartment. She paces the wall furthest away from the balcony, as if afraid to go near the burglar who remains trapped out there, sitting on the cold hard floor, covering her face with her hands.

'Have you called the guards?' Solomon asks.

'The what?'

'The police.'

'No! My husband! His friends will come.'

'No, no, no,' he says, trying to take the phone from her to explain to the man on the phone, but she whacks him hard on the arm and takes him by surprise. The baby howls, the little boy tries to kick him.

'Katja, listen,' he pleads, trying to calm her, to stop her screaming down the phone. 'This is a mistake. She's not a burglar. She's my friend. The burglar on the balcony. She's my friend.'

She finally stops and looks at him suspiciously.

'This is a misunderstanding. My friend was trying to surprise me. She went to the wrong balcony.' In actual fact, Solomon has absolutely no idea what Laura is doing on this balcony, she could be a burglar for all he knows, but he'll defend her till the end. He's seen Katja's husband. He doesn't want to meet his friends.

'It's a mistake. She got the wrong balcony.'

'Why would she want to climb to your balcony?'

'To . . . to . . . to be romantic, you know? Shakespeare. *Romeo and Juliet*. The balcony. You know? Trust me, she is not a burglar. It's a misunderstanding. Tell your husband to call his friends off.'

She thinks about it then fires a machine-gun drill of angry words into the phone.

As she does, Solomon opens the sliding doors and crouches down to Laura, who's still huddled on the ground, hugging herself even tighter at the sound of the door opening. Her face is buried between her knees, her arms wrapped around her legs, which are tucked tight to her body.

'It's okay,' he whispers, moving close, trying to see her face.

'I was trying to set it free,' she says, weeping.

'Trying to set what free?' He frowns.

'The bird.' She finally looks up. 'I could hear the bird. It woke me up. It was trying to get out. I was trying to set it free, but it wasn't there . . . '

He realises what she was trying to do. 'Oh, Laura.' He wraps his arms around her and pulls her close to him. He squeezes her tight, feeling her skin beneath her top where it has raised on her waist. He kisses the top of her head, breathes her in. He could stay like that for ever. She clings to him as hard as he holds her, and he's feeling this embrace with every fibre of his being, wanting this moment more than anything.

She moves her face from where it is nestled to his bare chest and looks up at him. Her forehead brushes his chin as she moves, his skin tingles, hers is on fire. Their hearts pound with the closeness. She lifts her chin to gaze at him, their lips so close, their breaths already touching. She searches his eyes and finds her answer. His pupils are dilated, she sees the want in them. She smiles.

Then Katja comes to the door, the baby still crying on her hip.

'Let's go,' he whispers, not wanting to move but wanting to get out of there before the husband returns. Laura moves with him, their hands finding one another and linking tightly. As they stand, Solomon sees a figure on the balcony next door. On his balcony. It's Bo. She's been watching them.

★ ★ ★

'I'm sorry,' Laura sniffs, pulling her legs under her body as she curls up on the armchair. She wraps a blanket around herself, shudders. She can't look them in the eye.

Bo and Solomon view her from the couch. And while it's back to two against one, the positions have changed. Bo sits as far away from Solomon as she can, perched at the very edge of the couch.

'I had a nightmare, I woke up feeling trapped, I could hear the bird.' She shakes her head.

'What did it sound like?' Bo asks, testing her.

Laura thinks about it, then shakes her head, no sound coming. 'I think I'm going crazy.' She rubs her eyes tiredly. 'What was I thinking?'

'No, you're not,' Bo says quietly, and Solomon looks at her in surprise.

She ignores him. She takes a chair from the kitchen table and moves it close to Laura's armchair, so that she's in front of her. Solomon's not sure whether she's deliberately blocking his view of the woman he hasn't been able to take his eyes off since he met her, or if she just wants him out of her own eyeline. 'What has happened to you has been crazy. How on earth you're expected to deal with it is beyond me. This has been your way. Becoming a cat burglar.'

Laura looks at Bo in surprise and they both start laughing, breaking the nervous tension.

'The bird is a canary. I had one as a kid. It stays in the cage. It sleeps inside at night,' Bo explains.

'Oh.' Laura sniffs. 'I should have known that.'

'I think it was less about you releasing the canary and more about you feeling trapped, you wanting to get out of there,' Bo offers.

Solomon is stunned by this exchange. He remains silent, feeling, probably for the first time, that Bo can handle her.

'Everyone has been so kind,' Laura says. 'I didn't have any reason to feel that way. You and Solomon have been so good to me, welcoming, hospitable.' Her eyes flicker quickly in his direction and then back to Bo again, not wanting to betray the woman who is being so understanding. 'I didn't want to ruin things for you, embarrass you, let you down.'

'You haven't,' Bo says, annoyed — but not with Laura, with herself. 'We . . . I can only speak for myself, but I should have protected you. I threw you to the lions, I watched it happen. I told myself it was for your own good, but it wasn't.'

Laura and Solomon look at her in shock.

'No, you didn't, you saved me,' Laura says. 'I'm so grateful for everything.'

'Don't be,' Bo says quietly. 'Please. We all got so excited about you, about how precious and rare and exciting you are, that we lost ourselves in you. Your talent — '

'Oh, I don't have a talent,' Laura interrupts. 'Alan, he has a talent. He's up all night, every night, working on his routine. He writes it, performs it, even sews his own dummy when it needs to be repaired. He's travelled the country for the past fifteen years, taking every gig imaginable. He's been shouted at, laughed at, paid next to nothing, just to hone his skill.'

As she says the word hone she sees Gaga with her knife, but no sound comes to her or from her. It's gone. This enrages her even more.

'Alice, for all her shortcomings, spends four hours in the gym every day — every single day. Nothing passes her lips that isn't for a purpose, she folds herself into a thousand little pieces, has dedicated her entire life to her craft. Sparks has been doing card tricks since he was seven. Seven! He spends six hours practising every day. Selena sings like an angel, and there's a twelve-year-old girl who leaps through fire on the lawn. *That's* talent. What am I? Some weirdo who opens her mouth and mimics sounds. There's nothing original about me. I'm like a parrot, or a a a . . . monkey. I'm a freak of nature. A weirdo, I belong in a circus, not in this talent show. I'm a con, a liar. They're right in what they say about me. I'm not original, I'm not unique or authentic. I mimic sounds and half the time I don't even notice what I'm doing. I shouldn't be here, I know that. I shouldn't have forced my way into your lives, I shouldn't have forced you two apart — I know that's what I've done and I'm sorry . . . ' The tears fall. 'But I didn't know what else to do. I don't have anywhere else to go, I can't go back. I'm trying to move forward all the time but I'm grasping at everything and can't catch on to anything . . . ' She trails off as the tears fall.

Solomon's eyes fill. If Bo wasn't here, he'd stand up, he'd go to her, he'd take her in his arms, he'd kiss her, every inch of her, tell her how beautiful she is, how talented she is, how perfect in every way she is. How she is the most unique, talented, authentic person he has ever met. How she captivates him just by being. But he can't, Bo is in the room and any sound he makes or any move he makes will betray him, betray Bo. So he sits in silence, feeling trapped in his own body, watching as the woman he loves falls apart at the seams, in front of the woman he tried to love.

And the woman he tried to love speaks for him, stronger than him, stronger than he'll ever be and he's grateful to her for that.

'Laura, let me tell you about your skill,' Bo says, speaking with conviction. 'Part of your ability is that you showcase the world's beauty. You recognise the tiniest details in people, animals, objects, everything. You hear things that we don't even notice or that we've long stopped hearing. You capture those things and you display them to the world. You remind us of what's beautiful.

'People say that's what I do in my

documentaries. I show the world characters and stories that have been hidden. I find the story, the people, then I help them to tell the world. You, you do it all through a simple sound. One whiff of my mum's perfume and I'm transported back to my house as a kid. One sound from you moves every single person to another time and place. You touch everyone, Laura. You have to understand that.

'Solomon told me that when his mother heard you mimicking the harp music at her birthday party, she said it was the most beautiful sound she had ever heard. She has been making that sound for fifty years, but she heard it for the first time through you. Do you understand how important that is? When you met Caroline in wardrobe, it took you one minute to bring her to tears; you made her feel like she was six years old again, sitting with her mother in her workshop. I don't think you have any idea of the way you touch people. You find the beauty in the world, the sadness in the everyday, the extraordinary in the ordinary, the whimsical in the mundane. Laura, you got into the show through mimicking a coffee machine for an entire minute.'

They laugh.

'You are important. You are relevant. You are unique — and you deserve to be up on that stage just as much as anyone else. So what if you don't have to rehearse — that doesn't mean you're not good enough. Should we all have to *struggle* to be truly great? Because it comes easily to you, does that make you any less talented? Or does that make you even more astounding? It's the greatest lesson that you can teach us: what you have comes from within. It's a natural, rare, God-given skill.'

'It's gone,' Laura whispers.

'It's still in there. It's like the hiccups. You got a fright and they went away, but they're in there. You'll find it again.'

'How?'

'Maybe if you remember how it began, that might help bring it back. You stopped feeling curious, or intrigued, you fell out of love with things. You'll be inspired again.' She glances at Solomon, almost as if she's handing the baton over to him. Does she really mean what Solomon thinks she means? The awkward look in her eye, the sad but resigned tone. She stands up. 'You have until tomorrow night. I've been helping Jack today, trying to figure out a set-up that will help you perform, that will help you feel comfortable. No more dancers in spandex, no more dancing bears in the woods. You're going to feel right at home up there. Well . . . I better leave you guys . . .' She looks around awkwardly, gathering her things under Solomon's watchful gaze. He wants to say something but doesn't know what. He's not sure if he understands correctly. She disappears into the bedroom and he hears her unzip a case. His heart pounds.

He looks at Laura, wondering if she understands the greatness of what's happening, but she's in her own world, her mind mulling over all the things Bo said.

Solomon makes his way to the bedroom. He finds Bo packing her things.

'Bo — '
'Bo — '
Solomon and Laura speak at the same time.

'Yes?' she answers Laura, going to the door.

'You said if I could remember where it came from in the first place . . . ?'

'Yes, it was just an idea . . . '

'Have you got your camera here?'

Bo's cheeks pink. 'That's not what I meant. I wasn't asking you to . . . '

'I know you weren't. But I want to tell you.'

'Laura we're not allowed to continue with the documentary. StarrGaze Entertainment lawyers have been very clear on that point.'

'I don't care what they say, this is my mouth, my words, my thoughts, they don't own them.'

Solomon and Bo look at each other. He gives her the nod.

Rachel is with Susie at the hospital, Susie is in labour. But Laura wants to do this now so Bo sets up a camera on a tripod. Solomon takes care of the sound. It's done quickly without fuss. Laura is ready to talk.

37

Isabel got sick very fast. She weakened quickly. She'd been taking all of their home-made medicines, everything they could research and make for themselves. At no point did she want to take hospital drugs. She was against chemo-therapy, she wanted to try alternative therapies, specific nutrition plans. She was very thorough in her research, Gaga too. They had always been like that, almost like everything they'd learned in their lives was all for that moment. She did liver-flush therapy, high pH therapy, which ensured she ate foods high in alkaline and balanced her body pH. And then when she couldn't eat whole foods any more she was on a liquid protocol.

'If I'm going to die,' her mother reaches out and wipes a tear from her daughter's cheek. 'I'm going to die healthy.'

Laura smiles and sniffs her tears away. She kisses the back of her mother's hand.

The work studio is in the house so that Gaga and Laura can work on the clothes alterations and care for her at the same time, though Gaga still deals with the customers in the garage.

Their home is private. Protection of Laura has always been their main priority though now Gaga struggles with leaving her ill daughter. Laura often thinks that even though she is by her mother's side, Gaga wants to be there herself. She is letting the business go, letting standards drop, just so that she won't have to leave her. Her mother's health has deteriorated fast, they sit up with her all night, supposed to be taking their shifts in turns but neither of them wanting to be asleep when the moment comes. It is on one of those days that Gaga is dealing with a customer in the garage, that Laura is alone with her mum. Laura can tell by the change in her mother's breathing that something is happening.

'Mummy,' Isabel says, in a raspy voice, sounding like a child.

It is the first word she has said in days.

'I'm here, Mum, it's Laura,' Laura takes her hand and holds it to her lips.

'Mummy,' she repeats. Her eyes are open, they look around as if searching for Gaga.

Laura's heart pounds. She hurries to the window and peeks through the blinds toward the garage. There's no sign of Gaga, the customer's car is still in the drive. She looks back from her mother to the garage, feeling trapped, the most trapped she's ever felt in her life. If she calls Gaga, the customer will hear or see her. They'd all made a pact that Laura would never be seen, not until she's the legal age. It was long understood and long unspoken. The idea of her being out in the world before she's sixteen terrifies them.

Laura is torn. Her mother's breathing is shallow, she knows she's leaving the world, she can't call Gaga and risk anybody discovering her existence, but she can't let her mum go thinking that she's on her own.

The panic. The hot feeling that overwhelms her body, as sweat breaks out on her brow and trickles down her back. The palpitations. The cold fear. She is losing her mum and while she wants to shout to the world for help, she knows she can't risk being taken away from Gaga too. She would lose everything.

She doesn't want her mum to die thinking she is alone, just as she will feel without hers. She doesn't want Gaga to know that her daughter died without her thinking she was there. She sits beside her, closes her eyes and wills every single part of her to solve the problem, to save her in the moment.

She opens her mouth and sings, and when she sings, she hears Gaga's voice, the voice of an older woman with a Yorkshire accent. Isabel squeezes her hand.

The broken tree, with a broken limb,
Stands where the grass is brown, and the sky
   is dim.
Flowers are forever buds,
   A skeleton tree in the luscious woods.
No spiders crawl, no animals reign,
On the broken tree, with a broken limb.
But on the branch a She Bird props,
With her beak held high, and her eyes apop.
As she sings her song for all

406

The buds open wide and the petals fall.
The spiders crawl and weave their webs,
The fruit flies flee from the strawberry beds
The broken tree is broken no more when the
  She Bird sits to sing her lore.
The tree's alive, the limb's repaired,
The animals inhabit because they all have
  heard.
Children climb, and laugh and play,
The broken tree comes alive for just one day.
The She Bird's song stops and she flies away
And the broken tree returns that way.

Solomon and Bo are holding their breath as they watch Laura. It's not just her voice that has changed as she recalls the song from her mother's deathbed, somehow she has managed to allow the spirit of her Gaga to inhabit her. It is nothing short of magical. Bo turns to Solomon, looks at him for the first time since she effectively left him; her eyes are wide and filled with tears. He reaches for her hand and she takes it, squeezes it. Laura opens her eyes and looks at their hands, joined.

Bo wipes her cheek and Laura smiles.

'Was that . . . ' She clears her throat to remove the emotion and starts again. 'Was that the first time you realised you had this skill?'

'Yes,' she says softly. 'It's the first time I realised it. But then, when I realised it, it became clear it wasn't the first time I'd done it.'

Bo nods at her to tell her more.

'Gaga brought it up with me one day, years before. We were lying on the grass, behind the house, I was making daisy chains. Mam was reading a book, she loved romance books, Gaga hated them. Mam would sometimes read the sentences aloud, just to annoy Gaga,' she laughs. 'I can hear them, at each other. Gaga blocking her ears *la la la la*.'

★ ★ ★

Isabel isn't reading aloud. It is silent. And suddenly Gaga starts laughing.

'That was a good one, Laura,' she says.

Laura has no idea what she is talking about.

'Stop it,' Laura's mum says to her, glaring at her over the book.

'What? It was a particularly good sound. She's getting better, Isabel. You have to admit it.'

Laura sits up in the long grass. 'What am I getting better at?'

Gaga raises her eyebrows at her daughter.

'Nothing, love, nothing. Ignore your Gaga, she's going senile.'

'Well, we all know that. But there's nothing wrong with my ears,' Gaga winks at Laura.

Laura giggles. 'Tell me.'

Mum lowers her book. She glares at Gaga, but there's submission in the look, like she's giving her permission but warning her to tread carefully.

'You make these wonderful sounds, dear child. Haven't you noticed?'

'Sounds? No. What kind of sounds?' Laura laughs, thinking Gaga is fooling her.

'All kinds of sounds. Just then you were

408

buzzing like a bee. I almost thought I was about to be stung!' She gives a belly laugh.

'No, I wasn't,' Laura says, confused.

Her mother looks at Gaga, there's concern in her eyes.

'Oh, indeed you did, my little bumble bee,' she closes her eyes and raises her head to the sun.

'No, I didn't, why would you say that?' Laura says, voice shaking.

'I heard you,' she says simply.

'Enough now, Mother.'

'Okay,' she replies, looking at Mum through one eye, then closes it again.

Laura stares at the two of them. Her Gaga lazy in a deckchair, Mum reading her book. Rage rushes through her.

'You're a liar!' she shouts, then runs from the garden and into the house.

★   ★   ★

'How old were you?' Bo asks.

'I was seven. It didn't come up again for a long time. Maybe a year later. Mum didn't want to talk about it, she knew I was sensitive about it, and Gaga was under strict instructions not to say a word.'

'Why do you think you were particularly sensitive about it?'

'Do you know what it's like to be constantly told you're doing something that you don't even know you're doing?'

Bo smiles at that, she bites her lip. She glances

at Solomon, a cheeky look in her eye. 'Let's say yes, I do know that feeling. It makes you feel like you're going crazy. It makes you resent the person who's saying it.'

Solomon hears her.

'Even if you know they're only saying it for your own good,' Laura says. 'Even if you know they couldn't possibly be making it up, because you trust them. It makes you question everything. I made a sound once that really startled Mum. It made her want to talk about it.'

'What sound was it?'

'A police radio.' Laura swallows. 'The sounds I made were only ever sounds that I had heard. I could have got it from the television, of course, but it felt to Mum like it was real. She couldn't ignore that sound. That's the sound they'd both been afraid of for a very long time. She wanted to know where I'd heard it, but I didn't know what sound she was talking about, I didn't realise I'd made it. We managed to narrow it down, though. It was the police radio. I'd heard it one day when they'd both left the house. I'd been in my bedroom, the curtains were closed just like they were supposed to be. Living in a bungalow, we had to be careful about who would look in the windows when Mum and Gaga weren't around.'

'They left you in the house alone at seven years of age?' Bo asks, concerned.

'They were in the woods, they were foraging. I decided to stay home, read a book. I heard a car approach the house. I got down on the ground and hid under the bed. I heard footsteps on the

410

gravel. They were close to my window. I felt like somebody was outside the window. Then I heard the sound of the police radio.' Laura shudders as she tells the story. 'I didn't tell Mum and Gaga about it when they came home, I didn't want them to be afraid. Nothing had happened, so there was no reason to tell them, but then I revealed it anyway in my sounds.'

'How did your mother take it?'

'She panicked. She called Gaga. Made me tell the story over and over, exactly what I heard, over and over again. I was confused. I knew they were nervous around the guards, but I never knew why.'

'Did they tell you?'

'I asked them that day. I thought they were afraid I'd be taken away because of the sounds I was making. As soon as Mum heard that, she sat me down and told me the whole story. Her and Gaga. They told me everything.'

'Everything . . .'

Laura looks at Solomon. She takes a deep breath. 'About how my granddad died.'

Solomon takes his headphones off, 'Laura, are you sure you . . . Bo, maybe we should turn the camera off . . .'

'Already have,' Bo says, turning to look at him, her eyes wide. She and Solomon had both read the tabloid article about Isabel and Hattie's alleged involvement in Laura's grandfather's death, a story Bo had heard in Cork when she had asked around about Hattie and Isabel. It was the story she had been digging for when she interviewed Laura at the Button cottage, but

411

now she's afraid to record it. She's not sure she wants to hear the truth. How everything shifts.

'Laura,' Solomon says gently as he places his equipment down, 'you don't have to tell this story.'

'I think that I do.'

'You don't,' Bo urges. 'Please don't feel that you have to. I'm not pressurising you.'

'Neither am I,' Solomon says firmly. 'In fact,' he adds, getting to his feet, 'perhaps we should take a break, stretch our legs. It's late. It's almost three a.m. It's been a long night, an emotional one. Tomorrow's a big day, we should — '

'I have to tell it for them,' Laura says. 'He can't hurt them any more.'

'Who can't?' Bo asks. 'The garda? Or your granddad?'

'Both of them. I have to tell the story. For Mum's sake, and Gaga's. When they hid me, they hid the truth. They were trying to protect me, but now it's my turn to protect them.'

Solomon looks at Laura, tries to read her. Laura looks at Solomon and Bo studies them both, as they do the thing they've been doing since the moment they saw each other. This non-verbal communication.

She looks away to give them space, to give herself space, to disappear from the weirdness of the situation. From the beginning she saw something between them and pushed them together. She pushed them together to get the story, she used Solomon to get closer to Laura. She can't deny she did it. He wanted to stay away, he knew what he felt, and she pushed him closer to her. She can't blame either of them. She certainly doesn't blame herself, but she sees it all for what it is, realistically and balanced. There is something large between them, something that connects them, something that she's not even sure Solomon sees himself. Solomon, who is so observant of her flaws and so ready to judge others, can't stand far back enough to see himself.

Whatever passes between them helps to move a decision along.

'Fine,' Solomon says, brushing his hand through his long hair. 'If this is what you want.' His voice is so soft, so gentle, so understanding, Bo wonders if she's ever heard him use those tones with her, if he even knows what he sounds like.

'It is,' Laura says firmly. A nod of the head that sends her hair tumbling down over her shoulders. She takes her seat in the armchair in front of the cream curtains that have been drawn, the lamp gives a light warm glow beside her, an earth green cushion and throw are over the back of the chair, helping to bring out the colour in her eyes even more.

Solomon sits down, eyes on Laura the entire time. Bo feels like she's interrupting something here, realises she has felt that way every time they've been in the same room together. She watches Solomon from the corner of her eye as he places his headphones on his ears, adjusts the sound again. She thinks of the countless times he has gotten lost in his own world beneath those headphones, either for work or for his own

413

music. He uses sound as his escape, just like Laura. She looks from her to him. She thinks they really have no idea. Or they do and they have been utterly respectful of her the entire time. In a bizarre twist, she wants to hug them both, then squish them together, the idiots.

Bo turns to Laura. 'Are you ready?'

She nods firmly, a determined look in her eyes.

'My granddad used to hurt them both. Gaga and my mum. He drank too much. Gaga says he was unpleasant most of the time, but he was violent when he'd had a drink. Sergeant O'Grady, the local garda, was his best friend. They'd gone to school together, they drank together. Gaga wasn't from around there, she grew up in Leeds. She was a nanny, moved to Ireland to look after a family. She met Granddad and that was that, she stayed, but she found it hard to settle. She liked to keep to herself. The locals didn't like that very much, which made her keep to herself even more. Granddad was possessive, he used to pick holes in everything she'd say when she was around people, the way she behaved, and so she decided it was better not to go out any more. It suited her, she said. But then he started getting aggressive. He hit her. She went to hospital with cracked ribs. Eventually things got so bad she went to Granddad's friend, Garda O'Grady — not to press charges, but to ask him, as Granddad's friend, to talk to him, help him. He didn't like what she was saying, told her she must be doing something wrong to make him so angry — he turned it all around on her.

'She would never have gone back to Garda O'Grady again, but for Granddad hitting Mum. She told the guard if he didn't do something then she would report him. Garda O'Grady told Granddad what she had said. That night Granddad came home from the pub drunk. He hit Gaga, he said he was going to kill Mum. Gaga told her to run and Mum escaped the house and ran off into the woods. Granddad chased her, but he was two sheets to the wind. It was dark, he couldn't see, he was drunk. Gaga followed him. She watched him trip and hit his head on a rock on the ground. He was begging her for help, to call an ambulance. She couldn't help him. She said she was frozen. There was the man she had loved, the man who had just beaten her and threatened to kill their daughter, and she sat and watched him drown in a stream. She said that was the best thing that she could have done for both of them. She didn't hit him, she didn't kill him, but she didn't try to save him either. She said she chose to save herself and her daughter instead.'

Laura lifts her chin. 'I'm proud of her. I'm proud of what they did, that they were strong enough to defend themselves in the only way they knew how. She had tried talking to his friend, she had tried talking with the law, and it didn't do any good. Granddad died at his own hands.'

'But why did they choose to keep you a secret?'

'Because Garda O'Grady wouldn't leave them

alone. He dragged Gaga in for questioning almost every day for months. He made her life hell. He spoke so badly about her she barely had any customers left. He even tormented Mum, who was only fourteen years old, he brought her in for questioning too. He accused them both of being murderers. He used to drop by the house at all times of the day and night. He scared them, threatened he'd lock them up for the rest of their lives. They lived in fear for so long, but they stayed where they were.

'When the work dried up, Mum had to look around for another job. That's when she started working for the Toolin twins. She had an affair with Tom Toolin. I don't know how long it went on for, but I know that it ended when she became pregnant. She never even told him she had a baby. She was terrified that Garda O'Grady would take me away from her, that he would find a way. Gaga felt the same. So they kept me secret. They didn't want me to have the same life as they had, they didn't want him to torment me. They protected me in the best way they could.'

'Do you think now that what they did to you, the life they chose for you, was right?'

'They were doing the best they could. They were protecting me. I could have left the Toolin cottage at any time, but I was happy there. Growing up, I liked to hide, to be hidden. I liked looking at things from outside, from afar. If I hadn't, I couldn't immerse myself so much in all of the sounds around me. They all became part of me. I absorbed everything, like a sponge, because there was room for it in my life. Where other people have stresses and strains, endless pressures, I had none. I could be complete.'

'Complete,' Bo muses. 'Do you feel complete now that you've left the cottage? Now that you've become immersed in society?'

'No.' Laura looks down at her fingers. 'I don't hear things as much as I used to. There's a lot of noise. A lot of muddled . . . ' She searches for the right word but can't find it. 'I feel a bit broken,' she says sadly.

38

Solomon brushes his teeth, taking longer than usual, staring at himself in the mirror but not seeing himself. He looks up to see Bo standing at the door of the ensuite, bag in hand.

Tears glisten in her eyes.

He spits out the toothpaste hurriedly and wipes his mouth. He moves back into the bedroom, banging his hip off the corner of an open drawer. He hisses with the pain then searches for something to say to Bo, but nothing comes to mind, nothing appropriate, more a feeling of panic that this moment is here and after everything, does he want it to happen? No relief, just panic, dread. The awful feelings of having to confront, deal, not hide from it. The natural wonder of second-guessing that comes with being confronted by change.

'Jack?' he asks, clearing his throat, awkwardly.

'No,' she laughs lightly. 'Just not you.'

He's taken aback by the harshness of it.

'Oh, come on, Sol, it's hardly shocking to either of us.'

He rubs his hip absentmindedly.

'You're in love with her,' she says quickly. She

rubs a single tear away from her cheek. Bo never did crying very well.

Solomon's eyes widen.

'Whether you know it or not, you are. I'm never sure with you. What you know and pretend not to, or what you genuinely are blocking out . . . Sometimes you see everything so clearly and other times you can't even see yourself, but then, isn't that all of us?' She smiles sadly.

Solomon goes to her and wraps his arms around her, tight. She drops the bag and returns it. He kisses her on the top of her head.

'I'm sorry I wasn't better for you,' he whispers.

'Me too,' she replies, and he pulls away and makes a face. She laughs and picks up her bag. 'Well, it's hardly my fault, is it?'

'Never,' he grins, shaking his head, feeling a little lost, like he's losing a part of himself with her.

She stalls at the door, lowers her voice. 'You were great. We had moments of greatness. Something happened to us when we met her. It's what you said once: she holds a mirror up to everyone. I didn't like what I saw of us, not when I saw what you could really be like.'

He feels his face burn.

'She saved us, I think,' she adds, eyes tearing up again but trying to stop them. 'Whoever heard of a saviour that breaks people up? We must have been bad.'

'We weren't,' he says defensively. Their relationship may not have been perfect but they had a lot of good times, or at least, mostly good, but not forever good. He won't see it tarnished.

419

'Where are you going?'

'Not my parents.' She makes a face, backing away.

'Jack?' he asks again.

'You need to get over him,' she says, annoyed.

'So do you,' he replies, and she rolls her eyes and turns away.

And despite the situation, Solomon hates Jack even more and wants to hit him even harder.

'I'm helping *StarrQuest* with Laura's final performance, you just need to get her to the studio tomorrow. I'll come back for the rest of my stuff during the week. Stay away from my underwear drawer.'

'I'll try,' he says, folding his arms and watching her. 'It's just the feel of the lace that gets me.'

She tries not to smile as she opens the door. 'This is the weirdest break-up ever.'

'It was the weirdest together ever.'

'I can think of weirder,' she says, looking over his shoulder.

He turns around, expecting to see Laura and is faced with the closed door of the spare bedroom. By the time he turns back to Bo she has left, and shut the door behind her. He only realises then that his body is trembling lightly, from the shock, from the loss. He looks at Laura's closed door again and thinks of what Bo said.

In love with her.

Of course he is. He knew it the second he saw her.

He knows now the solution to his dilemma, whether it's better to protect something precious and rare, or to share it. His love for her was precious, and the intensity of it was rare. His love for her was better not shared. She'd do better without him, he brought her to this point and he hadn't done her any favours. He was no good for someone like her. Precious was better kept protected.

His role now is to fix the mess he got her into, the mess he made of her. He took her from her nest, fractured her life, left her. He'll do everything he can to mend and rebuild. He closes his bedroom door and hears a sound from Laura that breaks his heart. Silence.

39

Close to five a.m. Solomon wakes to the sound of the television in the living room. Laura is still awake. He doesn't hold out much hope for her performance that is technically tonight now that the sun is shining brightly and the morning has begun, and he's not sure he cares. He weighs up the damage if she doesn't show up at the studio; Laura doesn't owe anything to the show, but she certainly owes it to herself. The public have got the wrong impression of her, and while nobody should care what people they don't know think of them, when somebody has something so beautiful to show the world, when people can benefit from her just being, that's when they should be understood. She owes it to herself to perform one final time, as herself, in the way that she wants to. He has no idea what Bo has up her sleeve, but he trusts her. The woman she has been for the past twenty-four hours has cemented in his mind her greatness, the reason why she's won so many awards this year. She's a champion in her own arena, she can capture hearts and minds through her storytelling.

He can't go to sleep, and while he's trying to

stay away from Laura, especially in such intimate surroundings, he can't lie here while she's out there. He's hardly going to jump on her without her permission, but he bloody well wants to. Best to stay away. Yet knowing that, he gets out of bed, doesn't bother with his T-shirt. He opens his bedroom door. She is sitting on the couch, her back to him. She's watching *The Toolin Twins*.

He watches her. Wearing one of his T-shirts, her long legs folded on the couch beside her, her hair falling lazily down, messy from her restless lie in her bed. His heart pounds. He's about to say something, something comforting, something warm about her father and uncle, when she rewinds it for a few seconds and plays it again. He doesn't want to disturb her hearing whatever she wanted to see or hear again. He waits, watching her. And then, when it's finished, she rewinds it and plays it again, her back straightening. He looks at the TV, at the brothers on the mountain surveying their sheep. She rewinds and plays it again.

It's not the right time for him. He was right about it probably never being the right time. He closes his door softly and falls asleep to the sound of Laura rewinding and replaying her father and uncle.

★   ★   ★

Laura keeps her eyes on the television as she hears the door behind her open. Her skin prickles, goosebumps rise on her skin. She sits there, frozen. Just him and her in the flat; she heard Bo leave, heard some of their conversation, tried not to listen as a mark of respect. She has felt so in the way of their relationship she should at least stay out of their goodbye, let them own that. So she'd lain in bed, eyes wide open, not at all tired despite the hour, the room smelling of Solomon, the same smell she'd smelled in the forest the first day they'd met.

She'd sensed him before she'd smelled him.

She had smelled his scent in the wind long before she'd seen him.

She'd watched him long before he even sensed her.

Watching him from behind the tree she had an overwhelming desire to be seen by him. Not like when she was a child. She'd watched other children playing in the woods and she'd wanted to play with them, but she knew better; most of the time she was happy just observing. That felt like enough. But in the forest on the day she first met Solomon, she had lost all reason and selfishly wanted his eyes on her. She'd deliberately made a sound so he would turn around. That moment had made her life change. It wasn't her mother dying, Gaga moving her to the cottage or her father dying. The biggest risk Laura had ever taken was in making a sound so that Solomon could see her. A man like that, she wanted him to see her.

And for a moment, in those woods, he'd been hers.

Everything for her changed; life before she'd met Solomon, and life after.

She swallowed the hard lump gathered in her throat. She's dreamt of his hands on her body, his kiss on her skin, she's imagined his touch, what he would feel like. Would he be gentle or strong, how he would kiss? She's watched him with Bo, from the corner of her eye, she's seen the tenderness he's capable of and wonders, would he be that way, or different with her? She can't help but wonder how his skin tastes, the feel of his tongue. From the moment she saw him, she hasn't been able to stop these thoughts.

She knew it was wrong to feel it. She'd tried to stop, but she kept being pulled back to him. She knew from her mum and Gaga that there was no place for a woman who took another woman's man. They would have disapproved; she already disapproved of herself, even though they were only private thoughts. She'd clung to him, like a life raft, not thinking about anybody else. She'd thought being so far away from him in Australia would end it, keep her away from him, the other side of the world. It hadn't. She'd thought meeting other men would distract her. Maybe because he was the only one she knew, that's why her feelings were so heightened. That hadn't been the case either. It seemed ironic, romantic and twisted that the first man she'd met would be the only one she ever wanted.

None of the distractions in the world would work. And his scent . . . it wasn't just his cologne, it was his skin. Sleeping in his room, living in his home, she felt like she was embraced by him. When she turned her head to the pillow and buried her face in it, it was like burying her face in him. She'd groan lightly with frustration because it wasn't enough. To be surrounded by him, on the outside of him, near him. It wasn't enough. She'd moved to the couch to distract herself.

She's afraid to breathe as she senses him behind her. She closes her eyes while the documentary plays and she imagines him coming up behind her, his lips on her neck, hands on her hips, then everywhere. Startled by her thoughts so close to him, she opens her eyes and focuses hard on the documentary, on what her uncle and father are saying. Her heart pounds, and not because she is seeing her father alive again.

Watching the documentary hasn't provided her with any solace at all so far. If anything, she feels even more alone. She was hoping to feel connected, rooted again, stop her floating head from drifting, ground herself with what is happening in her life. Start feeling, start hearing again, start making sounds again. However, she can't help feeling that throughout the entire documentary she was living only metres away and yet there isn't a trace of her, a hint of her.

'You never wanted a wife, or children?' Bo asks, on the documentary, and suddenly Laura sits up.

Joe shakes his head, amused by the question, a little shy. A *woman*? Even with his lined aged face, he looks like a schoolboy when faced with this topic.

'I'm busy here. With the farm. Lots to do.'

'Sure who'd have him?' Tom teases.

'What about you, Tom? Have you never wanted marriage or a family?'

He spends more time thinking about it than Joe did.

'Everything I have, everything I need, is right here, on this mountain.'

Laura pauses this, her heart hammering in her chest, and yes, this time it's because of her father. She rewinds it, then plays it again. She watches Bo ask the same question of the two men in caps bent over hay bales. Whatever about Rachel's stunning cinematography, the sight of the identical twins alone is beautiful. They have aged in exactly the same way.

She plays it again.

Her father.

'Everything I have, everything I need, is right here, on this mountain.'

On this mountain.

Laura's heart is pounding so much. To stop herself getting carried away, she scans the background to make sure it's the right mountain. Just in case. Maybe there's another child on another mountain, another woman who came after her mum. She's sure it isn't true, but just in case, something so big as this, she needs to understand correctly. She rewinds it again. Plays.

By the time she has watched it for the fourth time, she's sure. He had time to think about it, so much time that even Joe looked at him with that shy schoolboy grin on his face. His brother's being asked about girls, he sniggers at him.

What was on Tom's mountain? Joe, his home, his business, his sheep, his dogs, his memories and, yes, Laura. She lived on that mountain, so that meant he was including Laura too. He might not have loved her in a conventional way that fathers love their daughters, but he acknowledged her, he recognised her, he valued her. And that means the world to Laura.

Only once she has thought it all through does she remember Solomon. She turns around, a big smile on her face. He's gone. His bedroom door is closed. Her smile fades fast, until she remembers her father's words, then she goes to bed feeling as though he has just given her the hug she longed for but he never gave her until now.

40

Solomon gently raps on Laura's door. He's tentative at first and then he knocks with more confidence.

'Laura, I — '

The door opens, she's wearing his T-shirt, that's all. She looks at him, sleepy green eyes barely open or used to the daylight. She has a sleepy smell, a warm cosy bed smell and he wants to fall into her, literally. He looks her up and down while she rubs her eyes, her long legs, lean thighs disappear beneath his T-shirt.

'Sorry about the T-shirt,' she apologises. 'I should have asked you but . . . ' She can't think of an excuse and he doesn't care.

'No, don't apologise. It's fine. It's great. I mean, you're great. It looks great on you,' he flounders. The neck is too wide for her, there are three buttons on the top, they're all open so that he can see the curve of her breasts, one side gapes and if he leaned forward he would probably see . . .

She looks down at the plate in his hand.

'Oh. Yes. I made you a chicken salad. With pomegranate. Just because pomegranates are in everything these days.'

She smiles, touched.

'You should eat before we go to the studio, this'll be better than that plastic crap.' He looks down at the dish again. 'Or then again, maybe not.' He feels like he's waffling. He's a grown man, who wants desperately to go to bed with this woman, he needs to act like it. Though he can't go to bed with her, that's the problem. He will ruin her. He's already done a good job of it so far. He straightens up, takes a step backward as he realises he's practically leering at her. 'We need to leave in a few hours. You slept all morning.'

'I couldn't sleep last night.' She looks terrified at the thought of the show tonight.

'Me neither.' Their eyes lock. He'd swear she has a hypnotic effect on him. He snaps out of it. 'The show starts at eight. You're on first. You don't need to be there until six. Later than usual, but they said you don't need to hang around. They'll do the sound checks without you.'

'What about a rehearsal?' she asks, confused.

'They said you don't need one. You'll be absolutely fine, Laura. It's the last show. The last two minutes you'll ever be up there. Make it count.'

'You were making me feel better until you said that.'

'What I mean is, you need to show them who you really are. In fact, don't show them, just be you. And they'll see.' When she smiles at him, he laughs. 'I'm shit at this, aren't I? Last time I had a warm-up gig for an act, twenty people left before the main act arrived.'

She giggles. 'Maybe you could do that for me tonight, make it easier.'

She takes the plate from his hand and walks to the kitchen table. She sits down. He watches her eat. She crosses one leg over the other. She's barefoot. His heart thumps. He should leave, but he can't leave her alone in the apartment, not when she's been entrusted to him to bring her to the studio in one piece. She might start climbing balconies again.

He smiles at the thought of what happened last night.

'What?'

'Nothing.' He sits at the table opposite her. Whenever he thinks he should get away from her, he does the exact opposite. But then, the way she looks at him is distracting. 'I was just thinking of you being the super ninja last night.'

She bites her lip. 'I'm glad her husband didn't come.'

'Hey, if he calls around here today, I'll be straight out that window. You're on your own.' He leans down on the table, head on his crossed arms and looks up at her.

'Hey,' she grins, kicking him lightly under the table.

Silence. He watches her eat. He watches her think, studies the furrowing of her brow. Her seriousness makes him smile, every fucking thing she does makes him smile, and when she looks at him his face twitches from hiding the telling smiles. He feels like he's an overexcited twelve-year-old.

'I was in rehearsal for two days for the last performance. A big elaborate dance routine. This week, nothing. I'm not sure how to take that.' She looks at him. 'Did you see it?'

He can't stop smiling, and now she thinks he's laughing at her.

'Of course I saw it,' he says. 'It was terrible.'

She groans, throws her head back, her long neck stretching.

'It wasn't your fault. Bo suggested a link to the forest to their artistic director, but Goldilocks and the Three Bears wasn't quite what she was thinking. It wasn't your fault.'

'I told Jack I didn't want to do it, but they asked if I had any other suggestions and I couldn't think of anything.'

'So it was their way or nothing.'

She nods. 'Was it shocking?'

He thinks of how he felt when he saw her. It had felt like such a long time since he'd seen her: she'd moved to the hotel, been to Australia, he felt completely cut off from her. 'I was just happy to see you, it had been a while.'

She smiles, her eyes shining.

'But I know you can be so much better. Bo's working on something for you for tonight. She's putting a lot of work into it. I think she wants to redeem herself, show you that she cares.' He wants to do the same, but he's not sure how to.

'She doesn't owe me anything.' She frowns. 'All those mistakes are mine. I own them.'

'Well then, on the theme of owning mistakes . . . About what happened with Rory . . . '

Laura cringes, can barely think about it.

Solomon sits up. 'I let you down. In a big way. I'll never forgive myself for that, but I want you to know that I'm sorry. I should have protected you better. I just didn't want to . . . I thought I should give you space. For whatever reasons, my own reasons, I didn't want to crowd you and this new path you're on.' He looks at her, wondering if he should continue.

'I saw you three years ago,' she interrupts him suddenly, as if she didn't hear a word of what he'd said, though he knows she did, she was listening intently. 'On the mountain. I was foraging. I was looking for an elder bush. Tom had cleared them all away, because he was trying to keep the hedge stock-proof, which bothered me because the berries are tasty in autumn and the flower . . . it doesn't matter.'

'Go on,' he urges her.

'The flower has the real power. It adds an incredible flavour to wines, drinks and jams. Gaga used to make the most delicious elderflower cordial, at its best after only six months. I was on a mission. I wanted to find an elder bush that Joe and Tom hadn't destroyed, so I moved away further than I usually would. I came out from the woods and you were standing there, with your eyes closed, the headphones around your neck, that bag over your shoulder. I didn't know what you were doing at the time. Now I know that you were listening, for sounds, but all I knew then was that you looked so peaceful.'

'I didn't see you.'

She shakes her head. 'I didn't want you to see me.'

'This was three years ago?'

'May.' The fourth of May, she remembers. And not just because the elderflower was in bloom. 'I asked Tom who you were. He said you were making a TV show. That you liked sounds too. That's all he said.' She swallows hard before making a confession. 'I watched you a few times.'

'Really?' he smiles. His heart pounds. 'You should have said hi.'

'I wish I had,' she says softly. 'Every day that I didn't find you again, I wished that you'd seen me the previous time but then, when it came to it, I couldn't. So this time when I saw you in the forest, after not having seen you for so long, I couldn't risk it happening again. That's why I made a sound. I wanted your attention.'

She looks at him from under long eyelashes. There, the truth was out.

'Well, you certainly got my attention,' he says, reaching across the table and sliding the plate away. He takes her hands in his.

She wants him to kiss her.

He wants to kiss her so badly. He moves around the table, places a hand on her cheek and pulls her close. He kisses her gently at first, drawing away to look in her eyes, to make sure it's okay. Her pupils are dilated, the green rim around them almost luminous. She closes her eyes, then kisses him hungrily.

She sensed him before she smelled him, she smelled him before she saw him. She saw him before he saw her. She knew him before he knew her. He loved her before he kissed her.

41

The tension, adrenaline and excitement that emanates from the Slaughter House is visceral as Laura and Solomon draw closer in the SUV. There are hundreds of fans gathering outside behind barricades, waving posters, cameras in hand, singing songs of their favourite bands that have nothing to do with the talent show but everything to do with uniting these people in mutual fandom. They cheer as the SUV approaches, the sound of so many voices making Laura's stomach flip. Solomon feels it too, and he's not even going anywhere near the stage. He wouldn't blame her if she took flight now. She doesn't owe anybody this much.

Security men in black combat gear and high-visibility vests, with walkie-talkies, line the barricades and the entrance to the Slaughter House. The media have gathered, more photographers and journalists than ever, now that it's a global show, and they are anxiously trying to get a glimpse of who is arriving. It has become less of who will win and more will Lyrebird perform? StarrGaze aren't stupid, they know what the public and media want and they're not about to protect Laura now, not when she's kept them in the dark all week about whether she would perform or not, so despite Michael's newfound loyalty to Lyrebird, he warns them that he will open the car door that faces the media.

When Michael gets out of the car, Laura and Solomon know they have less than a minute before everything goes insane. Solomon takes her hand and squeezes it. They are far from their bed of safety where in silence, in peace, in absolute beautiful serenity they could explore each other. An entire afternoon of touching each other in ways they had both been fantasising about for so long.

Now they are exposed. The door slides open and their hands fall apart. Some things must be kept sacred. Laura looks out and she's faced with flashes, a sea of cameras, faces, calls, cheers. Some boos from those who are still resentful of her night out.

Michael nods at her supportively, he reaches his hand into the car, and she takes it. It's large, firm, warm, strong, it has knocked the lights out of more people than she'd care to know but his touch is gentle as he guides her out. She slides across the leather seat, protecting her modesty from the cameras that aim low as she steps out of the car. She's learned. She wears another of Solomon's shirts, a green checked one, wrapped with a tan leather belt, tan boots with suede fringing around the ankles. She layered his shirt with her own smaller denim shirt and her arms are filled with bangles. Lyrebird-chic, as *Grazia* magazine has dubbed the look. The crowd yell, the media shout at her for interviews. Unsure what to do, Laura waves, smiles apologetically to the boo-ers and allows Mickey to usher her to the doors. As soon as she's inside she's greeted by Bianca, who's grinning.

'Welcome back,' she says happily, without an ounce of sarcasm. 'We're going straight to hair and make-up. We don't have much time — everybody has done their sound checks, they're all dressed and made up, doing their pre-interviews and ready to go. You're not doing a sound check, you're on last at seven forty-five.' She lowers her voice to an excited whisper, 'You are going to *love* what they've done. Let's go.'

She starts walking and Lyrebird and Solomon follow.

'Have you been on the happy pills, Bianca?' Solomon asks, and Laura smiles.

'Fuck off, Solomon,' Bianca says.

'There she is. Our girl is back.'

Bianca struggles to keep the smile from her face. She leads them to wardrobe and when they step inside they see Bo, with a man that Laura has never met before.

'Laura, Solomon,' Bo says, a little nervously, looking from one to the other. Laura feels her face burn at the thought of what she and Solomon have done that day. Her cheeks betray her and Bo must notice, but she doesn't say anything. 'This is Benoît. He's the artistic director for tonight's final. He worked with Jack on his previous tours and Jack asked him to come back for you. He's an absolute magician in his field,' Bo says, barely able to contain her excitement.

Benoît is bald, wears head-to-toe black, but the most stylish black silks and velvet that Laura has ever seen. He wears gold round glasses and is elegant in his stance and posture. When he speaks, his voice is relaxing, hypnotic, lyrical.

'It is an honour to meet you, dear Lyrebird,' Benoît says, taking Laura's hand warmly. 'I'm a great fan of your work. I hope you will like what we have done for you this evening.'

'No trips to the woods?' Solomon asks.

Benoît looks insulted and also offended by the idea of repeating the semi-final disaster. 'No, dear, this show is in the hands of the professionals. We do not have much time,' he says eagerly.

'I'm so glad you're here!' Caroline welcomes Laura. 'My goodness, have we saved the best for last.'

Laura grins, feeling so loved, so surrounded by warmth and joy. Benoît sits in the chair beside her.

'Lyrebird — do you mind if I call you Lyrebird? I have known so many Lauras in my life, never a Lyrebird.'

Laura grins. 'Of course.'

'Thank you.' He dips his head. 'We have a spectacular display for you this evening. What Bo has done is mesmerising.'

'What do I have to do?'

'You just need to be you. No script, no horrific topless dancers dressed as bears, nothing but you and whatever you want to do.'

Laura's eyes widen in terror and he chuckles warmly. 'I know, my dear, to be your true self is

438

often the most terrifying. Tonight' — he picks up a drawing from a skctchbook — 'I have created a life-size birdcage. Only it is not for a bird, it is for you, dear Lyrebird. It's polished bronze — my dear friend made it for me especially. An expensive but necessary commission, I think the producers of *StarrQuest* will agree. It will suspend from the stage ceiling. I had to get special reinforcements soldered to the ceiling to make sure it would hold. It will, we have tested it.' He closes his eyes, splays his fingers. 'Perfect. Inside it, is a swing. You will sit on the swing. There will be a screen on stage for you to look at. Do look at it. Take in the images, absorb it, observe it, do whatever you wish. On that screen will be images and you will make whatever sounds you like. It is your story, your moment. We have taken you from you over the past few weeks . . . ' How honourable of him to include himself in this accusation, even though he had nothing to do with the show prior to this moment. 'And now we are giving you back to you. Express yourself as you so wish.'

Laura looks at the simple sketch and smiles. 'Thank you.'

'On your body will be a thin bodystocking. Gold. The finest silk upon which Caroline has hand-sewn three hundred delicate crystals. Of course your modesty will be protected by this flesh-coloured shape-wear. It is beautiful, yes?'

'Wow.'

'See how the crystals catch the light? Caroline did that.'

Caroline smiles excitedly and blushes.

Laura runs her hands over the fine silk, the jewels sparkling as they move. The stocking seems so tiny, too small to fit her body. She looks at Solomon, who raises his eyebrows suggestively.

'*Oui*, all the men will be hungry for you in this.' Benoît smiles.

Laura looks at Bo nervously, Solomon dips his head. Bo stands back, she looks away at the walls, at the rails of clothes, everywhere but at the two of them.

Benoît returns to the subject of her wardrobe, his excitement evident. 'Caroline, please reveal the final piece.'

His eyes don't move from Laura for one second. He drinks in her reaction, eyes gauging whether Laura likes what she's about to see or not. She plans to pretend that she does. It's evident that a lot of work has gone into all this, she can sense the importance of the moment for him, and she is grateful. But there is no need to act, what Caroline reveals takes her breath away. Tears immediately fill her eyes, the beauty is so great.

Benoît is enchanted by her reaction and gleefully claps his hands together. 'A thing of beauty, for a thing of beauty.'

'Wow,' Solomon says.

It's a pair of wings, a beautiful great big pair of wings, which will be attached to Laura's back. They shimmer with the same crystal embellishments as the bodystocking, but multiplied by thousands.

'Ten thousand in total,' Caroline whispers, as

if anybody speaking at a normal level will break the fragile wings. But they don't look fragile. They are big, and strong. The wing-span is six feet in total. They are grand, majestic, so beautiful as they sparkle in the tiny wardrobe room, Laura can only imagine how they'll appear on stage.

'Can I . . . ?'

'Of course, of course, they're yours,' Benoît says.

Laura stands to touch them.

'You did all this?' she asks Caroline.

'We did it together. From Benoît's designs. It was . . .' Her eyes fill. 'Well it was exhilarating to create something so beautiful. It took me back to my college days and . . . well, you deserve them.'

'Thank you,' she whispers.

As Laura takes the wings in her hands, the room is filled with the sound of a great flapping of wings, a bald eagle's, though most there don't know it, moving in slow motion. The sound fills the room and everybody freezes, eyes wide open. Laura thinks perhaps they've added the sound effects to the wings until she realises the sound is coming from herself.

Caroline's hand flies to her chest. 'I told you, Benoît,' she whispers.

'My word,' Benoît says, looking at her as though enchanted. Standing tall, back straight, he dips his head and bows as if meeting Laura for the first time. 'Let's get to work, Lyrebird. We have much to do.'

★　★　★

'I got the idea for the cage from one of my favourite films, *Zouzou*. Do you know it?' Benoît asks as they dress her.

Laura shakes her head.

He inhales through his teeth. 'Sacrilege. But you will. Tomorrow, everyone will. In it, Josephine Baker, the first black woman to star in a major motion picture, sings for her life, sings like a bird in a cage, twittering and swinging. It is an important scene, an important film.'

As Benoît talks, in the background Laura keeps abreast of what's going on in the show. It has begun already. Six acts in the final. The VTs recorded earlier this week, or during the course of today by her six housemates show how important tonight is in their lives.

'Now or never.'

'Do or die.'

'Sing for my life.'

'Performance of a lifetime.'

'Doing this for my children. So they will be proud of their mum.'

Benoît tuts. 'They will be proud anyway, but you and I know that, don't we, Lyrebird.'

Laura nods. He has a calming effect, an all-seeing, all-knowing soothsayer who has been here a thousand times. Nothing but his creations are a big deal. Everything will be fine. Laura feels calm.

Alice and Brendan's performance is flawless, heart-stopping. They've raised all the bars, taken major risks using fire, water, swords — everything is flying in the air. Alice looks strong and powerful, Brendan lean and mean. They work perfectly together.

Serena the soprano receives the longest standing ovation ever in the history of the show.

Sparks controls his shaking hands.

The twelve-year-old gymnast tumbles, leaps and cartwheels through hoops of fire.

Nobody puts a foot wrong. Rachel and her wife Susie arrive with their new bundle, Brennan. And Laura holds that little body in her hands and gets lost in his cries. And then, as Alan takes to the stage, walkie-talkies in the hallway followed by a knock on the door send Laura's stomach churning. They've come for her, it's time to move. She looks at Solomon and he glances awkwardly at Bo.

'Oh, kiss her, for fuck's sake!' she snaps, deliberately turning away and looking at the wall.

Rachel's eyes widen, unsure of what's happening as Solomon gives Laura a long lingering kiss. 'Just be you,' he whispers in her ear. 'As much as you can be in a gold bodystocking and six-foot wings.'

Laura snorts, then laughs and they break apart.

'Charming,' Benoît says, pretending to be unimpressed, but his twinkling mischievous eyes betraying him.

Laura's brought to the stage, her wings are closed down now, Benoît has told her to extend them only when she gets inside the cage, because otherwise she won't fit through the cage door. She stands by the stage and watches Alan bring the house down. His act has been perfectly honed, appears completely effortless despite the hours she knows he has put in. It consists of

Mabel telling him that she's breaking up with him. She's leaving him. She's found another man. A man who makes her feel different, sound different. That man is Jack Starr. To applause, Jack takes to the stage and puts his hand inside Mabel, which is odd for Mabel as only one man has ever been inside her. As soon as she opens her mouth she sounds completely different, a deeper, ridiculous voice. It's the second puppet that Alan was working on, the one whose facial movements he could control with a remote control. Alan fights with Mabel. She wants him back. He won't take her back. He stands by the wings, arms folded, and they shout at each other while Jack, in the middle of them, laughs until he cries. Finally Alan agrees to take Mabel back and they're reunited.

The crowd loves it.

He nails it.

And then Alan is finished and they're going to Laura's VT. She hears her own voice, the real her this time, talking about a journey, how her life has changed. It's nothing ground-breaking, but it's her and it's the truth. As she listens to the sound of her voice playing out to the country live, she passes Alan, who squeezes her hand and kisses her quickly on the cheek.

'You can do it.'

The cage lowers from the ceiling and though the crowd are supposed to be quiet, they can't help but go *ooh*. The cage door opens and Laura steps inside. Benoît was modest. It is not a simple cage as his sketch showed, but a beautiful, elaborate piece of art, with not just bars, but bars that appear to be twisted like vines, polished bronze leaves growing from them. She sits on the swing, somebody behind her clips her into a safety harness and the cage door closes. The cage is slowly suspended in the air. Her legs and body sparkle as it is raised, all eyes are on her. She feels beautiful, she feels like she is glowing, she feels magical and vulnerable trapped in this cage, high in the air. She sits up straight, perfect posture on the swing, not knowing what's going to happen but knowing that she must focus on the screen.

'I've come a long way,' she says on the screen. 'But I've a distance to go. My dream? My dream is to soar happily into my future.'

Then the lights are up, not all of them, a spotlight just on her. She turns to the screen and watches. She recognises scenes from Bo's *Toolin Twins* documentary. Sweeping views from the sky over the mountains of Gougane Barra, wind farms, sheep farms. Her mountain, her home. The tips of trees. She closes her eyes briefly and breathes in. She almost feels like she's at home. She imagines her morning walks, foraging, stretching her legs, exercising, exploring. The sounds of her feet on the soft earth, the rain on the leaves, the four seasons of living with nature. The birds, angry, content, fighting, building, hungry chicks. The distant sounds of tractors, of chainsaws, of vehicles.

Her cottage. Home. She thinks of the water boiling over the fire, the fire crackling on winter evenings when it gets dark so fast she can't go anywhere after three p.m. Onions frying, the smell that fills the room, onions from her own garden. The cockerel that wakes her up, her two chickens who provide her eggs every morning, the crack of eggs against the frying pan, the sound of them oozing on to the heat, her goat who gave her milk. The sound of a stormy night, the wind howling through the shed. Mossie's snoring, the owls, the bats.

Then an image of her home with Gaga and Mam. The studio. Jazz, a record player, the sewing machine, the hot iron, the sudden sound of the steam, scissors cutting through fabric, scissors landing on the other tools as they're thrown down.

A photograph of Mam and Gaga. The clink of glasses, the giggles and laughter of two women who adored one another, lived for one another, only had each other, only wanted each other and then opened their hearts for another.

The Slaughter House. Laura's first performance. Jack, chewing his gum, lights, camera, action, the applause of a crowd. The countdown, the security walkie-talkies. Laura's infamous night out. Photos in the press. Flashes, name-calling, heckling, the girl in the toilet who wouldn't help, who wanted the selfie, the high heels on the floor, the bang of the toilet doors, the lock, the flush, the roar of the hand-driers. Glass smashing, flashes, press yelling, everyone calling her name, blurred faces and blurred sounds. The confusion, head down a toilet, echoing, vomiting. Are you okay? The embarrassment, help help, nobody will help.

All the noise of Dublin city. Too many sounds, she can barely keep up with everything she hears in her ears. Ambulances, sirens, cappuccino machines, ATM cards, phones ringing, messages beeping, cash registers, video games, the hiss of buses breaking, all the new sounds.

The police station. A photo of Laura leaving, trying to cover her face.

'Are you okay?' She hears the sound of the kind garda.

Then suddenly the video ends and she sees herself. She is watching herself on the screen, a birdlike woman, sparkling under the lights. The journey brings her to now.

What sound does she make for now? For the end of her journey. She is silent.

After all of Benoît's work she has forgotten the wings, she was supposed to extend the wings. Panicking she pulls the string and they extend. They fan open and they are so strong they almost lift her off the swing.

The audience gasp. She looks at them, as they examine her.

It's not the end of her journey. She thinks of Solomon. His awkward throat-clearing, his satisfied sigh, his contented groans, a strum on a guitar. The happiness of the beauty of this afternoon. The magical sound of his mother playing the harp. The waves lapping on the beach across from their home. The seagulls. Just the two of them, alone, they don't need anyone else or anything else. This is not the end. It is only the beginning.

She thinks of Rachel and her beautiful little baby Brennan and suddenly she hears his cry in the studio. They must have brought him into the studio, Rachel and Susie will be embarrassed he has made the sound, broken the silence but nobody seems to mind, or to look around. Most people are smiling, some are wiping their eyes. She likes the cry of the baby, it's not a sad sound, she could listen to it all day, and so she does and she starts to swing on the swing, her wings fully extended.

She looks to the side and she sees the people who have brought her here.

Bo is crying.

Solomon is looking up at her proudly, grinning, eyes shining.

Bianca is sobbing.

Even Rachel is struggling. Brennan sleeps in Susie's arms and she realises it wasn't him at all, it was herself who made that sound. She should have known.

The cage descends slowly. She hangs on to the swing until the cage gently touches the stage. The crowd are silent as she descends. And then she doesn't know what to do; her time isn't up yet. She has five more seconds. It counts down on the screen above her. On one, the cage door suddenly opens, automatically.

She smiles at Benoît's final touch.

42

Laura and Alan stand in the centre of the *StarrQuest* stage. Jack is between them, but Laura reaches across and takes Alan's hand. His hand is clammy, on his other hand is his loyal Mabel, who's covering her eyes with her hand in anticipation of the result.

Behind them, their fellow finalists stand in the darkness, their lights extinguished as soon as Jack announced they were eliminated in the public vote. Alice has a scowl on her face. The twelve-year-old gymnast has already had an argument with her parents in the corridor. And now it is down to Alan and Laura as the final votes are in.

The tension builds but Laura feels an overwhelming sense of calm. She has won already. She has achieved what she wanted, and more. She has truly soared. Reached her own personal new heights. She feels free, she embarked on an adventure, she changed her life. Hidden for so long, she's not hidden any more.

Jack Starr rips open the golden envelope. There's sweat on his brow and upper lip.

'And the winner of *StarrQuest* 2016 is

. . . ALAN AND MABEL!'

She grins. The cage door opens again. And she's free to go.

Part 4

From about the end of June until middle-July the singing of the male bird undergoes a curious change. During this period his powers of mimicry are rarely exerted and he concentrates on the rendition of his own peculiar notes and call and the long, mellow, warbling nuptial song of his tribe. This song is incomparably the loveliest item of his vast repertoire, and for at least a fortnight in each year he applies himself assiduously to its perfection, singing it over and over from dawn till dark. During this period the male and female birds are never apart. They tread a fixed round through the forests and the underbrush or bracken from mound to mound, and at every mound the male bird stops to display and sing.

Ambrose Pratt, *The Lore of the Lyrebird*

43

Laura is sitting on the balcony, in another of Solomon's T-shirts. Her long legs extend to where her feet are crossed on the top of the balcony, her hands are wrapped around a cup of green tea. Her eyes are closed and lifted to the morning sun. Solomon watches her lazily from the couch where he lies with his guitar, strumming gently, slowly concocting a new song, mumbling words here and there, trying to make things fit together. He could never do this in front of Bo, he always needed to be alone, he felt too self-conscious, but Laura's company is calming. She listens and occasionally mimics the sound of his strumming. He stops to listen to her, she attempts it a few times until she has perfected the sound. He practises his song, she practises hers. He smiles and shakes his head at the wonderful bizarreness of it.

Laura opens her eyes and looks at the folded newspaper that Solomon placed beside her. She felt him leave it there before sitting on the couch to strum on his guitar.

She sees the headline. SUPERB LYREBIRD.

'You told me never to read these.'

He continues strumming. 'You should read this one.'

She sighs and removes her feet from the balcony, needing to plant herself, to ready herself for possible attack, though she knows it must have positive content if Solomon is pushing it on her. It's a piece about the *StarrQuest* final by TV critic Emilia Belvedere. Laura braces herself as she reads.

My mother was a midwife but related more with being a keen gardener. She dedicated most of her spare time to fighting a war with unwanted plants between the cracks of her pavement, in the lawn, on her hands and knees muttering curses and threats. Cracks and crevasses in pavements are comfortable, sneaky hiding places for weed seeds, carried in the breeze. Pulling them from their cracks is futile. Dandelions, thistles, sticker weed, pigweed, yarrow — these were my mother's arch-enemies. I think of this analogy in particular when contemplating the part reality talent shows play in our society.

The judges, the finders, are not the breeze that carry the seeds. They have an element of my mother, in that they notice and they pluck, but are (at first) without her aggression or irritation. Their purpose is not to annihilate — though that is all too often the result of their efforts. They see something rare, something pretty, but in the wrong place, and they uproot them. The finders put them in a fancy vase or jar, a place where they will be shown to advantage for all to see. They convince the weed it is where it belongs. They convince the weed to fight with all of the other weeds who always stood out from each other in their own cracks in their own pavements and never had to fight before. This is both the skill and the downfall of the talent show. The finders cannot be keepers. They uproot, they pull, they replant, and it soon loses its beauty in its new habitat. It cannot grow, it cannot thrive, it has lost its chink where once it sprouted with vitality. It is lost to the great unknown, in an unnatural world that doesn't understand.

The finders' purpose is to shine a light, yet often the light is so bright it stuns or blinds them.

From their moment of conception, I have despised television talent shows. It is an hour of discovered talent displayed in the wrong place, nurtured, if at all, in the wrong way. It may not have been concentrated vinegar poured on these rare weeds before our very eyes, but it might as well have been. This year, one talent show changed my mind, the finder of the rarest weed, that has grown and flowered in the most distant of fissures . . .

Alan and Mabel was a worthy winner of **StarrQuest**, a likeable act, an act you cheer for, chuckle at, cannot help to be moved by with its veiled desperation, but Lyrebird stole the nation's heart — correction, the world's heart. I was transported, in that one performance, to my childhood ... not something that happens often. Usually it is escape we desire, to get away from what we know so well. Lyrebird brought me to the core of me.

Lyrebird's sounds came so swiftly, in waves, sometimes overlapping one another wondrously, that it's impossible for everybody to have heard everything, even in playback. Each sound speaks to every person differently. While dealing with the repercussions of one, another arrives. Doors opened inside of me, feelings came in surprising bursts, here, there everywhere. A flutter in my heart, a pop in my stomach, a lump in my throat, a prick in my tear ducts. I heard my childhood, my adolescence, my youth, my womanhood, my marriage, my motherhood — all in two minutes. It was so great, so overwhelming I held my breath and my tears fell while I watched a still creature on a swing, in a cage, tell us the story of her life. A life in sounds, her sounds, but parts of life that we all share. We came together, it brought us together, a collective gathering of hearts and minds.

It may have lacked the razzle-dazzle of other finals; no doubt the absence of pyrotechnics is something that others will attack, but its subtlety was its strength, its majesty. It took great power to be so refined, and of course with Benoît Moreau at its helm, aided by documentary maker Bo Healy, there should be no surprise. Yet there is. It was filled with humanity, emotion and warmth. It was raw, it was gritty, soft and gentle. It rose and it fell before rising again. Harsh sounds during subtle images, gentle sighs of acceptance when faced with unyielding sorrow.

Lyrebird's performance was captivating, enchanting, a real moment of not just TV magic, but the kind of magic that rarely occurs in life. Whatever happened in **StarrQuest HQ**, whatever conversations or alleged altercations took place, it was right, it was fair, it was necessary. Right won out. People will forget, as they usually do, what they felt in those two minutes. It dissipated perhaps in the time it took them to boil the kettle, put the children to bed, send a text message or change the channel, but the feeling was there in the moment, and that they can't deny.

A change occurred, not just in the TV talent show: it happened within me, too. As a result, I am a TV critic, a woman, in two parts; who I was before I watched Lyrebird's performance and who I am after.

Asking Laura Button to find the moment her skill arrived would be like asking mankind to explain the moment it was no longer an ape. It is part of her evolution. We know that Laura lived in seclusion for much of her life, ten years on her own, and sixteen years before that in relative seclusion with her mother and grandmother. What we know is that animals that live in seclusion for so long evolve in magnificent and curious ways. Laura is no different.

This lyrebird's lore travelled far and fast, deep and wide, from a fissure, a crack, deep into the human heart and mind.

It is not the spotlight that encourages growth, it is the sunlight. Jack Starr learned that last night.

The finders found her, the devotees such as I will keep the gifts she gave, now let us leave her be and may she fly free.

Laura finishes reading the piece feeling breathless, her eyes filled with tears. She looks back at Solomon who has stopped strumming while he watches her.

He grins at her reaction. 'Told you it was good.'

There's a knock at the door. Ten a.m. on a Sunday morning, he's not used to visitors.

'Stay there,' he says, protectively as he places the guitar down. He pads to the door and looks through the spyhole. It's Bo.

'Laura, Bo's here,' he says quickly, giving her a chance to compose herself before he answers the door.

'Bo, hi,' he says awkwardly, pulling the door open, tucking his hair behind his ears.

She quickly takes in his dishevelled look. 'Hope I'm not disturbing any . . . ' Then she sees Laura on the balcony and she seems relieved she hasn't walked in on anything unsavoury. 'Can I come in? I won't stay long.'

'Sure, sure.'

Laura puts her cup down and goes to stand.

'No don't stand for me,' Bo waves her hand

dismissively, seeming awkward as a guest in what was her home only days ago.

'Please sit,' Laura pulls the second balcony chair closer to hers.

Bo sits and Solomon hangs back. Bo notices the review on the chair beside her.

'Oh good, I'm glad you saw that.'

Laura smiles. 'She mentions you too. Thank you, Bo. I appreciate everything you did for me over the past few days.'

Bo's cheeks pink. 'You shouldn't be thanking me. It was the right thing to do. Finally. I should have stepped in sooner, but I didn't know how to. Have you any idea what you're going to do now? I'm sure there have been a lot of offers.'

Laura shakes her head. 'I have some thinking to do. You're right, there have been offers. Even a cooking show,' she grins.

'You would be great at that!' Bo laughs.

'I'd like to do something on foraging . . . outside the kitchen,' Laura says, but trails off. 'I don't know, everything I want to do, that's truly me, means going home. I feel like I can't move forward without going there. I want to sit down with Joe. There's so much that I want to talk to him about, ask him about, explain to him. I'm sure he's feeling so hurt by what Tom did, there's a lot I can tell him that will help him. And I want you to know that I'll honour your documentary. I'll keep my word on that, but if Joe will ever talk to me, I think we will need to be alone.'

'Gosh, Laura, that goes without saying,' Bo says, waving her hand dismissively. 'I came to give you this.' She reaches into her bag and retrieves an envelope. 'I got this from StarrGaze Entertainment.'

Solomon eyes the envelope suspiciously. He doesn't want anything from StarrGaze in here, though they were honourable to Laura in the end, he's cautious of what more 'help' they can offer.

Bo senses his wariness. 'You still don't trust me,' Bo says quietly, sounding betrayed and resigned.

'Bo,' he says gently. 'It's not you, it's them. I'm sorry. Of course I trust you, especially after everything you did for the final.'

Bo seems relieved. 'You liked it?'

'Loved it, but you used your documentary footage.'

She shrugs. 'Well, I still own it, it's not exclusive any more but I think I can live with that. It was the right thing to do. Look, they didn't exactly give this to me, okay? So . . . '

'We won't say a word,' Solomon agrees, watching Laura turn the envelope over and her eyes go wide when she reads the writing.

'What is it?' he asks concerned.

'From Joe Toolin, Toolin Farm, Gougane Barra,' Laura reads, quickly taking the letter out.

Solomon looks at Bo in surprise.

They watch as Laura unfolds the letter, note the light tremble of the paper in her shaking hands. She reads aloud.

To Whom It May Concern:

*Laura Button was born in Gougane Barra,
Co. Cork, Ireland. Her mother was Isabel
Button (Murphy) and her father was Tom
Toolin. She lived with Hattie Button and
Isabel Button until she was sixteen years of
age and then on my property, Toolin Cot-
tage, Toolin Farm, Gougane Barra, Co. Cork,
until recently.*

*I am her uncle. I hope this is all that you
need for the passport.*

Good luck to her.

Joe Toolin.

Laura looks up at Bo, her eyes filled with tears.

'He must have heard you on the radio,' Bo
says. 'Jack says he sent this without any request
from the agency. I would have told you sooner,
but I only recently found out.'

Solomon looks down at Bo, notices that she
looks thrown together, unusually for her. She
looks different, rushed. It's ten a.m. on a Sunday
morning. She got here as soon as she could. He
starts to wonder in what circumstances exactly
did she find out about the letter from Jack, that
would cause her to rush here on a Sunday morning. The familiar jealousy starts to rise within
him, like a burning in his chest, but he quells it
immediately, hating himself for even thinking like
this.

'I thought it would help with your . . . options.'
Bo smiles.

'Yes. Yes, it does, thank you so much.'

Laura stands and wraps her arms around Bo.

Bo reciprocates and they stand together on the balcony, embracing. One sorry, one thankful, one redeemed, one restored. Both grateful for each other.

★ ★ ★

It's six p.m. when Solomon drives through the entrance gate to Toolin Farm in Gougane Barra. Joe could have been anywhere on his acres of mountainous land, it could have taken them all day to wait for him to return, but Laura is lucky. Joe is mending a fence in front of his house.

He looks up as the car approaches, squints to see who's inside. An aggressive stare at the possibility of more journalists coming to aggravate him about Lyrebird. Solomon lowers his window and gives him a healthy wave. He seems to relax a little, recognising Solomon and the car. Solomon pulls in at the farmhouse.

Laura looks at Solomon.

'Take all the time you need,' he says. 'Wherever you decide to build your mound, I'll follow you and watch you.'

She grins. 'Thank you,' she whispers, leaning in, lifting her hands to his cheeks. She kisses him, this man she watched and adored, trusted in and followed until she found herself. As soon as she gets out of the car, Ring and a new pup come racing towards her, dancing around her legs with excitement to greet her after their time apart. Solomon gets out of the car, elbows on the roof, to watch her.

She climbs the fence in front of the

farmhouse, and walks down the mountainside, hair blowing in the wind as she joins her uncle. He looks at her for a greeting but she doesn't say a word. Instead she helps him with the fence, lifting the wooden pole from the ground and holding it upright so that he can twist the wires around each other. He watches her for a moment, taking her in, trying to figure her out and what she's doing here, and then he takes the wire from her and they work together.

A Summary

When we draw together all the threads available to us to approach an understanding of the Lyrebird, we are imperiously compelled to enter the misty realm where intelligence separates from instinct and merges into a form, however vague, of spiritual consciousness.

The Menura, as we have seen, willingly submits its life to regulation by a definite code of guiding principles.

It has a strong sense of property rights and values.

It respects the territorial rights of its neighbours and defends its own.

It possesses the power to impart ideas by a form of speech.

It is monogamous and is strictly faithful to its mate — even apparently (although that has not yet been exclusively established) after it has been bereaved of its life companion.

It has a deep love of melody, which it is able to express most sweetly with consummate art.

It dances prettily and accompanies its steps with a strange elfin music, spaced with throbbing time-beats which the dancing steps conform.

It is irresistibly attracted to reside in places of supreme loveliness and grandeur filled perennially with the most pleasing perfumes of the bush.

Its nature is amiable and kindly and it has a decidedly sociable disposition.

It is capable of loyal friendship with human beings, but its friendship cannot be won — as that of all other wild creatures — with offerings of food.

Its domestic life is exemplary and never disfigured by quarrels.

Ambrose Pratt, *The Lore of the Lyrebird*

Acknowledgements

It is with thanks to the insightful musings of Ambrose Pratt in *The Lore of the Lyrebird* that I was able to immerse myself in the world of the lyrebird, this peculiar quirky little bird that I fell in love with. Pratt's obvious love, curiosity and admiration for the lyrebird, and *The Lyrebird — Australia's wonder-songster* by R.T. Littlejohns, allowed me to take the characteristics and traits of a lyrebird and build my Laura, a woman with her own unique and powerful lore.

Enormous thanks to my little family; David, Robin and Sonny. Thanks for your support, your love, your energy. My heart is full because of you all.

Thank you my beautiful parents, Georgina, Nicky, my patient bonkers friends, Marianne Gunn O'Connor, Lynne Drew, Martha Ashby, Liz Dawson, Charlie Redmayne, Kate Elton, Roger Cazalet and the entire HarperCollins team for your creativity and support. I appreciate you all so much.

To the readers, thanks for going on a new adventure with me. I hope you all enjoy the journey as much as I have.

We do hope that you have enjoyed reading this large print book.

Did you know that all of our titles are available for purchase?

We publish a wide range of high quality large print books including:
Romances, Mysteries, Classics
General Fiction
Non Fiction and Westerns

Special interest titles available in large print are:
The Little Oxford Dictionary
Music Book
Song Book
Hymn Book
Service Book

Also available from us courtesy of Oxford University Press:
Young Readers' Dictionary
(large print edition)
Young Readers' Thesaurus
(large print edition)

For further information or a free brochure, please contact us at:
Ulverscroft Large Print Books Ltd.,
The Green, Bradgate Road, Anstey,
Leicester, LE7 7FU, England.
Tel: (00 44) **0116 236 4325**
Fax: (00 44) **0116 234 0205**

THE YEAR I MET YOU

Cecelia Ahern

Jasmine knows two things. One, she loves her vulnerable sister unconditionally, and will fight to the death to protect her from anyone who upsets her. Two, she's only ever been good at one thing — her job helping business start-ups. So when she's sacked and put on gardening leave, Jasmine realises that she has nothing else to fill her life. Insomnia keeps her staring out of her bedroom window, and she finds herself watching the antics of her neighbour, shock jock Matt, with more than a casual eye. On New Year's Eve Matt is also forced to take a leave of absence from work, after one of his controversial chat shows goes too far; and as the year unfolds, through moonlit nights and suburban days, an unlikely friendship slowly starts to blossom . . .

HOW TO FALL IN LOVE

Cecelia Ahern

Adam Basil and Christine Rose are thrown together late one night, when Christine is crossing Ha'penny Bridge in Dublin. Adam is there, poised, threatening to jump. He is desperate — but Christine makes a crazy deal with him. His 35th birthday is looming and she bets him that before then, she can show him life is worth living. Despite her determination, Christine knows what a dangerous promise she's made. Against the ticking clock, the two of them embark on wild escapades, grand romantic gestures and some unlikely late-night outings. Slowly, Christine thinks Adam is starting to fall back in love with his life. But has she done enough to change his mind for good? And is that all that's starting to happen?

PS, I LOVE YOU

Cecelia Ahern

Holly and Gerry had the perfect life. Happily married, living in Dublin close to their friends and family, and with a brilliant social life, they had the world at their feet. Or so they thought. When Gerry dies, Holly is devastated. On the eve of her 30th birthday, the man who was her love, her best friend, her rock, has left her. But Gerry promised he'd always be there for Holly. And he is: his last bequest to her is The List, a bundle of notes which form a monthly mission for Holly to get her life back on track. As the notes are gradually opened, and as the year unfolds, the man who knows Holly better than anyone sets out to teach her that life goes on . . .